Lion, Tiger, Bear

By
John W. Warner IV

© M60 Media 2021
Washington, D.C.
First Edition
Printed in the U.S.A.

John W. Warner IV
Lion, Tiger, Bear
Sequel to Little Anton: A Historical Novel Series
ISBN 9781734193572

Edited by Steven Parolini
Graphic design by Alexis Chng-Castor

No part of this book may be reproduced in any written, electronic, recording, or photocopying without written permission of the publisher or author. The exception would be in the case of brief quotations embodied in the critical articles or reviews and pages where permission is specifically granted by the publisher or author.

Although every precaution has been taken to verify the accuracy of the information contained herein, the author and publisher assume no responsibility for any errors or omissions. No liability is assumed for damages that may result from the use of information contained within.

*My father, Senator John W. Warner III,
former U.S. Secretary of the Navy*

For my late father and his beloved U.S. Navy and U.S. Marines. Thank you all for the great times, exotic adventures, and my most important educational years. No school or university could match the life-altering and fantastic experiences I was privileged to witness by dint of the generosity of our nation's military and U.S. Congress. Having never served, my only regret in life is that I wish I had, but I do have the privilege to work with wounded vets, and I listen carefully to their harrowing tales of war. All I possess now is my humble prose, but serve I shall.

For my dearest wife, twin flame, and muse, whom I love so very much.

Special Thanks

Steve Parolini

Alexis Chng-Castor

Nick Cook, Author, Aviation expert

Eric Hecker, Antarctica expert

Penny Bradley, German history

Daniel Liszt

Adrienne Hand

Cynthia Baumann

My wife Guadalupe

U.S. Naval Archives

U.S. Army Archives

Marine Corps Records, National Archives

British National Archives

German Archives

Porsche Museum, Stuttgart

Franklin D. Roosevelt Presidential Library

Author's Note

"I wrote my will across the sky, in stars."

—Colonel T. E. Lawrence (Lawrence of Arabia)

"Tomorrow we shall meet.
Death and I,
And he shall thrust his sword
Into one who is awake."

—Dag Hammarskjöld

Away we go.

I caution the reader by stating that it is highly recommended for one to consume or partly consume my first novel *Little Anton* in its three-part overbearing juggernaut entirety before reading this book, which is a direct sequel. Oh for shit's sake, just thumb through the darn thing! It's a good reference for this lump.

Little Anton was always designated to be the long-winded bedrock foundation of my Beatrice Sunderland-and-gang versus the world series; lengthy, yes, an elephant pill to swallow perhaps, but well worth it. Liberal amounts of hot espresso by day and chilled rosé by night are imperative, and don't spare the crisp almond cookies.

The past is important, history is important, for without understanding what really happened, or some semblance thereof, we are lost as a people, as one worldwide race in the sobering present. No matter who we are or what we do, life is either raucously hilarious or astoundingly horrifying, with only boredom, toil, bits of fleeting happiness, and drudgery in between.

It was said by the Nobel Prize-winning author Toni Morrison that "words have power, words are important." It's up to us who put fingertips to keyboard, pencil to pad, chalk to chalkboard, to understand that wisdom and make every word count.

Hell's bells, I've tried.

•••

Yawn. We live in interesting times...

Unabashedly a fun-loving conspiracy researcher, stalwart UFO enthusiast, and scandalous revisionist historian, I have embarked on this series of written adventures with a hearty disposition, steeled nerves, a healthy sense of humor, and my colorful imagination at full throttle not unlike Bea herself, although she is armed with more healthy skepticism than I. Perhaps that's a good thing. Like Dorothy in *The Wizard of Oz*, or Nancy Wake the Resistance fighter in WW2 France, Bea continues her "Hero's Journey" with gusto and renewed verve during an unimaginably horrible, huge, bizarre, and complex war, one where many experienced a shattered psyche, a tested faith, and a sense of diminishing courage and loyalty when confronted with heavily-protected secrets laid bare.

Luftwaffe pilot and lion cub mascot

None of the main characters are my avatar (many friends have asked me), but they all have little bits of me in them, the positive and the, uh, not so much. We are all at odds with the light and dark within us, our powerful Yin-Yang emotions, our duality, it's what makes us human, it's what relentlessly drives us to better ourselves whilst unconditionally loving, forgiving, and helping others come what may. Something like that.

Considering the changing times circa 2021, the world recovering from a pandemic and financial crisis, I must proclaim here and now that although I know a great deal about the history of the occult, secret societies, mystery schools, dogmatic rock-hard religions, sacrificial cults, and satanic practices that have flavored our history for many thousands of years, I am in no way, shape, or form, involved with them on a personal or professional basis. Though I greatly respect folk tradition and ancient culture, I loathe all boring, conformist, and inflexible religions, negative vibration "evil" folks, gargoyle-types, fidgety Fascists, teetotaling totalitarians, and their sickening satanic practices that secretly glorify the ancient Sumerian Anunnaki and negative-vibe extraterrestrial "gods" and "goddesses," but I do understand their horrific significance in regards to our hidden history. Chapter Three of this book, no doubt shocking to some, is inspired by true accounts, so I will not apologize for it. Sadly, pedophilic Satanic Ritual Abuse in conjunction with dark Babylonian-type rituals is a genuine occurrence in our world past and present, so there's no ignoring it. Look it up if you don't believe me. If we do not fully understand the twisted, sickening depths of the darkness in our world and reality, we will not fully appreciate the light. And I'm all about turning up the light.

Anunnaki goddess Lilith and her owl mascots

Like a few million free-thinkers scattered about, I truly believe that many interdimensional star beings have influenced human history over the eons, the so-called Nephilim, Watchers, Archons, angels, Jinn, winged gods, goddesses, and unseen demons, as it were, and I trust that only a minute few have done us great harm, the lion's share being wise and benevolent star cousins, teachers, mentors, farmers, scientists and great friends. Our beloved and notorious garden planet Earth is an important school of hard knocks and well-earned wisdom in the cosmos according to many philosophers, enlightened quantum scientists, sacred texts, modern-day researchers, friendly extraterrestrial advisors, and ancient mystery schools. Whew! There's lots of unconditional love and forgiveness out there yonder by all accounts, and our world will change for the better soon, it has to, for we are finally and irrevocably living in an age of whiz-bang technology, big "D" disclosure, fierce protests, and great spiritual awakening. Mother Earth is rising in frequency (Schumann Resonance), and so are we.

The benevolent star nations out there know all this well and are very excited for us apparently. *Wink-wink.*

•••

But let's get down to Earth, folks.

As for rock-solid alternative history narratives and theories, one only has to research and critically examine all the megalithic ruins, geomantic earthworks, castles, mottes, cathedrals, mounds, pyramids, so-called "temples," grand canals, and yes, "star forts" to see via satellite imagery that our true history has been hijacked by certain academic powers-that-be, and I mean *wholesale*. It takes an awakened eye and a vivid imagination. We are literally living on top of the advanced ancient world—the strange grids, pyramids, unending geometric lines, faded star cities, and geoglyphs—the mysterious and inexplicable telltales hidden in plain sight, ones that are usually highly ignored by academia. Ah-ha!

As a military historian, I'll say this: Although star forts make good sense most of the time as Byzantine, complex, 14th to 19th-century in-depth military defenses, it's quite possible the Freemason architects and engineers understood the value of placing sacred geometric fortifications along telluric energy Ley Lines. The subtle earth energies were once used by railroad telegraph lines to boost the signals down the line. I believe there is a correlation, since the Germans were known for placing concrete bunkers, radio towers, and above-ground fortifications along these misunderstood energy pathways. Each fortification or fortified city is unique.

•••

In this book, Bea, Lutz, Bernie, Alice, and Ferdinand Porsche are in rare form and ready for action. Bea and Alice continue the feminist fight for equal status, and prove without doubt that women can handle any job no matter the challenges. World War Two saw women in many new roles: Mechanics, ferry pilots, intelligence operatives, code-breakers, doctors, nurses, scientists, and much more. My books are a celebration of these women and the Divine Feminine.

My character Gwafa, a hard-edged African from Mali, tempers my cast of lily-white aristocrats, his innate wisdom, can-do temperament, and exotic bloodlines equipping him with a powerful soul; he typifies for me those soldiers during World War Two that had to fight racism and inequality as well as the enemy, so he's a true Vedic-style Light Warrior in every sense.

A few chapters may seem long-winded and they are, but I tried my best to simplify colossal issues in our history and explain complex science in a condensed fashion. Please be patient with me.

•••

The genuine characters in this book are many.

Aleister Crowley

Aleister Crowley, a truly sinister man in my opinion, was the world's foremost occultist in the 20th century; he was indeed a spy, double agent, and spiritual consultant for many nations and their leaders in both world wars. One story purports that he and famous JPL chemist Jack Parsons performed a covert "Babylon Workings" ritual at Nevada's Groom Lake and Area-51 military site opening ceremony in 1949. (See: TV show *Strange Angel* on CBS.com). In my next book, I will explore this purported story and many others.

Rico Botta, Rear Admiral, USN

Rear Admiral Rico Botta is mentioned in Chapter Twelve. He was a genuine naval officer, and one that is rumored to have been involved with the U.S. Navy's shadowy "Foreign Technology Division" in San Diego at Douglas Aircraft. My father and I could find precious little information about him via a FOIA request and a USN request other than his general involvement with naval aviation. Very strange for an admiral.

As for the Ahnenerbe SS and its scientists Bruno Beger, Ernst Shäfer, Ernst Krause, Edmund Geer, Edmund Kisse, Karl Wienert and others, they were all real-deal scientists and occultists. Their 1938–1939 expeditions to Tibet and the films they made for Heinrich Himmler are the stuff of legends. Reportedly, they were all Thule Society members.

An excerpt from the *Rare Historical Photos* website:

"Reichsführer Himmler was fascinated by Asian mysticism and therefore wished to send such an expedition under the auspices of the SS Ahnenerbe (SS Ancestral Heritage Society), and desired that Schäfer perform research based on Hans Hörbiger's pseudo-scientific theory of "Glacial Cosmogony" promoted by the Ahnenerbe. Schäfer had scientific objectives, and he therefore refused to include Edmund Kiss, an adept of this theory, in his team, and requested 12 conditions to obtain scientific freedom. Wolfram Sievers from the Ahnenerbe therefore expressed criticism concerning the objectives of the expedition, so that the Ahnenerbe would not sponsor it. Himmler accepted the expedition to be organized on the condition that all its members become SS. In order to succeed in his expedition, Schäfer had to compromise."

(https://rarehistoricalphotos.com/german-expedition-tibet-led-ernst-schafer-1938-1939/)

It should be noted that Bruno Beger and Dr. Hans Fleishhacker had Jews murdered at Auschwitz in 1943 so he could have their skeletons placed in a Nazi museum collection. Beger, a longtime friend of the Dalai Lama, was a convicted war criminal that served no prison time.

Ernst Shäfer witnessed Jewish prisoners at Dachau that were subjected to lethal high altitude tests in 1943. He was by no means a saint. None of the Ahnenerbe were.

Walter Gerlach

Physicist Walter Gerlach was also real, and his *Unified Field Theory* and antigravity technology work for the Germans was, in my opinion and others', highly successful. The U.S. Military has greatly benefitted from his work, to my mind, the circumstantial evidence tantalizingly clear, and the *Office of Strategic Services* "hired" many thousands of Nazi scientists after the war in Operation PAPERCLIP. My grandfather, U.S. Army Major Paul Mellon, OSS, was involved with this technology and "Brain Drain" operation with fellow agents Allen Dulles and David K. E. Bruce, and told me many stories about their wild adventures.

My Grandfather told me he worked with his boss "Wild Bill" Donovan on many super-classified aspects of the war, and it is known today that Donovan was intimately familiar with President Franklin Roosevelt's secret UFO File. It is my personal belief arising from my intimate conversations with Paul that he and other OSS officers were there with General Patton when his 3rd Army liberated Pilzen in Czechoslovakia on May 5, 1945; they were great friends, Grandad told me, and he loved serving under the great general. My Grandad has four bronze stars and thousands of classified WW2 documents at the CIA that my Dad and I were unable to acquire through multiple FOIA requests. What is so secret about covert operations that happened seventy-five years ago that cannot be revealed today?

According to authors Nick Cook and Igor Witowski, the story goes that in Pilzen resided the top secret SS E-4 Division, the very outfit that oversaw most of the super-classified German *Wunderwaffe* high technology: High-voltage plasma accelerator free energy research (zero-point), torsion physics, transistors, scalar and sound weapons, chemical lasers, antigravity experiments, atomic weapons, and rocket works for Himmler's SS under the overall auspices of SS General Hans Kammler. My friend Nick Cook wrote about Kammler in his highly acclaimed research book: *The Hunt for Zero Point*. Another excellent book on the general is *The Hidden Nazi*, by Dean Reuter, Colm Lowery, and Keith Chester.

SS General Hans Kammler

So for me the dots connect. The shadowy real-life Kammler—a building contractor for all the death camps and the originator of the infamous Third Reich slave labor pool—has a cameo appearance in this book, and will return in the future. He is said to have been the most important man in Germany save for Hitler in the spring of 1945, and yet mysteriously the mainstream history books conveniently ignore him. Burn this photo in your mind's eye and never forget it; this is the horrifying, cold-blooded man who was in charge of all the secret projects.

Though not a character in this book, President Donald Trump's uncle, physicist John G. Trump, is mentioned several times in my narrative because he was privy to Nikola Tesla's classified work and the presidential UFO File. I believe his research included much of Gerlach's, and that's why most of Professors Trump and Vannevar Bush's research is still classified today. You can bet your boots JGT will be in my next book as an official character, oh yes. If anyone knew all about the secret German technology during and after the war, it was Professors Vannevar Bush and John Trump.

John Trump   *Vannevar Bush*

•••

As for General Rommel and his vaunted Afrika Korps, most historians agree that the war in North Africa—with very few if any SS death squads—was indeed a more civilized conflict, one that harkened back to more honorable times. But war is pure hell, and no conflict has ever been a good choice, the horror far too great for any kind of romantic ideals. (Those people and institutions and corporations that aggrandize and take profit from war may have differing opinions, however.) Rommel remains a romantic figure to this day, mostly because he was an honorable and brilliant general, but also because he was part of the plot to assassinate Hitler.

During the North African campaign in 1942, Siwa Oasis was occupied by

Italians and Germans. It still is a huge oasis with much water and many palms. Look it up. Beautiful!

On the lighter side, the Germans really did print a hilarious Tiger Tank operator's manual as a comic book with naked women. Young enlisted men who knew how to work on a farm tractor comprised the lion's share of tank crews, and by all accounts they loved the book. Who says the regular German Army had no sense of humor back then?

If readers don't believe that Allied soldiers behind the lines could have learned to operate a German tank *somewhat* effectively in a short period of time, I must insist you are wrong. Well-trained and highly motivated soldiers in dire situations can do almost anything they put their minds to. Ask any combat veteran.

The electric hybrid Porsche Tiger tank was also real; three were built with an 88 mm gun, but the main contract went to the Henschel Works.

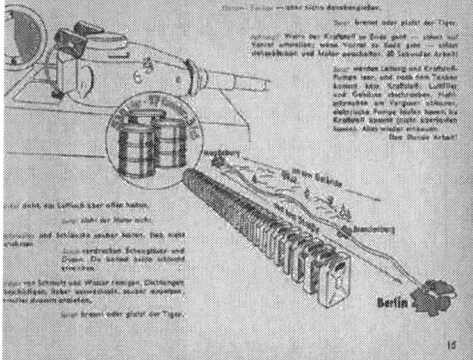

Herr Barrelbum

Porsche Tiger

According to Oxford scholar, author, and historian Dr. Joseph P. Farrell, the Germans really *were* looking for vast quantities of thorium in Europe, Russia, and the Near East—much more than they would need just for nuclear weapons development.

Did the Germans use atomic weapons in secret? The simply massive numbers of casualties on the Russian Front during the war is a strong clue, for how did the Germans kill an official 27 million (some say an unofficial 30-34 million) combatants and civilians with conventional weapons? Yes, many troops and civilians died from disease and hunger, but it's still a heart-breaking mystery we need to solve. I agree with Dr. Farrell's theoretical postulation: Thorium was most likely used in free energy research and for the making of low-yield, crude nuclear weapons delivered by German ground vehicles, big railway guns, and perhaps "dirty bomb" barrage rockets that were used on the Russian Front. Thermobaric weapons were also probably implemented *en masse* using coal dust and fuel oil. Plentiful uranium was found in Silesia and the Sudetenland, so be advised the Germans had plenty.

There is decent evidence to suggest that uranium was possibly purified at the I.G. Farben Buna synthetic rubber plant near the Auschwitz-Birkenau concentration camps due to Farben's very high consumption of electricity, and it is likely the Germans tested a small-yield atomic U-235 bomb in October 1944 on an island in the Baltic.

After the war in 1946, the USN produced a report by Capt. R.F. Hickey about the possible German Atomic Bomb. After extensive investigation, it was reviewed and signed off by a leading German scientist. It is the only known eyewitness report confirming one of the very few atomic bomb tests the Germans conducted. (See: *Zinsser Report*).

A wild rumor persists of a German atomic device dropped on the Russians in late 1944 near Kurland in the Baltic States, but it has not been confirmed either. And yet I must ask myself: what if it's true?

•••

Dr. J.P. Farrell's book, *Hess and the Penguins*, was instrumental in my fleshing out Rudolph Hess's personality and ethos. Many thanks to you, Joseph. Huzzah, old chap.

As for the history of Antarctica, the German explorations of 1938 and 1939—both sponsored by Hermann Göring and Rudolf Hess—are very interesting topics to study, especially since the Germans had been visiting there since 1915. All one has to do is look up just how militarized Antarctica has become over the decades since WW2 to get an idea how utterly fascinating and mysterious the continent has become.

My father was involved with *Operation Deep Freeze* when he was Secretary of the Navy in 1972, and he told me about the secret sub bases and missile silos under the ice when I was just a wee lad. He also said Antarctica was used for "space operations." Who knows what else they found? That's still officially classified, by the by.

Admiral Byrd and Admiral Nimitz sure had fun during the 1947 Antarctic expedition with 5000 Marines (Some reports say 10,000) and sailors in Operation HIGHJUMP. I suggest the reader investigate that intriguing bit of U.S. Navy "scientific research operation" history, especially since they had very little scientific equipment with them. There's even a U.S. Navy documentary film about it. What kind of scientific expedition needs aircraft carriers, warships, troops, fighter aircraft, and huge amounts of firepower? If Nimitz wanted to test new equipment in the sub-zero deep freeze, why not do it in much-closer-to-home northern Alaska or the Aleutian Islands?

Countless important dignitaries, presidents, royals, carefully vetted scientists, and world leaders have visited there, but the continent is extremely difficult and expensive for a civilian to visit, if not almost impossible. Most sensitive areas are sealed off by way of military force and airpower. Satellites have an enforced no-fly zone, and satellite imagery is whited-out extensively. China is now on its fifth military base. After reading this book, ask yourselves: Why all the fuss and secrecy? Why are there so many international military bases for a continent that was never supposed to be militarized?

•••

As I write this, many avant-garde historians are piecing together our hidden World War Two history, the bizarre role of the occult, and the sudden introduction of what General Jimmy Doolittle termed the "Foo-Fighters," which most now believe were some kind of friendly plasma ball drone-type observers from, ahem, "outta town," as Bernie Rodgers states in one chapter. (The famous rock band took their name from them in the 1990s.) These Foo-Fighters observed—and in a few cases caused electrical malfunctions—aircraft and ships from all nations embroiled in the conflict. Photos and mentions of them can be found in official U.S., British, Russian, and German military documents, so no naysaying! We have never been alone in this vast universe of ours, and we never will be, but hey, you knew that already.

Even after eighty years post WW2, we still don't get the official truth on this old story (I don't trust Wikipedia or the mainstream news media), but we do get modern *New York Times*, *Washington Post*, and U.S. Navy headlines on the lukewarm USS Nimitz jet fighter camera UFO sightings. Why was there no mention of the WW2 phenomena? Or the famous overflight of UFOs in Washington D.C. in 1952? (See: *Washington Post* front page of that year. The word is the UFOs were German). Today, officialdom only tells us the bare minimum, and considers everyday people unworthy of classified information or any semblance of genuine truth, lest we begin to ask millions of uncomfortable questions about our entire reality and historical narrative.

To my mind, writing an historical novel means sweating the details. In Chapter One, I have spent much time and effort researching and creating what I believe was the genuine agenda covered during the 1942 Oval Office meeting between Winston Churchill, General George Marshall, and President Roosevelt. They must have shouldered a supreme burden we can barely imagine: First they had to devise a global strategy to defeat the powerful Axis forces, then come up with explanations and possible solutions regarding the alarming *Foo Fighters* and their creators who were now involving themselves in the war to no small amount, the true story of the 1942 "Battle of Los Angeles" being one glaring example. Thirdly, they had to come to terms with the unavoidable notion that the Nazi SS were—possibly—receiving regressive extraterrestrial technology help in devising new wonder weapons, especially atomic, scalar, and antigravity ones. I believe the Vril Society's "Propulsion Workshop" was genuine, and the SS was far, far ahead technologically than the Allies. The official history narrative bears this out to some degree if one knows where to look and what dots to connect, but I'll warn you that it has taken me four decades to do so.

On page 18 is my re-created and touched-up copy of what I believe is a genuine FDR "Celestial Devices" (A.k.a.: *Foo-Fighters, UFOs*) document from 1942. There are many more tantalizing documents on this website to peruse: *Majesticdocuments.com*.

As luck and karma would have it, my good friend and cousin Chris Mellon,

"Battle of Los Angeles," Feb. 25, 1942.

> **TOP SECRET**
>
> Top Secret gm 25
> February 27, 1942
>
> THE WHITE HOUSE
> WASHINGTON
>
> February 27, 1942
>
> MEMORANDUM FOR
>
> CHIEF OF STAFF OF THE ARMY
>
> I have considered the disposition of the material in possession of the Army that may be of great significance toward the development of a super weapon of war. I disagree with the argument that such information should be shared with our ally the Soviet Union. Consultation with Dr. Bush and other scientists on the issue of finding practical uses for the atomic secrets learned from study of celestial devices precludes any further discussion and I therefor authorize Dr. Bush to proceed with the project without further delay. This information is vital to the nation's superiority and must remain within the confines of state secrets. Any further discussion on the matter will be restricted to General Donovan, Dr. Bush, the Secretary of War and yourself. The challenge our nation faces is daunting and perilous in this undertaking and I have committed the resources of the government towards that end. You have my assurance that when circumstances are favorable and we are victorious, the Army will have the fruits of research in exploring further applications of this new wonder.
>
> You may speak to me about this if the above is not wholly clear.
>
> F.D.R.   *Franklin D Roosevelt*

the former Deputy Undersecretary of Defense for Intelligence, was involved with DOD and Pentagon-approved U.S. Navy UFO disclosure via the *To the Stars Academy of Arts and Sciences* with senior intelligence and military contractors and scientists on the team. They had a rather bland History Channel documentary series that explored many extraterrestrial possibilities. I wish them luck, and I desire to read more of Chris' articles in the *New York Times* and *Washington Post*, but with much more transparency I hope. As of this writing, Chris has now quit the TTSA initiative.

What an interesting family I have!

•••

I would like to thank whistleblower *Nachtwaffen* veteran Penny Bradley for her testimony on occult German history, researcher Eric Hecker on Antarctica, researcher and journalist Daniel Liszt, Walter Bosley for his *Empire of the Wheel* series, and the late Michael Busby (*Solving the 1897 Airship Mystery*) for their informative and superlative research books.

I would also like to thank authors Nick Cook (*The Hunt for Zero Point*) and Igor Witowski (*The Truth about the Wunderwaffe*) for their groundbreaking research into free energy and antigravity programs during World War Two, and the surfacing of SS General Hans Kammler as an extremely important but shadowy figure in history. Well done, chaps.

Bosley and Busby both document the "1897 Airship Mystery" and "Sonora Aero Club," which only cements my belief that we probably had very basic electromagnetic antigravity and zero-point energy for the elite airship few in the 19th century, as difficult as that may be for most people to swallow given our false historical narrative that we all have been forcibly taught. Yes, this is wild stuff, I agree, but after years of careful thought I personally believe that Bosley is on the right track with his colorful theories on train robber Butch Cassidy, telluric Ley Line energy, the occult, and famous occultist Aleister Crowley. Newspapers the world over covered the mysterious Jules Verne-type story in glorious detail, and Americans enjoyed a mostly free press back in 1897 unlike today's, which is massively hampered by draconian national security laws, military secrecy redaction, CIA and DIA influences, and many corporate dictums, so please take heed. I am not alone by any means in this assertion.

•••

Our entire world history is peppered with grand lies, obfuscations, and fabrications, not to mention vast bits having been wholly destroyed or hidden away. It took me forty-five years of hard study and travel to accept the unavoidable "truth" of our moldy Swiss cheese history, or at least a sizeable portion of it, and I'm assured most will require the same amount of time to digest the new findings, whatever they turn out to be. I believe the U.S. Government, mainstream academia, and the Department of Defense will never give the public the full unredacted genuine truth of our world, therefore we must demand and expose it ourselves.

To complicate matters further, no historian or scientist can accurately sketch out our civilization timeline or human evolution. Not even close. There are so many holes, inaccuracies, and colorful fairy tales in the official versions it boggles the mind. There is no genuine consensus.

An example: No silly "Missing Link" has ever been found in primatology and it never will be. Why? Because it never existed in the first instance! Apes and primates are not humans, nor are they fanciful "proto-humans." They never were, and did not pack the gear for speech or higher consciousness, thought, or spirituality. Start there and move on is my gentle advice. Use that mind to think critically. Some researchers say we have many star cousins to thank for our unique 12-strand DNA mix, apparently. Go figure. Makes more sense to me, Mr. Darwin. (See: Author and researcher Lloyd Pye).

•••

As for colorful life experience flavoring my work, I literally carried my father's heavy leather briefcases (English-made suitcases; average weight: 45 lbs. each when full) all over the world with him from the time he was Secretary of the Navy until his retirement as a U.S. Senator of Virginia (Chairman of the Armed Services Committee, Select Intelligence Committee member), and after meeting many world leaders, U.S. presidents, royalty, Intelligence Community personnel, and plentiful top military brass, I have good reason to believe that the issue of extraterrestrial involvement—both positive and negative—in our history, militaries, and governments is not only genuine but ongoing, the hidden agendas uncountable. I asked uncomfortable questions and I received uncomfortable short answers, or no answers at all, but I got the damn message: *Shut up, be a patriot, stop asking questions about things that don't concern you, and move along.*

To my mind, extreme secrecy—military, financial, governmental, religious, and corporate—is a slow-moving death knell for our beloved nation and the world. At age 94, my father finally and reluctantly agreed before he passed away, at least partly so for an old fart, he said.

I cannot speak for the peoples of other nations, but over the decades as I've become disillusioned, weary, wise, and more informed, I now firmly understand with no

President Nixon and my Dad, 1972. Nixon was a family friend. I believe he tried to release the UFO File to the public but was warned off and impeached for his efforts. I was there at age 10.

*Grumman Aircraft, San Diego, 1972.
Prototype F-14 Tomcat.
Yes, that's me, and no, I didn't get to fly it.*

hint of doubt that Americans, we few, we mighty few, don't like being lied to by government officialdom, our highly compartmentalized military and its overwrought industrial complex, corporate-controlled media, religions of all stripes, secret societies, private roundtables, semi-public councils, whacky tech billionaires, and corrupt academia *what-so-ever*, and soon will not stand for it anymore.

I firmly support the U.S. Military for very personal and specific reasons, especially the U.S. Navy and Marines who are beholden to the Constitution, but not the secret black USAP programs that are unconstitutional and unacknowledged.

Sadly it is what it is, the reasons for the lies, misdirection, and cover-ups as plentiful as the stars in the night desert sky. Sir Isaac Newton, General George Patton, Nikola Tesla, Mark Twain, Albert Einstein, FDR, and Napoleon Bonaparte all said that history was a pack of lies written by the winners, so be advised.

Lastly, this topsy-turvy book is about the universal vibration of love: Love of country, love of self, love of truth in the face of lies, love of loved ones, and love of others everywhere. Forgiveness comes from love, and in the end all is forgiven. We are all one, one great consciousness, as in *The Law of One*.

Anyway, all this high-falutin' stuff aside, it's so much more fun to think and daydream out of the box, so my advice is to have fun doing so. An open mind, an unconditional forgiveness towards others, and a big loving heart to live life with are wondrous things.

1

Oval Office
Washington D.C.
July 19, 1942

Prime Minister Winston Churchill sat with a groan, tending to his tea. His Virginia-style buttermilk biscuit wasn't exactly a Ritz Hotel London scone, but the clotted cream and strawberry jam were first rate.

Franklin Roosevelt moved his wheelchair closer to the couch with a slight squeak. Being of stalwart upstate New York Dutch lineage, he had no love of the British Empire or any other one for that matter, but Winston touched him on a deeper level, always had, and their friendship mattered. Franklin would pick up the scorched, shattered bits of empire just like his cousin Theodore Roosevelt had done on a smaller scale, and an American-centric new world order would arise from the old, but only if they won the war. "We're going forward on our plan for the North African invasion, 'Operation Torch,' the Navy calls it," he began. "Americans must get into the action as soon as practicable, and General Marshall has appointed Dwight Eisenhower as overall Allied Commander. The Krauts will hate that—an American General with a *jur-r-mann* name. I'm at odds with many of my generals and admirals on this, it's a profound and...*unpopular* decision."

"But a good one. The traitorous Vichy will fight, I'm sure of it," murmured Churchill. "Or...they might surrender without a shot fired," smiled the president. "Keep the sunny side up, Winston."

"*Bum fodder*, but I like the way you think."

Prompt, Chief of Staff General George Marshall entered. "Mr. President, Prime Minister. Sad news from Libya." He handed Winston a pink telegram.

Churchill slowly put down his tea cup. "Rommel's taken Tobruk. 33,000 taken prisoner. 19,000 were British. The Suez is in his sights. God damn him to hell." He crumpled the missive in his meaty fist. "Tobruk...defeat is one thing, disgrace quite another."

After a few moments of silence, the president soothed. "They must have put up a helluva fight, Winston. All of them, the Australians and New Zealanders too. What can we do to help?"

Winston mused the question carefully. Too much of a favor could sour their relationship. "Sir, it seems I'm the most miserable Englishman in America since Burgoyne. That said, we need tanks. Jerry has more and more every day. Army Intelligence and MI6 reports say new ones are to be supplied in a few months' time to Tunisia, the upgraded and fearsome Panzer IV's. Tunis is swarming with supply ships."

Roosevelt looked to Marshall. "Let's send three hundred Shermans and a hundred artillery pieces, and by the fastest ships possible to the Suez and up to Egypt."

"Yes sir, that can be arranged quickly. Production has increased in Detroit," said the general, face pale, sitting across from Churchill in an easy chair. Suspicious eyes found their targets.

Churchill looked Marshall over. He knew Roosevelt had probably picked him as a five-star chief of staff not because he had great experience in leadership—he'd been promoted throughout his career curiously fast despite being a substandard regimental commander, and had worked hard on the President's Civilian Conservation Corps projects as a loyal officer—but because he had sharp understanding of the deepest secrets. Churchill suspected it was Marshall who had cobbled up the idea of letting Pearl Harbor happen on purpose after the Japanese communiqué had been read, the idea being to quickly galvanize Americans behind the war effort, but that was ancient history now and probably for the best, he thought.

Roosevelt reached out for Winston's hand. "Together we'll *beat* them. Grind them into that hot sand. We have to."

Cigar went limp. "Indeed, sir. New command is needed in Egypt, and I know just the chap: Montgomery. Controversial, unpopular with the high command, but tough and inventive. I'll be in Cairo in August to personally oversee the transition; bad blood may flow. The Nah-zies cannot be allowed to win even in a limited capacity. If they capture the oil fields in the east the war will drag on for years and years, possibly decades. And we three all have a good idea what the Germans are *really* after in that desert region, one that stretches from Morocco to India, a parched paradise of hidden treasures. And Europe is currently theirs to manipulate, underground facilities for war production increase daily. The facilities I worry most about are built upon Ley Line intersections—Poland, Czecho, Silesia, Romania, Bulgaria, Greece."

Marshall cleared his throat. "Shall I leave you two alone, Mr. President?"

"No, George. Stay. This warrants deeper discussion," said Roosevelt, sipping his coffee. "Besides, we need your input on our new whiz-bang science in the works, none of which will be shared with the Stalinists of course."

Despite his peaked depression, Churchill felt quite privileged. At last, Roosevelt was opening up on certain subjects heretofore highly classified and valued beyond measure. Full cooperation was needed, and now. Their intimate bedroom chat with cocktails the night before with Winston naked in the bathtub was finally bearing low-hanging fruit of the sweetest taste.

Marshall rummaged through his stuffed accordion briefcase. "The file, sir. Latest NRDC and Rad Lab reports and projects. MIT professors Vannevar Bush, John Trump, Varian brothers Russell and Sigurd. Tesla is a help, but he's getting on in years, frail. These are our top scientists, Prime Minister, all have the highest clearance in the land."

In pain, Roosevelt leaned back, grimaced, straightened his cramped and braced legs. "Enlighten our dreary morning, General. Cheer us *up*."

Marshall continued. "Due to their non-aggression pact, our west coast freighters flying Russian flags are reaching Vladivostok unharmed by the Japanese navy. Klystron tube microwave radar research has yielded the following: Long Range Navigation Radar or LORAN for ships, ground approach radar for planes, gun-laying units for the Navy, friend-or-foe beacons, and early warning systems are all moving along well. A defensive fire control radar is being tested on the B-24 Liberator bomber. Shows promise. Jet-assisted takeoff JATO rockets from JPL Labs are proving useful for heavy load aircraft. Chemist Jack Parsons and his team are moving fast on more powerful versions."

Roosevelt casually rotated his arm and finger to Marshall. "Isn't he the one..."

"Yes sir. I have the FBI watching him. He's an amateur occultist, a local lodge, but has engaged in written communication with the notorious Aleister Crowley."

Churchill snapped: "I know about him well, high-level *Ordo Templi Orientis*. Useful sometimes. MI6 keeps tabs on their back-pocket boy, but he's not to be fully trusted."

"Funny ol' world, ain't it now?" smiled Roosevelt. "Strange bedfellows we need indeed. Hired occult assassins, psychics and seers on the secret payroll, expensive and untrustworthy privateers and brigands, Russian psychic armies..."

Marshall cleared his throat and continued with his notes. "Boeing is well on their way with the XB-29 long range, high altitude bomber program. Computerized defensive gun placements and pressurized fuselage testing is slow but up-and-coming. They're scheduled to be combat-ready by mid-forty-four. The SC-5 Tesla-based scalar microwave testing is on schedule in New Mexico at Los Alamos. Professor Trump and the Varian brothers are hard at work at making it heavy-vehicle-portable when it matures in an estimated twenty-four months. It utilizes a neutrino tracking system, and if all goes well, any high-speed aircraft up to 150,000 feet should be disabled according to their data."

"Good. Let us move on to infamous File B," said Roosevelt. "Make sure Secretary of War Stimson is read-in on this."

"I'll brief him personally." Marshall pulled out the thick blue file. "File B, sir." Roosevelt smiled. "Winston, what do you know about our little aerial fracas in Los Angeles back in February?"

"Sir, only that the reports said it was a possible Japanese aircraft, a blimp or dirigible of sorts. Somehow it escaped unharmed to the south at a leisurely pace after much artillery and ack-ack ground fire."

Roosevelt squinted through his specs. "So far so good."

Marshall took the cue. He used his finger to trace the text under the heading *Battle of Los Angeles.* "I asked Professor Bush and his team about it after they saw the *Ultra and Cosmic Classified* footage of the craft molting smaller scout craft from its belly; we silenced a few papers on that detail. When Rear Admiral Anderson picked one up in the sea, Secretary Stimson ordered him to have it examined by a special-clearance Navy unit at the San Diego naval base; it had no markings, weapons, or pilot. Another craft crashed in the Santa Ana mountains, an Army G2 unit was quickly on the scene. No ordinance other than scout aircraft was dropped by the larger unidentified airship. P-40 pursuit aircraft with low-light cameras confirmed this action. Professors Bush, Lawrence, and Compton concluded it was most likely *not* Japanese. Since the antiaircraft fire went on for hours with searchlights having acquired the target, they said it's most likely, and I quote, 'non-Earthly, and therefore interplanetary.' All similarly classified reports from now on will go to the Office of the Coordinator of Information Director after my approval, Colonel William Donovan."

Roosevelt laughed a little. "Old Wild Bill, what a character. *Ultra and Cosmic* designations refer to my new little program headed by General Jimmy Doolittle, Winston, the *Interplanetary Phenomenon Unit,* or IPU. The General and his team will keep track of all the strange 'War of the Worlds' happenings for the war's duration, no Orson Wells narration needed. By the by, that radio program was a secret test cobbled up by Army Intelligence and the Secret Service Department to gauge the American public's reaction to a possible Mars invasion. A False Flag Operation on my order. It only proved that there were far fewer people who sincerely panicked than the vast majority of those who did not. Americans have naturally tough sinew.

They—" The black telephone buzzed loudly. "Who? Send him in." Fleet Admiral Ernest J. King entered.

"Ah! Come in Admiral," said the president. "I want you in on this particular part of my briefing."

Famously stubborn and hot-headed King sat next to Marshall. "Yes, sir."

"Read on, General."

Marshall continued. "Sir, according to Army G2 intelligence reports dated from January 1st to June 15th, prototype Northrup P-61 Black Widow night fighters have confirmed close-range sightings of what they term 'Foo-Fighters' over western Germany and northern France, but they did *not* appear on the experimental airborne intercept radar they have. The glowing unknown objects paralleled and zig-zagged our planes; one crew shot at the spheres but no return fire was given. Doolittle said they were spectators and probably 'not of this world,' but he also said there's a chance they might be of German manufacture, reconnaissance craft possibly. Television or camera equipped. Form of propulsion unknown."

Churchill said: "We thought they were Jerry's own as well, until MI-6 and the Air Ministry reported to me that the Germans thought they were ours. Bit of a mystery, but I can tell we're all of one mind on this."

Roosevelt pointed to King. "In the Pacific Theater…down Coral Sea way, the Navy informs me they've seen them too on occasion near New Guinea during engagements with the Japanese, as if 'they' were observing both sides. No interference was reported, but of course one popped out of the ocean one night and scared the living *shit* out of a destroyer's crew!"

Mild chuckles.

"Yes it did, sir," said the admiral, who found the least humor in it. "Next time… we'll shoot the little green bastards down if the order is given."

Cold silence.

Having been Assistant Secretary of the Navy in his younger years, and having absorbed much wisdom through hard political and personal experience, the president frowned at the admiral's arrogance. He tilted his head to the side and took a long drag, allowing smoke to slowly rise from his wrist and mouth, partially veiling his face. Through his pince-nez, he locked eyes with King and drilled a look into him that could punch a hole through steel. In a serene voice he said: "They're not green…they're *grey-y-y*. Very short or very tall, no empathy to speak of. Rather large eyes. Time travelers, spacefarers, and associates of the most elite Nazis, but that stays in this room. Other more benevolent races abound. Ours is not the only war going on. And the shoot-down order is…*not* given. Tell your admirals that. These…'celestial devices' as I call them, unless they fire upon you first, no action is to be taken. Make sure Ghormley, Halsey, and Nimitz are all keenly aware. Do I make myself absolutely goddam clear?"

An uncomfortable pause.

Without moving his head, King looked to Churchill then to Marshall. Both gave him the same hard look. "Aye, aye, sir. Very clear. My report," said the admiral glumly.

The president hefted the file up and down. "Ernie, I'll…have to ask you to leave us now. Many thanks."

The admiral got up and left in a huff, a bit shaken. He was not privy to the deeper and more classified conversation to be had and clearly resented it.

When the door closed, the president continued. "Perhaps soon we should bring him into the greater fold, but for now it's just us three."

"Agreed, sir," said Marshall. Churchill nodded.

The president went on. "Despite our harsh setbacks, Winston, Bataan for us, Tobruk now for you, our victory at Midway and the sunk Japanese carriers should remind us both to stiffen our spines with resolve and count our blessings. And I'll remind the both of you old soldiers that the Russians are taking the German brunt, and despite their own retreats, Stalin has tremendous Siberian manpower in res-e-r-v-e. Millions. And the industrial might in the Urals to supply them with tens of thousands of new tanks and aircraft."

"The wounded but rugged bear will pounce again, and harder," said Churchill.

Marshall added: "Reports state their casualty lists are growing by the hundreds of thousands from the new German thermobaric fuel-air rockets being tested, a devastating secret weapon system, but that's being kept classified by both sides. I know this, Mr. President, Prime Minister, because the Reds are tough sons-of-bitches and they fight hard for their Motherland, they're not cowards by any stretch. Why else would they retreat? It makes sense. No mention of gas or biological weapons. Luckily, the Soviets' improved T-34 tanks are the best medium tanks in the world right now because of their many numbers. Devastating and simply-built, a good main gun, sloping armor, reliable diesel engines, fast. Their production lines are quicker than the Germans' by far."

Churchill re-lit his cigar. "'Quantity has a quality all of its own.' Stalin's words, naturally."

Roosevelt perused File B; he took a lower tone. "Gentlemen, we are all top-shelf Freemasons here. Let's discuss freely what we think is *really* going on at the far fringes of this global conflict. As top dog in this fancy kennel, I'll go first. We all know a tidbit or two about our hidden world history that must remain secret for the war's duration, but it's my hope humanity as a whole will be enlightened when we've won, though we should spin it our own way to reduce panic. Now, as I've come to learn from others far above me spiritually over the decades, especially certain Zoroastrian gentlemen I greatly admire, God created duality and polarity for the loving and benevolent cos-mos to learn harsh lessons; low vibrational energy versus the high. Well, we got it in spades down here, I reckon. No pain, no hardship, no great loss to be had, equals no wisdom to be gained. 'Tough titties,' as my lovely wife and her she-men gang like to say, especially when boozing along in her baby blue Buick for forested parts unknown. She knows a wee morsel of what we're chatting about, oh yes. A woman after my own *hah-a-r-r-t*, you might say."

Churchill and Marshall laughed a little, the First Lady controversial, rebellious, warmly loved and bitterly hated, but a class act.

Roosevelt cleared his throat, his health on the downswing. "America as you both know has a secret destiny: She's *The New Atlantis* said Court Astronomer John Dee to Queen Elizabeth the First, a beautiful goddess of a land, this very neoclassical city under our feet being built upon the 77th-meridian crumbling remnants of the Atlantis Empire's western-edge colony. This city has been reconstructed over time in strict accordance to Hermetic Law, the Sacred Cubit, the Kabbalah Tree of Life, and the Megalithic Yard thanks to our fellow compatriots L'Enfant, Jefferson, Banneker, and George Washington, who's monument's obelisk is surrounded by the Sacred Feminine *Vesica Pisces*, bless her feet. And Winston, I *personally* chose the location for the new

Defense Department, one built around an ancient pentagon-shaped star fort that connects with the city grid using the sacred geometry of our illustrious ancient forebears; I knew we would be drawn into the war years ago; it was our destiny, the 'Arsenal of Democracy' and more. The subtle earth energy coursing through those long hallways properly channeled will help us achieve our inevitable victory."

"Impressive. I never knew the entire gist before," said Marshall.

Churchill removed his damp cigar. "I never conjured any doubts on your part, Franklin." The president said: "The Russians are cleansing what peoples and history are left of old Tartaria, their fine buildings, gold-domed mosques. In a few years' time, all we'll have left of her are the old maps and a few scattered stones. Lost high civilizations and their close associations with star people are being scrubbed from history. Pitiful, really. Sad."

"And the Japanese are doing the same to the Khmer ruins in Indochina," added Marshall. "Though we'll have their undivided attention soon enough."

Staunchly conservative, Winston said defiantly: "Perhaps that's *best*. If the common people wake up too fast about our true history and reality, our continuing visitations from extraterrestrials, then uprising, anarchy, and deprivation will befall the entire—"

"I *vehemently* diss-ah-gree!" snapped Roosevelt, suddenly emotional. "So help me almighty *God*, I'll stand up in Congress when this war's over and tell them the truth square in the eye, wobbly legs or no. Americans are *tough*, Americans are *smart*, from the farmer to the physicist, from the Negro shop clerk to the Mexican Rosie the Riveter, from the Appalachian sailor to the old money admiral, and they will accept the unacceptable with *stoicism* and *courage*, their life blood. They deserve that much. And so do your fine people. Am I *clear*?"

Churchill chewed his cigar with vigor as if to say something, but did not. He now fully understood why he admired his friend and peer so very much, a man who dared to accomplish the impossible against all odds, just like himself.

A cough. "Please continue, Mr. President," said Marshall calmly as the two men leered at one another.

The president flicked ashes. "Sorry, bit tired today. Now listen you two, we servants of the Brethren have kept the idea of true democracy alive for millennia and will continue to do so, the secret dream of all ancient philosophers. In case of sabotage,

I've sent my people to microfiche the entire Philosophical Research Library in California that Manly P. Hall has accumulated as a knowledge replica of the Library of Alexandria, Egypt, which we three know held the entire wisdom of the Atlanteans and all Prediluvian societies. The film will be stored underground at a new military facility in the Blue Ridge Mountains off Route Fifty. Ditto for the American Philosophical Society of Philadelphia. Let us hope that one day that benevolent destiny will be realized, my slight-of-hand New Deal a hefty start."

"Which the war has now stifled," said Churchill.

Marshall added: "Ruined, I'd say, but everyone has a job now."

"Undeniably," said the president. "Now then, as you both are aware, our loveable green, lush, and watery world of Eden, lodged firmly in a never-ending loop of time immortal, has been settled by many august cosmic explorers, farmers in their jean overalls, brainy zoologists, keen geologists, sharp-eyed geneticists, traders, miners, and various bloodthirsty conquerors over the mossy ages. In addition to her being a school of sorts, it's plain to us that Mother Earth is also a bitterly fought-over battleground. The dark minority against the light majority. All the world's a stage—she's the grandest of war prizes, and we are but mere thespians, slaves, and soldiers, I fear."

"Now I understand why you told the admiral to go," said Marshall. "He's... quite religious."

Roosevelt adjusted his pince-nez tighter, knowing full well that Freemasons and other occult philosophers clung to religion publicly in order to carry on with the universal truth—the "Light"— in the shadows without fear of modern-day Spanish inquisitions. The Egyptian goddess Isis represented the all-knowing, all-loving female-vibration cosmos, the big secret, the real threat to Rome's brutal spiritual totalitarianism based solely on patriarchy. Still, he chose diplomacy at the moment. "I-n-d-e-e-e-d. The Great Hermetica, or 'The Gift of the Lamp,' was passed down through history from antediluvian, predynastic Egypt to ancient Greece and Persia, then it was secretly adopted by the early Christian Gnostics, then it was lost for a while until the dualistic Cathar Knights of France incorporated it into their philosophy with help from the local nobles. From there, the 'Lamp' traveled into the arms of the Templars, then to the Rosecrucians, and onwards to the Freemasons. We must remain respectful and gentle on this, those that fastidiously tuck The Bible under their bed pillow must be slowly led by the hand through the dreamland of truth ever so mindfully and graciously. Personally,

I don't see any conflict with *God* over any of this, this is *His* doings, *His* designs, *His* cosmos, but organized religions will suffer someday when their more rigid adherents finally catch wind of the grand scam perpetrated by the illustrious but dubious Anunnaki and their despicable cohorts over the last thirty millennia. That rainy day will be a sad but necessary one."

"Should I be nervous?" asked Churchill with a slight smile.

Eyes dark and tired, the president tilted up his smoky quellazaire.

"No, my friend, you should not. But I know more about you than you think—la-dee-da. My troupe of Theosophical masters that tutor me are indispensable. How far up the pyramid are you...*r-e-a-l-l-y*?"

Churchill thought for a moment. "Three hundred fifty-seventh degree or thereabouts, near the top, but that doesn't matter as much as does the free-thinking person, I'm told. Bloodline must be pure."

"Illuminating and fascinating. Three fifty-eight for me and three fifty-four for George here. We three all know the risks, we all know that our darker-minded Masons, a small minority of rich and powerful fellow brothers to be sure, will want us hanged someday, so be on alert. Trust no one completely."

"Agreed in full."

"Yes sir. Are we sure this office is secure?" asked Marshall, a bit paranoid.

"*Very* secure. I've had security redoubled. So, where was I...ah! First, there were the biblical and mythical Hyperboreans in Pangea who suffered cosmic war, then it was the Lemurians in the Pacific, the descendants of which are now helping us fight the Japs island after island, then there was Khmer, then Mu, Lumania, Shambala, Zimbabwe, then Atlantis and her many foes from out yonder, amongst their own, and below; she destroyed herself in hubris, her technical achievements far outweighing her spiritual core. A great empire that rose and fell.

"From there we moved on to Egypt, Greece, Persia, Mongolia, and the grim Roman Empire that inherited much of their technology and architecture from the Prediluvian ancients, and yet still she fell to ruin. Today it's the fasces-wielding Nazis and Germans and Italians and Japs who are on the conquering path. Nothing has really changed. Since 1918, the unresolved war has simmered below the surface like an overheating Oldsmobile in a junkyard these past years and has now become our shiny new Cadillac, Tommy Guns blazing and running *flat out*."

"Hear-hear," blurted Churchill.

The president shook his head back and forth to accentuate his words. "Proxy wars for the mul-tee-too-din-ous and multinational forces of light and darkness from everywhere and beyond the heavens have been our tearful legacy, our primary focus as a human race despite our myriad achievements in the arts and natural sciences. Allegiances shift with the sands of time, old foemen become new allies and vice versa; pyramids, temples, and civilizations grew tall before their collapse, but the darkness...yes, the *darkness*, oozes and slithers its way in between the cracks of history, meanders around the fallen pillars of the ancients, and rears its head from time to time in purified occult form to feast upon the raw energy of ritualistic mass death, our Earth an abattoir, a Chicago *slaughterhouse*. The Nazis, Black Venetian Nobility, and the Japanese Black Dragons are the purified essence of that darkness, the pinnacle, the current unmasked head of that fearsome *snake-in-a-basket*, hidden in the shadows no more. Their evil, corrupt secret society factions versus ours. This time though, today, with our horrifying new weapons of unimaginable power on the drawing boards and in the sky, I fear the entire universe is watching us very, very closely. It is my belief...we are *all* on trial."

Winston stood and removed his cigar with vigor. He paced, then looked out the bay window. "I cannot but agree wholeheartedly. As I've always said, for better or worse, Stalin, you, and I must attain the ultimate in bully status over our global schoolyard. Otherwise, this joust may be the last for everyone." He then sat and massaged his belly, his headache worsening.

At this, the three men meditated for a minute or so, their countenances grave. "George?" asked the president gently, his voice jovial in its roller-coaster cadence.

"You're being aww-fully silent and sullen. Speak your mind. Or is it...that you require a martini?"

Marshall tightened his brown Army tie and squirmed uncomfortably; he usually kept an official distance from the president, but on this topic, *the topic*, he needed intimate proximity. "Mr. President, Prime Minister, there's one more issue. Professor Bush has had several conversations with Dr. Oppenheimer regarding the Manhattan Project in development; both are very familiar with ancient history on our level and beyond. Since we know that atomic-type weapons were most likely used in ancient times in India thereabouts, the Vedic texts warn us of severe complications and possible repercussions. I'm not sure I..."

"Do tell, General," said Churchill during another pause.

Roosevelt ordered: "Yes, do go on. If I remember correctly, it was in the Indus Valley region, Mono…Mohenjo-Daro, I believe."

Marshall gathered his wits. "Yes, sir, that rings a bell. Allow me to read Oppenheimer's personal note which is addressed to you specifically, Mr. President, since I'm not qualified to comment on it. It reads as follows: *'It is not known if a large fission explosion could ignite part or all of the Earth's atmosphere, rendering everything surface-wise to a cinder. In addition, from what I know of deeply ancient historical accounts, an atomic blast of a certain yield may affect more than just the local battlefield at hand. The texts strongly allude that a blast of such magnitude will rip through many of the twelve known densities and their infinite, concentric circle dimensions of our universe, causing millions of additional casualties in those higher realms. The spacetime rip can, for an instant, allow what's known as a 'portal' to and from these dimensions to form unnaturally with no safeguards. A situation could arise where many opportunist dark forces of a low vibration coupled with negative political agendas would enter, thus reinforcing our already perilous wartime reality and timeline.*"

Marshall then showed them an old engraving that was included by Oppenheimer for emphasis. It was the *Avri Potabilis Chemice Preparati, The Alchemical Preparation of the Golden Elixir*. It showed concentric circles with a plethora of occult symbols surrounding a pyramid in the starry sky, rays shining down upon the Tree of Life, Earth, animals, birds, phoenixes, a fiery volcano, the seas, and people of many races. It represented all the dimensions of the heavens alchemically affecting the physical plane, a direct symbiosis. "I can't even begin to imagine what might happen to our world, both seen and unseen."

"God in Heaven…" muttered Roosevelt, examining it. "How close are the Germans?" Marshall read another report. "Their multiple atomic programs are very active but slow. Heavy Water experiments in Norway, Hechingen isotope-enrichment units may be close to uranium U-235 enrichment with scientists Heisenberg, Hahn, Gerlach, and Strassmann, but reports vary on successes, failures, and dead ends. Minister Speer promised Hitler a bomb that would *'knock a man off his horse from ten miles distant.'*

The president said: "To hell with Speer. We must endeavor to pick up the pace! Non-terrestrial know-how in atomic and quantum science must be used for perfecting super weapons to affect the complete destruction of Germany and Japan. We should take firm advantage of every 'celestial wonder' that comes our way."

"Huzzah."

"Agreed, sir," said Marshall. "It's already been assigned to the *Non-Terrestrial Science Special Committee* per your order."

"Good. Keep on," smiled the president.

"Polish intelligence operatives claim that AEG and I.G. Farben are perfecting their Version Three chemical laser for isotope purification, but actual confirmation on performance is hard to come by. Telefunken and Siemens miniaturized transistors are being used in radar and U-Boat torpedo calculators and will likely end up in their rocket and advanced experimental aircraft programs. The Zuse Z3 digital computer is of course essential for all their high technology projects, and that's alarming in my book. But… what's really troubling are the unconfirmed rumors of special SS mining units that're scouring everywhere high and low for *thorium*, which is found in rare earth materials such as monazite and euxenite."

"Mining units?" asked Churchill worriedly. "*Thorium?*"

Marshall coughed. "Yes, sir, a possibility. Professor Trump told me thorium is used to coat tungsten filaments which are then fitted inside electronic devices such as radar. It's also used in making high-powered scientific equipment and high-quality camera lenses—Zeiss and Agfa come to mind in regards to optics on tanks, ships, subs, and aircraft. But those are just the nifty little side benefits, he said. If the rumors are true and I believe them to be, the Germans aren't just looking for itty-bitty inferior-quality amounts here and there in occupied Europe or captured Russian territory, but tons of high-grade ore found in select geological pockets mostly in the Middle East, northern India, and Egypt, and *much more* than is estimated for a bomb enrichment or electronics program." Here he paused, the enormity of the complex issues almost indigestible, the details unbelievable at best. "These elite units are in bed with the Thule, Vril, and Ahnenerbe societies. And, of course…we all know…what that means."

In a rare display of hot temper, the president pitched his coffee cup and saucer to the front panel of his desk where it shattered. "Damn!"

Nervous and overwhelmed, Churchill ground his cigar stub in the ornate John Adams ashtray, thought fondly of his wife, family, and finally his grandniece Beatrice, the hard-drinking, randy, always-on-report, irreverent Godless libertine he admired so much, mostly because she reminded him of his younger self gone irreparably wild and feral, only more so. He then low-growled: "Now we know exactly why the Foo-Fighter pilots are watching us all so closely: Quick advancement armed with little wisdom."

2

Same day
Libya-Egypt border

"Get that bloody arsehole off our fucking *tail!*" yelled Bea frantically, pulling up hard on the yoke and turning sharply into her pursuer at near full power, a lone Italian Macchi 202 dressed in spotted tan desert camouflage like a Cheetah, its guns ripping apart the unarmed, twin-engined C-47 *Gooney Bird* transport. The other two transports had peeled off to the north to escape.

Copilot in several pieces, windshield cracked, wind deafening, the starboard cockpit had been ripped open by 20 mm cannon rounds, but the American-built plane was tough, built to take punishment. Blood painted the control panel and Bea, dust from the diminutive sandstorm was everywhere, and shrapnel bits were lodged in her arms and face; she shook violently with shock and adrenaline. Wild evasive action was taken, throttles firewalled.

Tossed about in the passenger compartment, mostly wounded veterans from the recent fighting at the Jalu Oasis in Libya, ten Australians, four New Zealanders, and a Free French officer and his Malian sergeant bodyguard had smashed open the windows and were giving return fire with two Bren machineguns and rifles, but their arc of fire was limited even when Bea yawed violently back and forth with the rudder. "Put a hole in that sonofabitch!" she yelled.

The floor was slick with the blood from the dead and wounded; brass was everywhere, a mess. Big shell holes ventilated the compartment. Out of the twenty-two, fourteen were left alive. Panic, steady nerves, discipline, yells, moans of agony.

Screaming, the Malian let go a full 20-round clip with his Bren, hitting the Italian fighter and causing a vapor trail from the wing, his starboard fuel tank hit. The Italian plane fled.

An alarm. "Gods, no!" Hit severely, the starboard engine was now on fire; Bea feathered the prop, cut the fuel pump, and flipped the control for the extinguisher and the fire went out slowly. Control cables damaged, she had much reduced input on her yoke; the transport weaved back and forth on its own. "Now what?" Oil pressure warning lights on the port engine came on, a few stray rounds had found their quarry. Oil streaks plastered the left wing. "This is a bloody daymare!"

The Malian came rushing in head down, stepping over the dead pilot that Bea had removed from her seat. The man was six-foot-four, strong, black as coffee, a *sergeant-chéf* named Gwafa, and spoke a heady mix of French and English with a perfumed eastern African accent. "He's gone, *madame*! Eye-tie bastard! Many are dead. I clipped him with the Bren."

The rough desert terrain filled her view. "We're losing altitude! Port motor's losing pressure."

"*Mon Dieu, merde.*" Gwafa wiped blood and brain bits off the throttle quadrant, translating English labels in his mind. "We must try to re-start the starboard engine. It can run with many cylinders gone."

Bea struggled with the yoke, hands full, left rudder trim full, eyes wide, the vibration immense. Her teeth chattered. "You're a m-m-mechanic?"

"Yes. Mostly *les camions*, but I'm damn good. Flew a Mureaux-113 once or twice. *L'armée* trains us well, no questions asked. I used to steal motorcars and aeroplanes as a profession. A *voleur*, thief."

"Well done." Bea spied the port engine oil pressure gauge, it wasn't pretty. "Follow my instructions."

On the overhead panel he reset the generators, set the fuel and pumps, opened cowl flaps to half, mixture lever to half of maximum, flipped the primer switch two times, and hit the red starter button. The prop twirled as the starter motor strained. "Come on—*vite, vite!*"

"Burn out the booster coils—do it! We're drifting, rudder's shot up." Bea compensated for the reduced power, but she was way off course to the south, blown there by the sudden storm, her altitude 7300 feet and descending fast. Way points and familiar topography were long gone, but a large salt pan was off to port, probably Siwa. *Disputed territory*, she thought. *Under the horse's hooves of destruction* we are. "Errghhh! Come on you ruddy rudder, do your damn job!"

Gwafa eased off the mixture and hit the starter again. Prop twirling, the starboard radial engine repeatedly backfired loudly then came alive at seven then finally eleven out of fourteen cylinders spewing black smoke. He ran the throttle up slowly, checked the cylinder head temperatures, then eased off when the wounded engine found its sweet spot. Manifold pressure up a bit, Bea had an additional thirty-five percent thrust.

"God bless Pratt and Whitney!" she exclaimed.

"*Victoire*! R-1830 is as tough as the plane. That's what I read anyway." He pulled out his knife, cut the straps, then pulled what was left of the copilot out of his seat one chunk at a time; his stained kepi fell off his head.

The oil-leaking port engine became weaker, sputtering. The fuel pressure gauge died, the line severed. "It's packed up, we're going in. Help me with the yoke." Bea adjusted her trim, goosed the power up a tad on the remaining engine, and aimed for a narrow valley between two wind-blown plateaus. "Tell those wankers back there to get down on the floor, *prone*."

"*Oui, madame*." He leaned back and caught eyes with a stocky New Zealand corporal.

He used his hand up and down. "Get down!" The men did so.

Weaving, pitching, hydraulic pressure weak, she kept the wheels up for a belly landing in the desert northeast of the lake. "Just *once* I'd like to land a crate in good fettle…"

They hit hard, the rocky desert terrain unforgiving. The fuselage snapped in half just behind the trailing edge of the wings—cargo crates, mail, medical supplies, men, and bodies were scattered behind like so much confetti. At the bottom of a large, reddish rocky plateau, a stepped *hammada*, the front fuselage came to an abrupt halt, sand and stone filling the cockpit.

3

♈

Portugal
July 20

Up a steep hill in ancient Santo Alvaro, Bernie Rodgers licked his dry lips and adjusted his threadbare beret to block the hot sun. Dressed shabbily in torn dungarees and dirty boots, he led an old horse and older cart with a poor family in it. Six nuns followed on foot, their cornettes' starched white wings catching the slight breeze, hoping for flight.

Thin, his beard thick and itchy, Bernie was hungry and tired after his long trip and yawned accordingly. His repast three nights before included fresh fish, fig tart, and some of the best red wine he'd ever had. Ecstasy. Now he wanted a repeat performance after only meager oatmeal that morning. Dried dates and water only made him hungrier. Two frail, aged women passed his group going downhill with market baskets; they talked of their worthless husbands, the solstice, the price of tomatoes, and the war in Africa which they claimed sent up much more dust in the Sirocco wind. Bernie only understood a local word or two here and there. He doffed his wool saucer with respect.

A whining Alfa Romeo coupé, dark red and shiny, its Milan fiery dragon logo polished to perfection, passed them going downhill in first gear. The posh, spectacled man at the wheel looked satisfied, well fed, fat. He had departed from the fourteenth-century monastery at the top of the hill where an older model Rolls Royce sedan was parked behind the driveway gate like a rare caged animal. It seemed an odd pairing, sitting next to a monk's humble horse-drawn wagon.

Bernie put hands to hips as the red car purred out of sight downhill. He thought of the plentiful Standard Oil that was being shipped in from America and sold illegally to the Axis powers by the Portuguese merchants and grew a smile. "An 8C Alfa, eh? Fast and thirsty. Keep up the straw man deals. And my stocks will rise and rise."

"*O que, Senhor?*" asked the grey-haired mother, feeding her children small pieces of blood orange.

Bernie spoke the native tongue as best he could. "Hmm? Oh-h-h, just that some of the finest cars are wasted on the worst people, *señora*, that's all."

One of the nuns translated his mishmash gibberish.

They passed the ornate medieval entrance, its tall cast iron lanterns age-old sentinels, two robed monks stood there with smiles. One asked a nun what church they belonged to. The woman said Santo Martinho up ahead, whose bell was now ringing the hour.

•••

The long table, elegantly set with the finest Italian china, 18th-century silverware from France, a red silk tablecloth, and thick local bundles of twig greenery, shimmered in the dim torch light of the grand cellar eighty feet below grade. Multitudes of candles were then lit, and a heavenly glow descended.

Bishop Arruda, a local man fresh from Rome's intrigues and elegant private salons, a proud House of Savoy Venetian Black Nobility member, his telltale family pin shiny, held up a golden chalice to the twinkling altar that rose above him, eager to perform *Maleficium*. Speaking ancient Sumerian, he made an offering to male and female effigies. He finished up in Latin, shaking with devotional vitality. "Thy will be served; thy will is truth." Kissing the bare nipples of the granite statue, her three arms holding a key, dagger, and flaming torch laced with incense, he then bowed in ritualistic fashion over and over, massaging the delicate, fine carving of the iron-spiked wheel at her feet. More rituals followed, more deep-toned chanting, the smoky atmosphere fouled but energized. "O mighty Catherine of the Wheel."

Thirteen children, all under the age of eight, sat still. Tied tightly to their chairs with hemp rope, a few shed tears, others wore blank stares, their innocence and sanity long gone and shattered. Some wet their pants or dresses, the urine dripping down their legs to their bare, bruised feet that bore blistered burns from hot iron appliqués centuries old, rusty relics of the Inquisition. They had been locked in small boxes for days with severed body parts from rotting corpses, or put in cages with vicious monkeys or other animals to condition them, their personalities fractured into shards. Those that lived would be the strongest, yet the easiest to control. Upon adulthood they would become mindless assassins, their souls caged.

Four tall "priestesses" in symbol-embroidered black wool garb stood behind them, ensuring discipline, ensuring devotion; long red zodiac sashes cascaded to the floor. Their eyes were darkened in ancient Egyptian style, oddly predynastic yet different, their sumptuous black hair knotted tightly and covered in heavily perfumed beeswax that melted slowly in the heat. The room stank, its air thick with garlic, mismatched herbs, perfume, opium, and rank bodily odors.

Twelve middle-aged men—Serbian, German, English, Venetian, French, Egyptian, others—dressed in off-white hooded robes with embroidered symbols of the Maltese Cross hung below two Xs, their foreheads ashened with a reverse cross, faces behind thin gold wire masks, stood witness, their unvarnished enthusiasm clear to all. One man, an elite surgeon, had left in a hurry, the Alfa man. Family problems he said, "*uma emergência*," his own precious child in need of urgent medical attention at home.

Three loyal monks, the "servers," "informers," and "chanters," stood far behind everyone in the shadows, bathing in the low vibrational luxury of the event, heads bowed under brown hoods, unanointed but hopeful. They were also the "cleaners," and would scour the ritual room spotless after the ceremony. No evidence would remain, none ever had. Tradition.

All anointed ones had helped themselves to the tender pleasures from the children hours before during a slow-moving and laborious demonic mass in the lower chapel, its stone floor carpeted with dried white rose petals and spotted red from brutal rape and torture; men from behind, women in front, the children's pelvises spread like Monarch butterflies. Athirst, soon they would indulge their sinister spiritual lust, their unquenchable desire for unsullied warm blood and the highly purified occult power it possessed. A gift for their master and his minions of the dark; unpolluted and frightened children produced the purest fear-laden Vril energy, hormones, and adrenaline. It was just business, a transaction, a deal made sound for all.

Profitable.

"Cry not my little ones," said Arruda as he sat at the head. "This is a grand feast to celebrate our joyous and generous master. Just imagine how lucky you all are to have fresh meat for dinner when most of Europe is choking on rotten cabbage and dried fish heads."

Before them all on silver chargers were two naked adults without feet or hands, one man, one woman, both selected breeders, their legs tied back, their arms twine-tied together behind their heads like geese, mouths stuffed full of herbs and garlic and pine cones, roasted magnificently with generously-applied duck fat to make their crisp brown skin glisten in the dense candlelight. Meat thermometers jutted from their rectums, their eyes cooked to a milky grey. All their genitalia had been surgically removed off before roasting by trained butchers, the "cutters."

The lead priestess in a Medusa mask began to carve a slice of crackling skin and meat from a thigh with an ancient short sword, the burned rosemary carefully planted in the flesh looking like little trees after a forest fire. A dark aromatic sauce made from Madeira, butter, herbs, sacred mushrooms, and genitalia giblets was poured over the slice, ensuring a savory, ritualistic, culinary experience. Nothing had been wasted. No minute ritual detail overlooked.

The child began to shake, then vomit; the meat carved from her own mother, an honor said Arruda. The priestess cut the meat into small morsels while she chanted a flowery medieval poem, then forked several, forcing them into the child's quivering mouth while her strong hand squeezed her young jaws open, head back. The little girl gagged, a seizure ignored. More meat followed in quantity. When her toilsome meal was literally finger-shoved down and thus consumed in full, the woman unsheathed a curved dagger and slit the girl's jugular. "*Mortem est vita!*"

"*Sanguis est anima vivens!*" From behind, one of the greedy white robes pressed his gold cup to gather it all; he then drank, his white garment permanently stained in glorious crimson. He let go a tilted-back sigh of utter relief and satisfaction that stirred the anticipation of his excited cohorts, a hopeless drunk's long sobriety ended, quenched only by the exquisite drug most desired above all else, young adrenalized blood.

The other children, one by one, slowly began to endure their fate. All adults chanted in low tones: Latin, ancient Greek, old Slavic, Armenian, Sumerian.

The bishop stood and toasted with his jeweled goblet of wine mixed with day-old blood. "We commit this flesh to our bowels from whence it originally came, and in turn our gallant masters shall feast the light emanating from within our corpulent souls. May they gorge well."

"Thy will be done," chorused the adults. "The Law upheld."

•••

Behind the monastery at the rear entrance, or what passed for it, a small rusted gate bolted shut centuries past, Bernie let go of the horse, sending the family on their way with a leather purse of small gold coins and a smile. Peering everywhere for civilians, he gave the all clear sign.

Two of the nuns ditched their robes and habits; they were beefy British SOE, Special Operations Executive, former coal miners from Clyde, skilled commandos.

Brigadier McMaster had finally gotten his wish for a full-fledged training program back in England. The two men grabbed their rucksacks, ammo belts, and rifles from the back of the slow-moving cart; one M1 Garand, one Enfield carbine, cocked and ready. Dark blue plateau berets were donned, borrowed Portuguese uniforms creased and sharp.

The four remaining nuns were women volunteers; a Portuguese, a Basque, and two Spanish. Bernie had chosen them personally—handpicked, fit, trained well, all keen.

Professionals from the Pyrenees. Bandits. Boinas in black.

"Over the wall," hissed Bernie quietly, opening his worn leather suitcase and removing his personal FBI standard-issue Thompson submachinegun from its tight fittings. He threw on an eight-magazine bandolier and inserted a stick clip into the action quietly.

The two Brits pitched canvas-wrapped grappling hooks which caught on the reverse side; they scurried up and over in smart fashion, hushed boots to wall, landing on a monk tending to flowers and killing him silently through the throat with their long triangular daggers. The gate cracked open.

The women, equipped with rucksacks and sharp knives in their tall boots, stuck heavy .357 magnum Smith & Wesson revolvers each into their thick belts sewn with extra ammunition. Their silk scarves had a big knot tied in them, deadly garottes. Two well-dressed guards were dispatched in silence, their pistols falling to the stone floor as the women choked them with quick, determined strength. The women were dead silent. Black cats padding softly.

Inside the luxuriously-decorated Moorish complex, one that Bernie thought may have been partly built millennia ago, he unfolded his three-nights-before-penned sketch of a map written on yellowed Marrakesh hotel stationary and stained with coffee. He quietly ordered: "Just as we discussed last night. Most of the monks are out and about doing good deeds, I hope. One man, one woman, at each exit here…and here. Follow the colonnade to the main entrance, the big wood doors under the arch. They bolt everything, it's that damn medieval craftsmanship, overdone. The locked cellar is directly below us. Set plastique, blow them, then stay low and enter guns blazing. Do it. They'll have armed guards in the outer chambers that flank the inner, here and here. Hopefully their arrogance will be in our favor. Be damned quick about it." *This fucking map cost me a lot of money and favors. Better be on the level,* he thought. *Goddam Golden Square assholes… untrustworthy at best.*

"Aye, sir."

"*Si, señor.*"

"*Bai jauna.*"

Charges set, the doors were blown. At each lower entrance, the two-person SOE man and woman team entered and shot the three armed Arab men in tan suits and tall black fezzes that stood guard. Stunned, their return fire was panicked, haphazard, and hit no one on Bernie's team. Amateurs versus professionals. It sounded the same on the far side. Shots. Yells.

"Now!" yelled Bernie, descending the ancient stairs. He almost tripped on a crack. "Shit!"

The two remaining women covered Bernie's rear. Jesuit monks came on the run. The women kneeled and squeezed off carefully-aimed shots, downing eight handily. "*Bastardos! Infantophiles!*" Some were innocent, some ignorant and naïve, some not, but they all had to go. The women spat on them. *Dios* would sort them out, they thought.

Bernie kicked the heavy main door to the cellar; it didn't budge a hair. Then with all three of them shoving, it cracked open after several tries. A shot found its way through the thick wood just above Bernie's head, then two more. "I've got the middle—the flanks are yours!" Bursting through, Bernie unloaded a blast at two men in robes, their pistols drawn. The SOE man shot three more to the left, and the Spanish woman downed two of the black-robed women at right.

The initiates had been armed only with short swords, their ancient inner sanctum always secured before now. Always.

When Bernie rushed to the table, six children were dead. He swiveled his Thompson. "Everyone down on the floor—now! Put your damn hands on your head, you." He kicked a white-robed man in the balls, collapsing him.

"Look who I caught, sir, the bloody *Black Pope* himself," growled the other SOE man, a grizzled sergeant. He pushed the bishop to the floor and kicked him hard in the ribs; a hidden ornate silver-handled knife fell from his silk sleeve, its tip stained with poison. "Fancy the nippers do ya, dogshite?"

Bernie took the butt of his Thompson and smashed the bishop's knee cap so the man wouldn't run or set about to mischief. "I need him alive. As for the rest of you goat-fuckers…"

"*Andiamo,*" said the Basque commando. Bonds cut, she and another woman led the alive but terrified children outside, carrying two on their shoulders. Outside at the entrance gate with an American-issue walkie-talkie, she called for the truck. "Sam Hill to Poncho Villa, package ready for pickup." Bernie had picked the mission's code words.

"Understood," crackled the receiver in Spanish.

An unmarked panel van arrived from a hidden downhill position at the front gate in a damn hurry for a Renault. Few pedestrians were near, fewer noticed. Sunday.

The woman kissed the man at the wheel, a known man, a trusted man. "Take good care of them, *padre*. They've seen hell. Parents are all dead. *Via con Dios*."

"God's mercy will prevail," he replied. "They'll never find them again. My word upon it." He shook a supplied Webley revolver in his lap. "Praise the Lord and pass the ammunition!"

She kissed him again on the mouth, harder. Her voice hard, the Spanish commando hard-slapped the hood. "*Vamonos!*" The padre gunned it.

The two black cats then stood guard at the top of the stairs, hidden. Iberian Lynxes. Guns drawn. Eyes and ears.

Shaking with adrenaline and emotion, Bernie scanned the sickening room; had he not seen the cursed tableau with his own eyes he would not have fully believed what certain human beings were truly capable of, millennia after millennia. It was one thing to read a classified occult history book or a report with photographs, *but this*… He told the two "bitches in black" to stand up and move back to the wall; they did not go willingly, and viciously cast useless spells and weaponized chants at their captors.

The whimpering, feisty bishop was thrust into his chair. "You'll all die for this at His Magnificent's command, your souls consumed!" yelled Arruda, unrepentant, defiant.

"Nah-h-h, I don't think so." Bernie calmly went over to the two eighteen-foot black granite statues set upon a white marble altar of unquestionable Renaissance quality and vintage, the skillful carving beyond first rate. All eyes fell to him. "Huh. Carved…or were they cast in geopolymer by the ancients? Doesn't matter. Let me guess, Baphomet, Ahriman, no, no, a bull with a royal purple and gold crown of the higher knowledge chakra? Must be *Moloch*, foul god of the Ammonites…and his galloping girlfriend Hekate with her sidekick owl and spiked wheel. Tsk, tsk, don't you shadow people ever tire of the same old gods? What about Inanna? She's an underrated Anunnaki starlet that *loves* fertility rites during wartime. Frisky old gal don't ya know. A real dish. The

Bohemian Grove boys in California just *love* her."

"Unwashed, unworthy infidel!" hissed Arruda, jowls fluttering.

Bernie smelled his stained armpits. "Actually, you're right. Anyway, nice joint. The polygonal block foundation here I'm guessing is far, far older than the monastery built on top of it, some of these stones must weigh hundreds of tons. Not exactly a *Juvenalia* going on down here, or is it, Nero fans? Plenty of gargoyles on witness I see, stone-carved or...otherwise. I'm guessing this, uh, *temple*, is built over a nodal point of intersecting Ley Lines as well? Fun and games telluric energy exchange between consenting occult and adult parties?" He neared. "Circus freak *Babylon Workings* and soggy-assed *May-gick* carnival side shows? Poshy ritual death dinners all the rage, such as this one?"

Arruda shook with fear and anger. "I know your kind. Y-you slithering grub worms, b-b-bow at our master's feet. His black love and conquering octaves feed us all."

"Pass. You know, cathedrals, monasteries, mosques, and churches were originally designed by the ancients to gather and magnify love and light, but for countless centuries they've been corrupted by religion and dipsquats like you all." He bent over slightly. "Remind me, Cardinal Richelieu, the deal is you hooded gentry believe you get favors and wealth and power from human sacrifice and torturing children in the name of these demiurge dilettantes. 'Give Lucifer his Loosh,' said the Old Testament. Now that's just the cat's pajamas all right. Sick and sad. *Pathetic*." Bernie unhooded the six remaining white robes one by one with the tip of his gun's barrel. "Oh, I'm not naysaying the energetic results per se, they're sadly effective if done absolutely correctly according to precise ritual, weather, place, and of course astrological timing. Some of the time, anyway." He then looked at each man's guilty face. "Hmm, don't know you, or...you for that matter. Ah! But I know you four fillies, oh yes-yes-yes." He enthusiastically withdrew photos from a file in his knapsack. "Yup. 'It's party time any ol' time, chaps,' as a girlfriend of mine once said."

Bernie's ad hoc commando team all laughed. They all knew he was a homosexual and didn't care a whit. One of the Spanish girls had tried and tried with him.

He rifled through the file. "Let's see here, folks. One banker, *Deutschebank* and Kuhn-Loeb. Financier to the Reich, kinda boring if I do say so. Ah-h-h, but a backer of commercial-sized, religious-order 'orphanages' in occupied countries it says here, and we all know what they're for, brothel and harem fans. One...retired major general, old English aristocracy, loaded to the gills, exemplary military record, *le meilleur*, oh my, that's not good, nope, not good at all. One Croatian merchant I think, Nazi party pin, gold, chemicals, and unnamed flammables, and very rich too it says here. Hmm…and you, blondie, AEG electricals. Aww-w-w-w, an old Prussian by birth, now a card-carrying Tunisian as a cover. I feel sorry for the Tunisians with you around, maybe the electric chair will suffice. And…where's my Argentinian? Down there? Whoops, I suppose I shot him." He shrugged in Vaudeville fashion. "Naughty big shots, all. And with a bizarre taste for…" Bernie leaned in slowly and dipped his finger, eyed the English general directly, then tasted it. "…unpalatable gravy." He snapped his fingers; an SOE man smartly brought him five briefcases from the corner padded pew. "And just look at the party favors we've found." He opened one and examined sensitive documents. "Sassy information here, by golly-gumdrops. Ploiesti oil fields, synthetics, I.G Farben chemicals—oh, they're a fun outfit, Nazi alchemists by the *score*. Isotope purification processes, lots of coded numbers here I don't know about yet but will soon enough, rare earth elements, something scientific called a *laser*, and so much multinational cash changing hands!"

"You'll die for this," said the Prussian confidently and calmly. "And your families."

The two SOE commandos laughed a little, their rifles pointed at the men's heads.

Bernie smelled the main course, waving in the scent to his nostrils. "Death is an illusion, *mein herr*. Do we look scared to you? And here I was hamming it up with my best James Cagney. See *The Roaring Twenties*? No? Good flick, Hitler's favorite they say. Anyway, too much garlic and rosemary as usual, I reckon. Chef's a bit untalented. You should eat *him* next."

Arruda added: "Y-y-you *idiota* filth should be concerned about the sacred entities in this room you *can't* see that will—"

Bernie laughed. "Really? Don't think so. My beaming smile and positive vibration ward them off with aplomb. Only weak-minded, greedy, knuckle-dragging dolts like you fine people are afraid of spooks, Archons, Jinn, and interdimensional Loosh-lovin' parasites. That's the gimmick, it only works if you embrace fear and *believe* they can harm you." A strange cold chill hit the back of his neck. "Ooh-h-h, there's one now. So cute."

"Who…*are* you?" asked the Croatian man. Malice flavored his words.

"Lil' ol' me? Colonel Leon Schlesinger, at your service, ex Hollywood. You all are going to be the evil ogres in my next Bugs Bunny cartoon courtesy of Jack Warner and his brothers. I pay top dollar. Free studio cocaine." *And Hollywood is chock full of your kind of swine.*

"W-what do you…*want*?" asked Arruda in a deep voice. He reached for his half-empty wine glass, but the Spanish woman put her knife through his hand, nailing it to the table. "Agggnnntthhhh…"

"*Un regalito de Dios,*" she snarled, nose to ear. The Prussian man stood in anger. "Leave him b—"

The other Spanish woman slapped him in the head with her pistol. "Show some respect, *diablo*! *Hijo de puta.*" She sat him down and put the barrel in his mouth, causing him to gag. "E-e-easy, *señoritas*, let's be gentle," said Bernie softly. "We're in polite company.

Quality folks only. A salubrious Dark Workers' union meeting."

"W-what is it you…*want*?" asked Arruda again as the knife was withdrawn and its blade cleaned on his silk red robe. She then put it to his throat, tight. "Gahgg…"

"Want?" Bernie rubbed his chin, then pointed to all the prisoners at the table; the SOE men forced them to eat flesh by pressing the barrels to their heads.

"Steak and kidney pie, lads. Eat up now, healthy appetites," said the sergeant. "Use your hands, grab that meat, open yer gobs. Don't spare the gravy." He then rifle-butted a man in his spine. "Eat, I said!"

Bernie sighed lengthily. "Want? Not much, your unholiness. Just some detailed information on your kiddie-loving pals bopping around Europe trading valuable secrets for gold doubloons or vice versa, and their polished-boot royal hosts in their lofty castles, all the Dracula types naturally. We love blackmail too, such a sharp tool for the shadow war, eh? All this shabby occult skullduggery that's—unfortunately—been highly necessary throughout history to balance things out far below the surface of our, *ahem*, 'agreed-upon' false reality. Oh-h-h, and we're greatly interested in your Vatican business dealings with jolly ol' Adolph and his SS boys, your little *Italiano* cliques of freaks." He cradled a dead child's head gently, running his fingers through the soft hair lovingly and felt sick, wanted to cry all of a sudden, but steadied his nerves with gritted teeth and a bit interior cheek. He swallowed hard, tasting his own blood and its earthy iron finish, his lightheartedness thick armor, intellect a war hammer. "A chummy German friend told me about you and your peculiar hobby, and your Nazi connections in Rome. He's safely locked up in Valhalla, and doesn't like the idea of mass ritual murder believe it or not, non-combatant children especially. We exchange sleazy favors. Tit for tat."

"He's an occultist!" spat the robed Egyptian man, gagging on his foul meal and pointing to Bernie with a shaking finger. "I can smell a White Illuminati dog anywhere. A bloodline *traitor*."

The other Spanish woman then poured the remaining genitalia sauce over his shaved head. "*Salud, pellejo.*"

Bernie bowed slightly with a disrespectful smile and arms outstretched as if in the court of King Louis XIII. "Guilty. The light, or in my case the dull grey, must always triumph over the dark, or try to with gusto. Business as usual. Nothing personal."

Furious beyond measure, Arruda angrily hissed like a snake from the back of his throat, flesh falling from his mouth.

"Open wide." Bernie removed the bishop's soft silk hat and stuffed it in the man's mouth. "You know, cowboys out west like to put their dusty boot on the head of a hissin' rattler before slicing it off," he whispered. "Feel *mine?*"

"What will you do with us?" asked the Englishman politely, a medal-winner from the Great War. He undid his white robe to show his old dress uniform and awards. It impressed no one. "The King knows me well."

"*You*, my dear general?" pointed Bernie, strolling about as if he owned the place.

"Fuck the King," growled the Sergeant, a sinewy Yorkshireman, aggressively pushing the general's head with his rifle barrel.

"You're going to a certain wind-blown island off western Scotland, a decaying castle for ver-r-ry special prisoners with dishonorable conduct charges and worse. No delicious children for miles and miles, just big standing stones erected by kind and loving women druids—armed with African double rifles of course says my girl—to mock you, day after day, all those angry Celtic mother spirits haunting you. You'll be debriefed by occult experts, nothing but the best.

"And there ye shall rot in a cold dungeon cell smelling of dead fish for five hundred years." Bernie then looked to Arruda and lied. "But as for the rest of you egg-sucking black magicians-in-training, if you roll over for us on certain, well, occult, industrial, financial, and *military* matters, I'll see what I can do pertaining to limited sentences or even possibly…a prisoner exchange." *After they talk, I'll personally have them all hot-pokered. That I swear.*

The general said calmly: "Since you're obviously a twisted mystery school initiate of a kind, why pick on us? Energy is energy, it's neutral. You must understand the necessity of what we're doing, the holy urgency behind it, that we're only abiding by Hermetic universal law and free will. As above, so below. Balance in all things. Polarity experienced in action and deed with—"

"*Polarity?*" Bernie almost tripped in a pool of blood, feeling even sicker, but held fast. "I'll go out on a limb and say the rest of the world has had a healthy snootfull of bullshit negative polarity for the last eon and a half. Hermetic law? More like finding *loopholes* in those laws, and we all know the world has been highly unbalanced towards the dark for the last nine thousand years—naughty, naughty, so-o-o *unsporting*, old chap. Above and below my ass. Nice little world war we have going on now, lots of belly-slithering combatants in *s-t-r-a-n-g-e* uniforms."

"You'll get *nothing* from me," said the general sternly.

"Oh?" Bernie motioned to his team. Two of his team grabbed the two unimportant white robed men by the hair and put them with the black-garbed witches against the tapestried wall.

Bernie put in a fresh 30-round magazine, cocked the action, and let go one long, deafening Tommy Gun burst. Down they went. He came back to the table and massaged the general's shoulders softly, attentively, as the others ate and gagged and puked. "We'll see about that," he whispered. "My dear prince Vlad, *Vlad the Impaler*, that is."

4

In a large dark tunnel, Bea awoke on a thin palm leaf mattress. She couldn't move, and began to fade into unconsciousness once again. One eye caught a blurry figure. When she focused, she saw a German soldier in full kit, short pants, garrison cap, and laced, knee-high desert boots, his head low between his knees as if asleep, battle-scuffed rifle tightly gripped.

Sunlight from the entrance bathed him and he cast a long shadow. He was blonde and bearded, his skin treacle brown from the reflective sand.

He suddenly shouted: "Get up!"

Bea tried to talk but couldn't, her throat bandaged.

His German sounded familiar. "Wake up! If you go back to sleep you will die."

"*Agghhhmmmmff...*"

The man cycled the action on his Mauser rifle and fired at the ceiling. The bullet ricocheted, and the thrumming noise went down the tunnel as if a hummingbird flew past.

In pain, Bea felt sedated; opium or laudanum.

The man grabbed her by the collar and shook her violently, bashing her head against the dry rocky wall. "*Awaken! Gott* damn your soul, don't die on me!"

Bea inhaled sharply as her eyes flew open. "*Lu-u-utz!*" she screamed.

Gwafa and another man held her. "Easy. Breathe slowly...that's it, madame, easy. Just a bad dream. Morphine, the last of it."

"Where's...where is he?" she hissed, her throat bandaged after all. It had been so real, and Lutz had worn an Iron Cross for valor, his breath smelling of strong grappa, face stubbled with a two-week-old beard. It was the most vivid, full-color dream she'd ever had of him, perhaps more of a nightmare. She felt like crying, but dehydration kept her eyes dry.

"Who?" asked Gwafa. "It's only the three of us here."

A New Zealander in his beret held her tight. "Just us, mum, just us."

She spied his cap. "Sorry I...lost my wits fr'a spell. Saw my dead husband. What...what in...fuck happ'nd?"

Gwafa readjusted her bandage. "*Madame*, you have been out for three days straight, we were worried about you. We're in a cave. We carried you here for over two kilometers. *Les Bosches* and Eye-ties are everywhere. They found the plane. Only one other survived, a wounded Australian, they treated him well and took him into Siwa. I covered our tracks and we walked on rock as much as we could."

"The whole town's crawling with enemy. Tanks, trucks, two or three entire companies." He stuck out his tongue at her in his native style, then smiled. "That's our war-look for the 28th."

She focused her eyes. "Twenty-eighth battalion…I reckon y'are. You're…you're a *Maori*…a Pacific Islander. I read about you lot in the service rags."

"Yes, mum. Proud of it. The enemy really hate us mad dogs. We'll fight with knives and rocks and fists when our ammo's gone."

"This will hurt," said Gwafa, rubbing more salt into her wounds. "All we have besides a little sulfa powder. Siwa is known for salt production. There's a lake and large oasis. Good water. *Très bon*."

"Damn!" she cried, her breathing heavy. "What about you two? Wounds?"

Gwafa smiled, putting his canteen to her swollen lips. "We both have only scratches and bruises. Luck of war. I picked out most of the metal from your arms and neck and sewed you up tight. You need to rest, your knee and chest are much swollen from impact."

She put her head back down on the stained rucksack. "I'll not argue. You speak decent English for a Moroccan. How old are you?"

"Thirty-three. A man learns well in jail for two years. I am from Timbuktu. My mother was half Berber, half Dogon, and I speak it, father Mali. When I am scared, only *Française*. I was in the battle of Bir Hakeim with the Free French. On the flight I was assigned as a bodyguard."

"What's your name, mate?" she asked of the New Zealander.

He wore his smile even more broadly, his ample chest and big shoulders a testament to his tribal heritage of fierce warriors. "Lance Corporal Penn Takuta. I'm from Taupo, a mine specialist and artillery man, good with a bayonet, and I can cook well if we had any fresh fish."

"Helluva handsome international squad to survive with. Name's Thruxton, Pilot Officer recently demoted, Women's Auxiliary. One of the few women ferry pilots on the

Malta-Alex run. Rations?" *Damn, an ashy blackamoor and a South Seas cannibal. Wonder if they raped me?*

"Five days of canteen water and a few British rations. One med kit. Two rifles and seventy-six rounds. Tonight, I will go back into the village and trade for supplies. A black man in the desert draws little attention." Gwafa held up a pile of local clothes. "*Très chic*, madame."

A cool wisp of a breeze ran down her neck from behind. "How big is this cave? Any animals? Christ, any scorpions? Camel spiders?"

Gwafa stood. "It goes far back; we need torches beyond here. No spiders. Takuta killed one scorpion outside under his boot."

"We'll keep 'em off ya, mum."

"Orders, *madame*?" asked Gwafa, handing her a moistened sweet biscuit to eat.

She groaned. "Let me think. If Jerry's this far south, he must be gathering forces and securing water supplies to head north to flank us—*cough*—Allies. Most of the fighting is still along the northern coastline. Reconnaissance aircraft will sweep the area, nowhere to hide in the desert. Lots of tracks."

Takuta added: "The tanks and trucks are hidden well under the thick palm groves. Under nets too. This is one helluva big oasis."

Bea thought for a few moments, chewing, her mouth dry. "We'll need to count their forces, I've had a little intelligence training. Then we'll have to cobble up a small caravan of camels and head west to the Nile via Al-Fayyum, then to Cairo along the Nile. I dunno, something. But we'll need money or something to barter. The locals aren't fond of any of us. Who can blame them? It's not their fight."

Gwafa dabbed her forehead with a little ointment. "We can't trust anyone. They might turn us in for a reward. You both will need desert attire."

She pointed. "It's a risk, but trade the rifles. They won't be much use to us. Unarmed we'll create much less suspicion. Two blokes, one hen."

"We could be shot as spies, mum," worried Takuta.

"I know, but we'll keep our uniforms on underneath. This is a voluntary plan for you two. If I'm caught, sent back to Tunis and possibly recognized by any SS personnel, it'll be a death sentence for me."

Gwafa dabbed her forehead.

"Why, *madame*?"

She coughed hard. "I've had dealings with the Germans, intimate dealings. They'll torture me to death. I stole something of theirs a while back that was quite valuable. An aircraft."

"So we are both thieves."

Takuta stood. "Well I'm in. No way in hell I'm going to rot and bake in some open-air prison camp. Everyone's short of water and food."

Gwafa locked eyes on him. "Brave talk, fisherman. *Va te faire enculer*. But I agree. I would be bored to death the rest of the war. Nothing to steal, no one to fight."

Bea managed a slight smile. "You gents are made of tough stuff. I'm honored."

"Rest, *madame*, rest."

...

Days later, morning light touched Bea's face and she awoke. She stood and steadied herself on the wall. Dizzy, she walked a bit in a circle. The dense silence of the desert enveloped her at the entrance, the odd breeze and murmur of the sand over rock the only sounds. She then sat. One could hardly imagine that war was in the north, the lonely beauty, rocky plateaus, dunes, and a rare oasis painting the whole of it just for her, an island of rocks and sand, an oasis of relative peace. The writers, poets, singers, and artists were all correct, the desert a canvas of surreal imagination taken to its limits and beyond, a burning sun of a dream within a dream come alive. It was so hot she felt cold. In the distance, the slow, raspy rumble of German *Iron Annie* aircraft engines could be heard to the northwest, then nothing. She cleared her mind and meditated, a technique she learned at the Shieldmaiden school in Austria; the negative thoughts dissipated when positive ones drifted in with the breeze, a slow effortless process like the gentle petrifying of a tree into stone. Mother Earth and her animal life were also being killed or maimed in the war she thought, especially the horses and camels; this was total war, everyone and everything was a combatant.

Takuta arrived from his patrol and handed her a tin cup with sweet powdered tea and water. "He's been gone twenty-nine hours, mum. We have about two days' worth of water left."

"Right. Nothing broken, but I'm sore as hell. Knee's still a bit swollen. As my father always says, I'll live."

He opened a can of bully beef and gave her some on a hard tack biscuit that he had soaked in a cup so they could chew them. "'Tooth Duller,' mum. It's hot at least."

"Thanks. My father cherishes this shite, but I'll not complain. Always a perennial favorite, and most likely favorable to my slender constitution of late. I'm not one for the heat, but the desert *is* rather beautiful."

He chewed loudly. "Take me back to my island and I'll never leave again. What I'd give for a fuckin' dressed pie and slice of cool pineapple."

She pointed. "Well, well, Colonel Lawrence has arrived as a one-man caravan, and with an *Equus africanus asinus*."

"Who?"

"Of Arabia."

Gwafa returned leading an old jackass. "*La!* Two rifles and ammunition go far, *madame*, but I had to negotiate hard. One deal after the next, one hand paid then another. I have robes for you both. Dates, olives, nuts, bread. A big goat skin of water. Salt. A crude map in Arabic that took me forever to negotiate for its ownership. Three torches and matches. And a small pair of Italian Army binoculars. The donkey I stole, but we will try to return him."

Bea examined the binoculars. "Well done, Sergeant. Top marks." Gwafa popped a nut. "How are you feeling?"

"Tired, dizzy."

"I suggest another day of rest, *madame*."

"Agreed. What's happening with the Germans?" she asked.

"More have arrived. Transport aircraft have landed with fuel drums and supplies from the northwest. They are readying themselves for a push north and west like you said. Or perhaps a last stand here."

Bea rubbed her chin, pacing a little. "All oases are valuable, but what the hell are they doing this far southeast besides water supplies? Our lads have stalled them up at El Alamein. Rommel's up to something dirty again. He'll definitely attack to the northwest from here most likely as a secondary thrust. An asymmetrical pincer movement. Something clever. Either that or they'll hold on to this place no matter the cost."

"It's getting hot, *madame*, we should go back in the cave. Our water will last longer." Bea yawned. "Could use a kip."

After an hour or so, Bea felt the cool breeze from the cave's interior again, causing little hairs on her arm to come to attention as she awoke from a half-sleep state. "That's certainly refreshing. You said you have torches?"

Gwafa undid a filthy canvas roll. "*Oui, trois.* Plenty of pitch left on them. Perhaps a water source is the cause of the cool breeze. Evaporation, yes?"

"What the hell, let's go on an explore. I'm bored to death sitting on my bruised arse." "I'd like a bath myself," said Takuta.

Bea took a lit torch. "The Kiwi's on to something there." She crawled through the small opening after about sixty feet of meandering cave.

The tunnel became narrower and darker. When they reached a wall of tightly stacked stone, Bea knocked a few down so they could crawl through the opening. When the three of them crawled through, the tunnel pitched downward steeply. "Who in hell built this rat trap?" she asked.

Gwafa held on to her arm. "Careful, *madame*, go slowly."

At the end of the long slope, another wall about ten feet high met them. But its large blocks were polished to a shine and were expertly stacked and fitted.

Bea rapped her knuckles on the stones. "Now what? And where's the cool air coming from?"

Takuta wandered a bit and found a chiseled stone out of place. His torch flickered. "Here. It's coming through from here."

They all peeked through.

"I see a floor, a little sunlight, and something black in the distance. I'll go first," said Bea.

Gwafa pushed her out of the way. "No, I will go, *madame*. Too dangerous. Grave robbers must have opened this place long ago." He slithered his tall thin frame through, flashed his torch around for a good look, then held his hand for her to enter. "Safe."

Bea struggled through, remembering the last film she saw in Alexandria. "Bloody Blackamoor Tarzan, you. And I'm the Green Goddess."

Takuta struggled with his wide frame and big shoulders. "Not a chance. I'm too thick, mum. I'll wait in here."

Bea smiled at him. "Right. Hold the fort. We'll have a look-see."

Inside, the domed room spanned forty meters or so wide. Bea shined her torch near the huge, perfectly-fitted polygonal blocks that walled the circular chamber. "Must be a hunnerd tons apiece, I reckon. Look how finely fitted these stones are, as if melted into one another. The odd geometric angles keep it all intact during an earthquake. Just like the ruins in Peru."

Gwafa took out his knife. "I cannot fit the blade between them. *Magnifique.*"

She rubbed her hand over them, their coolness to the touch invigorating. "Pink granite, hard as hell, and even harder to shape. Did they drag it here from the quarries at Aswan? I'm going to guess this lot wasn't carved with simple-dimple copper tools."

"Then...how did they do it?" asked Gwafa, running his hand over them.

Bea drew a deep breath. "Believe it or not, I was taught they used fancy diamond saws and tools that ran off sound vibration and electromagnetic-derived electricity. How all that worked I don't know, but history's a lot older and stranger than we're taught, gents. Tens of thousands of years older, hundreds. I'm guessing this chamber is predynastic. The finer and bigger the stones, the more complex the design, the older a building or pyramid is. Had a little classified archeology training once in Austria before the war, a mystery school of sorts." *Damned SS is good for something...*

"I believe that," said Gwafa. "Not the best at it, mind you."

"I hated history in school," said Takuta through the opening. His voice echoed.

"It's mostly a damned lie, anyway. Schools are rubbish factories my dear Lance Corporal, don't sweat it." A few stones down, Bea spied high-quality hieroglyphics and fingered them. "Found something. Don't know what this ancient scribble means, but I recognize this carving." Before her in stone relief were two lions facing one another with X-pattern sashes across their midsections, and an unusual crown of Egypt with Lotus blossoms and the Falcon of Horus above them. On top of the Falcon's head was the symbol of the sun, and within the sun disk an ankh. "This...this looks like *The Most Holy Trinosophia* symbol, or some much older version of it, probably the original iteration. See here? The ankh represents the soul's eternal life force, the sun wisdom, Lotus flower's rebirth. Two lions guarding an entrance to another world. Lions were the symbol of Atlantis, stood at the harbor entrance to the last, they say. The crown represents higher knowledge—our crown chakras in the Indian traditions. Two beasts to overcome to gain the kingdom of higher wisdom. The Bennu birds in the boat below it are symbols of rebirth and reincarnation as well, and the mast that's coiled by two snakes—the 'wise serpents'—represents the energy of passion, *Vril* if you will, that rises up the spine to the top, a pinecone, the symbol of our 'Third Eye' pineal gland, which will open the gates to the universe's consciousness. It's a type of Caduceus symbol, The Staff of Hermes."

Gwafa smiled. "The red dot, like the wise men from the far east, India."

"Yes, and women too. Wisdom and knowledge from multitudes of reincarnations and hard lessons learned. The lesser symbols below I have no acquaintance with. Well, I'll…be…*damned.*"

"Atlantis? Really?" asked Takuta.

Bea looked back. "Yes, really. But if you prefer Pacific Lemurians like your island ancestors, I'll still be impressed. When you get back home, take a canoe to see Nan Madol. A megalithic paradise."

"*What?* That island is haunted."

Gwafa's voice became nervous. "What is this place, *madame*, not a tomb is it?"

Bea looked around but saw no other carvings or inscriptions. "No, no I don't see a tomb or anything that suggests one. Most archeologists call everything they don't fully understand a 'tomb.' The floor is polished to a shine under the dust." She neared the center of the domed chamber. Above was a smooth-walled circular chimney about fifty feet in diameter, and she could see sunlight far above. Below it was a hole of the same diameter to match. "This looks like some sort of…*air* shaft."

Gwafa fell to his knees and lay prone. He inched towards the side of the granite hole and felt the edge. "Sharp. *Belle finition.* Very precise work, so smooth to the touch." He looked down, his torch held outwards. "Nothing. I see no bottom. *Rien.*"

Bea slithered up beside him. A cool breeze suddenly arose from the hole, covering them and chilling their perspiration. "Nor I, *monsieur*. Definitely an air shaft, and with a machined granite rim that could cut glass. But in heaven's name an air shaft for what?"

Gwafa held up an old leather sandal. "Here is what's left of our grave robbers. They must have fallen down ages ago, *quels imbéciles*. If Takuta and I hadn't felt the cool air coming from the rocks, we would never have found the entrance. Many stones to move." Just then a strong rush of warm air came down upon them. He raised his voice. "This zephyr would catch anyone off guard or *en garde*."

Bea held the sandal as it crumbled away. "Hell of a first step. Air goes up, then it's sucked down for a while. Very odd. A heat exchanger, perchance?"

"I can feel it, the breeze, mum. What's down there?" asked Takuta from sixty feet away. "Not sure. It's a deep-as-hell hole, though."

"Who could have built such a place as this?" asked Gwafa in amazement, his eyes circling the hole's rim the entire circumference. "And all the way inside a small mountain?"

"And *when* was it built, is another question. Ten pounds on the table says it's as old or older than the Giza and Khartoum lot. We're talking twelve to fifty thousand years ago."

"That is long ago, yes. *Madame*, what if I...?" "Do it."

Gwafa dropped his torch. It careened down the large hole, intermittently bouncing off the smooth wall as it plunged deeper into the abyss, a tiny ember, then just a pinpoint of light. After a minute it completely disappeared from sight.

"Did you hear it hit bottom?" she asked, astonished. "No. Nothing."

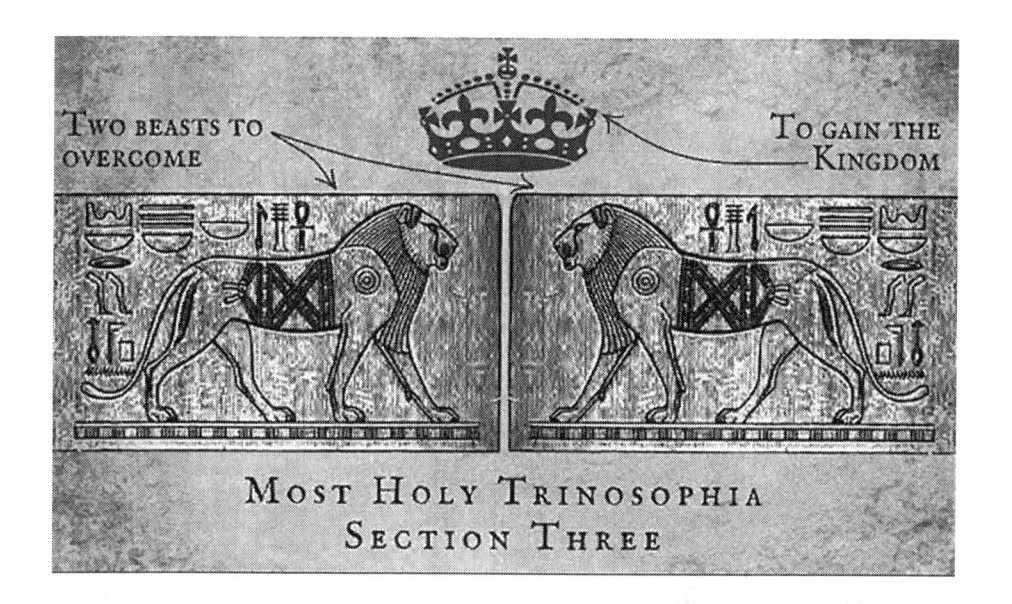

Two beasts to overcome

To gain the Kingdom

MOST HOLY TRINOSOPHIA
SECTION THREE

5

July 19
Abergavenny, South Wales

Under a gunmetal sky threatening more rain, Bernie strode through the damp grounds. He carried a heavy briefcase and wore his best Savile Row tweed jacket and dark green kilt; his mother's side of the family being Stuart, he felt more at ease blending in that day. He pulled his pocket watch from his vest. "On time and on target."

A brisk black Jaguar sedan missing a hubcap pulled up to the gate house; Bernie waited.

Royal Army Guards saluted.

Suddenly alongside Bernie was MI6 chief Stewart Menzies and his adjutant Royal Navy Rear Admiral Sykes-Picot, his silent escorts. They walked with purpose. All three men had questions that needed answers from their special prisoner held at secure Maindiff Court Hospital; all three had an agenda. An axe to grind.

Walking inside the unassuming red brick building, Menzies signed them in at the main desk. "Rodgers, here's the file. Read it fast."

Bernie did as ordered. *At last*, he thought.

On May 10, 1941, Deputy Führer Rudolph Hess flew his personal long-range twin-engine Messerschmitt Me-110 with special drop tanks to South Lanarkshire, Scotland, to meet with a fellow aviator, the Duke of Hamilton at Dungavel House. The official story leaked to the London press was that an ill-fated peace mission had been attempted, one that might end Britain's involvement in the war so that Hitler could invade Russia unfettered. A mission that failed when Hess, an experienced pilot, strangely ran out of fuel in the dark and bailed out. After his arrest and public denouncement by the Duke, Hess was quoted as saying that it had still been "the proudest moment of his life." Why, was unclear to all. Winston Churchill had stated publicly he was not interested in any peace negotiation, especially since London had been recently bombed with thousands of civilian lives lost.

Hours passed.

As Menzies and the Admiral interrogated Hess behind closed doors in Hess's quarters, Bernie quietly read the *London Times* in the hallway in a comfy chair adorned by the dim light coming through the wired glass window. He knew the cover story was bullshit, the flight made little sense given both German and RAF coastal radar, as Hess's unscheduled flight would have been intercepted in minutes by either side. Though the conversation was garbled, Bernie smiled when Hess raised his voice in temper while being peppered with intense, unrelenting questions, then became incandescent with rage. "Easy now, Walter. They're just doing their duty," he mumbled, then snapped the pages to attention as an army guard eyed him coldly. Yanks of all stripes, cocky *Johnny-come-latelies* were a plague to all English soldiers now that the Americans were flooding into Britain. His kilt hid nothing.

Menzies and the captain exited with a door slam. "He's all yours, Rodgers. Good luck getting him to admit anything useful, and you can 'eighty-six' that damn smug look on your face," said Menzies in mocking American military slang, snugging on his hat in a huff. He turned to the guards. "Carte blanche. Don't disturb them no matter what, *clear?*"

The sergeant came to attention. "Sah!"

"Thanks, Chief," said Bernie with a smile. "I'll do my best."

"A damn sight better than that would prove ideal," said Menzies down the hall. "You've got four hours precisely. We'll be waiting at the car when you're done with him. Right now, it's pints and pie for us in town. Train's at three sharp."

When Bernie slowly opened the second interior steel door to Hess's private room, Hess had his back to him sitting in his scruffy overstuffed chair. The threadbare carpet smelled musty, and the bed was unkempt, an unusual sight given that Hess had traditionally kept a clinically clean and tight bedroom. Clothes lay on the simple dresser, and a pitcher of water sat beside him. On the table was a framed photo of his wife and children.

Bernie spoke in German and pitched his tweed cap to the bed. "*Guten tag*, Walter. It's just me. They left."

"*Ja-ja.*" Hess motioned with his hand, his eyes staring out the window to the trees. "I only agreed to speak with them if they changed my room at the very last minute. No eavesdropping with electronics. I like the kilt, suits you."

Bernie sat on the creaky bed. "Been a long time. How-w-w are they treating you? How's your stomach these days?"

Hess sighed a little. "Oh, they delight in feeding me bland Welsh muck fit only for a horse, if that's what you mean. But a little suffering and torture is good for the soul, *ja?*"

The briefcase flipped open. "I suppose. Here's two books I brought you. *Esoteric Christianity* by Annie Bessant, and *At the Mountains of Madness* by Lovecraft."

"*Danke.* Theosophy and occult pulp fiction, always a good match." Hess frowned. "You're so thin these days."

"I've just come from Morocco. I...don't eat or sleep very well lately."

"That bad, eh?"

"Worse, but the operation was a success. The ONI, Menzies, and I greatly appreciate your help on that, we really do. A petite joint effort." He then pulled out a thick stack of forbidden Swiss chocolate and letters from Hess's wife. The intelligence he obtained in Portugal he knew would help the American plans for the November invasion landing in Morocco. *He'll never guess about that shindig. Finally, a second front.*

Hess took the bars and smelled them with eyes closed. "Like the Alps in springtime when I was a boy. The Swabian cows fat with milk." He opened a letter and smiled.

"The Bishop spilled his guts. Now we have solid intelligence on the Rome pipeline. That's...well, that's all I'm allowed to share."

Hess bit into the delicate confection. "He's a filthy swine. *Du Lusche.* They all are. A disgrace to civilized Aryan humanity."

"Coming from a true Nazi, that's really something."

He waved his hunk. "Don't be an *arschole*, Bernard. The Third Reich is pure at its core, it needs no such persons involved in its business in my opinion. Or at least it *was* pure. Himmler has other ideas for the SS, sinister ideas born of perversion and lower-caste breeding, the Black Sun concept twisted to his own specifications, the worship of Saturn and the darkness. Sour back door deals with putrid vermin. He hates homosexuals like Hitler does, but tolerated important ones like myself, two Prussian generals I know, also the Duke of Windsor and his cunt-licking wife. It would have been different if Göring and I had replaced Hitler...much different. Honorable, aristocratic, with pure Aryan rules, laws, and dictums to promote and nourish the State, not atrocities disguised as…as State policy. Not *genocide!*"

Bernie felt sad for all the Jews, dissidents, Russians, and captured undesirables in the camps. "It's going to get worse. Trains are being diverted from military use to haul human cargo; the Krupp works are making big furnaces with—"

Hess became enraged, and decided to go all in. "*Idioten!* We would *never* have made that mistake. Oust the filthy Jews and subhumans to…to Africa, to Palestine and elsewhere, anywhere, not murder them en masse like base psychopaths! What will the world think of Germans now? I warned Hitler, argued my points at the edge of his fury to no avail. He's mad, I admit that now, said I brought him nothing but problems, but I have been proven correct. They left me out of the planning for the invasion of Britain because I protested it too much. He was forced into the *Sea Lion* plan by the high command but was never happy about attacking fellow Aryans. The Dunkirk evacuation was possible only because Adolf kept his word on a pre-war agreement with the English to destroy the Russians together. But these new Hitler parasites have lost their German purity, their sanity, their military honor. By Nefertiti's cold breasts, we *deserve* Ivan's boot on our fucking necks now. Wonder Weapons or not, eventually there will be nothing left of Germany!"

They both sat silent for a while eating chocolate, wishing the war would end. Hess cooled down.

Bernie asked: "Just between you and I, and you know my word is my bond, did you have RAF help in getting through the *Chain Home* radar on your way to Scotland?"

"*Ja-ja*, yes, of course. Menzies knows that, and only two Spitfires were scrambled to intercept me, visual recognition only. He also knows that upstart Bormann took my place at Hitler's side. After I took off from Augsburg, Göring had General Galland scramble the fighters near Bremen twenty minutes too late on purpose as a cover operation, and they flew a different course heading on Göring's direct orders. Using Baur's maps, I was by that time nearing—"

"Hans Baur? Hitler's personal pilot?"

"Yes, Hans. I was nearing Denmark, with our own Luftwaffe radar units completely aware of my flight plan. It was a secret mission ordered by Göring; he had loyal Luftwaffe generals who hated Adolf and the SS in his pocket, including Galland. I refueled and re-oiled at a small secure strip just to be safe, the 110 burns through both fast. After that I flew west flat-out, zig-zagging a bit so the RAF would know it was me on radar. The King was supposed to be there with his Freemason lap dogs Lord Halifax, Duke of Hamilton, Prince George, and Lord Mountbatten, another queer of note. Haushofer had assured me they were willing to *negotiate* an armistice. It was Haus's prophecy, and what's left of the Munich Sumerian Brotherhood supported him. As for the Vril and Thule groups, they're watched day and night by the SS, but I was assured that nearly half of them wanted peace in secret, the SS and SD disbanded, commanders jailed, Himmler and Heydrich *shot*."

"Haushofer's an unreliable opium addict, you knew that. Christ, it's no wonder MI6 refers to all this as 'The Hess Mess.'"

"Ha! I like that."

Bernie whispered: "I've found out that Menzies hired Crowley to lure you here with fake astrological and occult messages. Did you know that?"

"I suspected as such. Even if they hadn't, I still would have come. Menzies wants to know how we use astrology to help the Kriegsmarine in its various operations, things like that."

"Seriously? The Navy?"

"Yes, the *Wehrmacht* too, Generals von Manstein and Paulus swear by predictions in secret, but I think it's too unreliable for military operations. It matters not. Crowley is a sick old man now, more perplexed than ever after a lifetime of service-to-self debauchery and loyalty to no one. Say what you want about us occulted Nazis, but what we do is for the *whole* of the Germanic and Aryan peoples."

"The Depression and America's staunch isolationist policies screwed us up. We're woefully unprepared for war even now, some of our recruits train with broom handles."

Slumped, Hess shook his head. "It was never in the original plan to declare war on your people."

Okay, hit him up hard now. "I remember you said you were *Reich Kommissar* of the Secret Technology Development for a while. How far along were they just before you left?"

"The Vril Propulsion *volk*? All programs were in infancy, but they have been using Tesla's body of work as a reference. Schauberger was working on new superconductors and has made vast strides with his vortex engine experiments, ones that run only on air and electricity. Schumann has made disc-shaped aircraft fly and hover, the RFZ2, but they are only unstable *toys*, wholly unsuitable as weapon platforms, useless and inefficient hangar queens. They glow bright colors depending on power levels, making them ideal targets. On a bigger experimental disc, the *Hanebu One*, the 30mm cannon rounds ignited from the strong electromagnetic field, then it crashed, the pilot killed!"

Bernie whistled. "Holy kittens."

"The Vril Society was originally a utopian sect, one based on their predecessors, the Templar-based *Lords of The Black Stone*. These Templars wrote and spoke in Sumerian, which is phonetically similar to German. The psychic Maria Orsic helps them with channeled information, her associates Sigrun and Gudrun too. The information on over-unity free energy and antigravity was given to them by the positive Aldebaran people for peaceful means, to end economic disparity and to eliminate the need for coal and oil. I was hopeful back in 1928, but it's all gone to hell now. The 'regressives' are in charge."

Bernie said: "It once symbolized friendship, good fortune, vortex energy, and harmony." Hess squirmed uncomfortably. "But no longer, now torsion vortexes will be used for war.

The *Gizeh* swine are involved, I think, a negative subgroup. I suspect…well, there were two strange men, very tall men in matching suits at a Vril Society closed meeting in Munich with a dozen of us and Himmler in January of '40." He took an odd tone, as if he were afraid. "They were…perfect *twins*, albinos with snow white hair and skin, striking pale blue eyes. They liked my groundbreaking homeopathic hospital in Dresden and its positive results with integrated medicine; they called themselves the 'Nazzara Brothers,' and said nothing else during the whole meeting, then left with the Reichsführer. They gave the rest of us great pause, a…mysterious pair."

"Albinos? That's a rare genetic condition. *Gizeh*, eh?" *He's bullshitting me again.*

"Orsic is one of us, trustworthy, a neutral person who errs on the side of the positive, but only when it suits her. She naively believes that Himmler will use the new technology peacefully when he sees the light, but of course he won't. The war has dragged on."

A grimace. "Gerlach?"

"*Ja-a-a-a*, non-linear gravitational physicist, the best. He has his fingers in many classified pies. He's made great strides with something called Red Mercury, an enriched plasma—*Projekt Cinnabar*. It uses thorium, beryllium, and monatomic gold. He's the lead physicist on electromagnetic free energy and exotic propulsion, and the SS are much enamored with his work.

"He's treated like a god and acts the part. They are working on a large-scale prototype zero-point energy generator near Breslau, *Die Glocke*, 'The Bell,' but it's in its design infancy, unreliable, dangerous. Many early versions have blown up, killing hundreds. 'Gestapo Müller,' the police chief of the Reich, has provided three rings of tight security around the Pilzen Skoda Works and Breslau, it's a marvel of compartmentalization. And do keep an eye on General Dornberger, Hermann Oberth, and Baron Werner von Braun—their rocket program, everything is connected, much cross-pollenization of technology. My fate here in England may be sealed by a radioactive fireball not seen since the Rama Empire."

"I'm here with you today in hopes of *stopping* that. Speaking of Gerlach, did you know about an experimental high-altitude Heinkel fighter project with Porsche?"

"A little. High-voltage electrical plasma expert Dr. Kurt Debus was working on that program along with a few of the physicists—*Electrogravitics*, but I remember it was too expensive, too complex, too time-consuming to be practical as a mass-produced weapons platform. An electromagnetic vortex field doesn't mesh well with recoil weapons. Propeller-driven aircraft are soon to be a thing of the past, the far simpler and cost-effective kerosene jet turbine is the future for fighters. At least until…"

"They're working on that jet system here too." *Mr. Whittle better get the lead out. Tell Menzies that.*

He slammed his palm on the side table. "A race then."

Bernie looked at him forlornly. "Look, Menzies doesn't have to know about our chat. I'll only inform my chummy little group, you have my word."

"Menzies is a fool, beware of him. Göring and I would have struck a deal with the King, the Duke, and Mountbatten, my dear Bernardo, an honorable *occultist's* deal, Churchill be damned, I'm sure of it. Winston wanted war, craved it."

"You as *Führer*, Göring as deputy?"

At this, Hess straightened up. "Yes, as *chancellor*, no more use of 'führer' as a title, but to be at my side Hermann would have to give up his morphine habit, his old war wounds killing him. Hitler and the inner circle would be publicly hanged, filmed by Luftwaffe newsreel cameras for all the world to see. I would have…*hated* seeing my old friend die, but it should have been done for the sake of Germany; war with England, France, and America is the wrong war and I and Göring knew it. Bormann would be our number three man in charge of all Reich finances, the 'Brown Eminence.' He's a genius at it, ruthless and quiet, ambitious. He was always nipping at my heels, displacing me at the Berghof meetings, the inner circle a pit of vipers. I hated those politics, everyone sidelined me at every turn. I was seen as weak, an occultist fool, an untrustworthy Anglophile. Adolph also hated that I brought my own food up there, clean food."

"Your insecurity is showing again."

"*Ja*, maybe so. Anyway, dangerous Churchill would have stepped down due to a technicality in the British Constitution, a hero to the British people still, and no more war with us would be in the new cards dealt. Certain areas of the Middle East would be German-controlled again, ancient Persepolis and Ur secured for archeology purposes. Then we would either crush the Russians or better yet make a deal with Stalin for Ukrainian farmland, that and oil from the Caucasus. Poland would be split in half again, Göring's Prussia saved. That was the deal to be made until I fouled up, missed my waypoint, and bailed out in the wrong place, late and off course in the pitch dark. A *Gott-*damned farmer stuck his pitchfork at me! Something else must have happened on their end too. Something went awry. A security breach perhaps. I was later met by the wrong people, angry people, suspicious. An idiot Polish officer too."

Bernie pitched his cap in the air and caught it. "Or they just had cold feet. The word is they had last minute reservations, the timing was off by a few months. The King supports Churchill now, all the way to Downing Street. The Duke was spared in this, Churchill thought it best for England to have him continue as a 'patriotic' commander in the RAF, and your story has been downplayed and misdirected in the press. There's enough royal scandal to go around. Morale is paramount."

He buttoned his cardigan to ward off the damp chill, sniffling. "Today, this very hour…perhaps that is for the best, but I still hope for peace between us. None of the English brats want to make a proper deal with me anymore. Rommel would have been recalled from Egypt, but that's just my fantasy, they said. Hitler is an asset to the Allies now, a loose cannon, insane; he makes terrible tactical decisions pumped up on daily narcotics, a nervous paranoid, a delusional wreck at times, physically ill. All they want is intelligence from me I'm not willing to give until we reach an agreement that's suitable to Göring and I, but you might be correct, it may be too late, the die cast. The Celtic and Germanic people should not be fighting, we should be common-ground *allies*. With new technology we can defeat the savage Russians, make peace with America, create a whole new Europe." He stood, tense. "Then we could raise the island of Hy

Brasil off southern Ireland, find parts of western Atlantis off Cuba, *Poseidonis*. Rebuild all pyramids and bastion forts to their former grandeur and restore the Earth's energy and defensive grid once again. Resurrect the Tuaoi Firestone and create another peaceful Aryan-ruled paradise of the *world*." He then sat, exhausted.

"Easy now, Walter, that's a *big* wish list. Anyway, how savage can the Russians be if they spawned geniuses like Tolstoy, Pushkin, and Dostoyevsky? Restored St. Petersburg to glory from ancient rubble?" Bernie massaged Hess's shoulders for a minute. "They have a small, intimate occult division at MI6 now, it's headed by a brigadier I know and trust."

Hess laughed. "Finally, some progress! Perhaps they aren't as stupid and inane as they appear to be. You do know they keep a doppelgänger of me locked up near London."

"Yes, an Austrian. They dye his hair, and he really does look like you except for your bullet scar. He'll draw any assassination attempts his way, not yours. Paid well."

"I had enough attempts on me back in Germany. I'll never understand why you and the American Navy Intelligence put up with the English brats and their silly schoolboy games."

"Politics, but they have their moments." Bernie sat quiet for a while, then said: "It's none of my business, but you and Hitler were very close friends, did—"

Hess coughed hard. "There was a time in the early days, the Freikorps days, when I was somewhat attracted to him, Bernard, but the feelings were not reciprocated, I mostly admired his luminescent aura, his sense of greatness and invincibility, in his presence one could sense the possibilities soon to manifest. We co-wrote *Mein Kampf* together in prison, and for a while we were two halves of the same Teutonic whole, a twin flame. But he has only one love, one desire: *Power*. He told me he sexually ejaculates at the *pinnacle* of a speech."

"I'm going to try and forget that bit." Bernie nodded and fiddled with his hatband that contained a hidden strip of actionable code numbers. "I'm heading for Cairo soon, Walter. And…I need your help."

"Ah-h-h, Cairo, *C-a-i-r-o*, so near my boyhood paradise in Alexandria. The warm hazy sunsets behind the pyramids, the lazy Nile on a sailboat with good Egyptian tea and fresh crusty bread. The old colorful mystics, eyes red with tobacco and hashish, sipping coffee and smoking hookahs into the night discussing Hermetic wisdom and earthly mystery. I hope to see it all again…my dream, someday." Emotions running high, he looked to the photo of his family and teared up. "I miss them so much, love them so much…"

Bernie held his hand. "I know."

After a minute or so Hess leaned over and wiped away tears. "Yes, yes you do."

He squeezed tighter. "Walter, I…I beg of you, what are the SS really after in the Middle East besides oil, minerals, and the Suez? The Ahnenerbe, especially? Are they after more hidden ancient technology? Artifacts?"

At this, Hess became sullen. His black eyes bored into Bernie's. "I can only speculate."

Bernie could tell he was holding back; he slowly grabbed Hess's cardigan and took a low tone. "Walter, so help me…if the war goes Hitler's way, we could all die or be enslaved. True Aryanism and peaceful Nordic philosophy made a *mockery* of, all ancient Celtic culture erased, no beloved Egypt or her treasures to benefit mankind, perhaps no more lush, green Mother Earth, only ignorance, only dystopian technocratic darkness swathed in black oil, atomic weapons, and endless wars!" He let go, calmed himself, then caressed the man's cheek softly. "Sorry, old friend."

Hess sighed again, smoothing his oily hair with a shaky hand. "It's obvious the darkest elements of the Anunnaki have certainly returned with—"

"They never really *left*, Walter! Some of them were always here, their offspring, you know that. Come on, come on, *think*, you know what I'm—"

"*Artifacts*? There's the Channel Islands and their tunnels and Celtic ruins that have provided much science. Heligoland too. And in Antarctica four years ago, the Thule expedition that Göring and I organized found ruins in *Neuschwabenland* much older than the Great Flood, *Kapitän* Ritscher told me so in his photographic report, the World Ice Theory proven true. An extremely high civilization once thrived there, rivals of the Anunnaki perhaps. I believe it was a southern outpost for the Atlantean Empire, a colony, perhaps a rebellious one. We are constructing a base there in the Muhlig-Hofmann mountains. England would have been given their slice of ice in our deal, America too if need be. I told that to Churchill but he's a stubborn ass. He always wants more than his fair share."

"Big deal. The SS supposedly has a copy of the secret map that Columbus and Admiral Piri Reis used, the one that shows an ice-free Antarctica, the huge one in the Spanish archives that's said to be older than the Great Flood. A U-Boat base in the works too, a stupid idea if you ask me. Look, I don't give a fat shit about the southern pole right now, it's not crucial to the war effort, I need to know about the *Middle East*. Please, Walter...*please.*"

Eyes shut, Hess thought deeply over the course of several minutes feigning memory loss, then decided to trust his friend and former lover to the fullest for the sake of Germany's future. "Yes, maybe...something. A strange conversation took place at my home in Berlin during a dinner party my wife threw for me. June of '40, I believe, hot. Haushofer, Speer, and Himmler were there with their wives. Thirty occultists of varying degrees. Everyone was drunk on victory and fine wine except for myself and the *Reichsführer*. Shameful. An Ahnenerbe man was there, an archeologist or zoologist named Schmitt or Scharffenberger, *nein-nein-nein—Shäfer*, he and my wife chatted with one another at the table. Drunk, he told her he was soon heading for the Iraq and Iran border via friendly Turkey, yes, let me remember...the Zagros Mountains there down south. He boasted he and his commanding general would be looking for something between Iran and Iraq, something ancient and valuable...yes...yes! Something that Alexander was searching for during his march on Persia, something paramount, something *important* for the Reich. They laughed about it as if it was just a wild fantasy, Haushofer as well. I was too busy with the other important guests to pay attention to their stories at first. Himmler scolded his friend Shäfer for drinking, told him to shut up, but the man was feisty, insubordinate even. They talked about a special SS Ahnenerbe team that would soon loot the Baghdad Museum for clay tablets and cylinder seals, and *that* did get my attention."

The brilliant but unstable Shäfer had been mentioned in Bea's classified report on the Ahnenerbe and her SS Shieldmaiden school. "Christ almighty, cylinder seals? Tablets? Alexander the Great? Walter, *scheisse*, what *exactly* are they looking for?"

Hess shook his head, confused. "I...I'm not sure. Shäfer was bragging, pawing at my wife in the kitchen, his hand up her moist crotch. After most of the guests had left, they went upstairs to fuck proper and for once I encouraged it. I love her, adore her...but she needs purposeful fulfillment from time to time." Hess became excited, eyes smoldering, hand making a fist. "Yes, yes, *now* I remember! She said to me the next day... he said something about an expedition to a sacred site, archeological ruins perhaps, a top-secret mission to a 'sacred and fearful place,' she said, one that could only be painstakingly found by careful and diligent aerial exploration. Not by fast, thirsty aeroplane or–or truck or on foot, but by a newly-built *airship* of some kind—a slow, hovering, loitering airship. One able to land anywhere, even on a mountain peak. I remember that vividly because I thought it was a silly idea, since as a fighter pilot I cherish speed and maneuverability above all. Any classified Luftwaffe program regarding obsolete airships would not be of interest to me, I'm an aircraft man. But you see I—"

"Zagros range?" Bernie stood abruptly. "By airship?" He paced, scratching at his beard. "An obsolete *Zeppelin*? Why would anyone, especially the well-funded Ahnenerbe, take a lumbering, flammable gasbag all the way from Germany over Bulgaria and friendly Turkey down to the Iraqi desert mountains with all the high winds and snowy valleys and…" Bernie paused to muse the unusual and confusing information. "Diesel engines, hydrogen gas, 30,000-pound cargo lifting capacity, but a lumbering antique today. That's just insane, by going low and slow in some deep gorge they'd be crushed into a mountain face by one strong gust in one of the most rugged, high-altitude places in the goddam Middle East, and it's in British hands now after the Iraqi uprising failed."

"Somehow I knew that Führer Directive was folly. Rashid Ali was no fool, and the Muslim Brotherhood is untrustworthy despite their ferocity. Hitler doesn't understand the desert peoples like I do. Too many competing clans and religious factions. You can build them up with advisors and equipment one day and expect loyalty, then the next they will turn on you like opportunist jackals. Who can blame them?"

Bernie looked out the window, guards were posted everywhere. "*Ja-ja*, I remember. The Brits and Arabs learned their lessons in the last war in Palestine. Anyway, the Russians are in Iran with the Brits as well, they invaded it. American troops are there too, we Yanks built the Trans-Iranian Line railway and shipped in locomotives. Sixty Russian divisions are supplied by our materiel."

"From Persian Gulf ports up to Russia via the long way? So the Mongol hordes will be supplied from the south too. Regrettable."

"Look, Walter, none of this makes sense. The Hindenburg never flew very high, mostly stayed below the clouds due to its pressure height, the gas loses its lifting power higher up. It can't possibly work in the high-altitude mountains, even a smaller airship."

"That is…all I can remember. There were many new *Wunderwaffe* projects on the drawing tables at the Skoda Works in Pilzen, hundreds, *thousands*."

"In any case, that's a hell of a slow, low-altitude target for an allied fighter or any armed aircraft to bring down. Why the Sam Houston would they go to all the trouble…

to…" Bewildered, he sat, staring at the carpet's loose threads. He tilted up his head and became excited. He neared, and ground his stained lips into Hess's, his chocolate-messy hands ripping apart their shirts in peaked passion. Naked but with socks on, they quietly put the bed to good use, going at it hard, then harder still, the straining bedframe creaking out a barrage of squeaks and groans.

Hess whispered: "How I've missed your strong hands, Bernard." And slapped his ass like a thunderclap.

6

♈

July 20

Wandering through the ancient town of Siwa, Bea, Gwafa, and Takuta, disguised in their Arab robes over their uniforms, sandals, and wrapped Berber-style turbans, climbed the mud brick stairs of Café Gil, its languid patrons smoking ornate hookahs and sipping tea since the Germans had bought all the coffee and generously overpaid. On the roof, hidden behind the crumbling wall, Bea put her binoculars up to her eyes and spied an officer's Kubelwagen in the distance. "Flag standards, Fifteenth Panzer Division. A company or two at least, medium-sized, probably about three hundred fifty troops in total, no, maybe more. Blue wool socks, *Fallschirmjäger* paratroops? Hmm... probably guarding the northern airstrip. Italians making up the numbers too, 136th Division, fashionable black caps with tassels, can't misidentify those fancy Spaghettis."

"Over there, beyond the palms, *beaucoup de camions lourdes*," said Gwafa.

Bea panned to the west and thought of Bernie, who always teased her that she performed precious little intelligence gathering in between mundane assignments, ferry flights, and romantic misadventures. "As my dear old beau would say, *Sweet Jesus Malone*. Tank transporters. Three Famo heavy halftracks and lesser ones too. Supply lorries, a gaggle or more, and many stolen British ones; that just steams my clams. They're up to something big all right, supply lines are insanely long, petrol is wanting. They're going to push for the Nile, a *Kesselschlact*, an encirclement of some kind, but down here they're on the edge of flaming nowhere." She scanned the dense palm forest that stretched for miles in many directions, the oasis one of the biggest and most beautiful. Fruit, olive, and date trees formed in vast rows.

Tanker trucks filled at the springs. "Water, food, and salt...and plenty of it. They're obviously here to secure it as a permanent supply for their move on Cairo, then on to the Caucasus through Palestine and Assyria, though I supremely doubt they'll make it all the way up there. Rommel has more luck, pluck, and bollocks than materiel. His fuel supplies are wanting, and he has to spare some for the Italians so he's quite thrifty with it. Bit of an ad hoc operation here, I count…five Mark III Panzers, two Mark IIs, a few smaller Italian Fiat jobs with small caliber guns, and three mobile 88 flak guns pointed northeast in the distance. Probably there's more stuff I can't see. They've been moving by night, keeps the telltale dust cloud out of sight. See over there? Tracks to the west are single file. Hard to evaluate their strength by air reconnaissance, and under those nets the tanks are well hidden in the palms." She watched as the Germans parked their trucks down narrow alleys to hide them, cleaning dusty air filters and patching split tires, the rocky terrain unforgiving to equipment. A few men tended to their bread bags, webbed belts, soft forage caps, and socks with stout sewing needles, and another carved his initials into his mess tin. One of the Mark III tanks was having its barrel swabbed out by three crew manning a long ramrod, its tracks repaired by five others, while two mechanics lifted out its engine for a rebuild at a tarped repair depot. Paint brushes went to work touching up the armor. A portable phonograph played scalding hot Swing. "Lots of maintenance happening."

"Over there, that man is frying eggs on his tank," said Gwafa. "This makes me very hungry."

"Showing off for the newsreel cameramen. Posh duty round here."

"The steep hill at the end of town, mum—spotters, I reckon," said Takuta.

She focused for long range across the shallow salt lakes. "Sure are. They're dug in everywhere like ticks on a dog's arse. If the Allies sweep down from the northeast it'll be a trap, especially for lightly-armed lorry patrols. I'd take a heavy bet on it anyway. Bloody Jerry, always up to sneaky maneuvers. Soon there'll be little to see by air. Wish I knew how to get word to Cairo, too risky to find a radio shack."

"We would do the same, no?" asked Gwafa.

"Sneaky defines me, Sergeant. Yes, we'd be up to something similar. This is said to be a gentleman's war in the desert. Honor and duty. Polite prisoner exchanges and good medical care. Up on the eastern front the Wehrmacht, SS, and the Russians are battling to the death with disemboweling sabers. Here we're just boiled eggs, a nobleman's rapier duel in a sandbox."

Gwafa shook his robed head. "Though I relish the action, I see little that is noble about war."

Takuta did same. "I second that, mate."

Bea was thankful for the lack of SS units and their murderous civilian policies since General Rommel had vehemently argued against them. His popularity in the German press, a gift from Goebbels, gave Rommel some independence from the stiff-necked general staff in Berlin, and Himmler's fanatical and genocidal SS. "Agreed. Let's keep moving."

As they meandered through the streets with Bea atop the jackass with a shawl, Gwafa and Takuta drew little notice from their dark complexions wrapped behind a thick cloth turban that Gwafa knew how to tie well and tight. Hiding in plain sight, a tactic that had always worked well for her, Bea kept her face behind a black veil, her lily-white hands well hidden, head low. A few Germans searched houses for contraband, others haggled hard via their Arab guides in the souk for sugar, salt, tomatoes, and spices very much appreciated for use with their bland Afrika Korps rations. Most troops were eating local grapes for newsreel cameras and bathing in the natural Cleopatra Springs nearby, a water-fouling practice frowned upon by the locals. Hordes of children harassed the smiling soldiers for Lire coins and Iron Ration boiled sweets under the colorful shawls, umbrellas, and carpets that ceilinged the spice-perfumed ancient street.

A German eight-wheeled armored car drove past, the troops atop howling and waving at the local women. Bea understood some of the banter; many Germans were eager to visit the nearby Temple of Amun, a local curiosity. "It's a damn holidaymaker's paradise here," she whispered in French, holding on to the donkey's neck and rubbing his ears.

Gwafa replied: "*Oui, madame, c'est tout.* A travesty."

"What a bleedin' strange war," whispered Takuta, overwhelmed by it all, wishing for the sea.

Weaving their way through the town's endless maze of mud brick buildings, built one on top of another, some with elegant white domes, they rounded a corner with a small bundle of locals. At the humble mosque's open square, the troops dismounted the armored car and scurried up to occupy the tall minaret and other high-ground spots. German soldiers in their pith helmets screamed at the locals to back off, aggressively pushing people out of the way with their Mausers held lengthwise so they could permanently block off a good portion of the palmed courtyard and public fountain with ropes and sidecar motorbikes armed with the new "Singing Saw" MG-42 machineguns.

A long, heavy and fearsome barrel pointed directly at Bea, her eyes wide. A young soldier then wrapped the bulky muzzle brake in a canvas bag and smiled at her, and another yelled at Gwafa to move back.

Under tall sand-colored tents painted to match the shadowed mud brick buildings, were three of the biggest tanks Bea had ever seen. Painted in desert camouflage, their wide tracks and heavily-armored fascines and turrets gave them a menacing stance like no other. Maintenance crews busied themselves, readying the heavy Panzers for combat; engine oil and fuel were added by the Jerrycan-full, and vital ammunition was loaded, the big 88-millimeter shells glistening in the hot sun before being lowered into the top and side hatches. From the air they would be almost impossible to spot.

An officer blew a whistle, and one of the tanks started its two engines one after another.

Bea could smell the distinct fumes. *Routine engine warm-up probably*, she thought. From her distance, she could just make out two maintenance crew reading what looked like a comic book.

"Panzer three, report," yelled the officer, a captain. The tanks were painted 101, 102, and 103 in red, with the Fifteenth Panzer division markings of a red circle with a white triangle and vertical line. The elite crews had also painted a jolly, smiling long-tusk mammoth on each of the turrets.

A *leutnant* spoke from the top hatch. "Herr *Hauptmann*, engine oil temperature and pressure normal, electric motors on standby and in good order. Cooling fans normal function. Chassis and sprockets lubricated. Turret electric motor needs adjustment."

Gwafa pulled on the donkey's reins. "*Vite, vite*, let us move."

As the crowd passed some German troops eating rations on a stoop, Bea could hear them bragging to one another. "Sixty tons apiece and ready for action, *Kameraden*," laughed a sergeant. "Fucking Tommies will fry in their shit cans!"

...

"*Arresto!*" An Italian patrol stopped them outside of town.

Bea moaned as if she were sick, gripping the donkey's neck under a dirty blanket that smelled horrible.

Gwafa spoke Arabic, and one of the Italians understood a little. "She is sick! The plague. She wants to die in the desert and we will bury her there by Allah's grace. We Berbers prefer this ritual."

Bea thought fast. There was only one trick that came to mind, the nastier the better.

Suffering a bit from dehydration, she hadn't had a bowel movement in days, thus there was a log jam in the river. She strained, and a pile of filth oozed out. She dug into her pants and smeared it on her face and hands.

An Italian peeked under the blanket and made a face. Bea also hadn't had a bath in weeks, but few had. "Ughhh. *Lei puzza de morte!*"

"She stinks of death already. You can go," said the Italian sergeant. "Praise be to Allah." Out of sight, Takuta lifted the blanket. "You right, mum?"

"Fine, just need a wipe."

•••

In the cave, Bea cleaned her hands and pants with hot sand. "What a royal mess, everything I mean. At least we got a decent walk around the entire oasis, lay of the land and all that."

"We must leave here or we will be caught eventually," worried Gwafa. "*Merde!*" Takuta paced. "We can't do much here, mum, and those big tanks…"

"Aren't supposed to be here, but they are. Look gents, we absolutely have to get word to the Brits up north. I'll let you in on something. Every few weeks I'm privy to a general security briefing back in Alex; I'm a ruddy sneakthief, a spy, at least when I'm not ferrying aircraft and doing odd jobs. Those are the new Tiger tanks, the sixty-ton buggers with 88 mm guns fresh from the Henschel Works in Kassel, and a metric ton is around the same for a British long ton, so don't get confused. The report stated the Germans wouldn't have them in the desert theater for another eight to ten months because of Russian front demand, but *here they are*, ready for action in a mostly ideal environment. Just those three big buggers alone could defend this swamp quite handily, they can reach out and touch someone in the worst way while quickly and safely maneuvering position to position. I'll bet none of our guns, especially the weak-kneed six-pounder antitank unit would punch much of a hole in 'em."

"No chance, mum. We've been begging for bigger ones every day."

Gwafa placed her pants in the hot sun so he could rub off the excrement when it dried. "What did the Germans say in the square, *madame?*"

She scrubbed her panties harder while the men kept their backs to her for privacy. "The officer asked about their mechanical readiness. But something struck me as strange, little tiddly things stick in my mind for odd reasons. As far as I remember, and I'm no Panzer expert, *gods no*, the Tigers are supposed to have a single Maybach petrol engine like most. The bushy-tailed *leutnant* said they started up two. He also said something about its electric motors. That says to me it's an electric hybrid-*mixte* power system. Very strange. I'll bet their range is pretty good for a big tank, and that's important. Everyone has fuel supply problems."

"Mum, you sound like an expert to me," said Takuta, scrubbing.

"As a pilot, I enjoy mechanical stuff on occasion. Especially new German designs; bit of a hobby, suppose. That and the latest fashion and gossip rags. Bit of a sponge, mind-wise."

"*Madame*, we must steal camels, use the stars to travel East to the Nile at night," said Gwafa, smelling her cotton twill trousers. "Much better now."

Bea thought for a minute or two. "Travelling day and night, it'll take us many days to reach the Nile even without harassment or unseen challenges, about three hundred plus miles, I reckon. That might be too late."

Takuta added: "We should pinch a lorry, but we couldn't carry enough petrol to make it unless we had a bunch of extra jerrycans."

"Stealing equipment from the Germans or Italians is dicey work, trust me. They'd track us down like hounds." She smelled her panties. "Ugghh, not exactly smart dress in Chanel, but it'll suffice; guess we're all soap dodgers for a long while. Anyhoo, a Kubelwagen might be better. Good mileage, but then we'd be a dandy target in a German vehicle once we reach allied lines—wherever *they* are—and God help us if there's a patrolling Hurricane or Beaufighter about, they'll strafe anything that moves. A camel is best, two even better. Let's have a think about it before we make rash decisions."

Gwafa unfolded the Arabic map. "Bahriya Oasis is halfway it says here by rough road, I hope the Allies still hold it, the Sudan Defense Force, all black men. *Oui*, many days by camel, but they are expensive. We have nothing to trade but the old jackass."

"We can steal some camels if we're lucky." She slid them on, then her pants. "Gads. Stuck at a romantic oasis with no camel, no beau, and no chilled cocktails. Sometimes, this war is a genuine bore, gents."

•••

Nighttime arrived accompanied by violet light and a lower temperature. Gwafa lit a small candle; they all ate rations while staring at the map on the floor. "Three and a half candles left."

Eating a hunk of dehydrated *Scho-ka-Kola* German chocolate from a tin that Gwafa had deftly swiped, Bea massaged their situation in her mind's eye. If they departed by camel during darkness it would be an understandable escape given the insane odds.

The three of them had a duty to perform nevertheless, and she mixed that into the dough, kneading it over and over with the stark reality. She couldn't just leave without performing some type of bellicose action, no, not that, it just wasn't her *modus operandi*. She craved some fun, some action, something, anything. "Got a taste for this stuff in Austria a while back whilst on skis. Dry as face powder, must be the tropical version."

The two men snapped off chunks. "You can ski, *madame*?"

"Spy mission. Trained with the German First Mountain Division. We ate a lot of cheese, nuts, and chocolate. High density calories and fat."

Takuta ate another chunk of the dry, sweet confection. "I miss the snow back in New Zealand, give anythin' fer a handful."

Gwafa liked it less. "*Merde*, what prayers I would trade for a bowl of sorghum millet with the fine leaf powder of the Baobab tree. Just a little sand to scour the stomach as my father once said."

Bea buttoned her jacket against the chill. "Duty calls, gents. What about some good, old fashioned sabotage before we hoof it out of here? At least when we reached Cairo we would have a decent action report to hand in."

"What about all their troops paradin' about, mum?" asked Takuta, now chewing a tooth duller. "We're outnumbered and out-gunned by a long shot, no pun intended."

"Any barley sweets left?" asked Bea.

Gwafa handed her two from the emergency ration tin, then dug out canned Bully Beef with his long fingers and licked them. "This is a big town and oasis out here in the deep desert, they are spread out fairly thin, *madame*. We could set fires with petrol perhaps. Slit a few throats. *Au revoir, bosches!*"

Bea scratched her dirty matted hair, longing for a brush. "Love a visit a Mayfair hairdresser. Hmm, three unarmed little pigs against a big pack of wolves. Jerry would never suspect three ill-trained commandos in their midst at this salty mud hole. They'll be on alert, but maybe not on high alert. A tad too much bravado and arrogance are two of their weaknesses, maybe the only two. The Italians just follow their orders. I say we blow up an ammunition lorry with a delayed fuse in the middle of the night. That might make a bold statement, and all eyes would be on the explosion while we scram, that is if we can steal camels and enough food and water for the journey."

Gwafa used his knife to draw a crude map of the oasis in the dust. "We are here, north of the oasis. To the west, here, are some of the fuel lorries and tank transporters.

We could—"

Takuta exploded. "Fuck all that! With respect, mum, I lost a lotta mates at Tobruk, hundreds. I want to kill as many of these bastards as I can, not blow up a single lorry and call it a day."

"Revenge is never a good battle tactic, nor is anger. Keep your head, and don't toss a *wobb*," said Bea sternly. After a few moments of silence, she asked: "When the plane picked you lot up at Jalu, what were New Zealanders doing there?"

He took a deep breath. "Mum, we were lorried down there with some Aussies to help secure that spot, oases are important to hold, right? After one bloody week it was time to evacuate when Jerry moved south in big numbers. I've been shuffled all over North Africa and I'm damned sick of it."

Gwafa added: "I was there to escort *mon Capitaine* to Alexandria as his bodyguard. He had important business there. His attaché was chained to his wrist. A pompous ass of an aristocrat."

"I know," said Bea. "My real job on the flight was to babysit him from a distance, a possible traitor, but that went south of course. I was having a go for a time with the pilot, we met in Alex on leave. Anyway, I love to fly, and I jumped at the chance for a flight over to Libya. As usual, I got more than I bargained for. Getting to be a bit of a habit, like betting on longshots at the Derby."

Quiet minutes went by as Gwafa composed his thoughts. "*Madame*...maybe the fisherman is correct. We are not pigs, but little mice, *petites souris*. I know it is suicide, but we mice should steal one of the big tanks, perform serious action, blow things up. They would never suspect. *Jamais*."

Bea giggled a bit, vibrating, then belly laughed. "Funny, you...you sound like me a long time past. But now I'm not as...as *reckless*. I tend to meditate things over and weigh the facts and risks carefully. No more rash actions for me. I've learned my lessons the hard way. Gads, a Panzer...that's just rich."

Takuta became enthused. "I'm in, mate—*steal* a tank. We're all going to die sometime. C'mon, mum."

Bea ruminated a bit. "Now you *both* have gone mad in the sun. No chance. I'll not consider it for a tenth of a second. We should concentrate on finding camels, food, water, and a compass, then hightail it to the east. Isn't there a Berber caravan coming anytime soon?"

Gawfa looked to his boots, part of one sole was coming apart. "There is a Tuareg caravan camped two kilometers south of town a man told me, but they are known for being shrewd traders and unforgiving slavers. Good warriors, *oui*, but tough negotiators. They dig fine wells. I don't know why they are this far to the east, but they are. Looking for extra good quality salt is my opinion. They are known to have the best camels."

She laughed again. "Tuaregs? As in bloody *Beau Geste*? The wild riders in the blue robes?"

"*Oui, madame*. But they are known to be opportunists as well. They guard the trans-Saharan trade routes jealously and like to steal and raid. Language is *Tamasheq*, close to Berber. Sunni Muslims. As a child in Timbuktu they were much feared and respected, but always had the most exotic goods. Their music and poetry are legendary." He smiled at the memories, face flickering with the candlelight. "They gave me expensive sugar once in a trade with my father, hard brown sugar, a lump as big as my fist. I remember the taste well, my first of it."

She smiled in kind. "My kind of nomads. Can we bargain for a ride east?"

He laughed in his deep voice. "*Madame*, we are unarmed, and you would be a valuable commodity as a *femme blanche*. A fine pale slave for a Sheik or noble chieftain with a taste for such. The fisherman and I could sell you to them for much gold!"

She rolled over and put her arm under her head. "That's just *lovely*. It's either the Germans or the ravaging nomads. Not much of a choice."

"Then let's pinch a tank, mum."

Furious, she sat up abruptly as if to slap him silly. She went face-to-face, eyes wide. "Are you *genuinely* certifiable, Corporal Pineapple? Hmm? Bit *risky*, that. Can either of you operate one? I can't, don't know the first thing about 'em. Pilot, yes, bulldozer driver, no. We'd be shot to bits just getting near one let alone firing it up and performing any kind of action. I'm for bolting out of here, *fast as possible*, or at least as fast as a camel can trot after we feed him a bag of cocaine-powdered coffee beans. No more hero stuff for me."

"And if the Allies come here? They will be slaughtered while we escape." Gwafa rubbed the insignia on his blood-stained kepi. "I don't have much, *non*, but I am a proud soldier of France and Mali. That is something, everything to me. *Tout*."

"I'm a Maori, mum. We prefer to *fight* when the odds are rubbish." She rolled over.

"Not on your lives."

The two men sat quietly, tending to minor repairs of their kit.

Something inside Bea rumbled like far-off thunder in the summertime, it rolled around her head, bouncing up and down the soft green English hills of her imagination. "Oh-h-h, no-o- o…" She tried to hide from it in the cave of practicality and good sense, but it oozed inside and flowed around her like brisk river water. Then, like a long-awaited orgasm after an hour of scalding sex, it pounced. "Fine. Dandy. Just great. Swell. What a fabulous idea 'n' all. Oh, what the hell, we're running out of water, we can't walk out of here without a luxurious caravan with parasols, and stealing a turtle-slow Kubel without being cut to ribbons by either side is a lot to ask. None of us wants to be captured or… *shite*, I'll consider it as a somewhat viable option.

"What's an entire company going to do against three mice? But you listen to me, my dear enthusiastic schoolboys, a German Panzer is one complicated son of a bitch, especially these brand-new ones with copious bells and knobs. It must look like a steam train in there with all the levers and valves and gauges, boiler too. We'd need solid intelligence beforehand on how it works, *detailed* information, and that's almost…an… imposs…" She snapped her fingers. "Wait a tick, I saw them reading something quite intensively, what was that? Wasn't that a comic book?"

"What? Why is that relevant?" asked Gwafa.

Takuta sat up. "I saw them reading something too, but I couldn't make it out."

"Could it be…no, it can't be that stupidly simple, can't be. Of course! The Germans are quite clever now and again. I'll bet sixpence to doughnuts it was their owner's manual, a detailed book with drawings on how to operate the damn thing in the field. It's brand new. Farm boys are the ones driving and maintaining those lumps, it makes perfect sense. Yes-yes-yes, the Yanks do the same for planes, I heard—Disney films, cartoons, and the like. Mickey Mouse."

"What're you doin' mate?"

Gwafa stood in the dim light, fingering his stone-sharpened knife blade. "If that is so, then I will use my private *armée* to steal one."

•••

Around midnight, Gwafa returned.

Bea awoke. "Shite, we thought you'd been—"

He opened the book as Takuta lit the two candles. "Moon is *parfait*. I bribed three of the young boys with half our bag of dates and nuts and the last of our boiled sweets to steal it off the tank. The Germans were in their mess eating and smoking by a fire. They distracted the guards and one boy grabbed it. It was a fun game for them, they like to sneak out of their beds and steal from soldiers, *any* soldiers."

Excited, Bea spread it out. "Great Nelson's gonads, '*Tiger Pz. Kpfw.VI P. Operator's Manual*, version one.' Pukka, chaps, top of the tree. High-quality Zeiss optics. Thick Krupp turret and hull. Says it's a prototype weapon, the Reich's newest Panzer, and great care should be taken with maintenance and the recording of defects or mechanical issues in the provided logbooks, then the information's sent back to Tunis. No wonder they're down here in a zone with little or no action, they're being *field tested*. This might be an idea, chaps, but it's a bad one. Usually I'm the one that's—"

Gwafa said: "*Panzer*, from the French word *pancier*, or the chain mail worn by the old knights, *les chevaliers*."

"A history buff, eh? Me too." She flipped though the many pages. "Holy Trappist monks' pants on fire, I'm not sure this is going to work, look how complicated this stuff is. It's a lot to absorb, a lot to…there's just no way we can learn all this…in a…" She read the facing page with her finger. "Let's see here, assembled by *Nibelungenwerke*, Austria, and designed by…by Porsche AG, Stuttgart. Porsche?—*Por-shuh*! Why…why that overstuffed, *wurst*-gobbling, pilsner-guzzling little 'Handyman'—I'll fix his *wagon*!" She shook the colorful book violently, tapping her finger on the pages. "I know the sneaky little bastard engineer who designed these lumps *personally*, gents. I read that Henschel got the contract to build their version, but oh-h-h no-o-o, seems the little 'Bohemian Braggart' built some too. That just *tears* it. By the heaven's celestial light, we're going to pinch one of those fat iron boilers and lay waste to this oasis if it's the last thing I ever do so help me God, Odin, Freya, or whomever by damn!"

"Now who is feeling the lust for revenge?" asked Gwafa with a hard stare.

She calmed. "I stand corrected."

"We must also be careful of the civilians, *madame*."

"Good point, hard German targets only."

"Porsche? Freya?" asked Tekuta, confused.

"Longest story, gents." She turned to page one and laughed. "It's full of naked women! So they do have a sense of humor about it. Look, this idiot Jerry's name is 'Barrelbum.'"

The two men laughed at the illustration of a smiling, skinny young German flexing his puny bicep, his tanker's cap at a jaunty angle.

Bea translated as she turned pages. "It reads: '*For platoon leaders and Tigermen: Frontal and turret armor 102 mm. Gun mantlet 120 mm. 8.8 cm main gun with 2000 meters effective range. Double baffle muzzle brake. Magazine holds 90 rounds total.*'"

"Ninety of those big rounds?" Takuta whistled.

"Listen to this propaganda, sounds like an advert for a motorcar: '*Leutnant S.V. killed thirty-eight T34 tanks in Russia in one sortie. 227 hits by antitank fire, 11 hits by 76.2mm shells, 14 hits by 52mm shells on the tracks, rolled over 3 mines—no penetration of the armor! Rolled along another 60 km to safety. Will shoot anything to pieces. Will withstand anything. Handles like an auto. Twin Porsche 310 bhp air-cooled 10-cylinder engines with electric 'mixte' Siemens motors with 3 speeds.*' I should have known better…electric motors? A hybrid drive? That's Ferdinand all over. Right. '*Power steering. Skoda-built suspension. 600 mm Tracks. Longitudinal torsion bar suspension. 45 kph on tarmac. 35 kph on rough terrain. 520 liters of fuel or 26 Jerrycans for a 105 km range. Can navigate one meter of dry snow. Can traverse three meters underwater. Smoke grenade launcher and defensive fire ports for use with supplied grenades, pistols, and two MP-40 submachineguns.*' Bloody ol' hell, what can't this lump do, fly like a buzzard and lay rotten eggs? That cursed curmudgeon Porsche, always upping the game, and I'll bet Hitler had plenty of input, the grandiose, bigger-gun-than-thou psychopath. These should be on the Russian steppes, not down here in the sandy frying pan."

"Perhaps that is why they are here…no one expects them to be." Gwafa then pointed. "What does it say next to the naked woman in the bathtub?"

"'*Danger lurks in the engine oil sumps. Remember then: Read your manual well, or else your Tiger will go to hell.*' Probably good advice."

Takuta laughed. "What's with the other naked bird in the shower?"

"It's talking about temperature ranges in subzero battlefields. Nothing we need to worry about, it's air-cooled. It overheats at 105 deg. C, and that we do need to mind. Socking great tits she's got, reminds me of my chum Drumm."

"How do we start it? I can steal anything," asked Gwafa, suitably perked.

Bea turned a page. "Here it is. T-handle ignition key, choke operation, rpm to 1500 for warm up, spark plug fouling prevention, fuel vents, fuel pumps, fuel valves, battery switch, fuse box, blower ventilation, directional lever at neutral position, steering wheel, clutch operation— crikes, this is like an oversized jumped-up bulldozer with twin engines and a naval gun. Lots of tidbits to remember."

"Simpler but similar to the C-47 starting procedures, *madame*."

"In a way, yes. And no gears to shift other than forward or reverse, only electric motor speed, remember that. Says here the bottom vent plug must be open or the Tiger will blow up from pressure, or be closed or it will fill with water when submerged. Well, it'll be open, not much mud or water here except for the oasis. Blowers on at full speed for tropical operations, engine bay and cabin. Keep debris off the rear deck grills for the cooling fans."

Takuta pointed at the illustration. "What's this kraut bird doing in the sun rubbing on tanning oil?"

"She says here it's about the oil coolers and reservoirs. Fill to proper levels and don't put too much in. That geezer Porsche is keen on oil and air cooling. Twenty-five liters for each engine, two nipples, two engines, she says." She turned another. "Reduction gears, turret drive, other bits. Dust is the tank's enemy, it says by all means keep the filters clean. Brakes are assisted by compressed air tanks. This picture of the handsome waltzing couple is meant to illustrate the driving and handling. '*2600 revolutions is best for a dancing Tiger, 3000 is maximum.*'"

Gwafa reviewed the detailed but simple cockpit illustration and driving diagram for turns. "I can drive it, *madame*. Once, I drove a *grand camion. Je suis confiant*, but I am not used to driving with only a tiny box to see out."

"No roll-down windows, lads. We'll all have to adjust to the limited visibility, and fast. The vision blocks are small, but made of thick armored glass. Think it's hot outside? Inside this bloated kettle it'll be near unbearable. See her drinking champagne? That's a carbon dioxide and monoxide warning. Fans must be kept running to vent fumes. Right, see the two yacking *fräuleins* here on the telephone? We'll need to use the intercom system, it's going to be loud in there and Gwafa will be somewhat separated in the forward compartment from the two of us in the turret. No door between them. '*On the intercom it works as good, as with a female in…early womanhood.*' Why those cheeky, slimy, sons of—"

The men laughed.

"Funny, old sods. As my old American beau used to say, 'put a sock in it.'"

"What about the gun?" asked Takuta. "I'll be the loader, I fired a lot of artillery during training."

Bea flipped a few pages more. "Here, an 8.8cm Pak 43/2. The big bugger. '*Muzzle velocity 1000 meters per second. Shrapnel bloom as far as 200 meters with an antipersonnel fragmentation round. Can penetrate 148 mm of armor at 1500 meters with a solid tungsten core armor-piercing round.'*—Are they bragging?"

"We call the fragmentation round a 'frag.' I've seen those guns cut our lads into pieces, mum," said Takuta sadly. "Great big plumes of sand and shrapnel, the devil's own dynamite."

"Sorry, mate." She placed her hand on his shoulder and squeezed. "Moving on. Says to keep the shells out of the sun and rain. Hmm, *'clean the lock, clean off the muzzle break, inspect the breech, unload a hot barrel if there's a pause in firing. Recoil buffer, electrical switch, release circuit, hydraulic safety valve, contact open/close, floorplate with breechlock, recoil brake, lubrication chart, fuses, short circuits, unjam procedures for the MG-34 machinegun. Stadiametric rangefinder with reticles.'*

Here's how the turret rotates, by foot pedal. Christ, we'll have to go over all this junk in a jiff. Fourteen checks with a numbered system on various components. Think you can handle this cannon?"

"Never met a gun I didn't like, mum. This spotted donkey here must have some meaning to Barrelbum-Jerry here."

"It's a visual procedure. I know how the coaxial machinegun works, I was trained on one, 400 meter range. No worries. See this diagram for the main gun? These are the notches for the reticle, says the bikini-clad *fräulein*. It's all in meters; 1000 meters maximum range for targets two meters high. The big shells will drop via gravity according to this scale; estimated to be farther away in sunny conditions, funny enough. Gwafa will give a guess as to range as well, and I'll divide it with mine if time allows. I'll also estimate the range popping my head outside. Looks like I'll be gunner and commander in one, the usual crew is four plus and extra radioman slash bow gunner if need be."

Gwafa said: "No radio need for us."

Bea looked at the diagram. "I can work a German shortwave radio no problem. If by some miracle we can escape with this thing maybe I could transmit a signal that the town's occupied by heavy armor. Range might be a problem."

"Right." Takuta read the diagrams which showed short, medium, and tall girls with red-marked bellybuttons. Then an artist painted a portrait of a fully naked woman pointing at trucks, jeeps, tanks, and other hard targets drawn with meters. "Distance is not range; I think I have the idea, mum. Solid armor piercing shell marked as #40, frags are #50, and high explosive #60, etcetera. A 600-meter shot goes right through her bellybutton."

"As rank amateurs we'll keep ranges short, point-blank even, peel everything open like sardine tins." Bea then read a highlighted caption. "Look, chaps, it says: *'Achtung! Barrelbum. Shoot less, kill more, and keep tight! Reichminister Speer will take delight.'* I'll just bet. What a wankering bastard of a Nazi hobo, just look at Speer's smile, and rubbing his hands in delight. Arsenic arsehole."

Gwafa laughed. "You are very familiar and *agréable* for an officer, *madame*."

"I'll second that, mate."

Bea sighed, sipping the last of the powdered tea in a tin cup. "Never was much of a leader, just a dim bulb Light Warrior with a dubious and colorful military record. Let's use up the candles and train ourselves." She wandered out the entrance and looked up at the stars, thinking of her Shieldmaiden school and her German friends Roxann and Ursula. *If only they could see me now as a desert mouse.*

•••

By early morning, candles melted, they had gone over the manual five times. Sunlight poured in.

Gwafa sat on the dirt, legs out while Bea held the cockpit illustration up to his right.

She asked: "Right, see the tachometer? Oil pressure and temperature gauges? Voltage output left and right?"

"*Oui*, I have it. Prime. Fuel switch on #3 main tank. Master ignition on. Red ball choke on. Starting procedure complete. Start. 1500 rpm. Engines warm. Good voltage. Forward lever engaged."

"Okay then, fourth time's the charm, gents. Driver! Accelerate and turn right… now." "Right turn." He did so by turning his steering wheel.

"Gunner, wait, that's me. Adjust to left for the optics. Loader, A-P."

Takuta simulated pulling out an armor-piercing shell from the magazine and loaded it into the invisible breech. "Frag ready."

Bea held up the range and windage angle illustrations. "Target acquired. Panzer! Range 200 meters. Watch out for the breech recoil. *'The reticle compare, to the girl's bellybutton where you stare. To the distance you add, notch by 100 not so bad…100 meters times the notch is how far you can be off.*" Bellybutton notch. Half meter to left to compensate. Height set!" She held out her arms clasped together to simulate the barrel. "Foot pedal back, turn turret to left. Hold below target. Firing—*bang*!" she yelled, pulling an imaginary trigger. "A kill, chaps. Driver, turn left. Stop. Full ahead. Slow. All stop. Rotating turret fifteen degrees. Loader, frag."

Takuta repeated his movements. "Ready."

"Target acquired. Infantry! Range 100 meters. Foot pedal back, turn turret to the left.Barrel down five degrees. Half meter to left. Height set." Bea yelled: "Firing—*bang*! All right, let's remember where the escape hatches are. Now, abandon ship. Go, go."

Gwafa opened his imaginary round hatch. "I think we are ready, *madame*, but that is just a guess."

Bea studied the various enemy tanks at the end pages of the manual. Diagrams showed weak points and effective ranges. "I agree. According to this, the tracks, the rear ends, and the space between the hull and turret are good hit points. The Mark III Panzer has a short, low-velocity 75 mm gun and I'm guessing it won't penetrate a Tiger unless he's pretty damn close. The only thing we have to really worry about are the other two Tigers and the flak guns."

"That's a helluva lot to worry about, mum," said Takuta.

"Agreed."

Gwafa lay down, exhausted. "Let us sleep, then at sunset we will visit the Tuareg camp.In the cool, they will be singing."

Bea slowly drifted off. *This is madness.*

7

As the sun began its lazy progress towards the horizon, Bea, the men, and their jackass, with what little supplies they had left, reached the campfires of the Tuareg two kilometers south of the oasis. Italian patrols had been sniffing about, but Gwafa had slipped through them by hiding in the deep wadis dry from the summer heat. At a distance they looked like anyone else, and moved slow as to not arouse suspicion. Agonizingly slow.

Singing, the Tuareg men dressed in azure robes and black turbans roasted locally-obtained goat meat over a fire and drank milk from a gourd, celebrating some religious holiday, wedding, or celestial event. Women and children performed chores and ordered young slave women to help them. One of the women pointed, and a few of the men stood. One of them mounted a camel and brandished a rifle; the camel moved quickly side to side, obviously highly trained for close combat.

Gwafa told Bea and Takuta to stay put and marched up a rocky hill to meet them. He veiled his face as was customary with Tuareg men and talked with them in Berber for fifteen minutes or so. He then waved for her and Takuta to come up.

"*Madame*, I told them the truth; they don't fully trust a Mali from Timbuktu. I informed them we are lost British soldiers, that we are but mere travelers caught up in the maelstrom of war. They do not care about you or the Germans or Italians or English much, but they do respect the fact we are warriors. Otherwise I believe they would have shot the two of us and captured you. The battlefront means little to them, except as an opportunity for trade in weapons; there have been violent rebellions in the west against the French. They are *Kel Adagh* clan and are here to trade luxury goods for salt, fruit, and vegetables, and will not head east. Tomorrow at dawn they head southwest back to their territory. They have all the salt bricks they can carry."

Bea looked to the two Tuaregs dressed in blue robes with weathered red-brown complexions, dark eyes narrow and forbidding; both had French pistols and unusual-looking Takouba swords in their belts; faces veiled, they eyed her with suspicion. "Ask them if we can trade for two camels, food, and water for two weeks' ride to the Nile, ask them what they want in exchange." *To hell with the nutjob Panzer idea…let's live to fight another day. For once be a level-headed officer and gentlewoman.*

Gwafa did so, haggling with flair. "They want gold, or better yet ten rifles and ammunition, *madame*."

Bea held her nose bridge. "Offer five rifles, plus the jackass."

Gwafa bargained hard. "They now say *eleven* and the jackass. Or they will turn us over to the Germans for ransom."

"Right, I'm getting the gist. Ten it is."

"They agree. You must stay here in good faith, *madame*. The Chieftain wants to meet you, he has never seen a *femme blanche*, and wants to be sure you are not an evil spirit, a *Jinn*. Tell him you believe in the teachings of their prophet El Maghili and the Islamic tradition of honored guests." Gwafa whispered some words in her ear discreetly.

Bea trundled over to the Chieftain's tent with the two Tuaregs. She was met graciously by the big-nosed Chieftain who sat on a cheetah skin and spoke a wee dram of Mali French with a thick accent; she nodded and listened, nodded and listened. *Long-winded chap, he is...*

Gwafa and Takuta went off out of sight.

Bea was heralded with music, singing, and poetry, none of which she understood, but she enjoyed her cheese, dates, millet, melon, and a rare treat for them, a roasted goat meal. *Their singing really is terrific I must say*, she thought, sitting on a beautiful carpet and eating ravenously next to the old leader, who then reached for her chin, turning her face from one side to the other, an inspection of potential trade goods. Enchanting and colorful nomads, yes, fine artisans in jewelry of course, a legendary culture to be sure, melodic singers, but still patriarchal slavers and fearsome raiders, she mused. With a smile, she toasted him with sweet mint tea. "*Tanmert, Saha*. Love old El Maghili, Allah be praised and all that." *Get back here soon lads, or I'll end up chained to a camel in a Sheik's harem somewhere with my arse in the air...*

•••

Two very long hours later as the sun began to set, Gwafa and Takuta returned with the jackass and six Italian rifles plus leather belts of ammunition. Bea met them.

Gwafa panted. "An Italian patrol was eating their pasta supper. An easy theft, *madame*. They will think the local people stole them, or perhaps us *nouveaux* Tuaregs."

"Pretty lazy lot, one was sleeping by the fire," panted Takuta.

She inspected the rifles for damage or malfunction. "The Germans respect them.

They battle hard, but to my mind they're romantics mostly, and I heard their hearts aren't really in the fight." She inspected the action and barrel in Seaforth Highlander fashion. "Don't they ever clean these things? Anyway, I think you caught a lucky break. Nice job."

The three of them sat by the fire and Gwafa haggled with the two Tuaregs he met before. "They were hoping for more accurate German Mausers, but the Eye-tie rifles will suffice. The women prefer donkeys for travel anyway. He says one old camel in trade, but plenty of food, salt, and water, *beaucoup*. That is the best I can do, *madame*. His name is Udad. 'Trust in Allah,' they say, 'but tether your camel.'"

Bea looked the old camel over; he blubbered, deeply gurgling as if he had a mouth of molasses, his drool soiling her robe. She wiped. "Ugghhh, he'll do. Look, I know it's a disappointment, but I'm responsible for your lives. No tank theft. We'll take shifts and travel by night. I think this slobbering Udad trek is best given the shite odds. Discretion being the better part of valor 'n' all. We'll depart at four in the morning while it's still dark. Make sure there's cheese in the deal; it's delicious beyond compare if a bit salty."

Eating fresh dates, Gwafa relented. "I must agree with your decision, but with great regret. I desperately want to drive a big tank before I die someday."

Takuta, sullen, said: "For the record I *disagree* with your decision, but...you're in charge, mum."

"Sorry chaps, for the best. No moon tonight. Get some rest; that's an order." Bea got up and wandered a hundred meters to the west of camp to view the stars away from the campfire light. In the desert, the skies were crystal clear. At a hundred yards or so distant she sat, gazing upwards, the golden orange sunset all encompassing, slowly transforming to purple and light blue. She searched the heavens for her favorite star in Orion's Belt. *Alnilam*.

Gwafa unveiled his face and pointed as he sat. "I worry. Let's keep one eye on her. You sleep first, fisherman."

Takuta laid down in a soft, sandy spot. "Cheers, mate. Us Kiwi diggers never get a chance at some real excitement, just sandy trench death an' boredom. She's an odd one for sure, a ruddy 'charlie,' maybe even a coward."

Blue light painted his concerned face. "Who is not odd? Look around you. *Non*. She is no coward...that I am sure."

"You're wrong, mate."

Tortured with indecision and concern for her men, Bea hummed an ancient chant she was taught by the Buddhist monk Kunchen back in Austria to clear her mind. "Oh-h-h-m, soh-o-o, *hum*, Oh-h-h-m, soh-o-o, *hum*..." It finally soothed her, and she calmed and relaxed, her eyes full of stars. It meant in Sanskrit "I am that," or "I am one with the cosmos," but she felt utterly alone and despondent.

Time lazily passed in twilight. From a distance, a man walked up from the dim purple horizon dressed in black Arab robes and sandals. He sat beside her and chanted in unison. After a long while, he got up and reached for her hand. It was Lutz, his beard thick as a bush. "Let me show you something my love, something that will heal you."

Bea did so, holding his hand tight while he led her deeper into the darkness. "You dress up well in the desert," she said.

He laughed. "I should say the same thing about you. Now, tell me, vhat do you see...now?"

"I..." At a snap, the sands around her lit up a pale blue and there appeared more and more stars until the heavens filled to ten times the normal amount, a blizzard of lights, crystal shards, and fireflies, all of them moving, swirling, dancing, singing a Siren song. Bea could see galaxies and other spider-web universes spinning around her, the growing mass of it all revolving in on itself clockwise versus counterclockwise, suns and star systems, gas clouds and nebulas, all alive, all rotating, all vibrating, all with souls burning bright, filling hers with a powerful violet flame. She held out her palm and a small galaxy twirled within it, casting a glow upon her weathered face. "...can't believe it. Where did...?" A herd of pastel green giraffes with wings passed her on their march to infinity's horizon; one turned to face her with the head of a spotted dolphin. It gave her a smile. Smaller unknown animals swarmed past it amongst amber balls of light. Sparkling gold eels fifty feet long swirled before her eyes like giant ribbons.

"Zhis is the cosmos we live in, Lady Bea, that we are all an equal part of. Everyone and everything as one, as *Source*." He held up a spinning blue and white orb to her utter amazement. "Here iss Mother Earth, *Terra*, our beloved and nurturing home. We are an integral part of her, and she us. We are all one."

"Yes, yes the *Law of One*, I remember. But to see it all with my own eyes..."

"*Ja-ja*. But you are seeing it now with your Third Eye, zhat iss why there is no end, no horizon, just infinite cosmic seas, infinite life, infinite consciousness. See our Moon? It's hollow, and the only one in our solar neighborhood that does not spin; it is in tidal lock. Vhy? It iss chock full of exotic and curious star beings below ze surface with spyglasses trained upon ze Earth. An international meeting place for diplomats. Earth is next to a large trading route with other galaxies, a 'star-gate' of exit and entry, and we haff many visitors."

"*What?*" Stars and planets passed through her, matter and antimatter danced, torsional gravity wells and plasma eddies swirled, photons of consciousness begat quantum strings of blinding light, black holes stretched and sucked galaxies in and out like taffy, the sun's soul beamed bright white, soaking her with a warm vibrational bath of unconditional love and all-forgiving sentience, a deep knowing of *The One*, the *All There Is*. "Why…why are you here? Why are you showing me all…all of this?" A hollow red moon with many races of star beings living inside went in one ear. She gasped, hearing their voices all at once as one high-pitch frequency of friendship, love, family, and comradery. For an instant, her mind was one with theirs, mother and fetus. When it emerged out the other ear she gasped.

"Ha! I am here as an advisor at ze behest of your Higher Self, viss permission of course." He furrowed his brow. "A *misfit* bunch to be sure, *unglaublich*! They argue a lot about your erratic behavior. A few hundred of them bitterly wonder aloud if they are really, truly related to you, common soul or *no* soul."

"Let me think…my Higher Self is comprised of all my incarnations and lifetimes, all of my various selves from the past and future, yes?"

He kicked sand. "Indeed so. Anyway, your Higher Self gives you subtle information and wisdom from time to time inside a gut feeling or ze sixth sense, but they haff authorized me at this moment in time, even though time does not exist as you once told me in Norway, to interact viss you on a strictly limited basis because of our being in love, our unique twinning flame. I did not want to at first, but they are a determined lot, stubborn. I was to visit my parents and Albrecht but *nein-n-n*, I was urged to do zhis instead!"

"As you know, the meaning of every lifetime is to learn, zhen to be service-to-others, which I am attempting to do at zhis very moment, but this war, Lady Bea…is going ze way of the darkness, those who have chosen to be selfish and service-to-self, and zo Light Warriors like you and myself are losing this very ancient battle. Its ferocity has now drawn much attention from everywhere out there. Very bad situation, the vorst they say, and the darkness must be stopped here, now, or it vill spread uncontrollably throughout our universe like a virus.

"Benevolent star nations have volunteered to help by the hundreds, many agendas, many unique ideas. The dreaded but highly respected Anunnaki have many allies, genetic brigands, and hired mercenaries, but the worst elements are their jealous rival cousins from the Alpha Draconis, Aldebaran, and Orion star systems—some are very intimate vith Himmler and the SS, I heard. A bad bunch, *ja*."

"The SS? Doesn't surprise me. Just look at what the Nazis have accomplished so far, things like *Anton*, ever more successful conquest, and a plethora of new equipment. And all their humor is based on bloody *shadenfreude*; misery is joy to them." A luminescent green and pink butterfly flew around her, landing on a planetoid. "We're losing alright, and Jerry's on the advance everywhere. What about the Americans, won't they be in the fight soon?" The butterfly left a gift of a golden Merkaba behind and flew off. *The very shape of the cosmos itself*, she thought. *What does it mean? Does it even need a meaning? I just don't...*

"They will be, yes. Roosevelt is one of us, and they have good generals to lead them, like George Patton soon to arrive in Morocco, a misfit mystic, a rough-tempered man who has had many thousands of reincarnations as a soldier always and has said so publicly, even as Hannibal, but now he has chosen to fight solely for The Light, for our very survival. The German field marshals and generals vill fear only *him*, respect only *him*. A pure, dauntless warrior, a soon-to-be powerful and arrogant leader not unlike Julius Caesar."

"I read about him in *LIFE* magazine. Smart uniform. Love the cowboy Colt pistols."

"General Montgomery vill be in Egypt soon, Herr Churchill's own choice—brave, honorable, and imaginative like Rommel. Let us hope these two Allied generals can make a difference here. The Ahnenerbe are active in the region and are up to much mischief. No guarantee for anything exists." Lutz snapped his fingers and they instantly appeared on a snowy mountain with tall pines that smelled wonderful. He wore a brown fur coat, Patton's initialed ivory-handled pistols in leather holsters, and a tall black Hussar's *Totenkopf* from the 19th century, the German Death's Head insignia busby fur hat. "Ah, I love ze Canadian Rockies. So clean and fresh iss the air. And I like moose. Being in a higher dimension allows one to ride animals with their permission, but beware of those big antlers for they are *not* like a motorbike's handlebars." He shook his head hung low. "*Autsch*! How I miss my old BMW…"

She shivered as an elk or two ran past; animals could see into other dimensions she remembered. "Bloody hell, Stick. I'm freezing."

He wrapped his mink around her. "Sorry. In the astral world there iss no suffering from ze frostbite, but there is a lot of cold politics and hot debate. One day I hope you meet my new friend Herr Field Marshal Mackensen, who was—"

She hugged him. "I miss you old Stick, love you, every day, every hour, every second." He ran his fingers through her filthy hair. "I know, but you must be strong, for all of us."

Tears pooled. "I'm *exhausted*. I want to go *home*, I want to be with Poppy, I want to lay flowers on Peachy and Dee's graves, light a fag and sing with the birds, I want to eat clotted cream blackberry crumble with Miss Margaret in the warm kitchen with Nestings and Keats, I want to be clean and washed and sleep forever in my own bed entwined with you an—"

He shook her violently. "Peachy und Dee told me to ruffle your feathers when you become teary-eyed! Zhey haff moved on, reincarnated as children somewhere to anchor *The Light* on Mother Earth, to again be Light Warriors in their own right, fancy Hussar uniforms or no. It was their time, they chose to die in zhat hospital when the bomb fell during ze Blitz. They did their *job*."

Tears gushed as a darkened London night swelled her frantic mind—searchlights, antiaircraft fire, thundering explosions, body parts hurled onto roofs and gutters, craters and piles of debris, alarm bells, fire, firemen, death. "Dee, she…she was searching for a *child* with a doctor after the first bomb hit the ward, then Peachy desperately searched for her in the smoldering rubble when the second bomb—"

"I know!" In an instant they appeared on the Russian front in Ukraine in filthy German uniforms. Tanks, armored vehicles, and trucks were everywhere as far as the eye could see on the vast steppes, Stukas blackened the sky, and dusty infantry on both sides were being slaughtered in the summer heat. "Look at me. *Zhis* is reality for us! The *Eighth Sphere* that philosophers Steiner, Bessant, and Gurdjieff all talked about—a vicious circle *false* reality of constant misery and hell, a demiurge bulge between dimensions and out of time, one that keeps mankind from evolving into peaceful, loving galactic humans like our country cousins out zhere—ze Pleiadians, ze Arcturians, ze Andromedans, Vegans, Lyrans, an-an-and the *Telosians*. I meet more and more of them every day. War is a mass death ritual—the many missing are taken as prizes! Our innate creativity and twelve strands of hearty DNA make us ideal combatants, ideal *slaves* for the dark ones, a war prize of valuable cattle covered in fleeces of gold. Vhy? Because we have special genetics that allow us to literally create our own reality while others cannot. But Universal Law prohibits the 'benevolents' direct intervention on our behalf, the 'Law of Non-Intervention.' Remember zhat! But the darkness abides by no laws but their own, dirty deals made daily, war crimes committed hourly. We are destined to be a unified, peaceful celestial race one day with immense abilities, and many greedy people do not want zhis to happen, ever. Soon our *Wehrmacht* boys vill be in Stalingrad, the entire Caucuses secured for oil, then on to Jerusalem and Tehran. The filthy SS *Einsatzgruppen* killing civilians by the hundreds of thousands, enslaving millions for the mines and factories, experimenting on pregnant women and children in ze camps, torturing and dissecting the innocent in the name of Aryan Science.

"Genetic material, missing refugees, children, and soldier corpses are the very currency of the galactic black market, the most valuable commodity, and the SS are in business by *Gott*! Working hard for the highest bidder and receiving much technology and advanced science for their black efforts. Remember Enlil, Enki, Kullasina-bel, and Gusur?"

"Yes, the Anunnaki kings that lived for 1200 years or so apiece. But I—"

Lutz made a fist. "They were *war profiteers*, criminals, devils, and so is most of their royal offspring today. Zhat iss why we have had so many horrible wars, but this one dwarfs zhem all! Rommel's *Panzer Armee Afrika* will soon reach Cairo, and the Middle East will be lost if the Allies do not push them back by some utter miracle of cosmic fate. The future iss nothing but a blurry haze of varying possibilities coming and ze going, while the past and present constantly change before my weary eyes."

"*Your* weary eyes? How 'bout my—"

He shook her harder. "Viss advanced technology and illegal atomic weapons Hitler vill soon rule England, Europe, Russia, and much of the Middle East if he is not stopped; Japan vill rule the Pacific, Australia, China, Mongolia, and India. If America is threatened by Germany and Japan sufficiently, she may give in to an armistice or may even be defeated, then slowly over time raw Fascism will rule her, rule ze vorld, the darkness unstoppable. Everyone must perform their duty above and ze beyond." He kissed her passionately. "Use your intention to survive, do the job you set out to do, that you *promised* to do before you were born in your 'Soul Agreement.' While you are alive and corporeal in zhis physical lower dimension you must fight, *Becämpfe die Nazis*, Lady Bea, gather your Divine Feminine inner strength and wits, forgive, meditate, and be caring of others when you can, balance the lion and lamb within you…but concentrate your mind, pull up your *Gott*-damn boot straps, and fight for *freedom*!"

8

⊗

July 21

Gwafa had fallen asleep, his head on Takuta's legs. One eye opened.

Bea stood before them; she checked her watch, 5:03. "It's party time any ol' time, chaps. Let's brace ourselves to our duty."

•••

Bathed by the dawn's emerging light, Takuta led a gurgling Udad by the reigns, passing the old crumbling and wind-eroded fortress made of mud brick and salt chunks, the older south end of town partially deserted. Bea rode atop a colorful, embroidered saddle that draped low on Udad; Gwafa covered their rear with eyes of discretion. "Drink some water, chaps. No dehydration," she whispered through her veil, with only a narrow slit for her eyes to see out. "Eat a handful of dates and fill your pockets."

In the middle of town, they wound their way through the crooked alleyways and dusty streets among locals and two other camels carrying heavy loads of goods and fresh-smelling sacks of coffee beans. All seemed calm, and they blended in perfectly. Long shadows cast a beautiful but ominous pall, the night's cold whisked away by warm gusted spirits of breeze.

Wide, the sparsely-populated town stretched for a mile in all directions. Troops were thinly distributed. Near the souk, several platoons of bearded Germans ate their melon, olive oil bread, tinned British corned beef, and date breakfast on benches by their camouflaged trucks andnetted armored cars safely parked under wide palms; a few complained of sand and dust in their teeth, others the olive oil taste. White cross-painted jerrycans of water lay neatly stacked near shiny mess tins of beans and pork and cabbage that would be their common-issue *mittagessen* in a few hours, the mobile kitchen boiler burning dried camel dung and whisking up steam, its blackened smokestack painted with the nickname "Kamel Kanone."

Shaking their wool sweaters and jumpers of sand and talcum powder-fine dust, enlisted *Landsers* read letters from home, smoked cigarettes and pipes, laughed, and played pranks on one another; they were just boys fighting far from Germany or Austria or Italy, and it was obvious they missed their families and loved ones, proudly showing their comrades photos and keepsakes from the mail, little bits of sanity from home they would keep in their pockets so they wouldn't go mad at times or lose faith. Soldiers treated the locals with respect, and a minority of them were flushed with victory, drunk on adventure, and having the absolute time of their lives. They were brothers, a family; they fought for German glory, each other, and father Rommel, not Hitler and his bastard Nazis.

Three officers were yawning and stretching as they leisurely exited commandeered houses used as barracks. The smell of tea, spices, and coffee filtered through the gentle breeze, stiffly punctuated only by the occasional jackass or camel dung pile buzzing with clouds of flies, the only true conquerors of the desert. A few empty bottles of Italian *Doppio Kümmel* filled the trash bins, and piles of brownish greatcoats fresh from the night's chill lay neatly stacked near a medical corps station adorned with the *Afrika Korps* palm tree and swastika. A dozen Germans and Italians were sick from lice, diphtheria, dysentery, and the hated skin sores, the hot, dry desert fighting harsh, thirsty, unforgiving, testing, a burning cauldron of death despite the little paradise all around them, a calm little water island in the eye of a dusty, raging sand sea, a *Ghibli* sandstorm of war.

The scent. Fruit and vegetable markets were just opening for the day's trade. Far off, there was a call to prayer, a melodious chant that stirred the hearts of all that held Allah dear.

Slowly plodding atop Udad, Bea absorbed everything that was around her, the fresh tomatoes being sliced and consumed making her nostrils flare. They passed a camouflaged Volkswagen Beetle with oversized off-road tires and flag standards, obviously the command car. *Porsche's greasy little fingerprints are all over this damn oasis.* "Gwafa, think you can find a quick way to the palm groves?" she asked quietly in French.

Chewing, he pointed above the rooftops. "*Oui, madame,* to the north I will use the Shali Mountain as a guide."

"Got the book handy?"

Takuta patted his robed chest. "Right here, mum."

"Fingers crossed, chaps." *Stay with me, Stick.* "Sneakthievery, offense, surprise."

As they followed the romantic call to prayer by the Mu'ezzin that led the devout to the mosque, huge palms ceilinged them as they drew nearer to the plentiful waters. Under the tightly-knit trees in the shadows of the early morning it was almost darkness, a dense coolness that almost made them shiver. Or was it just nerves? she asked herself grimly. A startle; birds shot out and took flight as if knowing Bea was leading a funeral procession of three plus Udad. The sheer calmness and serenity of the stunning environs both unnerved and soothed her, imagining herself a landscape artist of old, painting furiously, soon to lose the magical light.

Crossing an intersection of carts, Bea could scarcely believe their luck. Townfolk were casually entering the mosque for prayers, and that would prove to be a plummy situation, for there would be fewer civilian casualties if the fighting began in earnest. She spied two Tigers under the tarps and nets, backed up to a shadowed corner of the mosque complex, guarded. One was missing. To the left, fifty meters down a street was the headquarters, the 15th Panzer Division flag atop a stepped wood door entrance above an old Italian drop-top sedan painted desert-fashion and dusty, the sun-beaten leather seats long ago ripped. A small commotion commenced, strange noises and laughter, the commanding major exiting the house. Bea dismounted. "Let's have a casual look-see." *Shite, so many people, we'll never get close now.*

A crowd of Germans, Italians, and excited Siwans gathered in the street to view the bustling excitement. As they neared, Gwafa parted the seas for Udad then stopped in his tracks. A large wooden cage had been placed in a shaded alcove; in it was a roaring female lion with her two cubs, all three hundred-plus pounds of her. His eyes went wide. "*Merde!*"

By some miracle of poking sticks, distraction, and sleight of hand, one of the cubs was now in a German's arms, with other troops patting and fawning over the fierce little cat.

"No tigers to be had in Africa, *kameraden*, but she'll do!" Laughter enveloped thesergeant. "Our new mascot."

The cigar-smoking commander, an aristocratic major by the jaunty jodhpur look of him, paid a trader in silver coins and ordered crates of local vegetables and fruit loaded up into an old French truck, payment in full to a robed pack of black marketers, eager to make the conquering Germans happy with whatever they desired or lusted for. The major fitted his olive pith helmet on and turned to his translator. "Tell him a cub or two would have sufficed, but a whole shitting family, *Gott…*"

"Let's name her Marlena!" yelled a soldier, thinking of actress Dietrich.

"Look how cute. What about the male cub?" "We'll name him Irwin!"

More hearty laughter, as if their deployment at Siwa were nothing but a holiday or exotic excursion to the back of beyond, an arid trifle, a much-needed rest for a battle-weary and threadbare arm of the vaunted and undefeated *Deutsche Afrika Korps* under *Generaloberst* Irwin Rommel, one that desired an equally exotic pet to reinforce their esprit de corps, reinforce their gilded reputation via glamorous photos sent back to Berlin. For them it was pure adventure.

The lioness roared louder, pawing violently outside the confines of the sturdy cage, eager to get her precious offspring back. The mesmerized crowd "ooh-o-o-od" and "aww-w-w-wd."

Bea couldn't believe her eyes. "Arrogant dolts, what're they thinking?" *She's pissed- angry. What mother wouldn't be? Talk about the Divine Feminine...*

"Perhaps not much thinking was performed beforehand. *Pauvre animal*," whispered Gwafa.

Takuta partially hid behind Udad. "No one said we'd be dealing with ruddy man-killers out 'ere, mum."

"Shut it." Bea then nudged Gwafa. "Take Udad and get as close to that tank as possible, the 101. It's nearest to the wall. Do so at the quick without causing suspicion. Now go."

"But *madame...*"

"Go." Bea watched them wander through the growing crowd of soldiers and distracted locals more interested in a graceful and dangerous animal than prayers for the moment. Still the enchanting call from atop a minaret—"*Hayya 'ala-s-Salah...*"

Gwafa began to chat up a German guard near the tank closest to a neighboring brick wall, pretending to be selling tobacco along with some Arabs proffering sweets, cinnamon sticks and cloves. The burly German shook his head repeatedly, pushing them back with his rifle held horizontally, cursing. Temper ignited, he pushed back an Arab hard, then felled Gwafa with a mild butt to his ribs.

In the dense crowd Bea moved closer, thinking that shooting the German commander would be the best move; she shook with fear and indecision. *What the hell, we'll probably die today anyway.* A loose leather flap on an Italian officer's belt offered itself as an opportunity, and she gingerly reached for the pistol.

Abruptly, the snarling cub jumped out of the German Sergeant's arms and fled. With laughter, other soldiers began a wild goose chase.

"*Achtung*! A savage beast is loose!"

"Capture him, or Rommel will come for our balls!" yelled the major. "Pride of the *Afrika Korps*. A pride of lions!" More laughter.

Time slowed to a worm's pace. Universe elegantly aligned, the Zodiac clicked into gear; as all eyes were on the cub chase, Bea changed tack in a millisecond and ran towards the cage, pulling the latch open and ducking underneath. The lioness lunged, scattering everyone as she growled and attacked in a whirling fury. The panicked townspeople fled towards the mosque with Bea following.

"*Hafaznah Allah jamieanal*! Allah save us all!" German soldiers ran for cover. "*Scheisse!*" "*Heilige Mutter!*"

"*Gottverdamtt*! Don't shoot her, I just paid a ransom in fucking silver, boys," yelled the major, ducking into the doorway as his men tried in vain to corral the angry lioness with rifles and lengthy sticks. She bowled over a screaming soldier and bit into his leg, dragging him in a circle, shedding blood as a sizeable chunk came out.

As the crowd ran into the mosque, the Germans guarding the tanks took notice of the commotion. Gwafa whimpered and cowered behind Udad, pretending to be afraid and talking in Arabic. "It is written somewhere…if the wind blows, *ride* it."

Hidden, Takuta snuck along the base of the brick wall and silently shoved his knife into the back ribcage of a maintenance mechanic, puncturing a lung and downing him, palm over mouth. Tools clanged as the box fell.

Bea ran frantically towards Gwafa and the German, waving her arms. "*Achtung! Ein Löwen ist locker! Hilfe! HELP!*"

"Halt!" yelled the guard, pointing his rifle at her.

Udad fled, a young boy tugging at his reigns, a war prize.

"*Au revoir, Bosche!*" whispered Gwafa, slitting his throat in one fluid, professional motion. Bea took the man's rifle and covered her men. "Get in the driver's hole!" She ripped her turban and veil then shot another guard who was firing at Gwafa, the rounds ricocheting off Tiger 101's thick armor.

"Alarm!" yelled a few Germans. Shrill whistles. Tank crews frantically came on the run from their mess, napkins still tucked. "Mount your Panzers! Wind them up!" yelled an officer. More shrill whistles, louder, sharper.

Gwafa shed his robes and hopped up and slid feet first into the narrow round hatch, scraping skin in the process. A bullet grazed his head and hit the hatch. "Ahh-h-h!" He barely made it in, shutting it firmly. Fumbling around in the dim light, he thought of the starting procedures. "*Boules de feu*. Lights. Main battery switch on, fuel valves open…"

A *leutnant* emerged from 101's commander's hatch. "What the fuck's happening out her—"

After ditching his robe, Takuta stabbed him from behind, and with all his strength lifted the thin young German out, rolling him off the side. He was now in his New Zealand uniform and could not be shot as a spy, he hoped.

Using the big dead German as a sandbag, a prone Bea inserted another five-round clip into her Mauser and kept felling soldiers.

The lioness charged a group of Germans in the square, scattering them. Gunfire and panic, confusion and mêlée.

Under fire with the scene in boiling riot, Bea chose that instant to remove the canvas muzzle bag and scamper up the front glacis with her feet on the tracks, hands on the stepped armor. Rounds ricocheted and pinged.

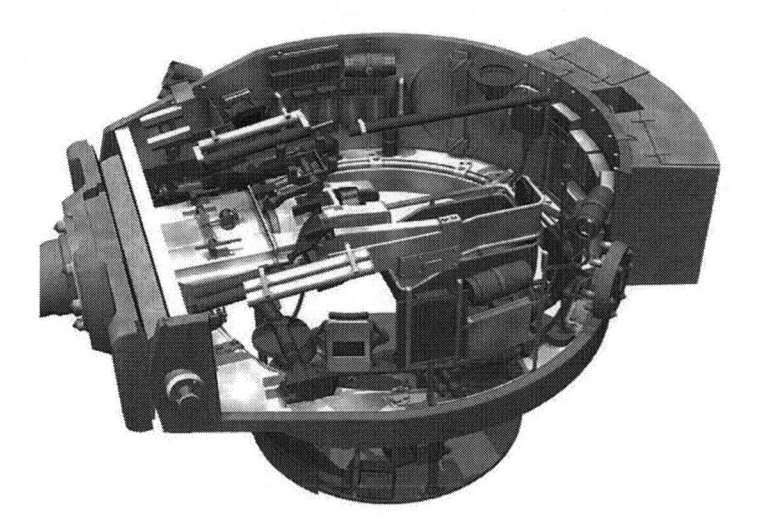

Turret Interior

Finding it just where the book said, Takuta shoved a clip into the tank's MP-40 submachine gun and began firing out the commander's hatch, covering Bea. "C'mon mum!" *Tak-tak-tak-tak-tak*. He shot two Germans climbing up Tiger 102 next to them, then ducked out of the way to reload. Return fire was fierce.

Losing her robes and scarf, Bea dove in headfirst, her legs flailing. "Shut the hatch!"

At the front, a German opened the radioman's round hatch and fired inside. Gwafa pulled an automatic pistol from a mounted holster and fired back, then squeezed his upper torso through the small gap between the front hull and the radios, shutting the lid and locking it. In a flash of inspiration, he barely managed to cock the action of the bow MG-34 and let go a few blind bursts in all directions to get the Germans' undivided attention. *Bur-r-r-r-r-r-p*. "Yah-h-h-h-h!" He then squirmed back into his seat. After thirty agonizing seconds of priming, he twisted the T-handle key two clicks, adjusted the red ball choke, pushed the starter button, and one engine fired up in a loud, smooth rumble, its coupled generator producing voltage. The dial flickered. 1500 rpm. 400 amps.

"*Nein–ne-e-e-ein!*" In the cloud of thick exhaust, undaunted Germans hopped up on the 101 tank and began pulling at the hatch. *Saboteure*! *Kommandos*! Kill these fucking rat vermin!"

Takuta and Bea pulled at the latch handle with all their strength, but there were three Germans pulling outside in a tug of war. More troops arrived, shouting, screaming.

The other engine fired. Full electrical power. Interior lights went on, vent fans whirred to life. The radio hummed, tubes warming.

"*Yar-r-r-rg!*" Using all his formidable strength and bracing his legs on the low ceiling, Takuta summoned the power of his ancestors and almost closed the hatch, but a yelling German was trying to insert a rifle barrel. He fired, and the round nicked Takuta's arm and ricocheted around the interior, finally grazing Bea's left breast. "Hell, mum!"

Bea pushed the end tip of her submachinegun's barrel against the German's invading barrel; she fired a three-round burst, clearing the threat. "Nice try, but no *nipple*!"

But Takuta still struggled, strained. "I'm losing the tug!"

"Hold on!" She rummaged around the beige-painted interior. "*Stielhandgranate*, where?" She found one in the small arms bin, quickly unlocked the small rectangular loader's hatch near Takuta and pulled the ceramic ball on the cord. "One, two, three…" She pushed up the hatch six inches and plopped it out; the Potato-Masher grenade went off the instant she shut it, sweeping the top and rear deck of screaming troops. Locking the hatch, she mumbled: "That's a little present from a former *Shieldmaiden*."

Takuta secured the commander's hatch, the rubber seal engaged. "We're in, mum, tight as a *drum*." He then laid out the comic book manual and let go the breech lock for the gun.

Bea fumbled around. "Right, fourteen checks. The red numbers—*go one by one*."

The warm, potent smell of grease, oil, live electrical cables, fumes, and gasoline met them—the *Panzer Odor*. Everything was clearly labeled, well organized, and painted a bright beige or medium grey to separate components. Pictures of pretty girls, snowy alpine valleys, and a Swiss calendar with days crossed off were taped to the inside hull.

Gwafa saw a German firing directly at his rectangular vision block; he quickly twisted the handle, closing it, but a fragment of one round just caught the left side. The thick ballistic glass was only damaged a tiny amount. "*Bosche* bastard."

Takuta quickly checked the turret's vision blocks and each numbered item. He cocked the coaxial MG-34 machinegun mounted forward next to the main gun then crawled forward through a tight hole to the bow machinegun at the radioman's cramped station. "Done, guns charged, all checks complete, just like the book said."

"Headsets, let's get 'em on." Bea turned knobs on the communication panel and inserted their cables, then clicked the headset microphone to life. "Gwafa? Can you hear me?" She looked through the commander's hatch's thin 360-degree vision blocks to see what was happening. The neighboring tank, 102, was firing up with three crew aboard. The *leutnant* shut its hatch. "Gwafa, we need you!"

Germans began pounding the top hatch with sledgehammers and big chisels, desperate to get it open. "Filth! Worms! Rabid dogs!" *Pound-pound-pound.*

"Gwafa-a-a-a!"

Takuta could see Gwafa through a gap and rapped on the floor hull plate near the front with the folding steel butt of the submachinegun. "C'mon arsehole!"

Cramped, Gwafa hastily slid on his headphones, his head almost touching the top of the hull. "I am here!" He moved the electric motor lever into number one position, increased revs, and opened the vision block slightly. "Ready, ready to *proceed*."

Engine noise filled the turret. Breathing now steady, adrenal glands pumping rivers, breast tricking blood, Bea calmly commanded: "Fisherman, load a high explosive round. Let's let 'em know we mean business."

Thud-bang-thud-bang. "*Schweinsärsche*! Pigshit-lickers!"

He rummaged the shell magazine, flipped open the safety clips, hefted one, and slammed it in the breech as it automatically locked. "*Loaded*, safety off."

She searched the floor while the Tiger lurched forward, causing her to headbutt the overhead breathing tubes. "Ow, gods! Where's the damn turret pedal?"

Takuta flipped a couple of memorized pages and pointed. "There-there!"

She jammed down her sandal and the turret traversed to the right as the electric motor gave off a loud whirring sound. "Wrong way dammit!" She then pointed her toes, pushed the forward pedal, and the turret traversed left. With her right hand she grabbed the elevation wheel handle and twirled it. She looked through the gunner's slightly magnified binocular sight, her head resting on the rubber pad; the long barrel was on her right, the optics and triangular reticles clear and concise just as the book had illustrated. "Elevate, reticle on target. Fire!" The report sounded like a cricket bat to a metal trash bin next to her ears.

The powerful round blew apart the command house in a huge plume of dust and debris, scattering troops as it collapsed. The men atop the tank rolled off in a hurry. Yells. Screams.

She clicked the microphone. "Gwafa, turn slightly left, follow the contour of the square. Where is he? *Where is he?*" She then moved to the thin vision block to her immediate left—all tan and jolly mammoth.

Without warning, Tiger 102 rammed them at an angle, trying to force them to stop. Both Panzers crushed the fountain as they moved along, scraping hulls, groaning, wet.

"It's like being *blind* for fuck's sake." Bea left-traversed the barrel under the opposing tank's barrel. Hers stopped at the 102's thick mantlet armor; it was akin to two woolly mammoths locking tusks at a water hole brawl. "We've got to get off the first shot or we're dead. All stop."

Gwafa hit the brakes with a loud hiss of compressed air from the tanks.

"Reverse full!" she yelled. As they backed off barrels scraping, the other tank began turning its turret with Bea's. "It's going to be *close*."

A deafening *clang*. Tank 102 had fired point-blank, but the solid core projectile ricocheted off Bea's turret, the angle not sufficient for penetration, denting it and leaving a bulge and paint chips inside. The disfigured round tumbled in the air at over 1800 feet per second, taking down a corner of the mosque in a cloud of dust.

Bea held her ringing ears. "Christ!" Eyes glued to her stereoscopics, she pulled the trigger. "Fire!" The gun boomed but barely shook the heavy tank as the breech recoiled, plopping an empty shell onto the leather recoil pad and into the spent shell bin. Her shot bounced off her opposer's round turret and dug a big hole in the dirt, covering them both in dust and debris. "Load another!" Their tank stopped when they backed into a tall minaret, collapsing it on top of both tanks. "What the shitting hell was *that*? Gwafa, all ahead full!"

The temporarily helpless German and Italian troops took cover far away and watched the battle in awe. None had imagined or prepared for such a gladiatorial spectacle.

Tiger 102 moved position then pivoted on its axis to get a shot at their side where the armor was thinner, but the long barrel was a hindrance at close quarters, the tanks designed for long-range fire over vast open terrain.

"Pivot right—no, left, *left*!" It seemed like a dogfight to her, but unlike planes these heavy tanks were agonizingly slow to maneuver. The second her optic sight caught the rear side armor she fired, putting a round at an angle through the side of the rear engine compartment and disabling her adversary's port side electric sprocket motor. "Take *that*, Herr Barrelbum!"

Tiger 102 kept pivoting with one track and fired a split second after, hitting the curved turret slightly and taking a massive chunk out of their armored rear counterbalancing storage compartment.

"Another one," she yelled, aiming for the thin gap between 102's turret and the hull. Takuta rammed one home. "Ready."

"Fire!" Again the thundering gun recoiled, the intense muzzle blast causing a dust cloud. A part of the deformed round jammed itself somewhere in the thin gap between 102's turret and its hull while splinters of it flew asunder, shattering walls into powder. "Got him! Gwafa, get around him, let's put one up his bloody *backside*."

Defending itself from just such an attack, Tiger 102 spun on its axis, trying to get another shot at them while protecting its vulnerable rear end. It fired, taking a chunk of steel out of the angled rear hull plating and cooling fan covers.

"Forget that idea." Bea traversed and aimed at 102's tracks. She fired, blowing off the rear-drive sprocket, separating the tracks. Tiger 102 stopped, temporarily disabled. "He's had it! Gwafa, move down the street full chat, get us to the fucking palm groves. Fisherman, watch our rear."

Gwafa gunned it, the electric motors and engines whirring at 3000 rpm.

Takuta positioned himself in the commander's seat and checked the hatch's circle of vision slits. "Just a few Jerries and Eye-ties scurrying around in a panic. They... they shot the lion!"

Bea saw the blood-soaked lioness in the middle of the street. "Poor old girl. *Bastards*."

Tank 102 spun on one track and rotated its damaged turret slowly, Bea's shot only partially successful. It fired, the solid round hitting 101's side armor and ricocheting off into a building, the attached steel tow cable and shovels on 101's side falling off in pieces. 102 fired again through a wall, clipping off a chunk of the top mantle before they went out of view. Blind, its next shot hit the building on their left, exploding it to dust in desperation with a high explosive round.

"What the *hell?*" she exclaimed, rattled, having fallen on the floor while the tank bucked. Turret to the side, she got up and noticed out the gunsight that the heavy barrel was now plowing through the mud-brick sidewall of a dwelling, collapsing it. She traversed it forward. "C'mon, make it right, Sundy-Undies…what would the girls say back at soddy Wycombe?"

Gwafa opened his vision block all the way and saw German trucks and a wheeled Pak-36 gun down the street being positioned. "Antitank gun! Two hundred meters."

A loud *bang* hit them in the frontal armor. Gwafa yelled an unfamiliar Malian cuss word so loud they could hear him through the steel.

Bea put eyes on. "Fisherman, high explosive round." Another round hit them in the turret, no damage.

"Ready."

Another hit them, only a gouge.

"All stop. Two hundred meters, elevate." Bea put the triangular reticle on target and fired, blowing the gun to bits and killing many caught in the massive blast of cloudy dirt and shrapnel. "That's what you get for the lioness! Load another one of those if you please my good man." Germans ran into a house, and an eight-wheeled *Panzerspähwagen* shot them with its 20 mm autocannon just to rattle their nerves with a loud *pack-pack-pack* on their hull, then moved off down a side alley. "Gwafa, forward, slow." She traversed a tad and let fly on the run, putting the armor-piercing high-explosive round through a wall and into the lightly-armored vehicle, blowing apart the aft section and igniting the fuel. She put another through the same spot and disintegrated the mud brick house. Flames grew from the stricken machine, its rubber tires on fire. "Now we're getting somewhere."

"*This* is what I call action!" said Takuta, sweating, heart pumping, viewing the carnage from a vision slit.

"Quiet, you!" She swatted a few flies. "How'd they get in here? Gwafa, pick it up a notch." Then coughed at the fumes, sweating pints.

"We are almost there." Gwafa moved ahead faster, the engines roaring, the generator, electric motors, and cooling fans whining a din. Powerful sun began to warm his cramped compartment, and exhaust fumes made him gag a little. Hands sweaty, he turned the wheel hard over, locked up one track, pivoted, and turned down a wide street while collapsing a wall, heading towards the glimpse of the Shali Hill, his waypoint. Directly ahead at the edge of town was a thick grove of palms, their shade dark and green.

A flash. *Bang*. A direct hit on their frontal armor. Little damage.

"Hidden Panzer! Load an armor-piercing high explosive," yelled Bea. Two Mark III tanks were already waiting in the palm grove. A trap.

"Ready."

"He's moving," yelled Gwafa.

"Fire!" Her shot missed just behind the moving Panzer, slicing through two palms and felling them like dominoes until it exploded in the ground. "Another goddammit."

Takuta loaded the same type of round. "Ready."

"Breathe steady…take aim…fire!" This time Bea's round hit the rear of the Mark III, slicing through its engine and igniting the fuel tank and exploding it, the back half of the hull in shambles; tank crew escaped through hatches. "Bloody *hell* this is fun!"

Backing up into the grove, another Mark III fired at them from 250 meters' distance, a direct hit on their front glacis resulting in a large gouge, but the German 75 mm short-barreled gun had much lower muzzle velocity and was largely ineffective against their thick armor. Still, Gwafa felt the strong hit through his steering wheel and pedals and cursed the war till his dying day.

Takuta slammed one home. "Ready."

"By Thor's jackhammer, I've got him! Ruddy beige bastard." Remembering the story of Wild Bill Hickok her father had told her, she took an extra three seconds to aim properly and fired, hitting him squarely in the shell magazine and blowing his turret and gun completely off the chassis in pieces, the explosion severe enough that Bea and the men could feel it in their chests. Suddenly she felt like a Shieldmaiden warrior again, eyes alight with blood lust. "Holy *alleycats*…Gwafa, turn left."

Takuta held his ears as he looked out the vision slit. "Jesus! I felt that one."

From a hidden position, another antitank gun fired; furious Germans and Italians from rooftops and back alleys swarmed their tank with smoke grenades, trying to blind them and ignite the notoriously leaky fuel lines with wine bottle Molotov cocktails. One German threw a wire-tied, six-grenade bundle at the tracks, blowing off a road wheel.

Gwafa weaved the tank back and forth in a jerking fashion. "Where should I go—*where, madame? Allo?*"

"We're surrounded, mum!" panicked Takuta, peering out the right side slit. "Smoke grenades?"

"Do it!"

Takuta pulled the trigger and five smoke grenades popped out of the top canister, filling the area with thick smoke. Germans fell back.

In the lightning-fast intensity of battle, Bea's over-stressed mind eased and she lost vision. Hearing Turkish music echo, she saw in her mind's eye the wondrous Sufi and Sarmoun Whirling Dervishes dancing in counter-rotation, a high-performance meditation, a two-way communication with the cosmos's all-knowing, all-loving Universal Consciousness. A slow-motion Dervish stopped on a penny; it was George Gurdjieff the mystic wearing white robes and a tall conical fez of scarlet, his piercing eyes ablaze; he pitched a vase of pink roses to the floor, the glass shards flew asunder. He pointed an ornamental curved sword at her face and yelled: "Love and forgive, but *defend* thyself from darkness!" It was all over in a split atom of time.

"Takuta, *fra-a-ag!*" Bea furiously twirled the barrel lever, depressing the barrel as far as it would go. On the move, she fired the gun point-blank at the ground. A huge explosion right in front of them sent a shock wave and bloomed shrapnel bits everywhere, killing and wounding all troops close by; some caught fire from their shattered handheld cocktails, screaming. "Gwafa, spin on your axis, don't let them put one up our arse. Can you manage the bow gun?"

"Yes!" He cranked the steering wheel all the way left with his left foot, wood stick jammed on the accelerator, his right hand just reaching the trigger under the radios.

"Fire on my command. Fisherman, another *frag*." She pointed. "Fire your machinegun on my mark. Three guns—*Whirling Dervish*."

"Aye, mum." Takuta shoved in another fragmentation round and made ready on the right side of the main gun, his left eye pressed on the MG-34 sight, nothing much better than a small hole in the mantle armor.

Bea traversed the turret full speed in the same direction of the faster-spinning hull. "Now! Fire–fire!" She blasted another hole to the left of the tank; troops fell. She ejected the smoking shell and grabbed another from the ready rack, straining, eyes bulging. "Oof!"

Gwafa jammed the stick on the gas pedal.

A full sixty-second, 360-degree traverse ensued as Takuta and Gwafa fired their machineguns in long bursts, felling troops and scattering others using up three-quarters of the ammunition from the lower magazines. She fired another devastating shot into the ground behind them causing a plume of shrapnel, then loaded another after dropping it—"Shite!"—the intense blast wave putting out the fire on their rear deck like a blown match, the tiny shell fragments nicking their hull, an action akin to a boy throwing a fist of pebbles at a passing Bigboy steam train, their besieged Tiger defending itself well, the comic book manual spot-on in its tutelage when consumed by a highly motivated crew high on combat fever.

"Fire!" *Thanks George*, she thought. Remaining troops fell back at the onslaught; a few wounded were ground into the reddened sand under their wide tracks. An unholy mess worthy only of *Dante's Inferno*.

Another Panzer, a Mark II, fired at them from behind at 300 meters' distance. Its low-velocity 50 mm round hit their vertical, flat rear armor and D-rings, damaging them, then changed position quickly. Light and fast. Blitzkrieg tactics.

"That plump little pig, always taking a pot at us from nowhere with its gobshite *pop gun*." Bea then spied a big brown lump through the palms at a distance; she twisted the magnification lever to high. "Wait…sweet Moses in Manheim, the Famo halftracks, parked in a row, heavily camouflaged under nets, yet juicy targets. Gwafa, half ahead. Takuta, high explosive round. Let's start a fire or two, shall we?" She elevated the barrel and calculated the 1000-meter distance. "All stop."

Takuta fired a burst of tracers at the target.

Remembering mere fragments of her Newtonian physics, she took a guess that the larger round would follow the same arc. She elevated a tad more and fired. The first halftrack blew apart when the round fell slightly short, bouncing into it. She elevated a little more, fired a second round, and the halftrack behind burst into flames and bits. Nearby a fuel truck caught fire from piercing hot shrapnel, then another. Flames rose high as a house. German mechanics in a nearby slit trench scattered, the burning fuel everywhere.

Antitank guns, more troops, and another Mark II Panzer began their assault from two sides at 100 meters.

Depressing the barrel to level, Bea thought fast. She fired one high explosive round to the right, then traversed and let go one to the left into a house, killing dozens on the roof. "Gwafa, get us into the palms, go-go-go!" *Where'n hell is Tiger 103?*

9

Bea swung the turret to the rear, covering them, firing a high-explosive round for good measure at a partially hidden antitank gun squad behind a wall. The entire building fell on them.

Takuta let go another burst of MG-34 fire, the turret traversing back and forth.

Gwafa mowed down palms, weaving amongst them when he could. If the Germans shot at their rear from the path, they would have a clear shot, so he veered left and right, zig-zagging a snake trail. His interior temperature gauge read forty-five degrees Celsius and climbing.

"Gwafa, do you know where you're going?"

"*Madame*, I think we are slightly northwest of the Cleopatra Springs, but it is hard to tell. I've lost sight of the hill."

Antitank rounds sliced through trees all around them. No hits.

She clicked the mic. "Jildy, Sergeant, step on it. Keep moving in a zig-zag."

After ten heart-pounding minutes they touched the corner of a large pond. "All stop. I'll have a look. Gwafa, pop your hatch and get some air. Find a canteen." She pulled the lever on the commander's hatch and the spring-loaded lid eased up. The relatively cool air of the shade filtered in. "Takuta, find a canteen if there's one in the supply bin. Be quick about it."

He found several. He took a few gulps, dehydration a soldier's worst enemy. "Here, mum."

Bea swigged the tea-warm water and tugged on her headset cord. "I'm going to test the waters. Keep a lookout." Standing with feet on edges of the cupola just as the book's woman illustration had shown, she carefully and diligently scanned the palms for movement with the commander's powerful binoculars. None. *What are they up to?* She climbed down and kicked off debris that clogged the cooling fans—one made a high-pitched bearing squeal from partial damage—then hopped down and waded into the waist-deep, two-hundred-meter-wide pond. Lily pads formed islands, birds scattered, and Lotus flowers bloomed blue and pink. Springwater bubbled to the surface, and papyrus and date palms shadowed it all, a bejeweled botanist's paradise fit for Nefertiti's own royal bath. Bea splashed herself, gasping as her overheated body suddenly cooled. She then tested the bottom, walking in a wide circle, soft but rocky and firm underneath.

Gwafa stuck his head out of his hatch. "*C'est bon?*"

"Yes, all good. Takuta, throw me a mess cup from the bin—quick, man." She caught it, and filled it with water, then splashed Gwafa. Refilling it, she scurried up the armor noticing all the hefty gouges and minute hits that looked like a sculptor had dug holes out of a solid block of clay with a round spatula, slipping here or there. "Tough ol' bugger. We can make it, I think. We need to throw off the dogs as to our direction, at least for a few moments, then set a trap of our own. We are very much wanted persons by now, and probably surrounded." She poured it on Takuta's head. "Close all the vents. I'll button up tight the bottom vent too." In a few moments they were ready, the turret now facing forward again after winning a barrel battle with a flexible tree. "So he can swim, eh, Professor? He'd better. Let's go! Don't spare the horses, Gwafa."

Hatches secure, Gwafa gunned it.

The big Tiger sank into the pond, the water a meter and a half up to Gwafa's vision block, the barrel temporarily submerged. The tank made a wake, looking for all the world like a giant prehistoric beast covered in lily pads, reeds, and Lotus flowers, the barrel well-adorned as if an Indian elephant's Howdah during *Vijayadashami* day. The hull provided some buoyancy as per design specifications, she thought, and didn't sink too far despite its elephantine tonnage. Her head outside the top hatch, Bea clicked her mic. "Go-go-go, don't stop whatever you do. C'mon, old boy—swim!" The tank surged forward at high rpm, churning up mud and sand with its aggressive metal tracks that acted as claws; it sank a little more near the far edge.

"That's it. Keep going!"

Gwafa hit the side edge, the tank groaning for traction. It churned and churned, plowing up acres of mud and grass, water churning, frothing. Slowly it emerged, a filthy, muddy mess.

Bea clicked. "Okay, Gwafa, all ahead straight as she goes for fifty meters." Takuta pointed. "Depress the barrel, mum, drain the water if there's any."

She did so. "Gwafa turn left. Now…turn left again. All stop. Now back up so I can traverse the barrel some." They pointed southward right at their original trail eighty meters ahead, the bent palms a giveaway to the original pond path.

Gwafa reversed slowly, and a narrow clearing surrounded their front view, the trees bent. A myriad of palm species and plants hid them well. He then climbed out halfway and cleaned his vision block of flowers and sundry greenery. "*Baise la guerre*! A long way to come to die in such beauty..."

Bea grabbed the binoculars and stood on the edge of the cupola. She scanned the forest carefully, looking for any signs of tank or troop movement. The Tiger hummed at idle, all twenty cylinders purring away; steam rising. She bent down and clicked the mic. "Gwafa, how's our fuel?"

"*Bon*. Three-quarters full."

"The left deck at the right corner is shot up some. Overheating?" "Hot, *madame*, but fine."

"Electrical bits 'n' bobs?"

He read both voltage meters. "Normal."

Nothing but dark green shade, patches of light, and palm fronds filled her view; it was surreal, beautiful, menacing. "Takuta, armor-piercing, please. Let's ambush *them* for a change."

"Ready, mum."

Bea panned. "Whoopsy-daisy, I see palms swaying, troops. Here they come!" She closed the hatch, hopped down, and pressed eyes to the gunsight. The lead tank, another Mark II, followed her trail and stopped at the pond's edge, confused. Behind him were two smaller FIAT tanks and some troops fanned out. The noise of their own engines kept them unaware of Tiger 101.

"Let me have a go, mum, please," asked Takuta. "Fine by me."

Reticle on target, he squeezed the trigger. "Fire!" Palms were sliced in half, falling this way or that as his shot peeled open the side of the Mark II, setting the fuel tank on fire after the round had passed through the engine.

"Nice one." Switching stations, Bea added: "We're really getting the hang of this, chaps." She then put another round in its turret.

Flaming gasoline covered the Mark II and fouled the pond. The two Italian tanks pivoted and fired, their small rounds bouncing off 101.

"Thin Italian armor. High-explosive round." Bea put one into the rearwards tank, blowing it to bits in a fireball, its ammunition magazine igniting like a pile of fireworks spitting sparks. "Frag."

"Ready."

Troops scattered and fell in the resulting explosion, the air shredded with hot steel bits.

Bea sent another downrange and destroyed the last tank in line, blocking the trail. "Three tanks burning, troops turning tail. They're done, retreating. Gwafa, remind me, you should have a fancy electric gyro compass in there, see it?"

"Yes, *madame*." "Head north."

After ten minutes of hard going and smashed foliage, Gwafa found a sandy road. After 300 meters they came upon a clearing.

"All stop." Bea used her binoculars out the hatch. "No enemy movement, but I see ruins ahead."

Gwafa checked his folded Arabic map. "Madame, must be *Umm Ubayd* temple." "Forward. Let's follow the road north. We're sitting ducks here."

Bea scanned in all directions as they passed over an irrigation creek, cracking the small bridge to splinters and stone bits with their enormous weight and grinding their way across, the rear tracks in water. At a crossroads, they stopped. "Small settlement ahead. Let's breeze through it." They sped along at 15 kph.

An Italian supply truck and troops were ransacking a building. "High explosive."

"Ready."

"Fire!"

The truck vaporized, troops obliterated.

As Gwafa held steady, the right-side voltage meter began to fluctuate, the electric generator causing the motor to surge, then reduce power. "Madame, problem with the right-side motor."

"What? Go as far as you can. Bloody *Porsche*, always designing something far too complicated and dodgy." A whining, surging sound enveloped her, the tank lurching from moment to moment.

At another crossroads, Gwafa halted. "One engine is overheating, hard to steer. An oil leak perhaps."

Suddenly, heavy artillery fire had located their position, explosions dug craters all around them. A heavy smack on their left rear shattered the main sprocket and track. "We've been sighted—it's the other Tiger on our left, 900 meters, flak guns have the range too," yelled Bea, traversing the turret and tossing a round at Tiger 103 as one last gesture of defiance. The round damaged the turret a bit, but it kept marching on, filling her optics. "We're sitting ducks—abandon tank!"

An 88 mm armor-piercing round found its way through the front side armor, passed in front of Gwafa's face with a windy thud through the radios and pierced the other side, landing outside in a cloud of dust. He undid his hatch and scurried out, headphones still on. Another round hit the barrel, disabling the main gun like a rifle shot through putty. Tiger 103 had a full crew and was deadly accurate.

Bea and Takuta oozed out the commander's hatch. She pointed. "They've stopped firing, Jerry wants the tank back, I reckon. Let's set the petrol tank ablaze. *Roast the sonofabitch.*"

Tiger 103 ceased fire upon seeing them exiting. Troops gave small arms fire, yelling at them to surrender.

On the right side of the hull, Takuta took out his knife and cut a rag off his tattered trousers and stuck it in the opened fuel filling port.

Tiger 103 fired its bow MG-34; rounds plastered the 101.

Bea gave return fire, then used the submachinegun to ignite the fabric, and a column of smoky, oily fire erupted out. "Run for your fucking lives!"

Using 101 to cover their rear, the three of them ran northeast up the road, crossing another ditch under fire.

Ten Italians rounded the corner of a building, stopped, and gave fire. Bea and Gwafa hit the sand, but Takuta caught ones in the upper thigh and stomach. Down he went.

"No-o-o!" she shrieked, waving her arms in surrender and quickly losing the MP-40. Gwafa held him. "*Non!* Don't die on me, Fisherman, I'll kill you…"

Takuta moaned in agony.

In the distance, they could hear troops and Tiger 103 approaching with a smooth roar and a metallic *clank-clank-clank*.

10

All was lost, thought Bea, arms on her head, hands clasped; Gwafa stood next to her, proud and unflinching, uniform filthy. From engines start-up at the mosque, only forty-two minutes had elapsed.

Tiger 103 arrived bathed in a dust cloud. Two squads of accompanying Germans pitched sand on the burning 101 with their entrenching tools, finally extinguishing the fire, but much damage had been done. The angry officer called on the radio for a tank transporter and halftrack.

The Italian officer had Takuta placed between two of his troops on rifles between them as a stretcher. He bled badly, and they pressed old-looking cotton bandages to his wounds.

A stout German *oberleutnant* gave orders in Italian for them to take the prisoners back to headquarters for questioning. He looked at Bea—she was dusty, greasy, sweaty, and stained with Takuta's blood. He vigorously fingered her tatty, ripped tan tunic, belt frayed and many buttons missing, the WAAF rank cuff insignia barely visible through the dirt. "*Scheisse in Brand! Ein schmutzige Frau und ein stinkender Schwarzer...*" He grabbed her hair and pitched her to the ground.

Another German hit Gwafa in the chest with his rifle butt, Gwafa fell to his knees, breathless.

She ever-so-slowly saluted in British fashion, palm outwards. "*Jawohl, Herr Oberleutnant*, a filthy British woman and a stinking French darkie, their shit indeed on fire. Remember this day, old chap, remember," she said in authoritative German. "And *don't* forget the Maori."

•••

As the day's sun grew stronger, Bea and Gwafa grew weak as they marched. An Italian soldier gave them both sips of his water. After an hour or so they stopped at a canteen to have lunch with the Italians. A medic tended to Takuta as best he could. Wine and water were passed, and hot macaroni with olive oil and garlic eaten. Starving, Bea and Gwafa ate, but both had no real taste for it. She thought it odd how cordial the Italians were, and she smoked an offered cigarette. Speaking German, she and a lieutenant talked of peacetime and the Amalfi Coast during the winter season.

An Italian sergeant perked up and stood. In the distance they could hear machinegun fire and the faint whining of gears—not tanks, but heavy trucks. Bea turned to Gwafa. "Hear that? I wonder who's—"

In a flash, a tan lorry burst through a wall, gunning down half the Italians with a Lewis Gun as it flew past, nearly hitting them.

Bea and Gwafa hit the ground hard while the Italians scattered.

A second truck, a desert tan Chevrolet with rugged tires, heavily loaded with jerrycans, thick tow ropes, crates, rucksacks, and armed with a .50 caliber Browning machinegun and two .303 caliber Lewis Guns followed the first, then slowed; they shot all the remaining Italians point-blank, the mess table running red with wine and blood.

The first truck, three hundred meters' distance and out of view, blew up in a fireball when the hidden Tiger 103 blocked its path, the lorry's many fuel jerrycans igniting all the debris and extra ammo. All five British irregulars were dead in an instant.

"You bleedin' idiots! That's a Tiger tank up there—you'll be cut to ribbons in a tick!" yelled Bea, prone, dust in her mouth, her spotted napkin still tucked. "We're Allies, don't shoot!"

"A *what* tank? Allies, eh? Get in then!" ordered an English officer with goggles and a Tuareg-style blue scarf wrapped tightly around his head. "The Moor can't be German, that's for sure."

Bea and Gwafa loaded Takuta on board and climbed in. A third *Long Range Desert Group* lorry gave dense return fire up the road, both machinegun and weak anti-tank grenades, which did precious little against a charging Mark II Panzer; the little pig had returned.

They drove off briskly with a heavy whine from the notoriously whiny gearbox; Bea tended to Takuta's wounds as best she could, but he had passed out completely. Steady on the big Browning, a corporal gingerly tossed her a med kit.

"Who the *hell* are you?' demanded the captain, reading a map in the wind and not looking up, one hand on the trigger of his Lewis.

The truck bounced hard, nearly tossing everyone overboard.

"Section Officer Thruxton. Women's Auxiliary," she yelled.

"*Sergeant-chéf* Gwafa, Free French. Our wounded man is a New Zealander."

As they rounded a corner near the salt lake, the crew gave withering fire from all three guns at a confused Italian mortar team who had no idea what was happening. The remaining truck then caught up with them north of the lake and they convoyed northwest at full speed. Dust cloud trail thick, the 88 mm flak guns opened up on them from 3500 meters away, lining their escape route with a forest of plumed explosions eighty feet high as they weaved back and forth, making themselves difficult targets, a hallmark of the infamous LRDG—hit fast from all directions, disappear faster in the confusion.

She looked to Gwafa with eyes of deep concern. "I'm so terribly sorry."

"For what, *madame*?"

"Nothing." *Not such cannibalistic and savage chaps after all…*

•••

He kicked rocks and dust in the fierce wind. "*This* one says they stole a Tiger tank, whatever *that* may be, and the blackguard sergeant here says they shot up the whole damned oasis with an 88—just the three of 'em!" yelled the captain, face filled with thunder. At thirty miles northwest of Siwa, safe from enemy reprisals and not having spotted any pursuers, they had stopped to bury Takuta. Gwafa and two other men had begun digging in the unforgiving hard soil as the dusty wind burned everyone's eyes. It grew stronger, a genuine zephyr.

Dismounting the other armed lorry, another Royal Army Captain, tired, his beard heavy, kicked his trousers of dust. He and a corporal rubbed their dust-fouled eyes, a common hazard if one were short a pair of goggles or at the very least a pair of pilot's sunglasses. "Dammitall! Anyway, let's bivvy up here for the night. Good cover in these ditches despite this slight…*breeze*." Calm, collected, he yawned, stretching. "Terrible luck Terry and his crew had, caught a big shell from something, somewhere. *Damnable* luck! Need saline drops, can't see. Goggles broke."

Bea and Gwafa could barely hear them talk, but they knew something was amiss.

He handed him some. "You're ranking Captain, Peter, but don't you see something wrong with these two so-called refugees? Deserters more likely. They said they crashed a wounded Dakota north of town and hid in a cave. A wild tale of nomads, shady deals, and mysterious heavy tanks with ruddy flak guns tucked between their flanks—*disinformation* more like it. They could be German plants, traitors, *spies*. Ones that could spread wild rumors, lies, fear. Our lads up north caught some last month, a

Jerry nurse who spoke perfect English was with them. God-dammit *man*, remember?"

The heavily-bearded captain—and in fact they all had beards of varying length—watched the burial detail in a blur, the cutting wind rising in ferocity. He raised his voice. "Spies, eh? A black sergeant, a dead Maori lance corporal, and a British WAAF officer…I-I-I tend to think not, Whitehead."

Whitehead yelled above the wind for all to hear. "Fine, but I lodge a formal protest…*sir*. Gut feeling. Their story is rubbish, Peter, come on! It doesn't meet the bill. Our mates *bought* it, what if it was a damned trap? I asked her if she could speak German, she said *yes*. It's obvious. Jerry's always up to something queer out here. Rommel's dirty little tricks and fast maneuvers, sand traps and mirages, phantom Panzers and armored cars in great numbers, fuel, ammo, and water cans buried inside endless mine fields that butcher our lads by the bloody thousands. Even us *Road Watchers*. One minute in Tobruk, another down *here*. I say we shoot them."

Hearing his impassioned speech, the highly-experienced and understandably paranoid LRDG men slowly turned their cocked weapons on Bea and Gwafa.

At this, Peter grew concerned, the loss of their comrades bitter. "Very well. Miss Thruxton, *over here* if you please," he waved. "There's a good girl." He rubbed his watering eyes, his vision obscured at best in the wind, so he closed them, sheltering his face with his cap.

Too exhausted, wind-chaffed, and disheartened to be concerned, Bea lazily saluted. "Sirs. How may I be of—"

Peter strained. "*What?* Speak up. I can't hear y—"

Pitching down his shovel, Gwafa quickly put himself between Bea and the pointed machinegun, his eyes fierce. "*Non!* We just attacked the enemy and lost a friend, and all for you! Fucking kill me first, you *bastards*."

The feisty, twitchy Brit in the lorry let go a burst of automatic fire at Gwafa's feet, causing a dust cloud that blew away in a second.

Kill us and be done with it? Bloody madmen, thought Bea.

"Hold your fire, damn you!" screamed Peter.

Reeking of battle fatigue, Whitehead pressed his revolver to Gwafa's dust-caked perspiring forehead and cocked the hammer. "Back off, Sergeant darkie, or I'll split you in *half*, nigger-boy," he growled with guttural angst, his red eyes flushed with revenge and bloodlust.

Eyes wide, Gwafa pressed back. "*Tirer, Capitaine*—shoot!" He then gave Takuta's Maori extended tongue war face. "Hrr-a-a-h-h!"

"Stop it!" cried Bea, now in between them. We're *not* enemy spies, damn you! Oh, you blitherings…"

"*Whitehead…*" Casually aloof and calm as was his habit, one that put the men at ease in hot, tense action, the ranking captain pushed away the pistol and cleaned his binoculars with a rum wipe, knowing full well that his men and Whitehead wouldn't shoot unarmed soldiers without a direct order, no matter what the unusual circumstances.

"Honestly man, 'Hothead' would suit you better, your intemperate nature will be your end." He turned to Bea, dabbing his burning eyes with a wet hanky. "Ah-hum, now look here, *madam*, regretfully, I must put you two under arrest. Is this true that you speak German?"

A scarf around her face, Bea raised her voice to be heard. "Yes, sir, but I—"

"Since Siwa was once our forward 'ops' base, and we do want it back someday, we were reconnoitering the oasis at a distance, checking up on old Jerry the new tenant, saw smoke, and heard the artillery and tank fire. Eventually we became curious as to who exactly was fighting who—though I must say we're still not quite sure for that matter—then breezily moved in for a bit of fun and sport, our specialty. We've had a *grave loss!*"

Bea pointed to the grave and snapped: "So have *we*."

"And then there were you three conveniently eating with the Eye-ties, chatting and *socializing* in German, I reckon. Highly irregular, as we, the tip-of-the-spear as it were, have no wireless reports of a downed Dakota *transport* or any allies in the area."

Even louder. "Why you shite-smeared orangutan…"

He neared her uncomfortably, nearly blind and deaf from dust. "*Both* of us want to know, once again and in greater depth, exactly how and why you and the—"

"…gong-farmers, back to your filthy nightsoil pits!" Bea shoved him back in knee-jerk defiance, the Tudor-era shit-shovel reference highly amusing to the men, but not to Whitehead.

"No, wait…" Stifling the man's pistol again, Peter approached her with friendly arms held high. "Peace be between us." He squinted, his mind rushing with the growing wind. "Only one person I know would say something like that."

"*What?*" asked Whitehead, eager to kill a turncoat spy, anyone.

He slowly undid her scarf. "*Beansy?* Is that…really…you?" He moved her dirty, matted hair out of her dirtier face that had swipes of crusty blood and turret grease caked with fine powdered Sahara. His hands shook as he cleaned. "No!"

"What?" With dry eyes, she squinted in the angled sunlight, pulling at his brownish-blond briar patch beard, feeling his sore-laden cracked skin, her mind in disarray but flooding with irregular and unfamiliar delight at having met Peter once again, a specter from years past. He looked seventy-five years old if a day. "Oldhubby? Peter...*fucking* Younghusband? *Captain* Younghusband? Of the famed LDRG? Shitting hell in a dry well..."

He mashed her closer than was possible and she back. "Gods, it's a g-goddam desert miracle, you're...you're a state, just l-look at you!" he breathed with great sudden emotion, tearing up, losing composure and pitching down his scarfed hat with a *smack*. His lungs heaved in and out, shaking her, no more the calm, cool commander his men had known for a year and a half of constant combat, death, thirst, and scalding-sun deprivation. On a whim and a heartbeat he'd lost it, completely and utterly overwhelmed by the day's events like a lost child finally reuniting with his parents in another lifeboat after a sinking had nearly taken their lives. In a cracked voice, shaking, he bellowed for all to hear: "Of all the...*people* in this d-damn war...oh please, n-n-no..."

Bea could manage no better, emotions at hair trigger. She bawled her eyes out while he squeezed the life out of her, the tears cleansing.

Gwafa smiled.

Shocked and outgunned, Captain Whitehead tactfully eased off. "Family reunion in the desert, chaps..." He re-holstered his pistol and perched on a jutting ribbed tire.

"Shattering."

Securing their guns, the men laughed a little, relieved beyond measure. Sometimes it just happened during the insanity of it all, lost brothers, family, or close friends reunited in the oddest and remotest of places, a chance tropical meeting of star-crossed and mismatched loved ones in a scorched-earth war zone so far from peaceful home and hearth that it seemed a miracle indeed, or so read a torn, sun-bleached, Tommy-handled magazine article or newspaper or book. But in person...

•••

At sunset, Bea and Gwafa sat with Peter near Takuta's grave drinking hot powdered tea with a dash of standard-issue rum as the wind finally died down to a comfortable level. The enlisted men had formally given apologies to her and Gwafa, suddenly enthralled by their insane story. Whether they believed it or not was another question.

As Gwafa turned his back for privacy, Peter sewed up the bullet furrow on her breast and applied a bandage and ointment.

"Ow! Watch the embroidery, Patches, I need both in good fettle."

"Nothing I ain't seen before, old thing. You've a nice farmer's tan line, anyway. All done." He smeared on some ointment and applied a plaster.

"He was a helluva gunner, smart and strong as an ox too," she whimpered, jangling his dog tags and wrapping them around her wrist like a coiled scarab bracelet. "Top man."

Having said a silent prayer, Gwafa rubbed his hands of cleansing dust. "A brave man, *monsieur le capitaine*, the best. He said he was from a fishing village, so I called him 'Fisherman.' He was my friend, and I will miss him forever." He then got up and helped with the pitching of lean-to tents and the preparation of supper, leaving Bea and her dear friend alone.

Captain Whitehead walked over and grudgingly saluted him while Gwafa returned the military formality that lasted a hair longer than usual out of hard-won mutual respect. All was forgiven. Passions had run hot.

"Corporal, give this…coal-dusted, preening, prancing *Panzer driver* another tot of rum on me," ordered Whitehead as he walked off amongst chuckles, still sore, still showing signs of severe strain and bent nerves.

Not one for spirits, and in fact he'd never touched any, Gwafa downed his second rum ration anyway with a following smile of healthy ivory, receiving many pats on the shoulders.

A man handed Gwafa porridge. "Oi, mate, not bad, not bad, have some soggy burgoo…" "How many you killed? Well done you dirty black bastard…"

"Run over a lion you said, eh? Feelin' a touch homesick for the jungle are ya?" "Where? Tim-buk-what? You mean *Tim-fuck-you*, eh, mate?"

"She got loose? Wait, was the lion *in* the tank wit ya?" Pure laughter. "Well hell, I didn't know…"

Peter, disjointed by the day's action and his emotional outburst, let go of a handful of sand as if an hourglass. "We've all lost good men. Good friends. It's their way of coping with the horror, picking on the new boy, brushing it off. They haven't had any rum in months, but today's special. Last of it, a few sippers left. Dash it all Beans, I despise this war, I really do. Up to our chins on all fronts and bleeding badly. The foul tang of death, it's *sickening*."

"I'm not too fond of it either." She paused, thinking sophomorically. "Funny thought, I know machines and aircraft have no souls, but...I must say that overwrought beast of a Dutch oven was...*wondrous*, obeyed commands like a loyal gun dog, shot everything to bits and beyond with that socking great cannon despite my iffy aim, saved our lives. The tank took the heavy punishment with aplomb, grace even, deep scars and all. You should have seen it covered in colorful flora and fauna, an Absinthe-addled artist's sweaty nightmare in a lily pond. We shouldn't be alive, Peter, not by a long yard, especially given my amateur's effort."

The temperature dropped fast. He took in a cool breath of dry air and exhaled, placing his filthy greatcoat upon her shoulders. "Oh, don't sell yourself short, Beansy, you tend to at times and it's even more *boring* now than before; you're as capable as any man and what's more you know it, or you'd *better*. Wondrous, eh? I've no doubt given the Germans' penchant for over-durability and mind-altering complexity. The high command continuously downplays the importance of the Jerry eighty-eight gun for morale's sake, the men's sake—its long, long range, flat trajectory, brutality, deadly accuracy—but we all know it's their best weapon out here besides Rommel himself, slices through anything and anyone when not shooting down plentiful aircraft by the score." He spat, unsuccessfully ridding his lips of dust. "So the big Panzer broke down, you said? I'll pen a letter to Porsche in complaint. Sadly and pitifully romantic, all of this, the desert fighting."

She lit a fag with Peter's American-issued lighter that made a *ping*. "Poppy said it was the worst of combat lies, the romance. El Zippo in my book, none, the exact opposite even." Suddenly, it hit her. "Gods, I wonder how many civilians are dead because of us?" She put her head in her shaky hands, squeezing it hard, then dug in her dirty, cracked nails. The fag fell.

He gently put it back into her lips, grabbed her hands, and held them gently. "Easy, you always were too hard on yourself, too damn insecure and melancholic like your mother. C'mon, stop it! Always feeling sorry for yourself. It's a damn business this, and innocent people *die*. No way round it." Their eyes met and fused, the past rushing in. "Christ, don't you understand? Even back at dear old Cambridge you always complained you felt as if you were daft and inept—missed lectures, poor marks, failing exams, disciplinary action called for on a weekly basis by every don in a dungeon. Bottom rung you were and strangely *proud* of it, your fertile imagination and dry-bone humor the true marker of high intelligence for those of us who recognized it, and I did. Few decent female friends, but the ones you had would fight to the death to defend you. Puffed up Lady Sunderland…boastful, contradictory, gruff, racist-minded in public, but it was the little insignificant people you'd go out of your way to staunchly defend, male or female, rich or poor, to the point of fisticuffs, verbal, intellectual, physical."

"Tosser's paradise, Cambridge. Hate bullies. I was only—"

"Don't deny it. That…pretty little Jamaican girl you defended from that pompous, rapist upperclassman rugger, the one you hit with the cricket bat in all the right places? The only son of the Baronet? Put all two hundred sixty pounds of him in the damn infirmary, out for the season, jaw and kneecaps asunder, cup finals lost."

"He was a right swine, that one. I'd forgotten all—"

"The snotty club girls chastised you for weeks, called you a traitor to your social class; teacups smashed, books stolen, spat in your face and I saw it, lurking behind a wall like the frail, bookworm coward I was, that is…until I meshed with you, the sparking match that touched off my powder charge. Then you stood up to bully Mosely the Nazi-boy that night at your father's dinner, stabbing his black soul and souring the meal but making us all proud in the process, even tough ol' Poppy. I noticed those things, remembered them, even if you didn't."

Tears ran. "I look down upon no one now. It's just that I…"

"Oh shut it, *Thruxton*, that's an order. Don't you understand you're *different* from the rest of us? You were never a berk or bottom rung, never an 'oversexed twit with an itch betwixt' as the jealous Mitford sisters blithely referred to you. Jolly ol' jammy-juggy this and that, an idiot hell, I realize now you were smarter than all of us put together, you could see between the delicate layers of shadows as you skipped along without a care, between the filthy lies and lines of text; you always maintained that they were teaching us mostly rubbish and now I finally believe you, my inglorious and hilarious King James ripped in half, bullet-stopper or no. Walk between the raindrops? Hell, you damn well *parted* them like a misdeeding Moses, girl. Unlike most of us toffs you loved common people, learned from them—where others shunned the lower classes, you flowered amongst them."

"Well, they aren't as brush-daft and boring as the Monaco set diddling each—"

"That day at Stonehenge, when you strained against the giant stone for a laugh? I actually *believed* you could push it over and uncover something truly remarkable, the rest of the sodden gang just swigged, shagged, and took snaps, mindless and oblivious while you spun reams of Wycombe-Aelfric revisionist history." He pointed to the grave, his tone a hammer. "Those...two...men followed you because you gained their *respect*, their trust, they fought alongside you, *hard*, and Gwafa probably would again, no doubt in my mind; I can see what's in the eyes of men. He would have killed me if I had laid a hard hand anywhere near you."

"Yes, but he—"

He took a firmer tone, flavoring his words with spice. "You know what I finally realize? Hmm? Ol' don Aelfric was right and said so to me that day at the picnic reunion. 'It's not the size of the dog in a fight—"

"'It's the size of the fight in the dog. Mark Twain.'"

"You're *special*, damn your eyes, against the plywood grain, and people *hate* that, they'll put you in your proper place and fetter 'n chain you there any which way they can; the higher-ups will always want everyone status quo and hive-minded like bees. But not a chance for dear ol' *Bea*. Oh-h-h, no. You've never been inside, never even *seen* the conformist iron box let alone thought inside of one, and God-damn you for it says the world. I'm surprised you're still in uniform. It's odd ducks like you that attract the admiration, respect, and hidden talent in others, then together as one you change everything. I loved you for all that...always *will*."

A long pause happened upon them, easing their frayed and worn nerves not unlike their worn uniform cuffs that needed constant mending, the small warmth of held hands reminding them both how much they really meant to one another. War was the ultimate hell they knew, but within its granite-hard foundation were tiny inexplicable fissures, ones that brought out the very best in civilians and combat-hardened soldiers, the little golden half-moments of fleeting ecstasy and peerless fire sparks of happiness that were invaluable in the constant mire and grind of wartime life, like floating, hard-to-catch Dandelion seeds in the summer whirlwind.

Bea tried to calculate all the grains of sand in the world, then, thinking of Lutz and the cosmos, she contemplated the infinite spaces between all those grains. "When did you sign up for the desert?" she asked, gazing at yet another stunning sunset that bathed them a burnt orange. She entwined fingers tightly. "Lost track of you."

The wind blew softly causing swirls of fine silica, the infinite spaces reshuffling. "Oh...in December of forty. Got bored with the artillery and jumped at the chance for a crumb of adventure out in the Libyan sandbox. Cambridge Library, the Arabic language book that I showed you. I learned it all, the hidden secrets too. Besides, I'm sure you remember that I like to drive fast, I take my turn at the wheel."

"At university, the MG, I remember." She pulled at it. "Love the beard, by the by."

"A necessity in wadi-land. Look, none of my business of course, but what are you *really* doing out here, Beansy? Last I heard you had some special training and all that, some intelligence work under your belt. I'm guessing 'Thruxton' is a cover name?"

She explained in detail the story of their ill-fated flight, the oasis, the cave—omitting the part about the ancient chamber which she deemed classified. "That's the grand gist. Up till now I've just been doing my bit, odd jobs and ferry flights, very little solid intel work. I once had a mission dealing with Porsche a few back during the peaceful racing seasons; he's a genius, but his engineering is a bit flawed Panzer-wise. Probably rushed it into production. This time round I was damned lucky to have two good men at my side, some divine intervention, that. Believe it or not, the tank escapade was *their* idea, not mine."

He laughed. "Only *you*. You! I swear it reminds me of when I first met you that day in the school library—petulant, resourceful, flammable, truly remarkable if a little scary. God, I was shaken and equally enthralled with you those first few days, from the first rain-droppy kiss onward. Whomever taught you soldiering did it well, taught you the ropes *proper*. Christ's flabby arse, what I'd give for a crack at a German heavy tank, in the turret I mean. Give 'em a taste of their own damn 88 mm tonic. Bloody marvelous, miraculous work the three of you— sunny dispatches by me of course, but no one will believe it back in Cairo. I can only report what I actually see. We'll need aerial confirmation of the big tanks. Ah-hum, field tests you say?"

"Yes, field tests. No one does believe, ever. That's war for you, life in general, stranger than fiction they say. Funny enough, the Germans taught me a great deal once upon a time. Can't relate the precise details. Top-shelf secret don't you know—the occulted SS and Himmler, female Viking training in mittens and furry boots, Vril and Thule flying carpets, King Nebuchadnezzar and the anal retentive Anunnaki, drunkard

Norwegian physicists and their home-brewed Aquavit, some halfway decent flying hours under my belt. The usual boring mix. You're a mystical sort, you understand."

He leaned back on an elbow and made a pebble pile. "Loud and clear. Did you know…it was I that recommended you to McMaster for the Porsche job? I'll bet Uncle Winnie was flushed with pride when you gave in. I only recommended a woman, but later on I found out via Drummy that they zeroed in on *good ol' Beansy*."

She pinched his arm while he laughed harder. "You? It was *you*? Bloody…old…hell…" "Don't be miffed old girl, awfully proud of you. Really was, you know."

"Don't be. I mucked up the job…most of it anyway." "Sorry. But as I just said—"

She perked a bit. "Wait, did you and Alice ever…?"

He sighed audibly. "A dalliance. You were off wintering somewhere in the Alps in '39-'40 with Jerry, lost and out of touch, she said. Dead maybe. Just a whimsy, mind. Said I was a rarity, said she doesn't prefer us great white hunters of little note and smaller manhood."

Bea giggled. "She'd scrub up well in pearls, perfume, and Chanel for old Gwafa over there. In her blood 'n all. Congolese *Heart of Darkness* and all that. Miss her, too."

"Great book. Your two other school chums?"

"Dee and Peach are dead. The Blitz. A hospital was hit."

He straightened up. "God almighty. I'm so very sorry. Your Poppy?"

She drew deep breath. "Fit and fierce. Supply job back in Blighty, guns and butter, salt beef and dried peas. Miss him dreadfully. Letters are few."

"My father actually got out of his stuffed chair at White's, put down his beloved whiskey, donned a tatty uniform, and joined the Observer Corps. One night during a raid he was searching for incendiary bomblets and…accidentally fell to his death at St. Paul's, the roof you know.

Funny, he and I thought very highly of Hitler once, and now…I could strangle that filthy dog Führer personally, the *lot* of them. Bare hands."

She cried again, overwhelmed with the war's suffering and loss and the day's stress. "I'll be at your side, Patches, by God's holy light I truly will be someday. I don't care if revenge is a fruitless endeavor, this unholy fight has me in botheration up to my sandy eye sockets. I've killed so many of the enemy I'm beginning to like it, *crave* it."

He held her tight, the nightly chill creeping around them, uncomfortably cooling their grungy pockets of sweat. "Easy, Beatrice, the men might hear…" he whispered.

"I've long been going mad, round the bloody bend, and now I think I've reached the limit, the *very* edge."

He rocked her back and forth as he did in days long past when they were truly young, innocent, and incomprehensibly human. "So've we all."

She kissed him deeply and he liked that, needed that.

11

August 9
Cairo

Bea flew awake in a sweat, gasping, crying.

Alice got up from her bed and walked two steps in their tiny room, and held her. "Bad one?"

"Shitting hell. A lucid one at that, clear as a glass, vividly colored."

Alice cracked opened the shanasheel window. "Let's get you some air." She looked out past the palmed inner courtyard of the modest hotel where many female personnel were billeted. In the street she spied him and inhaled. "It's him again, gods what a heavenly smell."

Bea inhaled the scented air. "The simply adorable and talented chicken man with his fresh bread. Maybe for a snackie." She then gagged.

"I tried to stop you after the tenth whiskey, but you said you needed it for… medicinal purposes." Alice helped her to the sink, steadying Bea while she puked, rolling her eyes. "Oh yes, a bad one, that dream. Do tell mommy, good for your soul 'n all."

Bea slid down the tiled wall to the floor, underwear askew, moist all over. She fidgeted her breast wound, now healed. "Hate being a ruddy-fuddy Light Warrior, the mystics say you fight the darkness by day and then by night in your dreams in the dreary ol' Astral world. Fairly exhausting, I might add. No extra pay given."

"Tough. The local universe is calling, and all of us must answer the duty call." Alice lifted her paper-thin nightgown. "Well? I'm on the pot with nothing but time on my hands. W-e- a-v-e thy tale of existential woe, beastly Boudicca."

"Filthy cow, always mocking my battle fatigue by degrees of insults."

"You do *not* have battle fatigue, it's good old-fashioned *shell shock*. You'll live. Now tell us your dreamy dream."

She reached for her purse and lit a bent fag from a crumpled pack of Lucky

Strikes that were fresh off an American supply ship; everyone was smoking them furiously after a shortage.

"That's an antiquated term, old bitch, and I'm not shell *shocked*, just…shell-averse." She blew a sweet Virginia plume Alice-way. "Let me get this shite straight, you've been shacked up over there in Alex shagging an RN chap whilst hubby Dickie chases Italians on his destroyer. Training with radar and wireless units, dining in luxury, shooting snaps, and typing classified cow pats for the admirals has been your sched while I, the thirst-plagued desert mouse, fashionably thin from Jerry Iron Rations and dehydrated camel meat, have been dodging shells and bullets near the Libyan border whilst locked inside a ship's boiler hurling same. Grounded and impounded, I was then ordered to perform endless filing duties plus odds and sods at a dinky RAF supply base west of here for days before I was able to come here and meet you via sultan McMaster's return. Somewhere, not sure where, there's a disconnect…a *beep* in the line, old hen. Just can't put the old finger upon it."

"Still like ol' Dickie, just not in love anymore." Alice passed gas and leered at her with wide eyes. "I'm with the Brigadier in regards to your wild tale of nomads, asses, and *Afrika Korps* hare-e-e-ems—no aerial photos of big mythical Panzers, no sympathy. For all I know, you stole a Kubel and schnapps and buzzed around an oasis lobbing off tennis balls from an old flintlock blunderbuss at naked wankering Italians swimming in a waterhole and cooking red poppy orecchiette. Now *ple-e-a-a-se* tell me your disturbing dream. Bored silly."

"Fine, love you too 'n all. Let me gather some wits." She drew a thumb furrow on her forehead just as her father did. "I was with Mumbly in the South Pacific somewhere, lots of palms, sandy beaches, both of us wounded. Takuta was dead in our arms, a bloody mess. We cried and screamed at the long line of Maori warriors jogging up a hill—they were half-naked, tattooed, with ornate necklaces, furry neck thingies, brandishing all kinds of weapons, clubs, spears and the like—to a huge, grassy step pyramid or something close to that. You've never seen such buff and muscular chaps in your life, oily, sweaty, bloody magnificent specimens of our species. Faces of stone if not sticking out tongues in a war-cry. Some were women, fiercer still. We shrieked and shrieked at them to stop, begged them, but they didn't pay us any mind. They kept charging and yelling, fearless, reckless, unstoppable. The Germans were dug in with Tigers ahead in the jungle, couldn't see them, but they were there defending the mound or pyramid. Tracer rounds flew and

I awoke. The end. Happy?"

Alice flushed, wiped, hoisted up her panties, and kissed her softly. "I'm so dreadfully sorry about your chap, truly, and your mother's in the metaphysical fight, so no worries."

"Do you really not believe me about Siwa?"

Alice smiled and hugged her. "Oh, of *course* I do. If you said you saw a tan-painted Bismarck with signal flag mizzen masts sailing in the desert sands guns blazing I would still believe you."

"Thanks. Time?"

She picked up her Hamilton from the small arabesque bureau inlaid with fine ebony. "Zippedy-zap. Half past eight."

"Shitting hell! We've missed breakfast with Rodgers at his hotel. Haven't seen him forever."

Alice began to dress in her Royal Navy Wren uniform. "He's here?"

"Here. He's got something for us in the works, but you know him, probably just a routine job rooting out local Jerry spies using MI-6 hired harlots and hidden cameras. But I need to visit the brain chap at nine sharpish. McMaster's a horse pill on this one. Says I need an evaluation or some such. Bloody old codger, he could use one too."

"I thought you were sacked from the WAAF."

"Not quite yet but I'm on the mat, five charges. Frankly, I like your uniform better, maybe I'll switch. Where's my other shoe?"

"Under the bed. A psychological evaluation?" Alice opened a jar and rubbed moisturizing cream on both their faces. "You look dog-old."

"Feel it too. Yes, a window-licker test or something equally suspect. Put extra here." "It's supposed to smell of papaya and mango."

"Stinks. Blast, where are they? Anyway, the brain doctor is fashionable these days, a requirement they say. Maybe it'll do me some good."

Alice found Bea's watch and ID card. "Doubtful."

•••

Sharing a small chicken sandwich, they fast-walked through Soliman Pacha street with its old-world architecture. It was crowded that day; they stood apart amongst the many locals in robes. Cars and carts bustled about, one jackass-drawn cart held fifteen women in black robes, a humble taxi for the poor. In the distance the Mohammad Ali mosque shone like a jewel, and the Great Pyramids hazily loomed beyond as shadowed sentinels of the mysterious deep desert. Bea remembered that McMaster had said pilots needed to avoid all three pyramids because their radios and navigational instruments would go haywire near them. She had tried it once and it was true, the pyramids were still emitting strange energy waves.

Bea stopped in her tracks and looked at the dark shadows on the old buildings: a flash of déjà-vu hit her for a frozen-in-time second or two, a distant feeling of her sitting atop an ancient temple while water ran in a carved-out channel in the stone, one where she could soothe her blistered feet in a round basin of cool, swirling fluid. Always, it was the long shadows. The strange past-life feeling vanished as quickly as it had arrived, leaving her slightly dumbstruck and dizzy.

Alice stopped to admire a seller of silks. Bea grabbed her by the arm and pulled her out. "Come on, Doll Face, time's wasting. Let's take the tram."

"Oh, *you*!"

•••

At British Headquarters Middle East in Garden City, a block of commandeered flats surrounded by barbed wire, the nearby streets and alleyways swarmed with Czech, South African, Greek, Cypriot, Slav, Maltese, Pole, Dane, Sudanese, Rhodesian, American, and Indian uniformed personnel.

Bea turned to the grand old Anubis Hotel across the street on the corner, its intricately carved Beaux Arts exterior rivaling any ancient monument for grandeur. "That's Rodgers' billet. I see they don't spare the plush cushions and pet peacocks for the high-rank Yanks." Bursting with opulence and grace, the grand foyer shone. They walked through the hotel's salon with fine stone pillars, tall carved ceilings, checkered floors made from a dozen marbles, and gilt hanging chandeliers wrought in traditional Egyptian style. In the lush, hexagonal arabesque courtyard there were indeed a few birds and peacocks by the misting fountain, their shrill voices cracking the sunny calm. Cigarette smoke and mild incense mixed, and multinational patrons sipped Turkish coffee, rose water-infused potions, and mint tea, a scene that bore the hallmarks of timeless antiquity. The war seemed far away, and that's how everyone wanted it.

"Have tea for an hour or so while I attend to my skull physic down the way. Back in a tick."

Alice sat at a small table. "Plenty to read in the papers. See you soon. Break a leg." She looked back. "I'm not a ten-a-penny actress on Broadway."

Alice mumbled to herself: "No, but you could be."

Bea stopped but didn't turn around. "I heard that."

•••

12 p.m.

At BTE (British Troops Egypt) Headquarters at the Semiramis Hotel near the Nile and the golf courses, Churchill waited with General Alexander, commander-in-chief Middle East, and Bernard Montgomery, his new subordinate and commander of 8th Army. Three lesser generals—General Wavell's cast-offs no doubt—a few colonels with stiff field experience, and lowly intelligence paper-pusher Brigadier McMaster stood witness, the cream of Cairo military officialdom. Each one had need of conversation or argument with Churchill, and would get it. Some politicians and generals back in England were tired of Churchill's dictatorial, "yesterday's man" style, but not in Cairo; here they needed his stiff resolve, begged for it.

McMaster read notes and mused on his sultan-worthy surroundings, the large wood-blade fans above twirling a soft breeze. The old boy feudal network held over from the 19th century, the one that gripped burning afternoon Polo, tiled swimming pools, scented-evening dances, end-of-marriage trysts, languid hours of cards and smooth whiskey, and petty prince lifestyles tighter than ever, was entrenched body and soul in the Canal District and Gezira Sporting Club environs. Nothing had changed since the last war, he thought. Luxury painted everything for the officers, a fine silk overlay of exotica and intrigue, black markets, and the promise of clandestine fortunes made or lost in the shadows. The dwindling English aristocracy that had been brought to its knees by taxes starting in 1918 found new life here where the pound sterling bought so much more. Night clubs, cabarets, and Clot Bey Street brothels fancy or plain were packed to the vaulted ceilings, so much so that more and more women had to be imported from around the Mediterranean to fill the voids. Overflowing souks made Egyptian traders rich, and any lewd pleasure or intoxicant imaginable was readily available on the cheap for those with little taste and no discretion; the Bulaq "settling pit" had overflowed once again with heroin addicts of all classes and military ranks, the milder hashish and Lotus flower tea the order of the day for those in search of false enlightenment and genuine hallucination, temporary heaven or permanent hell.

British counter-espionage units and military police were brutally efficient in their duties to the point of criminality—though many Axis spies *had* been rounded up—anything to keep Cairo safe for the old guard; new boys, and their counter-spy prostitutes dressed as modern-day Third Dynasty queens, their perfumed dresswear adorned with gold thread and patterns so intricate they would dizzy any man who noticed. And did they, he mused.

Under strict orders to report directly to the hotel, Bea came in and saluted. No one had informed her of Churchill's sudden arrival. For once, McMaster noticed, her uniform was ironed and neat. Guards stood by the doors. Tight security.

Wearing a black Fez hat and casual desert uniform, Churchill stood, removed his cigar, and kissed her cheek. "Seal those doors if you please, loungers and idlers have gravitated to Cairo in droves, and, cleverly dispersed amongst them, spies too. Gentlemen, my grandniece Beatrice, an intelligence officer under McMaster here. No mentions of her by you lot, ever, clear? She doesn't exist, a puff of fine sand in the wind. Not prone to fancies. Good to see you my dear."

She smiled. "Prime Minister, a pleasure as always. My dear generals, an honor." Blasé murmurs.

Churchill motioned. "Sit, everyone, sit. Ah! Tea has arrived with brandy. We're saved once again by Gunga Din here. Despite the heat, hot tea remains the deepest dye in our fabric."

A trusted and vetted Egyptian waiter appeared with an assistant, pouring hot tea for all.

They left quickly.

Head pounding a jazz rhythm, Bea sat next to Churchill, plucked a sandwich, and ate. *Now what? Brass hat Cairo clubmen all, and they don't particularly like the looks of me.*

A general sipped tea, legs crossed. "Prime Minister, as I was saying, cotton seed oil, wool, hide-tanning, metal works, and sugar production have all increased with local labor under our constant tutelage. Oil refining, metallurgical production, cement, and chemical works have blossomed handsomely as well. We're on the move up, supply-wise. Strikes will be attended to of course, and harshly."

"Good news is what I want to hear. Oblige me," said Churchill, pouring a thimbleful of brandy in his tea.

Alexander added: "Prime Minister, if I may, it was the shipment of American tanks that have made all the difference in the last two weeks at the front, the Shermans, Grants. Any possibility Roosevelt can send three hundred more?"

Churchill puffed harder. "I'll see what can be done, it's a delicate dance. This combat theater may be Hitler's soft underbelly, but plucky Rommel must be pushed back at all costs until the Americans arrive in Morocco. Then he will no doubt suffer… the *squeeze*."

In his high-pitched and squeaky voice, General Montgomery piped up. "We'll have devil Rommel by the throat soon, Winston, I'll see to that. I know him at a distance, know his mind. Tricky man. He's a vain, arrogant prima donna who's addicted to risky, costly maneuvers— that's his *main* weakness besides long supply lines. I hear they rely solely on captured British rations, lorries, and petrol."

"Indeed he does."

"More bollocks than brains."

"Decent tactician, poor *logistics*."

"Damn his impudence, and his Panzers!" "Hrrrummph."

"Yes, yes…"

The Prime Minister ashed his cigar into an inlaid brass tray. "You had better, General, or we'll be belly-up like a beached whale at the mercy of harpooning Nahzies." Mild laughter ensued; everyone knew eccentric Montgomery was just as much of a prima donna, but it certainly wasn't a weakness. Still, thought Churchill, unconventional Monty needed to prove himself capable of the job. "What's so *funny*, I ask?"

Sudden silence.

"*Hmm?*" asked Churchill in a stern, cathedral voice. "Sensitive papers were being burned around the corner just weeks ago by the bushel, quivering officers were in queue at the madhouse railway station with civilians, their tickets to Luxor and Sudan in hand. The city still has an air of panic thanks to bloody Auchinleck, a weaker commanding general I know not. The Germans are everywhere triumphant; we've been pushed back in 'The Flap' all the way to our damn doorstep by a lesser force, and I won't *tolerate* any more retreat! Morale is low, we need a desert victory—now. The Med and Suez remain our swift conduits to precious colonies. Never has our Empire been so weak and our enemies so ruthless. If we lose this war, unimaginable darkness will descend upon us like a plague of old sextupled, our loved ones and families enslaved forever while they put wilted flowers to our common grave pit." He stood and raised his voice to its maximum. "Am I not *understood* by ALL?"

Montgomery and Alexander huffed while the others sat squirming.

Churchill sat and plowed ahead. "Now…to another smaller matter to cleanse our palates. Beatrice, my dear, enlighten our dreary day with your colorful privateering tank tale."

Bea stood, stunned and unprepared. "Well I…that is, well, it's not much of a report, sir, but—"

Churchill scolded: "Rubbishment, grand scale. Go on, m' lady, report I say!"

Tired, thoroughly hungover, Bea rushed through her story quickly and haphazardly, her mind hazy and unorganized. "…well, you see…then in the mosque's square stood three heavy tanks, biggest buggers you've ever laid eyes upon, hefty armor plating, sixty tons apiece said a German, I'm fluent. Heavily camouflaged under nets and tarps. I, uh…after a distraction by a caged lioness I let loose, yes a lion, we actually pinched one with great difficulty in the commotion. The commanding major paid gold to traders, well, she was to be a mascot for them, her poor cubs too. Sorry, bit of a headache today. You see, we managed—"

Montgomery blurted: "A caged lion? Were you attending a *circus?*" Then they all laughed at her.

"No, sir, certainly not." Bea sat in disgust, exhausted, her perfunctory and unconvincing report a patchwork mess.

Alexander turned to Churchill. "Winston, she's having us on, eh? What's this inane phantom Panzer gibberish all about? We've enough to worry about."

"Patience, Harold. She's been through some hell southwest of here at Siwa, and my advice to anyone arriving there is to keep going through that hell."

McMaster laid down a report for Alexander. "Sir, a reminder. Siwa is now occupied by elements of *Generale di Brigata* Di Nisio's Division, the GGFF, of four hundred soldiers' strength. The airstrips have been taken over by Caproni 310s from the 12th Squadron *Presidio Coloniale*, and of course a few Jerry Ju-87 supply planes. There are aerial photos of elements of the 15th Panzer Division, about a hundred and fifty DAK troops estimated. They've obviously secured a large water supply there, and may move northwest if given the orders and further reinforced."

General Alexander put on his thick reading glasses. "Oh? Interesting. Bit of a thorn in our side, but a minor force. Now look here, young lady, are you sure of what you saw? My intelligence reports say that no German heavy units have been employed via Tunis, and may never be. Blitzy Rommel doesn't need or want slow, heavy tanks. The Henschel Works— where's that page? Oh, here—is busy readying more of them, it states here, just a trickle, but by special train to the more temperate open-country *Russian* front, which I'm told is what they were originally designed for. We evacuated Siwa back in June, reluctantly, and these reports say that it's filled with Italians mostly. Are you sure what you saw wasn't the Mark Three Panzer? Perhaps a new Mark Four with thicker plating?"

He looked to his subordinates for guidance. "You're a damned ferry pilot it says here. A fairly experienced operative, yes, but are you trained in tank recognition?"

"No sir. But I know the difference now. My two men and I were—"

Another arrogant general chimed in. "What you claim is utter nonsense, madam. We have spies in Tunis swarming the place. With respect, Prime Minister, we would've *heard*. The LDRG commander vouched for her integrity, a personal friend, but reported seeing no heavy tanks when he rescued you and the French sergeant. He said one of his lorries was most likely destroyed by a Mark Three tank or antitank gun. No sense in letting this aggrandized 'Tiger story' leak to the troops without solid confirmation, or at *all* for that matter. Morale would nose-dive amongst our own armored forces."

"Agreed in full. Let's keep this under hats," said Churchill.

An RAF Commodore addressed Alexander. "Sir, aerial reconnaissance photos of Siwa show only a minor force of tanks and armored vehicles, a holding action only. A trifle."

Bea addressed him too. "With respect, they must be older snaps, sir. Look, I told you everything was *heavily* camouflaged, and the thick palm groves can hide endless equipment, but you see it was—"

A general cut in: "With respect, Prime Minister, she's sun-mad, there's no possible way in—"

Montgomery arrogantly blurted: "Too big, thirsty, and slow for the desert, that is *if* they send any to Rommel at all, which I sincerely doubt, his fuel supplies low. But if they decide to, by the time they crane one or two of those heavy lumps out of a ship's hold in ten months, we'll already be in Tunis to blow them out of the water.

Henshel can then stick one up their trumpets with my comp—"

Bea rose to attention and snapped like a parched bird bone, her adrenaline a fire hose. "They're not Henshel Tigers, they're *Porsche* Tigers! Panzer VK 45.01P to be exact. Air-cooled petrol engines and generators times two. Siemens electric motors coupled to the rear sprockets. 102 mm frontal armor of high-quality hardened steel. Flak 88 main gun, you know the one, the goddam flat-trajectory tin-opener of the desert, devastating firepower. How they snuck them in past our spies I know not, but they did by Allah's swollen arse, and probably did it in sections by night in tarp-covered crates conveniently marked 'Tinned *Wienerschnitzel*!' After a thorough dekko of the town, we stole a clever pornographic comic-style illustrated manual via indigenous child commandos, and my men and I trained ourselves to a fine pitch in a cave at the quick with candles. After some horse-trading with nomad Tuaregs that took a decent fancy to me, we then miraculously commandeered one of the buggers dressed in Arab robes with the greatest of luck, gunplay, lioness distraction, and grenade-pitching—the Tiger 101, *our* Tiger, the one that saved our skins. For fuck's sake the good Doctor signed the inside of the turret with the other engineers as a *salute* to the tankers. I know him intimately, a mad genius and sturdy ass of a man—none of you do, that's for *damn* sure. With a spot of heave-ho and a handful of tungsten-core shells we miraculously disabled one of the Tigers up close, the 102, in what must be known by now back in Siwa as the *Great Mosque Mammoth Match*."

She turned to face Churchill, knowing his passion for the American Civil War. "It was akin to the ironclad Battle of Hampton Roads in 1862, the U.S.S. Monitor versus the damn C.S.S. Virginia, just as you taught me years ago, two great smoking iron beasts at each other's throats ramming and scraping hulls at *point-blank range*. After escaping that battle by the skin of our teeth, we then destroyed several other sub-par enemy tanks and antitank guns before being shot to pieces by our only genuine adversary, the third Tiger lurking in the palms, the number…one…oh…three. The big Panzers can take monstrous punishment by anything thrown at them, like nothing we've ever seen, lesser shells bounced off like a child's cricket ball to an iron letterbox. We had a few victories before mechanical failure set in, and then were hit by 88 shells. The three of us then abandoned the tank before getting captured. Good luck attacking them at Siwa by air with aircraft like Mosquitos or the new Typhoons soon to arrive, you'd end up killing half the town in the process if you could even locate them. I may have killed some civilians in the action myself—quick, hot, and sharp it was, our ears blown apart by the noise whilst we were mostly blind behind vision slits. Anyway, after being taken prisoner, the marauding LDRG swooped in, shot everyone, and scooped up what was left of us with a spatula. One casualty to report in addition to the C-47 Dakota's complement, a New Zealander Maori, and a damned good one...*sirs*."

A moment of uncomfortable hush.

"You *forget* yourself, madam," hissed a general in disgust.

Shaking, she turned to Churchill. "And *you-u-u*...taking the lion's share of food from the Indians in Bengal and letting millions starve!"

The Prime Minister retorted: "War materiel. The unwashed hordes breed as rabbits...a beastly people with a horrid religion."

"Just like the Boer War when you said in the press that you protested the blackamoors firing on white men, all the while you commended the creation of concentration camps for the women and child—"

Furious, McMaster stood. "Sunderland, *enough!* Mind your place..." She sat, shaking.

Silence reigned again, then a wall clock chimed.

Fans whirring a delicate thrum above, Alexander leaned back in his crackling wicker easy chair. He said, in a mild tone: "Young lady, Brigadier McMaster has informed me...that this very morning you've just had a psychological work-up. Standard procedure now for...*select* operatives in the field upon return from intensely active areas. What did the psychologist say about your state of mind and physical being? Heavy strain, malnutrition, and battle fatigue, wasn't it?"

•••

Bitter, Bea joined Alice at the hotel courtyard.

"It's been hours! Where's your jacket, tie, and hat?"

Bea snagged a biscuit and whirled a teacup to the floor where it shattered; heads swiveled. "I've been sacked by the highest gents in the land, including dear old Uncle Winnie, the soddy *Golden Square* occult chairman of Cairo. In full fig he was, fat fez and all."

"Yes, I just heard he'd arrived." She showed Bea a Colonel Blimp cartoon that made fun of Churchill. "Blustering old windbag."

"And he was in rare form. I was ordered to report directly to BTE after my brain session with Dr. Quackmeister, MI-6's most brilliant moron to date. Alexander and his henchmen deemed my story and me unfit for digestion, McMaster the bastard, too. Then some fat RAF Commodore told me to turn in my blue couture at the desk whilst the entire high command and office corps stood witness in the lobby snickering, their fly whisks and swaggers tucked under their sweaty armpits. I'm surprised they didn't cane me the *hell* out of there. Poppy was right, they're all soft-arsed brass hatters and ignorant whore-mongering dimwits under it all. I'm a civvy now and forever, and that suits me jolly well."

An Egyptian boy in a pillbox hat arrived with a note on a silver charger. Bea tipped the boy generously. "Thanks, old man. Don't put it in Barclay's Bank, they'll steal it from you and loan it to the Germans." He then cleaned up the mess with the waiter. Alice nabbed the missive. "Says to meet Uncle Percy's nephew Sam in the restaurant. North corner."

•••

In a well-padded green silk booth sat Bernie in his tropical-weight white suit, impeccable tie, and pocket square, his spread newspaper covering his face. A forest of potted plants and fan palms partially hid him as well. He recognized them by the sound their shoes made, just as he did as a boy when pursued by his siblings in the family hay barn.

Bea snatched the paper down. "*Guten tag*, Herr Sam," she hissed.

He laughed, and hard. "A civilian, eh? I just knew-w-w it wouldn't last. Love the WAAF skirt, ugly shoes, and the now barren white-shirt look. The newest from Paris?"

"Quiet, you. It's mufti for me. Soon I'll be wearing the big Bergman hat and dress from *Casablanca*. My new uniform for *Le Tip Top Club*."

"I'm jealous already. Love all the outdoor cinemas they have for us." Alice slithered up next to him and ate a wispy breadstick. "Bernie, why so thin? Gads old boy, you look a bit trodden underfoot. What news have you?"

He kissed her, then Bea. "Not much news. It's really damn good to see you both. Thin? Oh, I've been on the new Mediterranean diet, you know, cottage cheese, lemons, fruit cocktail, dates, all washed down with cheap bootleg gin. It's an American rage." He snapped a breadstick of his own. A waiter brought his savory lunch and a bowl of lemons, Bernie's favorite fruit. "Sorry, couldn't wait. Starving." He cut a lemon in half, squeezed it into a small glass with brown sugar and drank it.

Bea sniffed the delicate bouquet of exotic spices. "And of course, some fish, Shakshuka style. I'll have the same, please."

"Oh, me too," said Alice. The waiter bowed and departed, then bowed again as a group of Arab men in suits and fezzes met with British dignitaries. "You know, back in England and Europe everyone is scrounging around for a lump of jam or crumb of bread, but everyone down here seems extraordinarily well fed and bedded. Doesn't even feel like the war's on."

Bea added: "What war? They ignore it unless it's profitable for them. Anyhoo, I drink to be numb nowadays, and only eat fruit cocktails because I need plumbing help. Well, mostly."

Bernie snapped fingers at another waiter he knew and twirled his fingers downward towards his glass. "He'll bring us a bottle of extremely good French champagne, extra cold. No cheap stuff. I have a system here. You're both right of course, but there's no reason to be downright uncivilized about it." He snapped the paper to attention and folded it.

Slumped, Bea poured mineral water for herself. "Maybe the Mohammedans are correct about spirits, just 'Anunnaki Ale' after all to keep us happy, dumb, and tired. Well's dry, filled in by nomads. I was somewhat overserved last evening by Doll Face here, King Anu's favorite olive-oiled concubine in waiting."

Alice said triumphantly: "Harems were the first all-female universities, they were taught religion, science, and history by the best in the land. The sex bit was secondary."

"Shut it."

He snapped in half another. "Funny. But you're right about the booze thing."

Alice huffed. "Don't hang that on me, Beans. You were the one flirting with the entire Officer's Club clientele and slapping colonel what's-his-name so hard he lost his glasses to the far side of the bar. Sorry, Bernard, she's had a shell-shocking day of it. The brain doctor gave her a poultice of belladonna and mustard gas, and the high command caned her for insubordination. Down in the dumps, you see."

Bea nursed another glass, sniffing the magical, healing bubbles and limes. "Kindly take thyself over to the biggest pyramid, scale it, measure the Ley Line energy with a brass meter, jot some notes, paint it up like The Jack, then tumble down the backside singing *La-la-la Marseillaise*."

He doubled over. "Goddammit, I love it when you two make me laugh, especially when there's little else to laugh about. Tomorrow I meet with our boss man once again. Big things are afoot, but I'm for quitting this theater of war for Miami via Bimini, it's swordfish and rum cocktail season with Hemingway and the gang, then it's on down to Antigua for the Mill Reef Club tennis match and some U-Boat watching. Hemm thinks he can find Atlantis ruins near Cuba, wants to write a new book. What have you two been up to lately?"

Alice said: "Two weeks' leave from my RN desk job in Alex. Now I'm regretting it. Been learning the wireless, radar, and photography some. You know Hemingway?"

"Met him in New York at the 21 Club. Went fishing south of Nantucket. Tuna. What about you, kid?"

Bea leaned her head to the soft silk, eyes closed. "Me? Nothing much. Been vacationing at Siwa Oasis via aeroplane, petty frissons abounded. Lily ponds, Lotus blossoms, date palms, ancient ruins, artisanal spring swimming holes, all courtesy of the *Afrika Korps* tourist board in Rome. Had a lovely hire car with a flak gun and French chauffeur, a big Porsche, the *VolksPanzer*. Shitty petrol mileage but decent legroom for five."

Bernie looked to Alice. "She…?"

"That's her story. Might be happy reading in the *Times* someday."

The champagne arrived with the fish. The waiter poured, then hid the bottle behind a plant in an ice bucket as was the custom for western guests in certain luxury hotels.

Bernie dug in. "I see. Well, let's eat and be merry while we can, ladies. Lemons?"

Bea took one, sniffed it, and asked: "Speaking of travel, haven't seen you in nine months. Where've *you* been if I may pry?"

"Oh, Morocco thereabouts, somewhere in Spain and Portugal, then I was in England and London to visit and old friend. Flew back here with McMaster via Gibraltar a week ago. Been hiding from you both."

"Spain? That sounds like fun, Barcelona I hope," said Alice dryly. "War's hell 'n all." Bea said: "Don't be fooled, he's been making the rounds at London's bugger clubs, shooting grouse and feasting at banquets with his foul Illuminati chums, and visiting his sick aunt. Which one was it this time, Mr. Chase? Aunt Agnes Overholt?

Or was it…Aunt *Walter*?"

Bernie separated a bone from the delicate fish, the old code names from their Argentina mission sparking memories. "That's not a bad guess. Both are correct. And for Jim Bowie's sake, keep your damn voices down. There's more German spies in this town than fucking Berlin on Hitler's birthday. They all fly home for that shindig, a guy told me."

"Sorry," whispered Alice.

Bea kissed Bernie passionately for all to see, easing suspicions. "Not sorry. But you do have a point."

He dabbed his mouth of lipstick. "Nice touch."

12

♈

After four o'clock tea in the garden, Bernie led Alice and Bea to his suite. "You two can take a nap in the spare bedroom while I read some homework. Don't wrinkle any of the thousand silk pillows, they'll pad my bill." He then proceeded to the balcony's wicker throne with his briefcase.

Upon waking three and a half hours later, Alice unpacked her diminutive portmanteau she'd been carrying. "Two dresses—one blue, one black—two sets of gloves and pumps. Let's order another bottle of bubb. Call down for it, Beansy."

Yawning, she tapped the cradle up and down. "Right. I'm ditching this headache straight away."

•••

At 9:11 p.m., they arrived by taxi at the Grand Continental-Savoy Hotel, arguably Cairo's finest. Walking past a herd of posh sedans and horse-drawn carriages, Bea gently extended a white-gloved finger to a Bordeaux-painted Bentley 8-Liter sedan's doorframe and hand-painted double gold coachline, missing her old sports motorcar and the rush of speed and romance it had provided when there was petrol to be had back home; here there was plenty, she thought. Her father had donated her unpractical car to the war effort as scrap metal, the bespoke engine highly prized as a naval sump pump. "This lump would dignify even the most miserable of misguided miscreants," she mumbled.

"*Rah*-ther," said Alice, fixing her hair in the window's reflection. She then kissed it, leaving a lipstick mark.

Bernie chatted up two American gentlemen he recognized in the foyer just as the orchestra was winding up for dancing. The crowd of civilians and Allied officers was thick, the cigarette haze thicker. A huge palm stood proud at the center of the ballroom, and the brass-railed bar was the best-stocked in all of Cairo—even the entire Middle East theater. To top it off, an on-site radio crew was interviewing patrons with a large microphone, broadcasting live for the BBC.

Sufficiently doused with alcohol and dressed in his just-cleaned white dinner jacket, Bernie sat at a table, tipped a waiter heavily, and ordered champagne and Iranian caviar. "Biggest and best deal in town. Nothing but the finest for you two."

Now in a better, more sedate mood, Bea smoked and swilled. "Love a spot of tennis tomorrow early at the Heliopolis Club. Take us both?" She then mindlessly tipped ashes from her long black quellazaire, soiling the crisp linen tablecloth next to the ashtray, the fine Egyptian cotton shining like silk. *Finally, some genuine relaxation.*

"Sure thing. Here's to Churchill's saddle sores and petty crimes. Down the hatch." Bernie shot back a whiskey and chased it with a glass of champagne. He then raised his voice above the bustling throng's hum. "That's how the Russians do it. Wow, never seen it so crowded in here."

Already tipsyish and the happier for it, Alice read a brochure. "Oh! The Empire Service Club is organizing a tour of ruins tomorrow with all the silly—"

Dodging crowds, inebriated British officers and their demimonde-looking ladyfriends bumped into the intimate table, spilling their bottle and ice. Bernie wiped off a caviar blini from his formerly spotless jacket. "Of all the…"

A waiter arrived to salvage the wine.

The colonel remarked: "Excuse us, so sorry old chap, I'll gladly pay for the dry cleaning…well, well, if it isn't the 'phantom Panzer girl.' I say, this is opportune. Did Prime Minister give you a proper spanking for your dubious efforts and lost wits my dear? Good gossip all round." The two women laughed. "Can I get you a blank aerial photograph for a placemat?"

Bea ignored him, drinking. "Piss off, brass hat. I see security protocols mean nothing to you lot." *This day just won't end…*

Bernie slowly stood, wiping caviar. "Apologize to her, Colonel, *now*."

Bea pointed with her prized cigarette stick. "Oh, *please*, not on my acc—"

Another officer, a South African-accented major, went face-to-face with Bernie. "Do us a favor and go home, *Yank*, we're doing the real fighting in this war. What're you doing here really? War profiteering? A *slave* trader, are we?"

Alice stood and slid liquidly into the small space between them. "Let's not have an inter-service tussle, gents. There's plenty—"

With all his might Bernie laid him out, the crunch of the man's jaw breaking in half audible to everyone nearby. Women screamed, men shouted. Sudden pandemonium. Spotlights came on and the orchestra went into full swing, playing a popular Tommy Dorsey tune.

Fight-or-flight switch flipped, Bea's interlaced fingers cracked at the knuckles as her adrenaline cascaded like Victoria Falls. "What the hell, load an armor-piercing round..." She tossed her champagne in the Colonel's face, kneed him in the bollocks, and punched him in the solar plexus hard with a yell just as she had been taught by the *Gebirgsjäger* Mountain Division, felling him like a small tree. Nearby, revelers gasped and laughed.

"You rotten little cunts!" yelled one of the shady ladyfriends, tossing her red wine in Bea's face and pushing her with both arms into Alice.

Alice pushed Bea in return. "Have at her!"

Bea socked the impolite woman so hard her paste pearls came apart when she hit the tiles. People tripped and fell. She then grabbed the champagne bottle, and, thinking of Lutz, Hans Stuck, and Rudi Caracciola in the old days, pitched it end over end with both hands like a tomahawk into the big mirror behind the bar that had hung there for eighty-two years of grand gilded reflection. "Fuck all of you!" That did it. Two French officers grabbed her but she kick-boxed and elbowed them off one by one. "*Vive la* bloody France!" yelled Bea.

Appearing from behind, Bernie then hit both Frenchmen square, noses smashed.

Organically the violence spread, table to table, palm to palm. Laughter and gaiety, horror and shock. Wasted spirits and precious ice. Waiters went down with trays of delicacies and the last of the chilled French Rosé. Another table was flipped, then another, and someone hit a British general nearby rudely calling him a German spy.

A disgruntled Egyptian man, tired of the British occupation and its history of imperial duplicity, pulled a pistol and shot three rounds into the ceiling's hand-carved centerpiece while yelling: "Long live Rommel and Hitler!" Ten officers of various nationalities tackled him, beating the man half dead. Photographers captured it all with flashbulbs popping, the BBC radio crew reporting on the fly.

Five ambulances and two trucks carrying Military Police arrived.

From behind, Alice jumped onto the other demimonde woman who then twirled around screaming trying to shake her off. "I've got *this* one!" yelled Alice.

•••

August 10
7:12 a.m.

McMaster vigorously marched down the dim muggy hallway at the military police jail, fist-held swagger under arm, polished shoes echoing off the shiny blue and white tiles. He stopped at a dingy cell. Bernie was on the floor snoring and Bea and Alice were sleeping on the single cot. Stained and ripped clothes were in a shamble for all three, and Bea and Alice had one shoe apiece. "Wake them *up*, sergeant."

"Sah!" The sergeant pitched a hefty bucket of brown Nile on them. "When they're *lucid*, escort them over to me under armed guard."

•••

In his office at MI-6 headquarters near the Middle East Command, a furious McMaster stood when his three damp prisoners entered the spacious room number thirty-nine escorted by two MPs. "Sit down, the lot of you," he commanded.

Bernie said: "My fault. It's true I threw the first punch, but he was—"

McMaster chested up to him. "Unbelievable. Or *is* it? You of all people, Rodgers. Christ almighty, and a man of your age, too. Always occasioning a damn breech of the law."

Tie was fumbled with. "I…"

Bea came alive with a slump and a moan, her black silk Dior a wreck. "We gave them what they all deserved and wanted, *entertainment*."

"*Shut up*." The brigadier paced, pointed a finger. "You'll pay for the mirror all right, out of your own *pocket* m' lady. Government ministers including Mr. Pasha, diplomats, two princes, an incognito king and queen from somewhere and their entire entourage have given us a formal protest…*in writing*. For God's sake, twenty-one people are in *hospital*. It'll be in the papers any minute now. And you, Drummond, you were supposed to keep an eye on her. Well, you work full time for *me* now once again, the Navy's handed you over this very morning, *official*. You begged a field assignment? Well you've *got* one, young lady, your wireless and radar skills will come in handy if indeed there are any. I need to get rid of you three fast—this is damn near an international incident! The mission briefing's been moved up to tomorrow, so sober up. I'm waiting for a boffin to arrive from Bombay."

Alice said: "Sorry, Brigadier. Bit of a cock-up all round. You see, two pearly strumpets were calling us nasty—"

McMaster snapped: "Be *quiet*, all of you, while I think." Twenty minutes of snoring went by while McMaster shuffled and signed papers. "Honestly…"

Sergeant Tillings knocked and entered. "They're here, sir. The Map Room upstairs." "Very well." The Brigadier walked over to Bea, asleep on her arm, nose dripping. "Rise and *shine*, Private Lassie!"

On the top floor of the well-furnished townhouse, Churchill, a general, and a colonel were waiting on plush couches, both officers subordinates of Montgomery, both in the armored corps. Large maps festooned the opulent silk walls, and an ivory-inlaid round table filled the center of the ancient circular Persian carpet with, ironically, reverse Hindu swastikas.

Somewhere down the hall, a local servant had lit fragrant incense. Thick sweet Egyptian coffee was served, lots of it.

Slightly swaying, Bea, Alice, and Bernie all saluted.

Churchill rose with the help of his cane. "Ah-h-h-h-h, the newest members of the vaunted Hellfire Club, Cairo chapter, one gent and two fillies—bare of foot and in formerly posh frocks. My hearty congratulations, my dears. Talk of the town, and that's quite an achievement in its own right. Reminds me of the Sudan War and Kitchener when I was a young man m' self here in Cairo, dueling with fisticuffs and whiling away hours in the perfumed bazaar admiring the indigenous beauties."

Bernie neared the table. "Prime Minister, sirs, I take full responsibility for our actions last night. If I may be able to—"

Churchill waved his cane. "Never mind that! This city puts Sodom and Gomorrah to shame, ditto the officer corps. All charges by Allied officers and old General Phillips—lost a tooth or two, poor old dog—have been dropped on my order to the provost marshal. Someone claimed it was *you* that hit the general, Rodgers, a real nose-ender."

Bernie tried unsuccessfully to repair a ripped pocket. "Not me, sir. But I admit I popped just about everyone else. My best Joe Louis."

Bea stepped forward. "My apologies, sir, you see we'd been done by rather harshly by these two heroin harlots that—"

"Never you mind," snapped Churchill. "Lay it out, Robinson."

The colonel opened a file on the big table and poured its contents out for all to witness. "Aerial photographs by low-flying Spitfire reconnaissance. He made several passes on the deck three days ago at full chat in the early morning hours with a new high-resolution, fast-firing camera; woke 'em up *proper*. Jerry never even heard him coming till it was too late. Took some small caliber ack-ack fire for it from rooftops. No disappointments on all counts."

"*What?*" Bea's imagination clearly showed the Spitfire's scalding pass in her mind's eye.

Bernie picked one up. "May I?" It showed two Tigers in the mosque's square being repaired under tarps, and there was no mistaking them for lesser tanks. "I'll be damned! Look at the size of them compared to the others. Long high-velocity barrels, definitely Pak-88s." Other photos showed destroyed tanks, trucks, and buildings. A Mark III's scorched turret and gun were clearly visible attached to a crane in the repair depot amongst lines of tank tracks in repair. Off to one side was Tiger 101. "They're cannibalizing one of the big ones for parts it looks like. That means these two Tigers are still operational."

Bea and Alice crowded in, relieved and bewildered. Bea waved one at Churchill. "Three days ago? Then yesterday you…"

The two British officers chuckled.

Alice wrinkled up her nose. "Looks like you flattened the *mosque*, old girl…"

Churchill soothed. "My dear, I had all the faith in the world that you would perform beautifully in front of the stodgy high command. A part played well. Apologies for the duplicity, but we were hoping it would open some jaundiced eyes, which it most assuredly did. My visit here was to get their attention on the war in the west, not the King Tut-worthy festivities hereabouts in biblical Tartarus. They needed a jackboot in the arse. Monty was in on the game, a good sport. I'm also here to sing his praises and raise morale."

"Well *done*, madam," breathed the general with emotion, a tank brigade commander himself.

Bea hugged Churchill, regulations be damned. "Loathe you." Then slowly turned to McMaster. "Why you brass-hatted, tin-horned, son-of-a-whore…"

He raised his palms in defense. "Sorry. For your own good. Especially after last night's debacle. You may be a civilian at present, but you still work for this branch. I expect professionalism, m'lady. Tell me…you didn't have *fun* running riot over the generals."

"You and those brassy Madras peg boys can bugger off to—"

Churchill pinched her face just as he did when she was little. "Leave him be, he's one of a kind and we need him alive."

"Beastly rotter," she mumbled.

The general held up a crumpled missive. "Oh-h-h, yes. One more thing. There was an exchange of seriously wounded men, and an Australian had this German letter pinned to him. It went through the hands of a dozen officers near the front before it landed on my desk two days ago. No one understood it. Allow me. *'To whom it may concern in the British forces, regarding the three foolish but courageous Allied infiltrators at Siwa recently, I wanted to personally state that although there were sixteen civilian casualties, none were seriously hurt or killed. In addition to our own casualties, the lioness was buried with… full… military… honors.'* Signed, respectfully, 'Commander X,' 15th Panzer Division."

Bea sat in relief, head in hands, then cried a little, her exhaustion acute. Alice rubbed her silky back. "See? Not all of them are evil-minded."

Churchill put his hand upon Bea's head and rubbed lovingly. "In an hour's time I depart for Tehran via swift Liberator. Then it's on to Russia to visit Joe Stalin for vodka and belly dancing. Then back to England via the northern route. Do you have mail for your loved ones I can relieve you of?"

Bea looked up, eyeliner dripping. "Yes, but they're in our f-f-flat a mile away."

The Colonel said: "I'll send someone straight away. Change of clothes for both of you too?"

"Yes, sir. Thanks," said Bea, regretting the destruction of the only evening dress she had. Bernie kissed Bea on the cheek. "Nice job at the bat, kid."

"Colonel, sir?" asked Alice, holding the silk fabric to her chest. "I'm afraid I'll need a new brazier as well. Snapped in half. And sir, please send Sergeant Tillings. If anyone's going to rustle through our knickers pile I'd rather it be him. Best of the bunch."

The Colonel smiled under his thick moustache.

McMaster gently dragged Bernie away by the elbow. "A car's downstairs waiting for you. You're wanted at the American Embassy post haste."

Bernie chugged a warm Coca-Cola and opened another. "The *embassy*?"

•••

American Ambassador Alexander Kirk rushed out to the black Lincoln sedan that delivered Bernie. They passed one another; Bernie tipped his fedora, but Kirk only gave him a long stern look before he slammed the door.

Inhaling a sandwich and descending the steps with vigor, Bernie suddenly slowed when he reached the bottom floor, then swallowed hard; before him were four Thompson submachinegun-armed U.S. Navy sailors guarding a steel door with a stern-faced young junior-grade lieutenant and his sidearm at parade rest. "Gents." They saluted, then briskly opened the steel door for him. "Oh for shit's…Allan! *Allan*! Jesus H. Christ sailing a skiff in his dirty underwear, why the, uh, Seventh Cavalry?" he asked, thumb pointing, genuinely surprised. He then gripped the man's shoulders, genuinely happy.

In dress whites, a tired Captain Allan Simpson shook hands with a broad smile. "Hiya, Bern. Oh-h-h them? They're my close companions for *this* trip. Orders from King. Top shelf. They picked me to brief you because of our long friendship. Small world."

"What? You mean—"

"They sent us by C-98 Pan Am flying boat to Cabo Ruivo, Lisbon, with some Allied top brass. First class travel and booze, she's one helluva classy bird. Then we hopped a drafty Gooney, snuck past the Luftwaffe in Sicily with Hurricanes on our flanks, refueled and did a mail pick-up in Malta, hauled in some Limey brass, and got here only hours ago still airsick. How are you?" He opened a military travel thermos of coffee and poured two cups.

"Need the Navy grind. I can't stand the local axle grease."

"Sore knuckles but I'm okay. Been busy as hell relaxing. Damn, it's good to see a face from home." They sat as the airtight door was closed like a sarcophagus, the frigid, air-conditioned room hewn from thick rebar concrete. File cabinets and locked safes lined the walls. "Nice and cool in here."

Simpson pointed at two olive drab wooden crates stamped USMC. "Happy birthday, shithead. I personally hauled these two custom Springfields you requested straight from Quantico. Big, long eight-power scopes, pistol grips on the stock, pretty damn rare. Two beefy top sergeants just won marksmanship trophies with them at 1200 yards and got steamed as hell when I stole them. Christ, I was afraid for my *life*. Going elk hunting, Doughboy?"

Bernie hefted one, cycling the bolt. "Thanks for the rush delivery. 1939 production with cheek pads. Much more accurate at very long range than anything issued by the Brits or Germans in my opinion, heavier match-grade barrels, smooth triggers, blueprinted actions, tighter tolerances, better steel. They can keep their zero under very tough conditions." He aimed it at a crack in the wall. "Jesus, King and the

ONI sent you all the way out here in person? For what?

I'm truly honored of course, but a little embarrassed too. Am I...*that* important all of a sudden?" Simpson sat, physically exhausted; he rubbed his hair. "Hah-h-h-h, man. Not only King, but Rear Admiral Harry Train, the new ONI boss. I'm here to secretly brief you and Churchill in the flesh. This case stays chained to my wrist even when I sleep, and the boys will be in my rooms upstairs with me loaded for grizzly. The ambassador doesn't care much for us, too much artillery, secrecy."

"He seemed pretty steamed when I passed him. Wait, does Knox know you're here?" "Nope. He doesn't have clearance on much of this, very scant knowledge. Sometimes a chief petty officer can be fully read-in while the Secretary of the Navy isn't, that's just the way it is now. You'll need to get used to a whole new level of air-tight compartmentalization back home, security has gone *haywire*. Our little department has been hermetically sealed off by order of FDR. Small and chummy. Not everyone can handle this shit or needs to know, especially most of Congress. Your, uh, last report got some big notice upstairs."

He pulled the trigger. "Oh?"

"Which reminds me...there's a certain rear admiral I know back home you should meet some time. Name's Rico Botta, originally an Aussie; he was a reserve naval aviator, big balls, smart, and competent. He knows everything via me and what's more he gets it like *you* do, an intuitive type, empathic, an ancient history buff, and he didn't go through our lame American education system, if you...get my gist."

He ashed his butt with vigor. "Probably a good thing. My year and a half at Yale taught me that and more. Academia doesn't like independent thinkers like us. Bad student, worse attitude."

"No kidding. By the way...what really happened back then that made you quit? You were always tight-lipped, and never did tell me very much."

"It's boring."

"Bullshit. Come on, spill. This is *me* you're talkin' to." He sighed heavily. "You *really* want to know?"

"Yes. I rate it by now, don't you think?"

Bernie hesitated at the harsh memory. "Legacy or no, I hated that damn school, mindless conformity was a virtue, brain-washing standard fare. When I got tagged as a freshman for Skull & Bones at a dumb naïve seventeen—you know, fancy bloodlines and such—I soon began to smell a fascist rat, but I went along out of curiosity, you know me. Weird Thule Society rituals in the buff, satanic magic crap in spades, so I began to read up on the occult and German secret societies, a local Theosophist guy I knew via my Uncle Terry loaned me rare books on the sly.

Wasn't...*pretty* reading. After some verbal scuffles, I threatened to expose them in the school paper, then some of the hard-boiled Bone boys began to threaten me with death after I quit in my sophomore year, 'no one quits,' they said. Guess I'm the only one alive who did. Of course the paper wouldn't have printed my exposé anyway, but like I said I was really a naïve pup back then. One night later that fall, some hooded thugs beat me and my girlfriend with baseball bats into pulp in the pitch dark near the theater; gang raped her, the cowards, left us for dead out cold in a pool of blood. I barely made it, Allan. So I took Dad's advice and quickly joined the Marines for two years with a broken arm and collar bone, grew up a lot during the Boxer Rebellion as a shavetail, you remember all that. Anyhow, Amy...Amy died of internal injuries and complications around that time in the hospital, she had underlying heart issues already, I held her tight to the last second the day before I shipped out. No one was charged, it was all covered up by powerful Bonesmen parents; my own wealthy family could do *nothing*, we rank lower on the Illuminati totem, harsh internal politics...something like that. Learned a big fat life lesson on that one." He lowered his tone. "Anyway, the threats followed me. Dad said he knew big people in the Navy who could silently protect me, so it was off to the Academy to learn something useful with you, Tommy, Matt, and Derek when I came back from China. I guess...those kind and understanding admirals still watch over me."

Simpson softened his tone. "Shit, I didn't...Jesus...I'm so very sorry, Bern. Right, right, I met you at Plebe Summer before we were cadets, the Annapolis Malt Shop. Daily egg creams with rum. Now I remember. I'm sorry I pressed you, it's none of my—"

"Forget it, water under the keel." Bernie placed his Coke's bottle cap on the sharp edge of the metal desk and popped it open with a fist. "You were saying about Botta?"

"Yeah, Rico...Rico. Marshall told him to forget reading any and all history books back home, they're all full of bullshit, disinformation, and outright lies like you said, so Botta's on his own for research, but he'll get help from the Theosophical Society eggheads. That really sobered me up when I heard that. Anyway, we might put him in charge of a small group of our guys that'll infiltrate the Germans pretty soon, check up on their weird stuff. Keep his name...*quiet*."

"Can do. So, what did you bring me?"

Simpson got up, took a deep breath, and regained composure. "I brought *the* file. Is *that* important enough for you?"

Bernie sat, searching his empty ripped pockets. "Spare a butt? When you say *file*, I'm guessing it's not mine, but something a little more important?"

He shook him out a Chesterfield. "Is your eye black? What the *hell* happened to you? You smell like a water buffalo covered in sweaty vinegar."

"Ahh-h-h, just a drunken scrap last night at a hotel barn dance defending the honor of fine English ladies." He inhaled tobacco sharply. "You know the score, one's my old colleague from the Argentine deal; she's on my team if she doesn't quit, sue me, or crack up."

"You always were a dead hoofer on the dance floor. Use your psychology, charm, and grace on her. What's that old Egyptian wise man you keep squawking about? The bird-brained one with all the barroom wisdom?"

"The Egyptian Thoth, also known as *Hermes Mercurius Trismegistus*. Ibis head. An Atlantean ascended master that specialized in Hermetic Law. A health nut teetotaler for sure."

"Call him up for legal advice, but I'll leave all that weird ancient mystery school crap to you and Botta, I'm just a nuts and bolts guy, strictly steam engines and torpedoes. How's your social life?"

Bernie stretched, yawning. "You know me, I always surround myself and the truth with a bodyguard of lies and indecent women."

"Good. You know how it is, most of the Navy couldn't give half a shit, but a small set of them give way too much. They're worried you could be blackmailed, Baron von Steuben. And FDR himself has a queer list for leverage purposes, you know, to get certain brass thinking *his* way quick, so be advised. I shouldn't have told you that, but you rate it."

He fanned himself with the photo. "Won't happen. Besides, I bat left and right, and don't care a whit if I'm labeled a faggot or not. Put it in the world papers and I'll retire to Rio, happy and forever rum-drunk with both sexes on my arm feeding me papayas."

"I'll visit." Simpson opened his handcuffed briefcase. "Always remember that our little club has three factions, first the oddball mystics like you, then the Freemasons, then the really conservative guys that think Hitler and the SS boys are not *all* that bad, so take heed. White hats, grey hats, and black, just like the cowboys. Here's the Navy's airship file you requested, *Project KITE*. It's all we have on that program; keep it for your group's briefing, but then burn it afterwards with *your* eyes on the furnace. Got it?" He then pulled out a large pale blue folder with a coiled metallic seal and opened it. "Now to the big one. *File B*. Direct from FDR via Marshall via King, the newly-amended version. Apparently, King wasn't read-in a hundred percent at first, but FDR finally relented, all covert hands needed on deck. What I heard was…King cried at his desk like a baby, his faith cracked apart at the waterline. Then he got boiled on whiskey and smashed up his office *but* good. Almost quit the service. (Assistant Secretary of the Navy) Forrestal calmed him down in the hallway at the War Department, told him to shut the hell up and take it like a Navy man. I was there with him. Unlike Knox, Forrestal is fully read-in. Tough politics."

"That rough, eh?" *This is going from bad to worse…*

"That's why they sent me with the cutlass-wielding boarding party and the handcuffs, the file's one seriously hot potato, the hottest. See this overbuilt briefcase? Courtesy of our gadget boys in Newport News. It's got an explosive manganese thermite cartridge in the side. I push these three latches in sequence and—poof!—up she goes with me at 3000 degrees like a goddam welder's torch. How 'bout them sour apples?"

He blew a plume. "Yikes."

"It's a five-second delay, so maybe I have time to ditch it, maybe." He tightened his tone for emphasis. "Christ almighty, Bernie, don't screw this one up! They read me the riot act and *meant* it. I'm to see to it personally that you memorize File B right here, right now. Eyes only, mac. It goes back stateside with me tomorrow morning. *To-morrow*."

Sensing his old friend's rare onslaught of concern, Bernie opened File B. "Pretty quick turnaround. So this is really it? Heavy. Hmm, *Foo Fighters*, eh? Is that what Doolittle's calling them now? Good a name as any, I guess. Whoa-a-a-a Nelly, *Project TETRAHEDRON, Project ASTRA*, now that's new to me, this shit too. What the flying…Admiral Byrd and Antarctica, *Project ICEHOUSE*, a future naval base in the works. Yeah, that jibes with Hess's story on the *Neuschwabenland* expedition a little bit. Personally, I don't see much benefit for us in that godforsaken frozen place. Uh-oh…

things are heating up in the Pacific I see, all ahead flank. What's Halsey's take?"

Simpson straddled the corner of the desk. "He and Nimitz want to shoot the Foos down. They rattle the crews, bad for morale and the sailors think they're Jap secret weapons—but the president gave direct orders to the top admirals: no hostile action to be taken unless fired upon first. No exceptions. And Bern…"

"Yeah?"

He neared. "This file…is classified *above* the atomic *Manhattan Project*. Am I loud and clear, Mister Rodgers?"

Sobering fast, Bernie hesitated, taking it all in. "As a ship's bell." He then slowly turned a page as if it were ancient, crumbling papyrus. "*Battle of Los Angeles*? That shook up Hollywood. I heard there were multiple craft in the sky, and one even looked like a cigar. Fifty bucks says *none* of them can be shot down, not by conventional ordinance anyway. Jesus, says here it was all over the *L.A. Times* as a possible Jap balloon, but that was only bullshit PR, right?"

"That was the idea. We cleaned up the papers on the censorship allegations, national security trumps all in wartime. I think you're right that these so-called 'Interplanetary Craft' can't be disabled. Very few of these things show up on radar either, and when they do they fly off the scope at unimaginable speed. Zig-zag turns, full stops on a dime, straight up and out of sight like a 15-inch shell. Turn to page eighteen. One of them augered in at Cape Girardeau Missouri last year, a real mess, an FBI shit-show before the Army G2 boys got their mitts on it and took the debris to Wright Field for analysis; they can't make heads or tails of the wreckage, but that's all I know. Certain hangers are now designated *Special Access Projects* or SAPs. The compartmented personnel in one hanger can't talk about what they're doing to others and cannot even eat together in the mess hall. Forrestal saw the crash debris too, he told me it shook him up bad, real bad, the, uh, strange bodies and…chopped-up human body parts in gelatin or something."

"Oh-h-h, *God*…"

"King told me that fat piglet Hoover has a featherweight chunk of the hull on his desk as a souvenir; Hoover's partially read-in on this stuff, and probably has a secret photo of Himmler and Hitler kissing in his closet, so be advised that he's a shining example of the Nazi-lovers. But I need your personal opinion, Bern, do *you* think any of these aircraft are possibly German or Japanese in origin?"

Bernie took a deep breath, thinking deeply and hard. "No. No I don't. But the Germans are up to their usual mischief in any case. The metaphysical word is they're getting high-end technical assistance from someone, and I suspect the worst from their Vril Society head gal Maria Orsic. Remember her photo?"

He tipped up his cap. "Yeah, a real dish. A Nordic type. Long hair like Rita Hayworth." "Longer. Tesla told me a while back the Vril longhair 'channelers' are the link in the system, the hair having some sort of…of antenna-like quality, they get the real psychic dope from above, so to speak, as did he, but for a *price*. Just like the Seven Sisters of ancient Greece chewing laurel leaves and getting high so they could verbal access the universe. Hess told me the Germans call it *Projekt Majik*. Just run-of-the-mill access to ye old Universal Consciousness, and of course, other more unsavory types like mercenaries. Get it?"

Simpson fiddled with his hatband, a habit he had picked up from Bernie when they were young ensigns. "Mmm, sorta-kinda."

He took another deep breath. "As far as I know that's the way it's been done for countless millennia—mob middlemen with moxie in on the deal." Bernie looked him in the eyes. "It's just nuts and bolts psychic stuff, Allan, no great shakes, okay? We use 'em, but the Krauts use 'em *better*. Both sides of the fight supposedly get very quiet technical help from what I call 'outta town folks,' so to speak. Have you ever met Cap'm Hillenkoetter?"

"Roscoe? Just a handshake."

"He's attached to Nimitz's intelligence staff, we became drinking buddies during my stint in D.C. He and I met with Einstein at the Cosmos Club after a small closed meeting with Marshall and a few select senators. It was a *deusey*. You missed it because you were stomach sick, remember? The three of us snuck out and had a very private lunch afterwards at Martin's Tavern, birds of a feather. Hillenkoetter had quietly invited an Army Air Corps colonel, Hoyt Vandenberg, but I didn't know him. Apparently he's another wild bird. We were all—"

Simpson's eyes flared. "You did *what*? Alfred is never supposed to be alone without bodyguards! German spies and assassins are all over that town. Christ, you and your damn bullshitting—"

"Look, eccentric genius or not, the man wanted a fuckin' decent hamburger, his guards were at the bar and we used the kitchen entrance. They had the back room reserved, privacy. Only one way in, no windows. You know me better than that. Now look, though it's a wild hunch, the four of us think some of their crashed Foos are probably done on purpose, discreetly, like uh, like a *gift*, a telescope or compass given to some Pacific Islander by Captain Cook, a technology transfer. It's some sort of Cosmic Law loophole I don't understand, probably a circumvention of the *Law of Non-Intervention*, but it doesn't always work that way, and the spacemen outlaws—the black hats—don't play by the rules. Lots of competing agendas, lots of angles. You read the report on physicist Hermann Oberth, right?"

"Yeah. Bright guy. Maybe he likes hamburgers too."

Arms were folded tight. "The British have had a German-born spy in their midst since '36. We have Oberth on record bragging that he and the SS scientists are 'receiving technical assistance from extraterrestrials,' quote-unquote. I believe that in spades; the Germans are making filthy occult deals with many competing devils, the worst elements. The extremely conservative command culture in America and Britain has delayed high technology from blossoming in my humble opinion, and *that's* why the Germans are so far ahead, they think *big*."

Simpson swallowed hard, thinking of his own family. "You do know you're the only person in the Navy that scares me."

"Good. Remember your English history? It's a theory in my shady circles, but we believe that Court Magician John Dee made agreements with interdimensional black-hat gunmen to sink the Spanish Armada using Babylon Workings and Satanic *Magick*, and Queen Elizabeth the First began the mighty British Empire as a result. It's said she painted her face white in honor of those tall, white-skinned galactic gunmen-for-hire; she was part of the royal Anunnaki bloodline that's come down through history. All dumbass royals are, the world over. Understand?"

"Thank God we're Americans."

He pinched his nose bridge. "Damn this hangover. Can't think. Look…how do I put this? We're all part of the same universe, in the same rowboat, but the Nazis and their new pals want to kick the rest of us into the sea to drown, *The Law of One* be damned. Obviously, the SS boys in charge could give a fat dump about that."

Simpson opened his wallet to show him a family photo. "I'll leave that timber to you and my Aunt Penny to saw. Back in West Virginia she can psychically predict the weather and people's health problems with alarming accuracy. Says she can silently talk to the animals.

People think she's a witch because her personalities change a lot. Is that related?"

He smiled at the image. "Exactly my point. She might be of the Merovingian bloodline believe it or not, higher I.Q. Some have the gift, some can channel higher dimensional beings and receive vital information. Sometimes it's...it's on love, sometimes on how to heal a sick horse, how to build an aqueduct, a star fort, or sometimes how to build a German ballistic rocket with an atomic warhead. The choice is ours, free will. You... *do* like your powerful Buick fastback don't you? Its short-wave radio? The fancy new television you saw in the window at Macy's? Klystron-tube radar for our ships and planes?"

"Yeah, so?"

He pointed upwards. "'You're welcome,' they say. Tesla said to me that's how he invented all his highfalutin' stuff. His daydreams were full of, and I quote him, 'gifts received.'"

Simpson thought for a moment. "Son of a..."

"Just imagine what our guys will learn at Wright Field when they start to pick apart and really learn how those Foos fly here from another star system or galaxy using a psychic navigator. Anyway, as for the Krauts, gleaming new toys emerge every week. I've learned from a contact that the Vril and Thule guys are working hard day and night on strange new propulsion systems with Gerlach and his cohorts; the Ahnenerbe's all over the Middle East in short pants and knee-high boots looking for quality thorium in big batches, lots of tonnage. Tell Oppenheimer that."

"Tesla, Oppy, Trump, Van Bush, and the Rad Lab boys at MIT are with you on all that Cosmic Law Foo stuff, but I was ordered to ask for one more qualified opinion." Simpson removed another file. "Oh, and good news, Commander, you've been promoted to Captain, finally, even though I vehemently protested it. I brought you a new khaki uniform and whites, courtesy of our Washington tailor since I remember you lost your luggage in that London bombing recently, or is that just a tall sea yarn? No way in hell they were going to trust a lowly commander with this stuff, clearance or no clearance. Regarding File B, they call it 'Majestic' clearance now. Highest one."

Bernie lit another. "Typical."

"Oh, yes...back home we have some stiff competition, the OSS, *Office of Strategic Services*, Wild Bill Donovan's new outfit. FDR said we needed another intel branch to deal with the Foos, Nazi high command, and the Thule SS, a diverse one that's close to the State Department, and it has a mess of boring intellectual swells that put *you* to shame."

"I heard."

"Redway's filthy rich candy-ass cousins and Rolling Rock Country Club chums are *flocking* to it, but Donovan has strict egghead requirements. Pointy-hat mystics like Carl Jung, Ralph Bunche, and that Wall Street asshole Allen Dulles are in it, so's Moe Berg the ball player."

"Jung? Really? The Mellon connection, eh? Then we do have competition, he'll have some deep things to share if he gets his specs on this file. You said Moe Berg? The Red Sox catcher?"

"That's him, good arm. Oh, and Mellon-head Redway said to say hello by virtue of a 'fuck-you.' He'll be here with the *Torch Invasion* gang in November if all goes well in that department. He's an ONI to OSS liaison officer now and isn't real happy about it."

Bernie tapped the file with an exaggerated up-and-down finger. "Good. Tell him the Germans have been quietly shipping in some new heavy tanks at Tunis, experimental Porsche Tigers armed with 88 flak guns. Might be a problem for the Army when they land in Morocco and Algeria."

"I'll tell that to Marshall direct. Personally, I fear the Foos more than tanks."

"You have a point." Bernie softened his tone. "How's Cynthia?"

"Wife and kids are fine. Send their best." He pulled out a manila with a child's drawing of a camel, a llama, a pyramid, and some palm trees in it. "This is the *really* important one. From Cynthia, she always loved you the most."

It brought a smile to him. "Thanks. Llamas are…South American not African, yes? Funny, she's always—"

Simpson pulled out another manila. "Here's a jazzy photo from an army transport in China that's been supplying Chenault's Flying Tigers. You and the ivory tower shitwigs back home were right about the big pyramids, this shows three of 'em. The same pilot flew over Mongolia and said he saw one *four times as big* as the ones over yonder here, but it's hidden in the mountains. His compass went haywire near them, no radio signals in or out either."

Bernie picked up a magnifying glass. "I knew it was true, and now we have evidence."

Simpson poked him. "You and your damned star forts. Where the hell do you meet all these elder hep cats anyway?"

"Low-life Tiki bars and noodle shops that lie in the shadows of gold-domed temples. Regarding the Nips, I hear they have a good general to grab and stash all their gold spoils in Malaya. Or...is that just an Australian intelligence tall tale that's been exaggerated by our pal Red?"

"How did you...?" Irritated, Simpson took a deep breath and paced. "*Urrggnnshh*. General Tomoyuki Yamashita, yeah, that's the guy, smart and snake-mean. Conqueror of Singapore, occult Black Dragon member. Redway said the pile's growing, an estimated one-half of the world's reserve if not more, so you can do the economic math on that one, kiddo. They're finding a lot of it in Burma and Thailand along those ruler-straight ancient canals, the old Khmer Empire ruins and deep tunnels that you told Red about. Well, the Japs have been all over it since the twenties. We're doing our best trying to find the smaller caches island by island as we go along in the South Seas. Tough slog, the worst. We're...*losing*...a lot of our young boys, Bern, a lot. It's a meat grinder. My nephew, he...the Marines..."

Bernie's heart skipped a few beats before it sank. "I know...God I *know*." He composed himself over the course of a minute and waved the China photo. "Is this one to go public?"

"Not till the war's won." Simpson stretched. "Keep reading. Inhale the file. Memorize every sentence, comma, number, detail, and photo. And for shit's sake don't share any of this with our esteemed allies here. As I said, your eyes only. Even Churchill only knows part of it, I briefed him at seven this morning in here, alone, but only on a select few pages that the president laid out with his initials. Anyhow, this prized lump might help you with your proposed assignment; it was in your last report that you said it's all connected somehow, the big picture. Oh, here's some mail and a *Washington Post* for you too."

He unloaded several envelopes. "Don't underestimate Winnie, Allan, he puts me to shame on some stuff. Ah yes, from my younger brothers Andrew and Nick, and one from my sister Binney. Thanks." He waved a clipped *Los Angeles Examiner* news article. "*Air Battle Rages over Los Angeles*...nice headline."

Bernie scanned the attached classified memo. "Wait, wait, wait, the Navy shot 200,000 rounds or so at the one over LA with *no* effect? The Army a hundred fifty thousand?"

"Aye-aye, sir, and for five hours straight. The big searchlights we had on it could be seen for fifty miles; over a million civilians witnessed it. Should've been a turkey-shoot, but it wasn't. Shells passed right through or bounced off it while the thing molted scout craft or something out its bottom like a pregnant salmon up river. The newsreel boys shot tons of footage and CBS Radio covered all of it live. Keep up steam while I hit the head down the hall."

Bernie remembered what Einstein had told him. "An electromagnetic time-space plasma bubble, that would probably defend them handily against…" He then looked up. "Hey, you're lucky there's a toilet, usually it's just a big hole and you squat."

"Great." He opened the door and a guard came in to watch over Bernie. "Lieutenant Hecker, so help me God, if anyone tries to come in here, or he so much as puts a foot outside with the file, *plug* 'em."

"Yes, sir."

Not looking up from the file, Bernie laughed. "That's not even the least bit funny, Allan." Simpson stood in the doorway and said seriously: "It's not *meant* to be, old friend. Orders."

•••

After two hours, six cups, and twelve cigarettes, Bernie carefully closed the file. "Shit-t-t- t-t…another fine Navy day, but now I have more questions than answers."

"No kidding."

"I have to ask again. Don't know if this is related, but Hess mentioned something about *Neuschwabenland* in Antarctica, a dumbass German U-Boat base project under the ice. Have you heard anything about that crazy idea?"

"Not a word." Simpson locked the file away securely in his briefcase and cuffed it to his wrist. "Look pal, I don't need to remind you the war's not particularly going our way, but this one's going to be the *big* one. Don't fuck it up whatever you do. If the Krauts find a way to drop an A-bomb on the Russians or the Allies first, we're shit-canned. All of us scuppered into the bilge. *Done*. Allied morale will collapse *en masse*. They'll crank them out by the dozens once they get it right, and Oppy says they'll weigh eight tons or more with lead shielding and no German aircraft can carry that weight…yet. Look at me, do you and I understand one another?

"King and Train told me to squeeze you by the balls and bite your tongue on this. And all us land-locked swabbies back home jerking off behind desks are counting on you and your team to do the job. No one else qualified in this parched sandbox would know what the hell they were looking at or what the deeper significance of it would be, just McMaster, you, and that…*nutty* gal of yours. Time is of the essence. Whatever it is they have going on out there, somewhere, *anywhere*, you need to stop it in its tracks. Find it. Secure it. Bring us back *superlative* intel, and if need be—"

"Destroy it all."

He paused. "Steal something too, anything of value. Make sure you have young, strong, and capable *male* team members too, you're not a young squirt anymore in the Rockies carrying a hundred-pound rucksack on snowshoes towing a sled full of beer. And listen, swigger, skip the bilge juice from now on until the mission's done. That's an order, sailor. I still have seniority."

Bernie stretched. "Don't worry so much, granny. I may be thin, but I can still hack it. I climbed the big pyramid the other day for exercise with a fifty-pounder, twice. It was a bitch, but I did it."

"Keep it up. Look, Churchill and McMaster are the only Limey brass you or I can trust here, and that comes from our pal Bill direct, so I'll say it again—be *damn* careful."

Bernie nodded. He respected the English spymaster William Stephenson, a close friend of Redway's. Stephenson in turn respected the Americans greatly, unlike others in his sphere back in London who still considered them lesser "Colonials."

Simpson leaned back in McMaster's occidental armchair. "Now, where can two old sailors get a decent beefsteak, French beans, fried potatoes, and a cold glass of creamy milk around these dusty parts?"

Blood sugar low, Bernie looked at his watch. "I know just the place. You'll love the belly dancing woman and her python."

13

August 11

The wall clock chimed seven a.m.

"Time flies when it doesn't really exist," said Bea.

Shutting a British history book on India, Bernie chuckled. "Funny."

Alice bit a cracked nail. "She's been strangely metaphysical of late. So boring."

"I've always wondered…why was it that you lousy Limeys always wore red uniforms back in the day?" asked Bernie.

"English Civil War," said McMaster.

Alice added: "Venetian red wool fabric was cheapest for a government contract. Typical."

"So you rapscallion Colonial Rebel turncoats could rudely call us 'lobsterbacks,' of course," snapped Bea.

He shut the book. "Made for easy targets. I find it interesting that British MI6 used to be called *Marine Intelligence 666* during the age of high-seas piracy, which greatly alarmed the devil-fearing Spanish. Then the British East India Company used opium and slave sales to expand your infamous empire."

McMaster cleared his throat. "Yes, well we—"

Bea laid both hands on the desk. "Look, Brigadier, he's the best soldier I've ever seen. Courageous, mechanical-minded, a good shot, and deadly with a knife. He can fly a bit, and understands an aircraft's engineering. A motorcar thief too. Read lots of old unsullied books in the mosques and libraries of Timbuktu, and speaks Berber. Smart as a whip, street clever too, and with an appetite to learn more and more. Steady. Strong as an ox." *Best leave out the jail bit.*

"I like him already," said Bernie, feet up, not bothering to remove his eyes from a classified textbook on archeoastronomy, a difficult discipline.

"Is he handsome?" asked Alice. Bea eyed her. "Shut it."

McMaster picked up the phone. "Well, we're short on trained personnel, and all of the SOE chaps are busy in Europe or Burma. Hello? Tillings? Get hold of French General Sylvie over at their headquarters." He waited a minute. "Hello? *Bonjour?* Yes I...who?"

Alice mumbled: "SOE? Ministry of Ungentlemanly Warfare chaps. I had a little training a while back with them y'know. Basic stuff. A rough go."

"'Inter-Service Research Board' members in good standing," sniffed Bea. Bernie added: "In America they're called 'Winnie's Secret Army.'"

"Or in our case, the Bureau of Unladylike Sand-Sappers," said Alice.

•••

An hour later, he arrived under guard, stiffly saluting McMaster; kepi was removed. "*Monsiuer le Brigadier*, Sergeant-Chéf Gwafa Jean-Pierre Modibo Mahamadou, reporting as ordered."

Bea got up and kissed him on both cheeks. "I'm officially a civilian now, so good to see you. Now I know why you wanted me to call you just plain ol' Gwafa."

He smiled. "And you, *madame, une honneur.*"

McMaster shook hands. "Your Colonel Rouyre speaks highly of you. Sorry about the, uh, 'Panzer fuss,' as it were, but we know it's the truth now. All over town."

"*Merci beaucoup*, sir. No one believed it. Why would they? A woman, a black, and a Maori."

McMaster looked through Gwafa's file. "All good. How much schooling have you had?"

Gwafa looked embarrassed. "Sir, I ran away when I was fourteen. All of Africa and everything in it has been my school, but she has taught me much. I read many books on Moorish Science, speak many dialects. I feel with my heart, see with my soul, hear with my mind."

McMaster smiled and put his hand on his shoulder. "Good. Any...mystery school learning?"

Gwafa looked puzzled for a moment. "By that, sir, do you mean...the Qu'ran, prophets, and the teachings of wise men? This perhaps I can say I know well. Sami's poetry, prophets Muhammad, Hud, and Salih, astrologer Ahmad ibn al-Buni, architecture and geometry, sundials, astrolabes. *Les cartes anciennes*, the maps of Al-Masudi and Admiral Piri Reis. Very little forbidden astrology, but I peeked at it long ago. I am Aries. Stubborn horns."

Alice was all eyes. "Love the accent. Africans always have the best—" "Pssh!" snapped Bea.

The Brigadier sat. "That'll do. These three will fill you in on occult particulars as you go along. Unbelievable at best, disheartening at worst. Espionage and the occult have always gone hand in hand throughout history. Our Royal Navy Remote Viewers are currently tracking the Atlantic U-Boats psychically. Good results."

His lifelong suspicions confirmed, Gwafa said: "U-Boats? Can this be true? So the seers and mystics are correct?"

Bea and Alice clapped. "Welcome to dreamland, Lionheart," said Bea. "Almost all books on Earth are filled with disinformation, outright lies, and confusing counterintelligence. Get used to it is my advice."

"What they mean is…most of what we're taught in western schools and universities is horseshit, Sergeant," said Bernie. "But you studied in the Islamic tradition mostly. Now you don't have to *re-learn* quite as much. The basics are okay."

He fondled his kepi. "I only had…"

McMaster sat. "Now, to business. We're offering you an important assignment. It's voluntary of course, but you need to sign my order and the Official Secrets Act before we brief you on any details. According to Bea here, you're well qualified for the job."

Gwafa replied: "Sir. There is talk that I may be promoted to lieutenant said *Général de Brigade* Sylvie, one of only two black Africans in the Free French *Armée* given such an appointment. Perhaps this will…postpone…" He looked to Bea with a face of fondness and respect, and she returned it. "*Merde*…I enlist! Anything to have more fun with *madame*. I would probably make a bad officer anyway."

Bea said: "*Ahem*. Lethal force can and will be implemented if you mention any itty-bitty fun details…"

Gwafa looked to McMaster, nodded, and quickly signed the paper. "Cairo is boring, sir. Mundane duties. I am a wandering soul in search of excitement and knowledge. Thirsty."

Bernie shook his hand. "Welcome aboard, you'll regret it." He then felt Gwafa's strong arm. "Shit. Another Joe Louis, I think. Call me Bernie, first names only. This one's name is Alice."

"As in Wonderland." Alice kissed him on both cheeks, then discreetly licked his ear quickly. "Charmed *monsieur. Puis-je avoir le plaisir de*—"

Gwafa reeled back a bit.

Bea pulled her away. "You're an *officer*. No dalliances with the enlisted personnel."

"Rats."

McMaster pointed to the large map of the Middle East behind him. "Right. Seats everyone. *Operation Frisland*, like the mythical island off Iceland. Action on this is imperative. Here's Cairo, here's Basra. You'll all be transported there by air in four days' time if all goes well. Gwafa, are you familiar with this region?"

"No, sir, but I speak Arabic. An expert on the Sahara, and I am well-trained in overland navigation. *Les étoiles*, the stars. Maps are no stranger to me, but I have never been that far to the east. Many dangers, many legends."

"Bloody Basra? What the hell's in *Basra?*" asked Bea. "Except for more sand, sun, and camels. Miss ol' Udad, eh, Gwafa?"

"He was a brave one, *madame*."

McMaster tapped a folder. "I'll let Bernie explain. This is *his* mission. His proposal. Took a devil of a time to get it approved."

Bernie told in detail his story about his Hess meeting and what subjects they had talked about. "So he said they were bragging about an airship expedition to the Zagros range. There's something or some place that Alexander the Great was searching for on his way to Persia. Something fearful and amazing, important—and important enough for the SS to get lathered up about."

Gwafa said: "I have heard of this man, the German *Hess*, but I never knew he went to England to sue for peace. Étrange."

Bea shut a book hard. "I worry about Schäfer in this, he's a mystic extraordinaire all right; his band of Ahnenerbe merry men and all." Bea quickly explained her Austrian Shieldmaiden SS School Nine experience to Gwafa. "…and just call me *Oberleutnant* SS Uta von Manstein, if you please."

His eyes bulged a little. "I would rather *not, madame*."

McMaster paced. "It's entirely possible SS scientists are involved, but we have no information on our end. You, Bernie?"

"Just Schäfer, but who knows? Now, on to the airship history if I may…" "Gas airships? As in the *Graf Zeppelin?*" asked Alice.

Bea added: "Have to say, sounds a bit dotty."

Bernie stood, stretching his legs. "No, not Zepps. A wholly different kind of airship. An antigravity airship, and a really fast one at that."

Bea perked like a spanked spaniel. "*What*? You mean antigravity propulsion like *Anton* had? Oh-h-h, no. Not that squirrelly shite again...it nearly killed Lutz and me."

Bernie nodded. "Yup. Ancient Vimana technology from India, but a very different application. Unfortunately for us, Dr. Häkkinen is in German hands in Norway. Heavy water production."

Bea looked sad. "Poor old bloke, I knew him in Norway, Gwafa, an excellent physicist." Bernie took chalk to the board. "Alice, Gwafa, a primer on German antigravity. Three German physicists named...Walter Gerlach, Viktor Schauberger, and Winfried Otto Shumann—and maybe a few others like electrical plasma expert Kurt Debus and rocket designer Walter Dornberger—were given decoded engineering schematics from the ancient Vedic Texts of India by way of the SS Ahnenerbe and the Vril Society. Tibetan texts as well, thanks to Schäfer and his crew. Back in ancient times before the Great Flood, worldwide high civilizations flourished with Vimana-type airships, submarines, sailing vessels, crystal power using different light spectrums, and some sort of land trains using sound vibration and Ley Line energy to propel them. Big dual tracks are found all over the Med in stone, especially in Malta and Corsica, where they meander into the ocean since sea levels were four hundred feet lower before the big flood.

"The legend of Atlantis is no mere legend, this was a seafaring empire of diverse peoples, the pyramids and big megalithic buildings worldwide are the evidence in plain sight of Atlantis' might and scope. You see—"

Bea snapped: "I'll explain the gist to him." She then explained the Freemasons, Ahnenerbe, Vril, and Thule Societies in plain terms. "Everything in the cosmos vibrates at a certain frequency—harness that hocus-pocus science and you can make anything work. Vril is the 'Pranic' life force of the cosmos and it flows through all of us, everything. Mystery schools and secret societies hoard all the forbidden ancient knowledge, wisdom, and history, like selfish rogues. Vatican, too. Huge secret archives underground, big bank above. Bastards, all."

"The mystery schools may have a point. Rudolf Steiner said that mankind may not be ready yet," said Bernie with a sigh. "But I agree with you, Bea, the hell with the Vatican."

Gwafa suddenly looked pale grey. "*Zut alors*! This is very complicated, but I do remember the legend of Atlantis, *monsieur*. The Egyptians tell about it on the walls of the Horus Temple, a wise man once told me. As a boy, my father and I toured Sudan and Khartoum and areas all over when we traded goods as far as Mecca. Many of us in Mali believe legends are just handed down history told by storytellers, *true* history."

"Exactly," said Bea. "Look, simple-dimple. April of '40. My friend Lutz and I pinched a Heinkel fighter from Stuttgart. Experimental. A Porsche 16-cylinder engine mid-mounted, bucketloads of horsepower. Fast as hell. Flew to Norway and crash-landed. When we patched it back together, we contacted a local physicist my friend Olaf knew, Häkkinen, and he jiggered with the engine's ancillaries. There was a black drum, a special motor, electrically-driven. It had two counterrotating drums inside filled with a special liquid mercury that turns into an electrified gas—a 'plasma' they call it. Free energy, tons of it, no parasitic loss. Cables from it electrified the special alloy airframe and wings, hence the term 'antigravitics.' We spun the doojigger up in flight, produced an electromagnetic field shaped like an invisible tire's innertube, and it reduced our weight by eighty-five percent. After that we shot straight up like a rocket at over 530 mph with very little G-forces. Simple antigravity, just like King Solomon's flying carpets."

At this, Gwafa smiled. "I think I may understand. *Magnifique*. Who knew such great and wonderful things existed all along?"

Alice bit a nail. "Apparently the Indians and *Germans* did. Just no sharing."

McMaster added: "In any case, I have an occult report for you to read later, Sergeant. My boiled-down version of the *Gift of the Lamp*. Grim but…enlightening."

Bea crossed her arms and rolled her eyes. "He's going to just *love* that one, my cherished Illuminati enthusiasts. British Raj and natural selection by colonial Maxim Gun."

McMaster scolded: "*Beatrice…*"

Bernie said: "Okay, great. Look, we have a lot to cover today. Can I have the floor back please? Now, back to the airship deal that—"

"One tick. I have a question," said Alice. "Though I'm familiar with your odd 'Lamp Gift Report,' I must ask again for my and Gwafa's benefit…why do the minute few at the top keep all the secrets and history of the world held so tightly to their vests? Wouldn't exposure of all this fanciful rigmarole benefit humanity as a whole in peacetime? Wouldn't wars and poverty and-and *inequality* be a thing of the past? Or is it that they…*want* it that way? The status quo, I mean. Perhaps I'm being naïve as usual, but except for Gwafa, we've all come from privilege, from fancy universities, rubbishing Illuminati bloodline families I suppose, why weren't we four toffs taught the genuine historical article? Or at least some *soupçon* portion of it?"

McMaster sat on the corner of his desk, playing chess with a pencil cup and inkwell. He took a tone of despondence. "Because in their eyes you don't *rate* it, none of us do, or we'd be in the secret club, blackmailed and threatened. As I've learned over the decades, since deep antiquity the minute and powerful few in the shadows, and that includes the Nazis now, look down upon everyone else with extreme distaste. They were and remain trustee slaves, overlords for their mysterious patrons the Anunnaki. Occult philosophers and Theosophists such as Plato, Socrates, Saadia Gaon, Blavatsky, Gurdjieff, Besant, and the great polymath Avicenna who famously said—"

Bernie interrupted with: "'The world is divided into men who have wit and no religion, and men with religion and no wit.'"

"That about...sums it," said McMaster glumly. "Philosophers and a few historians like Isaac Newton tried to warn us in their writings, but few have listened; their more extreme views suppressed. Sometimes even benign kings, queens, presidents, and heads of state are treated shabbily and childishly, it makes no difference even with them. Secrecy, immense wealth beyond imagination, access to hidden technology, mind-altering religious skullduggery, and raw unfettered power over life and death and the course of history are the ultimate aphrodisiacs, the *ultimate* euphoric intoxicants for those of a fascist bent. These...so-called 'illumined' secret elite feel as demigods, the superior caste among us all. Most are dark-minded men, ones you've never heard of and never will, chosen in secret usually at universities, or born into Anunnaki royal bloodlines or sub-bloodlines that provide a stock to choose from, and very few are chosen. Dark occult rituals, symbology, pedophilia, torture, blackmail, murder, extorsion, and their own hidden caste system identify them well, but rival factions abound—a potential weakness to my mind. Secret societies and roundtables, occultish clubs, the Order of the Garter, Knights of Malta, Order of Orange-Nassau. We've all known them—the bullies, the ill-tempered sociopaths bereft of any sense of humor, the deceptive two-faced Januses, the chronic liars. They're like drug-addicted little children, and they play their infantile games with aplomb using all of us as ignorant, compliant pawns in a never-ending chess game. Nationality, class, race, or religion plays little part I'm told, it's only the light versus the dark, the positive versus the negative, but it's my belief that the Allies are on the side of the light, even if only scantly so. Unfortunately for the rest of humanity, privileged or not, we must play their games and abide by their unfair laws simply to survive. As for us positive, so-called 'awakened and illumined few,' just as our ancestors and philosophers did, we must play those games rather delicately with open eyes, understanding, forgiveness, and loving hearts, just...*not* by their rules."

After long moments of polite silence for Gwafa to take it in, he said: "Many empires have come and gone in the Sahara, many kings such as Musa Keita and elite wise men with much gold and magical powers. The rule of might over the many. Some say he was the richest king ever to have lived. To me, from Arabic teachings, magic is nothing but undiscovered science. I remember an old French saying, *'science sans conscience n'est que ruine de l'âme.'* It means: 'Science without conscience is nothing but the ruin of the soul.'"

Bea put her hand on his shoulder and smiled.

"Quite." McMaster looked to the clock. "Tea and a loo break for a few minutes."

•••

Bernie laid out the U.S. Navy airship file and shared pages. "Let's start at the beginning. It wasn't just the Germans and Indians, but the Prussians as well. Old feudal Prussia was the main military state in early nineteenth-century Europe, the best, and they spawned good alchemical engineers, mystics, and philosopher-scientists via their disciplined high-quality universities. This was an era just before 'scientific materialism' officially replaced philosophy and the occult sciences, the bitter fruits of which we are eating today. The Prussian royal class had huge reserves of money, the militarists had ambitions of a unified Germany and European conquest, and the boffins had the esoteric knowledge and the burning desire for more, so it was a marriage made in heaven or hell, depending on one's perspective. Long story short, they must've figured out basic electromagnetic antigravity before anyone else did in the modern era, and hid their programs well. The technology may have been lost for twelve millennia. Remember Mary Shelly's *Frankenstein*?"

Gwafa said: "I read the French version when I was in jail. No sleep for days."

"What about her?" asked Bea.

Bernie had that mischievous look in his eye when he got excited. "She was on to something. She'd heard the wild, spiritualist salon rumors about southern Prussia and Silesia, the return to ancient Germanic pagan ways and occult knowledge; most of the literary salon aristocracy of Europe had, but it wasn't about resurrecting the dead with huge amounts of electrical charges with Van de Graaf generators, it was about good old-fashioned antigravity propulsion and exotic chemical production via alchemy. It wasn't so much a return to old Germanic ways as such, but a return to innovating science in the vein of the Renaissance, forbidden Prediluvian-style technology that required—get this—the spiritual consciousness of the alchemical inventor as a mandatory step in the procedure, the so-called *Philosopher's Stone*. Castles like Schloss Fürstenstein lit up the night in rural areas, scaring the shit out of the local peasantry with secret experiments and weird phenomena—who knows what else they were up to? Mineral and metallurgical wealth in that region is awesome; coal mine tunnels stretch for dozens of miles. Add it up."

"Fürstenstein Castle is now a Nazi high-command post near Breslau," said McMaster. "A fallback position or forward base for Hitler depending on future circumstances, a possible gold depository too. Tunnels to something called the *Riese Complex* are under construction, say our Polish operatives. We think they've developed some sort of tunnel boring machine on a rail line. I have reports that state many kilometers have been already dug. Speer hired a genius officer to oversee the whole project as head contractor, don't know the name, branch, or rank."

Bernie looked to McMaster. "Hess confirmed some of that too. Something about a *Project Chronos, Project Cinnabar*."

The brigadier shook his head. "Never heard of them."

"I rather liked *Bride of Frankenstein*. They showed it just the other week on the side of a building near the souk," said Alice.

Bea said: "The overwrought hairdo suits your Prussian pallor." "As do neck bolts for you, von Franken-Manstein," snarled Alice.

"Piss off on your bike down to the Valley of the Kings, open a sarcophagus, have yourself a French kiss."

"Bloody Watusi cow, I'll give y—"

"Easy, ladies, decorum. Cut the cackle, please." Bernie went on. "There were dozens of American eyewitness newspaper reports of colorful airships around Texas and Sonora, California in the 1850's. The U.S. Navy thinks the Prussians went to California because they had access to lots of Ley Line energy in that sparsely populated region, and also had access to German immigrant ranches with oversized barns that allowed them to tinker in absolute privacy. One eyewitness, a lone miner, saw them flying in the Grand Canyon. We suspect that monatomic gold powder was produced there somehow alchemically. The area was part of the 1849 Gold Rush, so it seems logical, and the airship men needed lots of it. A German engineer by the name of Peter Mennis and an engineering draftsman named Charles A.A. Dellschau were in charge; it was publicly known as the *Sonora Aero Club*, but there were other groups elsewhere we think.

"An unknown Prussian military officer was pressuring this group of aerial misfits into producing military versions, but no one in the club was interested by the time the ships took flight. The secret Prussian group, including the financial backers, was called NYMZA, an acronym. The ONI and myself think it stands for 'Nationalist Prussian Aerial Exploration Club,' or something akin to that. Someone murdered Mennis and all the airships disappeared, but that's all we know. As for how they were built and flew, all we have to go on are odd color drawings that Dellschau left to a mysterious widow. She died in strange circumstances, an unsolved case, and the book of notes and drawings somehow ended up at an antique junk shop in Galveston, Texas, an interesting strip of land that's favored by the wealthy for vacations. Who knows? Maybe the drawings were left there by Dellshau on his way to Mexico or elsewhere by airship, a parting gift to someone, a lover perhaps."

"Prussians all the way in California?" asked Bea. "Dellschau? Poppy mentioned that odd bloke once with Uncle Winn—I mean *Prime Minister*." She looked over a couple of the hand-colored illustrations. "The man's insane, but a decent artist. These craft make no aeronautic or aerodynamic engineering sense to me whatsoever. Big chains, hoists, odd wheels, discs, wild stripes, whirling spheres, Chinese hand fan wings, a mess."

Gwafa looked at them with Alice. "Bizarre," mused Gwafa. "This airship was big enough to have a chef and kitchen. *Incroyable*."

Alice added: "Long flights, one supposes. Good weather for airshipping in California too.

This one...this airship thingy looks like something from a 19th-century circus or carnival, or something gaudy one would see at an international world's fair or exhibition."

"Good points, since perhaps they were intending to show them off to the world in style at the *Universal Exhibition* in France in 1861, but they didn't, and no one knows *why*," said Bernie, revealing another etching. "This gets better. In 1863 during the American Civil War, an inventor by the name of Solomon Andrews showed President Lincoln and some top Union Army brass a three-tube airship that maneuvered surprisingly well and could attain 125 mph, and did it without airscrews or any visible means of propulsion. Gee whiz, now isn't that just a bit odd? Now where might he get such an idea? I think he was part of the Sonora Club. After the demonstration, Secretary of War Stimson told Andrews that the War Department wasn't interested in it at all.

"*Bullshit.* That project went underground in secret. A Secret Service man by the name of Ambrose Bierce, a former Union Army surveyor and balloon reconnaissance officer, was put in charge of the program and decided to take it out west for privacy on Lincoln's orders. He followed the Union Pacific Railroad and their telegraph lines that were built by U.S. Government geomancers upon telluric energy pathways, otherwise known as...*Ley Lines.* Ta-da!"

"Well I'll be a Confederate spy belle of the ball..." said Bea.

Alice added: "Nice job that, Bernie."

"The telegraph can't work without telluric electricity, but few know that. Though official paperwork is scant, we think that somewhere in Utah in the Wasatch Mountains, probably in a cave or large cavern with its own private railway line, is where they set up shop for research and development, probably built a small town. Railroad and telegraph banks like Wells Fargo and Bank of New York, even a few rich industrialists with European Rothschild money, were involved funding-wise to keep it off the books in a cash-strapped, post-war U.S. Congress.

Redway told me that Chemical Bank was involved for exotic chemicals, and his family's newly-formed Mellon Bank was tapped for steel and coal supplies in Pennsylvania. For all concerned, it was a private, multi-corporate operation conducted in the shadows, free from all congressional oversight or budget restraints. A robber baron's dream."

"This smacks of Jules Verne's writings," said Bea suspiciously. "Captain Nemo, *Robur the Conqueror, Around the Moon.* Stuff I used to read at school. Old Isambard Brunel would've been interested in all this, bit of a chancer like you."

Bernie pointed at her. "Bingo. It's believed that Nikola Tesla, Jules Verne, H.G. Wells, John Keely, Edison, and Gustav Eiffel were all in a small private secret society together, *Plus Ultra Six.* They knew about our true history: Atlantis, Lemuria, Khmer, Mu, the airships, and the esoteric truth of the world and universe—they wanted to build a new world, a peaceful one built on free atmospheric energy and antigravity, just like the one the ancients had."

Bea said: "I thought that was just a Wycombe Abbey tall tale by Prof Aelfric." Bernie crossed his arms in smarty-pants style. "Nope, it was real. Anyway, you win a

Kachina doll—Hopi, of course." "Of course."

"Verne's *Master of the World*, too," said Alice worriedly. "But I think we get the literary message."

"Hopi?" asked Gwafa.

"American Indians. Roy Rogers. Glen Ford. The Wild West films at the cinema," said Bea. "Spiritual in the extreme, wise."

"*Oui*." Gwafa nodded. "I like the hats and feather war bonnets. *Belle couture*."

"Many cowboys and cowgirls were black too," said Alice, a fan of Race Westerns, her eyes full of Gwafa.

McMaster said: "The annihilation of distance was not solely a British goal in the last century. The Germans were at it hammer and tong. Speed was everything."

"Ley Lines? What are those?" asked Gwafa.

"Wait, I'll take a crack at it." Bea went to the bookshelf, then carefully opened a copy of the Catalan Atlas from 1315. "These accurate *portolan* maps were highly prized as state secrets by the Venetians and Spaniards, and were most likely cobbled together from much older sources. The Phoenicians were successfully navigating the Atlantic for thousands of years. See the nodal points and lines on this Catalan navigation map? They never made much sense as the Wind Rose Network for prevailing winds, and many a sailor or navigator was frustrated by the Rose lines.

But are they Ley Lines? We think so, yes, it makes more sense. The Earth is covered in a sort of...sort of *grid* of them along tectonic plates; some gather like spokes on a bicycle wheel at nodal points like big-boy Giza over there. Tributaries flow off as if from mighty rivers, and the big ones connect major ancient sites—henges, pyramids, canals, megalithic buildings, temples, towers, cities, and star forts. We think Freemason-designed star forts may have stored telluric electromagnetic power, or what's also called 'Earth Energy,' for defensive purposes. It's all about frequency, whether it's a flower, formal garden, earthwork, or complex star fort that contains and perhaps amplifies all that heady stuff. Heal the Earth and you'll heal yourself, etcetera, blah-blah. As an example of drastically old technology, consider that Dowsing Rods detect underground running water's electromagnetic signature, it's an old Atlantean technology, simple and effective. There are said to be bizarre gadgets that do the same for Ley Lines. Or so I've read in the book *The Old Straight Track*."

"Ah yes, those rods I have seen," said Gwafa. "For the discovering of wells."

Alice added: "Crystal limestone and granite are *piezoelectric*, like in a crystal wireless set. Acoustic engineering at its finest, frequencies for all uses under the sun. Running water is electromagnetic too, that's why a shower at a waterfall is so luscious. All these forts and star cities are unique and quite beautiful, especially the ones in Italy like Palmanova. 'Voluptuous masonry,' said Cicero. Most of Amsterdam is inside one. I'd like a miniature one in my garden someday."

"A garden gone to weed, no doubt. Mirrors thy iffy intellect," said Bea. Alice asked of McMaster: "Can she and I be separated for lectures?"

"Let's keep on, shall we?" asked McMaster.

Bernie looked through his worn leather diary that Simpson had brought him. "You're getting the gist, Gwafa, unlike the giddy Andrews Sisters here. Now…when I was a teenager with Dad outside Denver in 1897, we saw a 120-foot long airship land one night near Fort Collins where Dad had some business dealings, and I know for a fact Fort Collins and Fort Morgan are built on Ley Lines and had telegraphs—the entire western fort system had them too—ta-da! The airship was out in the grasslands and lit up with electric lights, had strange little winglets and rotating metal wheels on big levers fore and aft, a spotlight, and had red and green navigation lights like a steamship. It was named *Magellan*. Two men who'd shot an elk asked us for help in carving it up and then invited us aboard for dinner and a ride. Their names were Samuel E. Tillman and Amos E. Dolbear, the pilot and engineer. Tillman was a U.S. Army engineer, West Point professor, mapper, astronomer, and one of the founders of the *Cosmos Club* in Washington D.C. You see, Dolbear was a professor of chemistry who perfected the electric gyroscope, something much needed on an airship. He also worked with early telephones and wireless communications, and successfully experimented with the conversion of sound vibration into electricity—*remember* those details. They said the ship was funded by private industrialists back east, and I'll bet it's a who's-who list of illumined robber baron men and their wives.

"There were two other men aboard dressed in long, black frock coats—serious-minded military types but not in uniform—and I suspect now one of them was our friend Ambrose Bierce. There were three well-dressed Freemason gents with good senses of humor, and there were two quite handsome women in red silk dresses as well, one Spanish, one Mexican. All were occultists I realize today, and I'm now positive one of the elderly men was John Worrell Keeley, the inventor of the *Etheric Vibratory Engine* and an expert in aerial navigation theories; he had a swell bulldog puppy onboard named 'Ether.' Dad recognized another as John Jacob Astor IV, a financial backer of Keeley; they talked and drank for most of the journey since my family was chummy with theirs during summertime in the Adirondacks. Quite the dash-fire party list!"

"I'll just bet," said Bea, arms crossed.

"You really get around, don't you?" asked Alice.

"I manage." Bernie continued. "So then we set off and were treated to a champagne and elk dinner in an elegant salon as we flew over the Rockies at high speed, the searchlight lighting up the snowy peaks. Remember, electricity was brand new, the world enthralled with it. Dad and I had the thrill of our damn lives! Once over Grand Junction—and we rattled a few ranchers on the ground with the bow light and blowhorn for fun—we turned around and flew back at even greater velocity. It was an exciting evening to say the least, lots of drinking, and I lost my virginity in ten minutes with one of the women, Guadalupe, in a posh stateroom that had all the comforts of home, even a hot shower with perfumed French soap. I was a tall handsome strapping lad in them-thar days."

"*Unbelievable*," snapped Bea. "Can't believe you were ever a *virgin*, old boy." Alice flashed her eyes. "How exciting!"

"You never mentioned this story to us before, why?" asked McMaster, keenly interested. Bernie waved his arms. "When I met with Hess it all seemed connected, especially with Bea's Heinkel fighter escapade. You see, Dad and I never knew what powered the *Magellan*, never saw the engine compartment. We just thought it was another gas dirigible marvel of the age, although a damn fancy one. It had only a thin metal tube with of some sort of gas at the top of the fuselage. Very odd I thought at the time."

"Gas tube? For plasma? Wait…did it have an Anton-like whirling drum or gadget?" asked Bea.

Bernie snapped his fingers and went to the drawing board. "Indeed, it must've had one." He drew a schematic of the airship. "It used torsion-field antigravity, I'm sure of it. Today, we know that antigravity aircraft have an electromagnetic plasma 'space-time bubble' surrounding them, which is why you felt very little G-forces while inside Anton during combat. It's like a slightly different reality inside. Einstein told me that over a hamburger lunch."

Bea added: "And when firing the big 30 mm autocannon it danced the *St. Louis*

Shag." "Or did you shag all of St. Louis?" asked Alice.

"Why you little rat-faced Dingo-dog with eyes of—"

"Stop! How that set of physics works I have no idea, but it does; Professors Oppenheimer and Bush at MIT think it has to do with an entirely new set of physics that exist inside that magnetic field, one that allows gravity a honkin' big leeway," said Bernie. "We made some sharp turns this way and that over Grand Junction, but hardly felt it. Dolbear told me they couldn't even shoot a Sharpes buffalo rifle from the airship because it would destabilize the field, causing the ship to wobble around. That's why they hunted animals by foot—but they *could* drop things by hand. They said *Magellan* was powered by a leather-covered ceramic device containing a thin layer of gold inside, *monatomic* gold I suspect. And it also had what they called 'Serum,' which had to be similar to the counterrotating drums inside Little Anton's unit, the ones full of electrified plasma with isotopes of something mixed in with the liquid mercury—'Red Mercury' the Germans call it—and that's *alchemy*. But alchemy only works when an engineer or physicist uses the transition of one mental vibration state for another, the lower to the higher, the male to the divine female, otherwise none of the technology will work. I know, sounds goofy as hell. Dolbear said that the ship was powered by 'traditional alchemical and electromagnetic cosmic forces,' and could circumnavigate the globe in just five days if need be—hell, the little library had all of H.G. Wells, Walter Rathenau, and Jules Verne's books in it. A gramophone and pipe organ too. Victorians loved those damn organs, lots of vibrating sound."

"Those chaps were awfully forthcoming with details. Why?" asked Bea.

Bernie pointed at her. "They wanted people to know about the technology, they wanted it public for the world."

Alice placed her chin in hand. "Please explain to us mere mortals what monatomic gold is, exactly? Is it fashionable?"

Bernie drew breath and closed his eyes in thought. "Okay. The Navy told me it's real gold, but it's gold that has been put through a classified alchemical process that turns it into a white powder. Moses' *manna*, from the Bible, if you will, and he mixed it with Magic Mushrooms, hence 'High Priests.' Talk about a consciousness boost."

"Oh, we just adore them at boring garden parties," said Alice.

"The gold is what they call an ORME material, *Orbitally Arranged Monatomic Element*. The lazy atoms are unclustered and loose, as in 'mono-atomic,' but the frisky electrons are in a high-spin rate, and that's *torsion*, which is directly linked to electromagnetism and antigravity, like a fierce tornado that picks up a car or cow. Viktor Schauberger's experiments with swirling water and air proved it to be so. I'm told that in the lab a near-weightless cube of monatomic gold hangs in the air above an electrified copper plate. Tesla said the theory is…it can exist in two dimensions simultaneously, and it's used as a non-crystalline superconductor of some kind, a key component, and one that can be used at room temperature, not frozen at minus thirty."

Bea said: "Well, *that's* not fashionable at all. So glad I took theoretical quantum physics back at Cambridge. Oh, wait, I most assuredly did *not*. So, if I remember correctly, a superconductor is a fancy material or alloy that conducts energy with no resistance or parasitic loss, yes?"

"You bet," said Bernie. "Once set in motion, electrical current will flow forever in a closed loop of superconducting material, an infinity figure-eight. Mother Nature's perpetual motion, if you will. A quantum tornado, macroscopically speaking."

Gwafa whistled. "*Ooh-la-la, trés compliqué*. But I have seen a tornado at work in the deep desert, very destructive."

Bea rubbed her forehead. "Tornado? Hold on a ticky. I was taught back at Shieldmaiden school that the Sufi Whirling Dervishes can meditate *trans-dimensionally* via the torsion field they create, thus they easily interact with the big cheese Universal Consciousness out there in higher dimensions of time and space, all points of which are connected for some odd reason, probably a draconian municipal law, no doubt. Could that be related to any of this zany stuff?"

"Absolutely!" said Bernie. "I think you're definitely onto something there. The Pineal Gland, or Third Eye, must be activated by the spinning when the Dervishes go into a trance state, then they can see beyond *The Veil*, beyond what the Persians and Rudolf Steiner called our *Eighth Sphere* of reality, a prison of the mind and soul. 'Dervish' literally means 'doorway,' the doorway to another world, a higher world. We'll go watch them tonight at a joint I know. It'll knock your socks off."

"I have seen these men dance for days at a time to the enchanting musical rhythm, they become one with Allah," said Gwafa wistfully. "I much admire that ability, but traditional Islamists are at odds with the mystery schools, fear them."

"Bingo," said Bernie. "Ask yourself *why*."

Gwafa thought for a moment. "Ah-h-h, now I understand. Forbidden knowledge of the higher realms."

Bea raised her arm as if she were back in school. "If I remember, old prof, the Persian Zoroastrian mystery schools predate Islam and Mohammed by many thousands of years. They may predate all silly religions."

"And their concept of monotheism is really about The Law of One at its core, that we are all one in the cosmos, all equal as it were," said McMaster. "Different races of people out there and down here have different perspectives of time and reality, but we're all part of the same cosmic 'Source,' the supreme creational intelligence of the cosmos. The Prediluvian ancients practiced and believed in cosmology and nature worship, not Anunnaki gods or artificial religions. And all these saucy bits of intelligence stay in this room, if you please."

"Sir, exactly who the bloody hell would even believe us?" asked Alice. McMaster breathed: "Good point."

Bea asked: "Law of One? You mean the law of confusion and bewilderment." "God created the world in six days, and was arrested on the seventh," said Alice.

Gwafa rubbed his eyes. "My head is going to explode like that tank we shot, *madame*." "You said it."

Bernie shook a fist. "Now we're on the dusty metaphysical trail, cowboys and cowgirls.

The key to alchemy lies in the practices of Turkish and Islamic mystics and Freemasons, my personal favorites. The airship engineers must have known about Sufi wisdom, because a person must go through a spiritual alchemical change within themselves for the technology to work properly, or even for it to be discovered in the first place."

"Right. Hence ye olde *Philosopher's Stone* once again, got it," said Alice. "I'm smarter than I thought."

Bea nudged her. "I wouldn't push that theory too hard, stone-head."

Bernie took chalk to board. "Alice is right. The *Stone* is the awakened self, it's called *Utam*, the vibration of a new universe within one's consciousness, a higher state of peaceful enlightenment, the merging of the male and female energies. It's happening here, now, to us five would-be mystics in this very room. Get it? That's why I think the 19th-century airship folks didn't want their new toys ending up in the hands of the military. No offense to all of us, but war is the ultimate lower state of imperfection and vibration, or more simply—it *stinks*. So the real question is: Do *any* of us have the wisdom to use the new technology properly at the present?"

"Well, the Nazis sure don't," said Bea. "Bloody ingrates."

"Perhaps not as *intended*, but they're using it to good effect, I reckon," said McMaster. "Higher knowledge and technology are both neutral. A knife can cut an apple or kill a person."

"Could use a cold apple about now," whined Alice, the room warm and stuffy.

Bea mumbled: "Braeburn crisp, Bramley sweet, Cameo, Cox, Egremont…"

"Oranges and pomegranate for me," said Gwafa.

McMaster picked up the phone. "I'll call for some fruit for lunch."

13 ½

After a long break, they kept at it.

"Just…roll…down…the hill gently with me on this, people," said Bernie, eyes closed, twirling his fingers like wheels. "So, where was I? Ah! Back in the *Magellan*. Some of the plasma may have been injected into that top tube for some sort of antigravity reason, I surmise. Anyway, I wasn't really listening at the dinner table to all the scientific garble, my eyes were on my twenty-year-old gal's heaving breasts while she and I talked steam trains and hothouse flower species in old Hispaniola. Dad was piss drunk because he remembered he hated heights but forgot all about it at first in the excitement. But it did catch my attention when Tillman said we were going 221 mph. Man oh man, I remember *that*. Nothing on Earth had gone that fast back then. Imagine the sheer optimism of a looming electrified 20th century—Tesla Towers, free-energy, safe airships, near utopia, free beer, etcetera."

"Steam trains were barely touching one hundred in the 1890's," said McMaster.

Gwafa asked: "High-speed flight in 1897? But that was well before the Brothers Wright in America took to the air. I do not understand…"

"That's the point," said Bea. "You're not supposed to." "Academia *sneaks*," said Alice. "Everyone's in on the con game."

Bernie soldiered on. "Powered maneuverable flight is as old as the hills, Gwafa, and it wasn't *really* kept secret. In 1897, newspaper reports of multiple airship sightings filled the minds of America with wild stories of high-speed long-distance adventures by mysterious inventors and nameless monied eastern industrialists. Thousands of reports and articles; the papers called it: 'The Great Airship Mystery,' and you can find them all over in American archives. The Navy sent some in my file here." He passed out three old, faded clippings inside folders. "I think even the *London Times* reported on it. By 1894 or so, we Americans finally caught on to the airship technology after forty years of secret development."

McMaster examined one. "Have to say, I barely remember anything about it. By 1900 all the press dried up."

"Well, don't look at us, that was well before *our* time," said Alice.

Bea read one. "*San Francisco Chronicle*. July the second. Says here one airship landed on Mount Tamalpais north of the city to acquire fresh water and drop off passengers and mail at around ten p.m. The witness was Mrs. Kathy Lamont, a local breeder of Huskies who sold one to the ship's navigator. Then it sped off to the northeast and was sighted again in Lake Tahoe and Carson City. One of the letters in the mail sack was from Argentina addressed to a Robert Leroy Parker, dated only two days prior to the landing. That's some quick post service."

"And it was from San Carlos de Bariloche, a town which is still the premier longtime German settlement, the one that transplanted their culture brick by brick and strudel by strudel. Wheat, cattle, and sheep farmers. Very little Spanish spoken there is what I remember when Dad and I visited in 1925. Lots of big bands, marches, flags, and beer halls."

"The one that looks like *Munich*?" asked Alice. "The report I read stated that there's a few lurid Nazis lurking about down there as we speak. Probably another decent fallback escape if old Adolph loses the war."

"*Brava*," said McMaster.

Bernie pointed at her. "Well done Alice! A while back I talked to an oldtimer general who was in the U.S. Army Observer Corps. On his death bed, he told me that the army wanted those newfangled airships for top secret military use only, but all the airship pilots, owners, and industrialists involved nixed the idea in 1901 or so. Sound familiar? They were all occultists like us, philosopher scientists and misfit mystics, bankers with a conscience, even. They wanted the technology for peaceful and public commercial use only, with little or no travel fees to boot. The word is they scattered to the wind…*due south*. Argentina anyone?" He rustled papers. "The Navy file here says none of the airships were commandeered by the U.S. Army or Navy, and no trace of any of them could ever be found—but then airship sightings appeared in Argentina all of a sudden. Lots of 'em. Documented in the papers, too. From my own research, I think that Etta Place was murdered in California years later under an assumed name, maybe she got too close to the Germans' secret. I suspect *Hermetic Order of the Golden Dawn* and *Ordo Templi Orientis* master Aleister Crowley was involved in all of this somehow, he was seen skulking around in the Ley Line-rich San Bernardino California area up to occultish activities. He was shadowed by the Secret Service and U.S. Army intelligence, and that means Butch and Sundance were in the mix. I'll bet he was whipping up some strange Babylon Workings along Ley Line nodes for someone, some nation, but that's just wild speculation on my part."

"Of all the barmy stories you've ever cobbled up, this has to be the barmiest," said Bea.

McMaster dug into a file he had prepared. "This was around 1915, wasn't it? That seems to jibe with my intelligence reports of the time; he was working for us Brits even back then. I've met with him twice. Odd man in the extreme, fiercely independent, wary. He was known for being a triple agent, or one that acted as such. No one ever trusted Crowley fully. Even today he's considered an unhinged liability within our unofficial ranks, said Menzies. I take a more balanced view, however."

"So what?" asked Bea. "One of my least favorite Cambridge celebrity alumni. Devil and bugger poetry master bar none, sadistic, masochistic in the extreme, though all that does bite at a bit of Ishtar-style orgy fun."

Alice added: "He's known as *The Beast*. The wicked man abandoned his family. His wife ended up in an asylum because of his penchant for violent sex bondage, torture, and witchy mistresses painted up pentagram. He should be arrested and *hanged*. Or bloody well given the Victoria Cross."

McMaster leered at her. "Don't judge. Mystery schools and symbology are mostly neutral, it's up to the adepts which direction they wish to go, what puddle they put foot to, a clear mountain stream or a cesspool. Those that intimately know the dark can be a valuable asset for its understanding; good and evil are *relative* concepts. Keep to positive or negative vibrations in all of this. No one is a saint. None of us. Crowley and other grey-area mystics helped us in the last war and may do so again. He and his wife honeymooned in this very house in 1904. In 1923 he was in Libya and then Siwa, doing God knows what at the oracle temple of Amun there."

"Siwa?" asked Bea. "I say, all this *is* rather odd, but then…I'd expect no less." "I do not want to meet this man ever," worried Gwafa.

Bernie went on. "Hess has helped me dozens of times, so consider him grey area too. Anyhow, I met Crowley back in 1925 in a Bariloche bar. We climbed a few hills in the Andes with an Austrian group of folks, and he and I discussed Sir Francis Bacon, John Dee, Enochian Magick and lost Prediluvian history, and that's when I took a greater interest in the occult. America's full of it, up to her tits."

Bea folded her arms. "Soddy Freemasons and the like, always keeping the good stuff to themselves."

"Honestly…" said Alice. "Snotty schoolboy follies."

Bernie said: "Agreed, but they may have good reasons for secrecy. Occult-minded SS spies literally infest D.C., and throughout America's history the Masons have been a great help, especially during our Revolution against you rotten lobster Redcoats."

"Rabble rebels, we'll soon have you back in the Empire." Bea then turned to Alice. "Funny how patriarchal societies keep secrets to themselves like guilt-ridden philandering husbands."

Alice snapped: "Toads, all."

Bernie kept on. "So…if there's an expert on Ley Line energy it's Crowley, a spy's spy. I think he was on the trail of the lost airships since he was seen in Mexico City in 1915 on his way to South America via the Yucatan and her Atlantean pyramid cities, all important stops along the way. He knew the significance of the technology—a formerly Prediluvian one that could transform the new 20th century. He's wrapped up in this story we know for sure, and probably working for the highest bidder behind the scenes. McMaster and I know Churchill meets with him in secret from time to time or at least used to. On what we know not. Crowley has been corresponding to some American rocket, JATO, and propulsion scientists, especially JPL chemist Jack Parsons. So he may be of use to us Yanks too, alchemically speaking of course."

Bea thought of Lutz and *Little Anton*. "*Jet-Assisted Take-Off?* I think I may have some rocket experience in that area."

"Inde-e-e-d you do," said Bernie with a wink.

McMaster said: "In London, Menzies and Commander Fleming asked me to call Crowley and arrange for him to meet with Hess, but I told them you, Bernie, would be a levelheaded and more trustworthy choice."

"And tryst-worthy…" mumbled Bea. "Good one, that," mumbled Alice.

Bernie bowed slightly. "I thank you all. Most likely they would have knocked metaphysical heads and gotten nowhere, but I'd like to be a fly on *that* wall. Now, regarding unconventional airships, the U.S. Navy cobbled a sixty-foot job together in 1935, named *Chief Crazy Horse* just to piss off the Army spies, but it was rudimentary and slow, about 180 knots sustained. Scientist T. Townsend Brown was called in for this project. Its altitude performance was so-so, about 18,000 feet or so. Very little lifting power, but quite good loitering capability for reconnaissance in the South Pacific; they tested it in the Philippines. The propulsion and antigravity data were primitive, and it's plain it wasn't too impressive, which means they missed a bunch of things, got 'em wrong. Unreliable, it had a slew of malfunctions and bugs that no one could figure out, not even Brown. One night it landed in the water off Puerto Princesa and nearly sank. After that, four-engine flying boats and bigger, faster aircraft took over the imaginations of the admiralty and the very costly program was shelved in 1936. Hard times back then even for the Navy."

"You Yanks should've stuck with helium dirigibles, old boy," said Bea haughtily. Bernie went face-to-face. "Three young sailors…drowned that night, so shut the *fuck up*, my fair lady!"

Thirty long seconds of silence.

"Sorry," whispered the girls.

"My condolences. Impressive history, *monsieur*," said Gwafa, easing tensions with a calm voice. "I must ask, is this man Crowley involved in African Voodoo?"

"Who knows? He may have been. Same idea really, African *Black Magick*," replied Bernie. "Same shit, different style. 'Black' just means *hidden*." Bernie wrote the words on the board with the odd spelling. "It's pronounced 'May-gick.' But…all of you need to remember that the genuinely horrible stuff is 'Satanic Magick.' There's a big, big difference." He looked at each person, his face steel-hard. "Am I *clear*?"

To everyone's relief, lunch arrived on a trolley with Tillings. "No apples today, but plenty of melon, cucumbers, dates, radishes, and figs. Healthy appetites, everyone."

Everyone dived in.

Chewing a ripe fig, Alice asked: "Right. So, what's all this magician jibber-jabber got to do with our proposed mystery mission exactly?"

Bernie sighed again, and stuffed in a cool slice of melon. "I know it's a lot of dots to connect, tons of strange information, but in due course all will become clear. We're all tired and stressed a bit, but please bear with me. Brigadier? It's showtime."

McMaster laid out large photographs on the table. "Gather round. These photos were taken by a Russian reconnaissance plane seventy-six miles east of Sebastopol a month ago, don't inquire as to how I got them. They seem to show a large silver cigar-shaped aircraft moving southeast at high speed. The pilot said he chased it at 380 mph plus at 28,000 feet but it climbed and sped away at almost twice his speed and altitude, an estimate of course. He chased it towards the Turkish coast but then gave up when it accelerated out of sight. He thought it may have had Luftwaffe markings, but wasn't quite sure. When Rodgers told me what Hess had to say I began ruminating with Menzies and the admirals. This...*could* be a German airship, and potentially a very big one at that."

"Blurry image, was the pilot sure?" asked Alice, using a magnifying loop and dripping melon juice.

McMaster said: "*Please* be careful. I've been told he's reliable and experienced."

"It's no Foo-Fighter, that I'm sure of," said Bernie confidently, mouth full of cucumber sandwich. "The Russians know the difference by now."

"A what, *monsieur*?"

McMaster passed a tray of nuts. "An unidentified and unexplainable aerial phenomenon. Round balls of bright plasma flying very fast. They can pass right through an airframe and make no damage. Unknown origin. Unknown propulsion. Most likely peaceful. Intelligently controlled. They gather data we think."

"Spies from...another world?" asked Gwafa. "Another dimension?" "Maybe," said Bernie. "Possibly."

"This one's even blurrier," said Alice.

Bea looked up from the perplexing photos. "All right, Rodgers, what's going on in that fat, Foo-Fighter-infested head of yours?"

Bernie dashed back to the big wall map. "What if...what if the Germans *perfected* the airship technology after capturing some of the originals in Argentina? What if they convinced some of the more technical and materialist science people to join their nationalistic cause? I think the Thule or Vril Society, both of which are much older than we thought, brought some of these people into the proto-Nazi fold before the last war, 1905, 1910 or so, it makes sense." He used a yardstick to plot a course. "Southeast from Sebastopol would take our supposed airship to the Zagros Mountains, the very place Hess said Schäfer was bragging about. It's a long shot, but I strongly believe the Ahnenerbe is involved with a thorium and rare earth elements mining operation somewhere in those mountains. Sure–sure, the Germans were there in Iraq a while back to try and secure oil reserves and sea ports, but what if they weren't the only commodity? Hess told me the Baghdad Museum was raided by an elite SS Ahnenerbe squad that stole Sumerian clay tablets and cylinder seals, and that *reeks* of Anunnaki science research. The Germans need tons of thorium and other exotic elements for their atomic bomb, electronics, missile, and antigravity programs, and there's very little thorium in Europe. High-quality thorium ore, monazite and euxenite, are mostly found in the Middle East and northern India. I checked with a geology professor and physics egghead about it. But there's something else the Ahnenerbe is looking for down there. Some sort of archeological ruins or ancient megalithic sites, I don't know what or where, but we need to *find* the whole shebang. Besides Schäfer, I smell senior members of the Thule and Vril in this too, oh-h-h-h yes. More than ever."

Bea folded her arms. "Have to say, this kind of odd stuff is right up their dingy street."

Bernie dabbed his finger on the desk. "Do the math. A large and powerful antigravity airship could transport many tons of ore back to Germany for processing into isotopes at our friends I.G. Farben with their fancy new chemical laser. It would probably fly mostly at night at very high altitude, which means well above radar detection and fighter range. From high altitude it could swoop down at a steep angle and land on a plug nickel. The Germans are obsessed with big railway guns, Tiger tanks, battleships, and six-engined transport aircraft, why the hell *wouldn't* they build a huge antigravity airship? It's Hitler's ego run amok, all of it. They are way ahead of the Allies on atomic research. Christ, not long ago their big railway gun *Gustav* laid waste to the Russian White Cliff concrete-fortified below-grade ammunition bunker at Sebastopol from twenty-six miles away; you've seen the pictures, biggest railway gun in the world, dual tracks. Was the gun really a stupid idea? The bunker blew up in a massive explosion. Was it a lucky hit with *Gustav*'s 800 mm conventional round? Or…was it a newfangled thorium or uranium *atomic* shell that did the trick? It's something to ponder. I know for a fact that the Russians are taking huge casualties—*millions*."

"*Gods…*" breathed Alice.

"Millions? No wonder Hitler wanted that oversized blunderbuss built years ago, he knew they would probably have exotic ordinance by now," said Bea worriedly, looking to McMaster. "I'm starting to feel very, very small at the moment…"

The brigadier replied: "And we thought it was just another white elephant of theirs, built only to destroy the French Maginot Line."

"Look…my ONI Navy pal I met with yesterday says it's *imperative* we succeed in our mission for the war effort, and that comes directly from FDR."

"*Le President Américain?* Roosevelt?" asked Gwafa, suddenly concerned and overwhelmed, wondering just how he had ended up in this stuffy room occupied by strange people with stranger ideas, but he was also spellbound beyond measure. Enthralled.

"And Prime Minister too," said McMaster. "Emphatically so."

A little nervous, Alice asked: "What about their radio signals? Any aerial photos of the Zagros? Do we even know where to look?"

McMaster shuffled his file. "Very few photos exist, and fewer available aircraft to provide reconnaissance; we've found nothing. No radio signals either, no triangulation of anything, nothing but *silence*. We don't want to let Jerry know we're sniffing about either, tipping them off could mean disaster. You'll be on muleback with a guide, low-key and dressed appropriately. A precision insertion. Get in, find it, radio us the coordinates, and get out fast. The bombers and ground attack Mosquitos with heavy guns will do the rest."

"If a base does exist, they're deep within a vast British territory, so they must be using some sort of new communication system," mused Bernie. "Perhaps a telluric one at that. It's a theory back at MIT that ultra-low frequency signals can be relayed through the ground along Ley Lines."

"A sound idea," punned McMaster. "As you all know, the Allies are quite thinly spread out from here to India. Very few personnel. The Germans could be acting with impunity."

Bea neared the map. "With respect, Brigadier, this crackpot idea has a lot of speculation, ifs, ands, and buts attached to it. Correct me if I'm wrong, but looking at this 'ere map, the Zagros is one helluva big area a thousand miles long by five hundred wide. Where would we even start? What if you're wrong about the general location, Bernie? It could be a base hidden somewhere else, maybe in Iran or parts east in Afghanistan. We could be searching for *years* with no—"

Bernie exploded, palm to map. "I'm telling you it's there in the *Zagros!*"

Silence.

A minute later McMaster broke it, fastening his briefcase. "The Indian chap I mentioned arrives this evening. Professor Simon Parkes-Jackson. Cultural and religious history, the best. Tomorrow, he may be able to help us narrow down a search area."

"I'll bet its bloody freezing at night up there too at altitude," said Alice.

"You'll live." Bernie sat with a deflation of lungs. "Look...I know...it's a leap of faith, but the dots connect pretty darn well, well enough to give the ONI good reason to trust me on this. These ideas must fall upon fertile ground and that's *you all*. We'll perform our due diligence and intelligence once in Basra. Hess wouldn't lie to me on something like this, I'm sure of it."

"Yes, I know, blurry photos, Russian pilots, Butch Cassidy, Schäfer's drunken bragging and tall tales, Vril, Thule, and Alexander the Great…but it's worth a go in my book and there's no one else anywhere near qualified but us. Other than a few scattered book-swallowers and mental cases, MI-6's entire Occult Division is here in this room, no offense Brigadier. I've found a reliable Iraqi guide, he knows the people in those mountains, every trail, valley, and goat path. Bottom line…if the Nazis drop a big-yield atomic bomb by high-altitude airship on the Allies or England, we might *lose* the war in a day. London and its surrounding areas would be incinerated with one single bomb. Now, are you three with me heart and soul?"

Alice slumped. "Nothing better to do." "*Oui, monsieur!*" said Gwafa, bolt upright.

Bea held her aching head in her hands and moaned: "Oh-h-h, it just had to be *Schäfer*."

14

August 12

Well-dressed in a white suit and bow tie, he stood by the map. "I…am Professor Parkes-Jackson. Mother is Indian, father British. Oxford and Calcutta Universities—religious studies, mythology, Middle East, Tibetan, Tartarian, and Indian cultures. I specialize in the historical *Puranas* which describe the ancient Vedic civilization that existed in India for perhaps millions of years. The Vedas tell us of advanced medicine, calculus, atomism, and quantum theories which the Germans seem particularly interested in. The ancient Indians knew that gravitation held the universe together. McMaster told me two weeks ago what you're looking for, an ancient site in the Zagros that the Germans might be after." He opened his large, locked valise and put on his white cotton gloves. "I may…have some answers." He carefully opened a huge, thick, forty-pound bookmarked volume that had a crumbling leather and reed binding with faded gold leaf. "In '38, the Ahnenerbe found a complete set of the multi-volume *Kang Shuur* in Tibet. In it, they found the Atlantean secrets and Vedic mathematics they needed for their various top-secret sciences and technology. Even so, they missed some things, vital information."

"Professor, we suspect they're after large deposits of euxenite for thorium production," Bernie said.

Not bothering to look up, he replied: "That is…*not* my department." He carefully showed everyone an open page with an engraving. "This…exquisitely-decorated book, possibly belonging to the great Raja Chola, is titled the *Kahnnhar*, an old Indian history text that contains Vedic and Buddhist history and philosophy, select portions of The Vedas, trans-Arabian wisdom, and a section on Alexander's march to India in search of higher knowledge; it's very old, written on parchment from around 1310, and translated into Hindu from an older Tamil-written book, possibly by the ancient Kadamba people. Throughout the ages it probably was moved time and again for safety. It was found in a secret chamber at Fort Vellore in the city of Tamil Nadu seventy years ago. My colleagues and I have visited every bastion fort in India; they are astoundingly complex and advanced." He looked to McMaster. "East India Company, the British Army, and the Dutch my fat foot! They were mostly built by the ancient Indians."

McMaster swallowed hard, hands in pockets. "Yes, well, there it is."

Parkes-Jackson continued. "Tamil is the oldest language on Earth by the way, it is Lemurian, and everyone used to speak it until the Anunnaki destroyed the Tower of Babel and created other languages to divide us, to confuse and conquer us. This text also mentions the *Vymaanika-Shaastra* on how to construct antigravity Vimanas—but it is purposefully vague and symbolic just like the *Kang Shuur*, the complete knowledge too dangerous to put into print verbatim. My colleagues and I believe the *Kahnnhar* is a unique volume, as I could find *no other* like it in my worldwide travels, and it completes the missing passages in the Kang Shur. I believe it contains information copied from various scrolls from the libraries of Apollo in Rome and of Alexandria, both of which were torched to the ground by dark forces of the era." He turned a page carefully. "Here is the *Epic of Ninurta*, which lists cosmic weapons captured in an ancient Anunnaki war that can devastate opponents in three separate dimensions. I suggest you four study the etchings carefully. I'm assured the Nazis have done so already from the cylinder seals they stole in Baghdad." Another page was flipped. "Now, in this section, a faded image shows Alexander and his generals at a pass in the Zagros in 330 BC, the *Persian Gate*, where a great battle took place between the cities of Babylon and Persepolis on the Royal Road. Legend has it that The Gate may have been a natural 'portal' of some kind to other worlds and dimensions at certain dates and times in history when the planets aligned in a certain way. If so, it was and may still be a very dangerous astrological place. There are many legends of people disappearing at sacred sites like this, never to return. Some say they end up in vast caverns under the Earth, the Moon, or asteroids, or even in faraway galaxies in higher realms of existence. Quite the...*unexpected* journey, I imagine."

"Wonderland Alice down the rabbit hole," said Alice, chewing peppermint gum, smacking.

"And with a bellyful of druid mushrooms," added Bea, popping a stick. "Quite the ponderous tome, this."

"Indeed."

The professor stared at the girls for a long moment, unsure of their intellectual and spiritual worthiness. "Ariobarzanes, the Persian leader, held Alexander's Macedonian forces off for a month before Alexander reached Persepolis and destroyed it like the bloodthirsty madman he was. Western history paints him as *great*, but he wasn't. Just another conquering psychopath. However…before Alexander reached The Gate, he and his forces traveled a circuitous route from Babylon. Along the way he stopped in the city of Susa, and while camped there for weeks he was told by a few elders of a mythical fortress that was built by the ancient ancestors of the Elamites far up into the mountains. This fortress was said to contain all the treasures of the universe one could desire— yet only if one's heart was pure enough to understand its spiritual function. The much wider area of Tal-e Khosrow, or today's Yasuj, is the place where Alexander was said to have located the fortress it says here, and this stronghold was said to be manned by the last of the pastoralist Uxians, a mostly peaceful and wise tribe. It is written in most accounts that Alexander refused to pay their traditional fee or 'Defile' for travel through the Persian Gate, and thus put most of them to the sword…or so we're told. All other accounts say that the Uxians paid Alexander a yearly tribute of many horses, cattle, and sheep after their costly battle."

"Pretty expensive," mumbled Bernie.

"Love sheep," muttered Bea and Alice simultaneously.

"*This* text…states that Alexander tried another route to the north to circumvent The Gate, but a splinter group of Uxians stopped him. They survived inside the fortress by holding off the Macedonians with mysterious magical powers and defenses, and eventually even Alexander and his large force could not penetrate the walls no matter how hard they tried, thus finally leaving it and its defenders behind and moving on. 'Magic' is just spiritual technology and science not understood by today's purposefully limited academic understanding. I believe…this is the *true* account, but I find it strange that Alexander and his generals would leave a stronghold of any kind in such a strategic place near a major artery. Very strange." The professor skipped ahead in the book and gently unfolded a frayed interior map which nearly covered the desk space available. "So, if this mythical fortress does exist, where is it located? I've found what can only be a Hittite Ley Line map from deep antiquity in this section on geomancy, mounds, pyramids, temples, and subtle earth energies. My colleagues and I believe it was carefully re-copied time and again throughout the millennia as the older texts disintegrated. My best guess is that it represents information from over 9,000 years ago, perhaps even to Prediluvian times. As you can see, the spokes of six major Ley Lines intersect north of the greater Yasuj and Persian Gate area. I *do not* think that is a coincidence of any stripe.

I believe…Alexander went out of his way to find this fortress, a possible gateway to the Anunnaki Orion star system, his lineage." His eyes went wild with imagination.

"No wonder the Germans are so keen on Iraq." Bernie examined it closely. "Looks like around a hundred-fifty-mile-wide search area, but that's a guess."

"This map certainly *looks* ancient," said Alice. "Written in Sanskrit?"

The professor traced a line. "Good eye. Now then, Alexander arrogantly called himself 'Alexander Zeus-Ammon,' which a few of us believe link him to powerful Anunnaki royal bloodlines. Therefore, this explains why he was such a naturally great conqueror—his special genetics—but of course we all know it was his many thousands of incarnations upon Earth and elsewhere as a warrior that gave him 'genius,' as it were. In any case, he was treated as a living god."

Bea nosed in for a look. "But that makes this legend even more odd, especially since Alex may have possessed a superior intellect compared to his generals. What would've been so special about a fort and its occupiers that he, Mister Great, couldn't handle?"

Parkes-Jackson wiped his glasses and smiled. "An excellent question. According to Vedic cosmology tradition, Alexander was an *Avatar*, or one who descends from a higher realm to a lower one to learn, experience, and teach. My colleagues and I *do* know with certainty that the Brahmins of Tibet were still using Atlantean consciousness technology in Alexander's time, that is, telekinesis, telepathy, and perhaps matter creation and destruction abilities of the mind. We think Tibet was Alexander's ultimate goal, perhaps even China for more and more wisdom; Avatars sometimes forget their true missions and get caught up in militarism and ego."

McMaster said: "Before the last war, a British officer witnessed Tibetan monks levitating a two-ton boulder with musical instruments and drums, and now I believe him. What else can you tell us, Simon? Anything about the Aryan myths or the Nazis?"

"I…can tell you what I've heard in Bombay mystery school circles, but you won't like or believe it. I've heard that certain members of the Nazi SS and Thule Society have been in physical contact with the infamous *Gizeh Intelligences*, and have gained much knowledge from them via trade for the last twenty-five years."

Bernie sat down. "I need a drink."

Bea slowly withdrew her arms from McMaster's desk and stood upright. "I'm going to sincerely regret this, but…who the bloody hell is *that*, may I ask?"

•••

August 13

Wearing his prized brown Stetson cowboy hat and Army Air Corps sunglasses, Bernie had commandeered a Dodge command car with four-wheel drive and drove fast. His remaining brim feathers took flight.

Alice and Bea held on to their pith helmets and nearly bounced out several times. "Slow down Herr Caracciola," yelled Bea. "You'll kill us *all*."

"Chocks away!" Bernie ran full chat over a sand berm and went airborne. Gwafa yelled with delight. "Faster! *Vite!*"

The Dodge slammed down; Alice and Bea bounced up.

Bernie laughed above the wind. "I love it when you Brits own Detroit's finest." He drove south past the three big Giza pyramids starting with Khufu, then Khafre, then Menkaure, pointing at them with his arm and index finger as if making a point of their grandeur. "All are claimed by those dimwit pharaohs, but *none* were built for them. All that trouble just for tombs? No way. No tombs were ever found. There are hundreds of water tunnels beneath us, somehow they're integral to the genuine function of these pyramids, perhaps hydraulic energy production of some kind. The King's Chamber was for Astral travel use only. And what in tarnation took away all the smooth outer casing stones? The Great Flood?" Finally, he parked it on the north side of the Bent Pyramid after a half-hour's dusty, bumpy travel. Except for Gwafa, everyone's nerves were a bit raw from lack of drink.

Bernie rubbed his lower back. "Egypt was said to be the agricultural breadbasket of the Atlantean Empire, and Giza was its regional capitol. The entire Sahara was once a green, lush paradise, a huge civilization."

"Well certainly not anymore," said Alice, throwing a handful of sand. Gwafa and Alice set up a military-issue tent, its sides open, and folding campaign chairs.

Bea gathered the canteens and ropes, piling them inside. "Oh-h-h, the back," moaned Bea, rubbing it.

Alice took a sip of water, wiping her lips. "Hot, hot, hot. What infernal reason do you have for lecturing us weary hierophants out here in the blistering shadows of the ancients? Damn, cracked another nail…"

Bea said: "Use glue. Takes a while to dry." "I'm not slopping hoof glue on my nails…"

Bernie sat on a big casing stone that had fallen off the pyramid long ago.

"My reason? Operational security and a powerful tableau. No chance of wired bugs or prying ears while I talk big-picture stuff. I wanted all of you to share my vision of the past, one that directly affects our future. It's inspiring to say the least, you know, all this, uh, crap."

Shaded, Bea eased into the creaky campaign chair. "It's okay, I guess. Great thanks for the glorified Paris to Peking race. Back's sore still from my usual crash landing in the desert."

"You'll live," said Alice flatly.

"I not only loathe your company in this life, but the next as well."

Gwafa felt the large stones, noticing the high-speed saw marks and spiral grooves on one of them. "I have never seen anything like it." He reached inside a deep bore hole, perfectly round. "*Superbe.*"

"That's nothing." Bernie tipped up his hat and gestured upwards. "Just look at it! Gaze upon what I consider the most significant pyramid of the whole bunch. It was purposefully designed to be bent at the top, the predynastic and matriarchal Egyptians knew *exactly* what they were doing out here during the Zep Tepi time period. See what remains of the smooth casing stones? Electrical insulation of some kind, all these pyramids were power generators of a sort. Inside, the two pyramidal chambers have staggered stones for sound vibration concentration, a 'corbelled ceiling.' A piezoelectric marvel of the Prediluvian age of egalitarian laws, equality of the sexes, wisdom, and massive electromagnetic power. Pharaoh Sneferu may have claimed it as his own with a chisel and hammer, but we four know it was built many thousands of years before *his* time—a much later age of royal arrogance, taxes, tribute, and Fascism. A time when the cobra festooned their crowns, a symbol of the imperious Anunnaki and their cohorts in my opinion, the demiurge, a worship of the underworld. The 'Wise Serpents.' Napoleon and his philosopher-scientists scoured this region for every last drop of ancient wisdom, Atlantis references, and artifacts that could help him grow his new empire, and they did it with firepower. The Rosetta Stone and the Paris obelisk were but two of them. Who knows what else they found?"

Bea tilted back her head and groaned. "And Freemason Prince Talleyrand backed that expedition, so there's our occult connection. Oh well, my old kingdom for a chilly martini, one with a wise gecko on the rim eating an olive."

"Make mine with a longish lemon peel." Alice sat, adjusting her wide white hat. "I just knew we were in for another windy lecture. Fine. Pyramids, pyramids. Let's see, let's see, oh! The one hundred forty volcanic stone pyramids of the Azores are probably evidence for dusty ol' Atlantis and her survivors. We climbed them as children. Wrote a paper at Wycombe about it once. Top marks."

Bea said: "Funny, I'd forgotten all about that, and you did *not* get a high mark. That porcine sheep's bladder you call an intellect wouldn't have been up to snuff."

"Did too, you rancid gash of a Napoleonic spy. And snorting snuff had nothing to do with it. Puffed a ton of fags though."

"Right. Moving on. You know, it's a thought, but maybe the strange air shaft Gwafa and I found could be some evidence of the supposed buried civilization under the Sahara that's even older than these rock piles round here. Perhaps all of North Africa was part of the Atlantean empire, and with free airship service to tourist destinations, first class of course."

"Of course," said Alice. "Chilly martinis, gratis. Paté, pedicures, and a foot massage."

Bernie gestured behind him. "Now you're with me…I think. None of these pyramids were tombs, that's just the cover story going back to Napoleon; no hieroglyphics or sarcophagi, no colorful murals, no toy boats for bratty King Tut. Inside the shafts and chambers here everything is *all business*, no frills, nuthin'. All of these pyramids were built for industrial purposes on an industrial scale; my guess is that Ley Lines the world over terminate here at Giza, which serves as an anchor nodal point, like a railroad terminal— all roads lead to Rome, right?"

Bea said: "Yes but—"

Bernie held up a palm. "The head archeologist at the museum here is a closet occultist like us, name's Bauvall. He quietly told me over dinner at a shadowy restaurant that sound and frequency were vitally important in ancient times. Each temple, building, or pyramid was built to respond to a unique musical scale based on its dimensions and sacred proportions, their construction stones containing various crystals that're highly electromagnetic. In addition to certain lights and colors, I think the music and sounds created an electrical field when the vibrations interacted with the walls and columns inside temples. Stones become piezoelectric just from the mechanical pressure of the ones above pushing down. Thus, each energized building had a different function—astral travel, medical healing, electricity generation, fertility, crop yield enhancement, water purification, enlightenment and learning, etcetera. Hell, sky's the limit. Cathedrals and mosques are *somewhat* similar modern equivalents to these old Egyptian temples, but much lesser ones I'd say."

"Buildings as spiritual machines, yes?" asked Alice. "Built using the sacred cubit? But if—"

"You've been perusing Lovcraft's tatty novels again," blurted Bea.

"Soddy ol' hen. Least I can read."

Gwafa added: "Then…that is why the chanting and singing at the mosques under the colorful domes are so beautiful to the ear, the echoing and haunting Azan. It *heals*."

"Pop goes the weasel!" said Bernie, pointing. "Give the man a ten-cent cigar. I believe many of the intricate patterns we see on Persian rugs and the walls of mosques are sound vibration and frequency patterns. The building blocks of the cosmos. That's why I, the MIT Rad Lab boys, and the Navy think that matter can be created by sound."

Alice threw a handful of sand to Bernie's boots. "You're bloody *joking*. Like Merlin's *Sidhe* staff? I don't remember it *singing*."

"But perhaps it did," laughed Bea in smarty-pants fashion. "Get this. The SS are keen on *Aryan Musicology*, and that included *cymatics*, visual-acoustic engineering if you will; they're on to something. Boring music therapy was part of our training at the school, the harp, violin, and drums especially…very odd stuff, and Minister Goebbels changed all German music to an unharmonious 440 hertz tune. I suspect an agenda."

"I didn't know that," said Bernie.

Bea continued. "As I remember, the SS boffins put fine sand on a brass plate and made various geometric patterns with sound, some of which looked just like the round Catherine windows in cathedrals. They said that star fort designs were most likely based on vibratory patterns called 'cymaglyphs.' One pattern looked like an octagon with a pentagon inside with an oval inside it. Sacred geometry, I might add. See? I'm a ruddy genius."

"Raving Nazi *bitch*. So that's it!" screeched Alice. "Each 'earth energy' star fort had a different frequency. Stonehenge and Avebury circles must have had their own too. I wrote a report for McMaster on them. Farmers told me they grew huge cabbages and root veggies on their farms that neighbor stone circles, and used dowsing rods extensively. Limestone for *Yin* energy, bluestone for *Yang*, so to say. People in Arbor Low and Stanton Drew believe the standing stones enhance fertility too. They call it 'paramagnetism.' We now know that Irish round towers were for farming enhancement primarily, Viking recognition secondarily. All this hopped-up magnetic stuff must be related."

Bea pinched her. "I may be a bitch, cabbage-patch, but I'm no *Nazi*."

"Oww! That's entirely debatable."

"Not."

"Is."

"You're *both* onto something. It's all part of the big picture. Celtic spirals and Cathar Crosses also come to mind when we talk of frequency." Bernie drew patterns in the sand to illustrate. The big ones that have whole towns inside the bastions must've produced some kind of frequency for defensive purposes on top of all the hydraulic engineering, canals, farming, and Ley Line power amplification…something like that." He then pulled out a National Geographic magazine and two drawings he had stashed in his rucksack. "Believe it or not, I've spent quality time in Cairo's libraries between hangovers. Here's a snowflake photo from a microscope, here's a Marquis de Vauban-designed French star fort etching from 1678, and here's a photograph of cymagraph at high frequency from the Caltech lab. See any resemblance?"

They crowded in. "I'll be *damned*," gushed Alice. "And that ruddy fop Vauban gets all the fort-building credit."

Gwafa traced a pattern. "Very beautiful and intricate designs. I can understand why a fancy noble Frenchman would need to take credit—*un* égoïste."

"Mother Nature hard at work, no doubt," said Bea. "A woman's work is never done." Bernie leaned back to the casing stones and stretched his arms. "Ah, the Marquis, otherwise known as Sébastien le Prestre de Vauban, and his Dutch enemy peer Menno van Coehoorn, both of whom get most of the credit for bastion fort design, but I believe they knew the ancient secrets of harnessing earth energy for defenses. Few if any books detail how they built their forts, but historians gave them all the credit. Some of them are so beautiful they can be considered harmonious sculpture."

Bea said: "Cheeky twits." *"Impressionant."*

Alice added: "Agreed. The enemy must have just wept at the artistry, laid down their arms and proclaimed them far too fetching and breathtaking to attack and destroy."

Bernie said: "Funny, and possibly correct in a way. Anyway, somehow, the ancient Egyptians implemented vibratory sound levitation to lift these giant blocks using music, horns, metal rods, those unusual scepters, tapping their long tuning forks, chanting in unison, probably an amalgam of all that shit and more. They softened edges and melted blocks together with sound. I believe we're close to figuring all that out. The U.S. Navy has been experimenting with various devices for long-range underwater sub location, and they stumbled on what they term 'acoustic levitation.' For fun, they tried it on a sailor in a bosun's chair and they were able to lift him up a few feet. They also used sound frequencies to rotate a small-scale propeller shaft in water, and it *worked*."

Bea twirled her hair into strands. "Oh-h-h, yes. The SS was also working on sounds that affect our DNA—it was a top-secret program for eugenics, I believe."

Bernie closed his eyes in disgust, pinching his nose bridge. "That's just *great*."

"Music soothes the savage beast, any girl knows that," chirped Alice. " The Aborigines and their didgeridoos, fantastic vibratory sounds. But…is this where we get the wild rumor about Nazi sound weapons?"

Bernie said: "Unfortunately, yes. The SS, Thule, and Vril people know that sound frequency has an effect on matter, it can boil water and crack granite in the lab; Joshua's horns at Jericho, the walls destroyed. Cellular healing or…destruction. Consciousness itself is a frequency, and I was told by Tesla that it can create matter. He thought the Atlanteans built their entire civilization that way. But the weapon knowledge may have come from the warlike Anunnaki, and those fancy dudes created weird hybrid animals and a few races of us humans from some sort of primordial goo using sound, light, tons of genetics, cubes of meat, buckets of blood."

Alice wrinkled up her nose. "Eww-w-w-w."

Bea did too. "You said it. And later their friends the sonofabitching Belial boys created pet-slave centaurs, Pegasus, chimeras, hydras, griffins, cyclopses, hippocampus, *yechh*…to perform all the menial dirty work before the fall of Atlantis, the big war."

Gwafa turned to Bea. "Do you mean…?" She nodded, eye to eye.

"Then…Kongamato, Gbahali, and Minotaurs as well?" asked Gwafa worriedly. "*Merde.*"

Bernie said: "Now *look* everyone, the point is…sound vibration, frequency, and its mathematics are key components of antigravity and propulsion, and we need to try and understand this for our mission. So let's stick to the program."

"Some African tribes put sand on their drums to divine the future, strange patterns appear as if by magic," said Gwafa, thinking deeply and connecting dots. "*Mon Capitaine*…they are the Anunnaki from the Qu'ran, no?"

"Call me 'Bernie,' no ranks or military anything. From today on we wear only civilian clothes and desert garb. Yes, they're the same sky gods, same deal. The word Anunnaki means: 'From the heavens they came.' Did you read McMaster's 'Lamp Briefing' last night?"

"*Oui*. I could not sleep much after that. If it is correct and I fear it to be, the world I knew was just a blinding mirage. In Sumeria, the lighter-skinned people tended to the temples, gardens, and kitchens for the gods. The brown people were their warrior caste, Blacks the worst of it in the harsh sun of the fields. Now I know why we *Noires* have always been at the bottom of the Anunnaki caste system that has survived to today. A clever tactic to keep all of us fighting one another, never to rise against our…*true* masters in the shadows. Racism was manufactured by…design."

Bernie soberly replied: "It's part of their divide-and-conquer strategy. It makes sense, and on behalf of the white race I'll say I'm sorry."

Nonchalant, Bea added a limp: "Sorry, old thing."

While Bea nudged her, Alice bit her broken thumbnail. "Mmm? Oh yes, sorry."

Gwafa made an unusual face constructed of bewilderment and resentment. "*Brule en l'enfer*. I should have sold you to the Tuareg!"

Bea kissed his cheek. "Thanks, old lion."

Bernie took out a book from his rucksack. "Let's review more of last night's homework—Hermetic Law courtesy of Thoth. I know it's a royal pain in the ass, but it's important. We have to have our metaphysical heads screwed on tight for this mission, and no stripping of the threads."

"Oh, gods 'n sods, here we go *again*," said Bea. "More druidic dribble."

"Quiet in the peanut gallery." He pointed to Alice. "Go."

She popped another stick of peppermint gum. "Right. *Principle of Mentalism*. Infinite cosmic intelligence. All is the mind; the universe is mental. And so will I be after all this medicine-man hullaballoo."

"You said it, sister."

"Good, I think." He pointed to Gwafa.

"Number two is *The Principle of Correspondence*. As above, so below. As within, so without, and the vice of versa. To explore the higher and lower nature of all things, as if...one holds a spiral seashell in our hands only to try and understand the beautiful patterns in all nature, to find the hidden solutions to a problem. Perhaps the desert beetle with its outer armor was an inspiration for the making of tanks. The world around us is a mirror of what is inside our hearts...which breaks mine. But if one thinks in positive terms, the world will follow your path, and I will try. And *mon favorite*...to take a breath is to breathe the sky, to sit on the earth is to be part of her. No divide. The unity of being. *Trés difficile, Monsieur Bernard*."

Alice clapped. "Beautifully said, old chap."

Bernie then clapped. "I'm impressed, now let's—"

"That's *peanuts*. Look inside yourself, beware the vicious circle, and don't blame others for your own dirty laundry. Understand the driving principles of the Nazis and you can defeat them," said Bea arrogantly. "Number three, *The Principle of Vibration*. Love this one. Nothing rests at ease, everything moves, hopefully *fast* mind you, and everything vibrates like a bloody radial engine on fire. Like a hummingbird's wings, the faster something vibrates, the harder it is to see, hence the snotty invisibility of higher dimensions. The old moldy Hermeticists believed that our thoughts had their own rate of vibration, thus we could tune them like a violin or engine, the results being whatever we desire, the sweet kiss of Mozart or fantastic rumbling horsepower. I'm guessing that's what the airship blokes did with the old technology from India, pretty damn smart, mmm, Vimana-wise that is."

Bernie put fists to hips. "Brava! Doing well, everyone."

"Vimana is the same as airship?" asked Gwafa.

"Yes-s-s-s," they chorused.

Alice said: "Ah! Four. *The Principle of Polarity*. Everything has opposite poles. North and south. Yin and yang. Like and unlike are the same. All truths are half-truths, all paradoxes can be reconciled, yackedy-yack. This is why Beans and I get along so well,

I'm the brains, she's the blunt instrument. Simple-dimple, zippedy-do."

Bea kicked sand. "Spoken like a true manic-depressive infantile infant. Fairly thin line between love and hate, I might add."

Alice leaned to Bea. "Give us a kiss." "A half-kiss only."

"For a half-wit."

Bea sighed heavily. "You have me there. In Norway I was deemed a half-goddess only by Pekke and Olaf when my river horse bucked—"

"*F-i-v-e*," interrupted Bernie. "*The Principle of Rhythm*. Everything has its tides—you should see the Bay of Fundy in Canada, forty-foot tides, and you can just pick up the fish to fry. All things rise and fall, like the stock market. The pendulum swing manifests in everything. Rhythm compensates. Rome rose and fell, Napoleon's empire too. Everything changes, everything ebbs and flows. The deal is you should put the gearshift in neutral and wait before you shift up or down; this way you can modulate your passionate emotions and remain calm and collected in the heat of battle. Keep to the middle path. Through the heightened awareness of this axiom, one can experience transcendental states of consciousness to rise above the swing of the pendulum. In other words, keep a cool head and don't let the tail wag the dog."

Bea mumbled: "I tend to blip the throttle before changing gears…"

"Six," said Alice loudly. "*The Principle of Cause and Effect*. Nothing merely happens for no reason at all. Nothing happens by chance or without explanation, unless one believes the two-bit, ha'penny Hollywood psychics in the gossip rags. Anyway, no escape from this one. Cement. If one becomes the cause, you don't suffer as someone who just reacts to circumstances. All that is done will be undone, or…something akin to that. Honestly, I've no idea what this one really means."

Bea said: "I have a sizzling suspicion that I quick-draw react too much to circumstances myself, but in my defense, most of those insane circumstances are hell on wheels. By the way, Doll, I want my latest *Confidential* and *Modern Screen* back, and *sans* lipstick stains."

"Not finished. The 'Eight Women Clark Gable Can't Do Without' article jibes with the one in *Silver Screen*. Before he signed up with the Air Corps, he and Barbara—"

"That's just *hype*. Bubblehead Stanwyck is out, super-smart Heddy Lamarr is in, she's a gifted scientist, and that slob loves an egghead brunette. The only real truth is—"

"That's quite *enough*," said Bernie. "Hollywood aside, let's apply *Cause and Effect* as best we can. That's the whole point of this review. A greater understanding of what we're truly up against is paramount. We're not going into the mountains to…"

Alice whisper-yelled: "Gene Tierney!"

"No, he's shagging *Lauren Bacall*, and mostly in a back seat. Put two blankets in the back of a wood-sided shooting brake and—"

In Bea's face, Bernie yelled: "…spy on goat herders! It's *station wagon*, not a dumbass 'shooting brake.' Are we done for today, twit-twins?"

The girls squirmed. "Gossip's more important in wartime," mumbled Alice. "Just connecting grapevine dots, that's all. Practice."

Bea snapped: "Pssh!" "Stop pssh-ing me!"

Gwafa stood, wiping his pants of dust. "I will go last, *monsieur*. Seven. *The Principle of Gender*. Both the masculine and feminine exist in all equally. To mix this wisdom with the other principles will give you an expanded toolbox from which you can repair many things. Masculine conquers and progresses, the feminine is receptive, sacred, protective, and treasured, she nourishes all life." He looked to the girls and blinked. "Just as…*Madame* Bacall does with *Monsieur* Bogart."

"Yay-y-y!" They chorused, clapping. "As it should be," said Alice.

"The masculine high-compression piston inside the feminine cylinder block, eh, Gwafa?" asked Bea.

He laughed. "You have a gifted imagination, *madame*."

"But she's no *gift*. Again, tread the middle path to self-mastery," said Bernie. "We're all addicted to extremes. My Jewish friends Marvin and Lisa back home have a good Yiddish-y saying when confronted with such." He shrugged. "Eh, what're ya gonna do?'"

"All that from a *goyisher faygala* with an Ibis head mask," mumbled Bea.

Bernie snapped: "I heard that."

"Don't *kibitz* around, Beansy. And this war is the embodiment of too much masculine force. The balance between these energies is what's desperately needed," laughed Alice. "We need more fillies in the game."

Bernie snapped fingers. "Actually, that's well said, Miss Bacall."

"You mean to tell me, Herr Ibis, that if there were an equal share of women as men in this war, we might have a shorter one?" asked Bea.

"That's a damn good notion. Maybe so," said Bernie. "Back home the Army is training women ferry pilots and mechanics by the score."

"Call Beverly Hills, Tremont 5467 collect, Ava Gardner. She'll round up the poolside gals," whispered Bea.

Alice hissed: "How did you get that private number?" "Pssh!"

Gwafa shook his head. "There is too much anger and confusion in this war, too many lies and deceptions. Nothing is as it seems."

"Agreed." Bernie reached into his haversack and gave him a book. "In addition, some wisdom from the wise man Averroes; it'll help. I want you three to review it all during our trip. Otherwise…we may all go mad with frustration, disillusionment, confusion, and fury, gossip or no gossip. Wisdom and esoteric knowledge on the fly aren't easy or efficient, but we must bend our intellects to the grindstone. Try to get a firm grip on all of this stuff, the big-picture from high up, that's why we're going to climb this pebble here."

"*What?*" asked Alice.

Bea looked up at the crumbling magnificence before her. "No way in hell I'm climbing this sunbaked crumbling biscuit. And yet, have to say, these piles are quite the impressive engineering achievement. Imagine the world they inhabited all those millennia ago when these parts were green and lush, canals and moats gushing with water. Priests and initiates inside travelling Astrally sky-high on opiated Lotus blossom tea, loads of electrical power for everything conceivable, fertile plains of crops to the horizon, a utopian paradise perhaps. It's all…a bit sad really."

Bernie touched a foundation stone, hoping for some sort of divine wisdom to rush through his arm. "They remind me of a haunting sight years ago, rusting steam tractors and old mining equipment in the Rockies, derelicts of a lost age dissolving slowly in a green desert of tall grass and aspen trees."

Gwafa looked up. "An engineering and mathematical achievement beyond imagination for so long ago. How was it done?"

"Acoustic levitation I think," said Bernie. "Electromagnetic power most likely relayed by large obelisks—lightning rods and antennas if you will—were probably used to power soundwave drills and saws. In effect, they had power tools, iron, and hard alloys. A simple type of antigravity papyrus mat for moving stones—just a tap of the long tuning forks and away you go. These 'scepters' split huge blocks if they knew exactly where to place them, and the forks created standing waves from the tines, they even used wires to connect multiple forks for greater power; pretty simple but elegant science. Iron pipes created the bore holes like the ones I saw in the museum. Diamond drills maybe, I don't know, but the evidence is right here."

"They had batteries too, didn't they?" asked Alice.

Bernie nodded. "Indeed. Maybe even electric lights of a sort. I believe it was an egalitarian effort in an age of peaceful freedom, a communal project for the benefit of all. After the Great Flood, the Atlantean survivors *must* have implemented traditional and harmonious matriarchal rule with both sexes equal; it was maintained for a long while—the age of Thoth, 'thrice great,' but the Hermetic wisdom that moved east to Persia and India and north to Europe was purposely lost over the centuries in the quagmire of war, foul regimes, enforced religions and their inflexible dogma. A Sufi elder once told me the darkness moves like a well-trained sniper in the tall grass, slow as molasses, drawing little or no attention, patient, steady, unrelenting. No one notices until it's far too late."

Alice wiped her sun-cheaters with a silk hanky. "So-o-o, once again…you *really* believe that Aryan galactic spacemen from the Alderbaran star system, after landing at the poles of course, set up a secret underground facility under this area eons ago as a base of operations for the entire planet? One that communicates to the Thule and Vril Societies? Honestly, it's a bit of a stretch for—"

"It's *madness*, all of it," spat Bea. "I think the SS and Himmler made up that fairy tale as a way to get more funding from the Reichstag. Though I concede Hitler may have been hatched from a giant Martian spider egg."

Gwafa waved his Australian-style hat at some flies. "I am not so sure, *mesdames*. Many sacred texts tell of gods, angels, demons, and Nephilim that fell from the sky to help create mankind in their image. We are all blind to the truth, whatever it may be. One Qu'ran passage reads: '*The creation of the heavens and the Earth is greater than the creation of mankind, however…most of mankind knows not.*'"

Bea rolled her eyes. "Oh, please…"

Alice pinched her. "Don't you go and piss in everyone's oatmeal with—" "It's rubbishing nonsense I tell—"

"*Madame*, you should be more open to—"

Bernie raised his voice considerably. "What the *hell?* This war has exposed some of our genuine cosmic reality, did so in Los Angeles, all over the newsreels and radio—you all saw them. It's like the time I briefed some lead-bottomed top brass and puffy senators back in the States—confused, ignorant, and religion-addled minds as shallow as the flats in East Galveston Bay, flys unzipped with their shriveled dicks in their hands, whimpering and bitching that it's all 'out of their league.' But *you* three Redfish? Really? With everything you've learned so far?"

Alice said: "Yes, but I don't think it's the right—" Bea pointed. "She's—"

"Look around us, *see* anything interesting? Here we are on this great big blue, green, and sand-tan marble flying through space and time at a billion miles per hour revolving around in a solar system amongst countless others in a universe with trillions of galaxies. Trillions! Who thought of all that? Allah is the cosmos, and the cosmos is us—*everything*. It's flat obvious Mother Earth has been *Grand Central Station* for hundreds of millions of years, pretty darn nice spot, and look at all the swell ancient megalithic constructions that are impossible to build today with all our fancy gear. The biggest Navy shipbuilding crane back in Newport News couldn't handle the 800-ton foundation blocks underneath the three big pyramids, ever notice those? What about the 1600-ton ones over in Baalbek? Not exactly something the tourist guides expand upon, now is it? Who really built the Panama canal and the Suez? On ancient maps there they are, plain as day, all we did was dig them out a little, but nobody in scientific officialdom likes that Whitman's Sampler chocolate box because it has a scantily-clad, wide-eyed Pandora on it stuffing her mouth high on cannabis oil extract."

Bea interrupted: "Well at least she's having a jolly ol'—"

Bernie exploded. "What's the *big deal* I ask? We've been conditioned by a conformist society, crapper schools, and false religious beliefs to somehow, some way, believe we're unique in the cosmos—*cowshit*! How self-centered and stupid are we? Look at the diversity among us, the Eskimo to the Aborigine, the hummingbird to the condor, the giraffe to the goddam Komodo Dragon. Trees, flowers, plants, fish, mammals, snakes, and insects so varied and numerous we're still recording them day after day in the damn Amazon. All that junk was brought here stick by stick, bug by bug from out there yonder by mostly friendly people. The ancients knew all this, it was just a simple part of their lives. Who's a space-man? Space-*woman*? Can any of us tell who's who? Around here on walls, Akhenaten is carved as being twelve feet tall with an elongated skull and face, his children and wife Nefertiti the same, and even taller Osiris is painted with greenish-blue skin, and don't give me that lame 'ancient artist's impression' excuse again, they knew *exactly* what they were portraying." He pointed at the stones.

"These…people…weren't…*stupid*. It's right in front of us but most don't see, or even *want* to. Are we truly narcissistic enough to say that unless you're born on this rock you're an other-world interloper not worthy of our attention, interaction, or friendship? A despoiling raider like Buck Rodgers' *Killer Kane*? Flash Gordon's *Ming the Merciless*? Read the Book of Enoch, *The Watchers*—guess who! If it's true there are civilizations of folks in vast caverns underneath us in Ultima Thule or shitting Agartha, should we shun them as tunnel-boring outsiders too? Always the rock-headed cynic, aren't we, Bea? Enough. End of story. Confirmed. We are all one. We are *all* star beings made of common stardust, light, and consciousness, all equal denizens of the universe. I *think* therefore I *am*."

"I *drink* therefore I *am* not," spat Bea. "Ol' Flash is a bit of all right, eh?" Alice nodded in agreement. "Oh, hmm…"

Bernie kicked a load of sand hard. "Look at all these incredible structures, they knew precisely what they were building, every last sacred cubit's worth, just imagine what's out there in the galaxy? Benevolent pyramid unions? Engineers creating stars and planets on their own dime for the sheer fun of it? Use your heads, use your imaginations, there's obviously a hefty bunch of star people who've taken a keen interest in this war for their own agendas, of which I surmise…there…are…*many*! All accounts state that most of the Anunnaki were not kind and generous, they genetically created a bunch of us as slaves, as cattle, as sex objects, as a commodity. So deflate your egos and get a grip on the reality we have because it's changing fast. But don't go round pointing judgmental fingers someday at other folks from 'outta town' that look and speak different from you, or even dismissing their right to exist at all without first remembering The Law of One, the bedrock basis for all wisdom teachings—or don't you get that clever shit? What you seek maybe seeking *you*. Do I make myself fucking *clear*?"

"*Oui, monsieur*."

Bea threw a pebble to the dust. "As mud, Herr Merciless Mingo." "Well, one would just have to question some of the—"

"Want more? Do you? *Huh*?" With great emotion, Bernie relayed the contents of File B over several minutes. "And that load of burning hay comes from FDR and Admiral King, so pull your collective heads out of your collective asses and grow up. That's my and the ONI's drunken *Gift of the Lampshade*, so take it to heart. This is classified information that's *above* the American atomic program, but I don't care that my orders said I can't share with the other school kids, oh-h-h no. In my book you three are more than worthy, much more so than the lazy, myopic four-star generals and admirals back home polishing their seats and covering their heads with burlap sacks hoping it'll all just go away, the bomber pilots just *hallucinating* the Foos from lack of rest. The top twelve scientists back home all agree with what I'm saying, all of them—Oppy, von Neumann, Van Bush, Einstein, John Trump, Lloyd Berkner, Al Loomis, etcetera.

"Yes, I know it sounds Hollywood crazy, but put it all in context; the SS is getting hush-hush advisory help from a select group of fascist Aldebaran Aryans. The Germans aren't stupid and we would do the same, that's the *official* word, and who knows what information they're getting from others with an interest in this killer-diller conflict? My guess is the Anunnaki, Indian Naga half-serpents too, and all courtesy of the sniveling Vril mystics and psychics probably, horse trading under the table with everyone's life in the flippin' balance. No one cares about anything but their own *ass*. What did that drunken Shäfer tell you that day in Austria in his office when he was groping you? About the, uh, the–the *currency*?"

Bea shut a book with a *slap*. "He said…that *genetics* are the top-shelf barter goods of the cosmos, the real treasure of the gods, he thought. All the rest of it is secondary stuff: diamonds, coffee, copper, cocoa, corn, gold…"

Gwafa asked: "Drinking chocolate? But—"

"*Genetics*, as in bodies, blood, and parts, like from a *chicken farm!*" Bernie said angrily. "It's an unpopular and untidy hypothesis back in Washington, but I stood up at a closed meeting and said that I think missing prisoners, war refugees, and children disappear without a trace a little too *conveniently* and often for my taste—the classified historical records backed me up. All I received in return was silence, the implications too horrifying and indigestible, 'too big of a fish to reel in' a gutless senator said to me later. We four know what the SS is up to now at the death camps—bizarre genetics, twins, mothers, daughters, horrifying experiments on human lab rats by the thousands, you've all read the foul reports, and they've only just *started* the process. Just a coincidence my fellow Jungians? I smell a sleazy galactic black market for slaves, genetics, and fresh meat, *don't* all of you? No? Too wild of an *assertion*? All through recorded history there's always been one down here, everywhere, why not out there? *Law of Correspondence*—put it to use. A minority of selfish assholes amongst a cosmic sea of higher dimensional love and benevolence. 'As above, so below,' kids. And don't ever talk about any of this shit with others, *ever*, or each of us will be silently shot in our beds by our own people, *understand?*

Christ, Bea, you were trained and schooled in some of this in the damned SS!"

Bea took a firm tone of authority. "Trained, yes, but training is not *believing*. We were forced to learn a lot of confusing pagan stuff and occult things, sky-high on narcotics, insomnia, and severe stress. Shäfer and others only alluded to Anunnaki-this and Aldebaran-that, dragons and griffons, fairies and goblins, no *questions* asked, no *answers* given. Gang raped, starved, brainwashed, and beaten senseless we were. Not exactly a comfortable mountain mystery school with fountains, pillows, and palms, everyone singing and dancing into the incense-scented night to soothe the enlightened soul. Trance state, Nazi State, state of bewilderment. My fine point is, I don't know *what* to believe anymore. No one does. So kindly go fuck yourself, Herr Pyramid." *And they say I'm mad...*

Frustrated, Bernie slowly put his back to them, arms outstretched on the massive stones. "Christ, I just..." A minute of refreshing silence passed as a small breeze cooled them.

"Beans?" asked Alice casually, peeling another cracked nail. "*What?*"

A long pause as a nail end was successfully chewed. "Kindly give Rodgers the benefit." She sighed. "Fine."

Alice nudged her the way she always had since childhood. "Fine." "And dandy."

Gwafa pointed to his head rapidly. "*Oui, certainement–certainement.* I remember the Dogon tribesmen back in Timbuktu who visited there, they said the great central sun of the cosmos shines its light onto the star Sirius, a focal point for the light of Allah in our galaxy, *The One*, the release of light and love for all, and it was the home of their ancestors. They wear many masks and have year-long festivals to celebrate their forefathers from the stars, and the wisdom they gave. This is all...making some sense, perhaps."

Bernie bowed to him, palms up. "A wise man speaks in humble tones. The Egyptian *Ark of the Contract* was representative of the contract between Earth and the star people of Sirius. Then they—"

"*Enough.*" Bea got up, deciding to take a long walk to clear her besieged and overcrowded mind.

"Where are *you* going? I'm not *finished.*" yelled Bernie, temper aglow.

"Science fiction is not hard science, *Buck-O!*"

"The hell it isn't—it's science *fact*. Science fiction doesn't exist, it never did. Jesus, of all people. Grow up and conquer your *fear*, Lady Chickenshit. You're scared of the truth!"

"What *truth?*" Furious, Bea pitched her full half-gallon canteen to his chest point-blank, hard. She then pushed him back with both arms with all her might. "What's *eating* you, anyway?"

Bernie reeled. "*Me?* What the hell do you mean?" Alice scolded: "Beans…"

Bea pointed here and there. "You know exactly what I *mean*. Except for Dolly, here, we've all seen combat and felt its resulting *fatigue*. Death and fire, blood and guts. The school of hard knocks is not a tuition-free institution, yes? But there's something else eating at you like a *cancer*. Well? I know you better than anyone else round here, maybe everywhere—lover, friend, and foe. I don't care a fat fig if you've chopped away our comfortable parquet floor of reality, it was rotten to the pegs to begin with. Now, I'll ask again, what's *bothering* you? What scarab crawled up your arse and sunk in its teeth? Lost a bundle at strip poker with a spacewoman? Got a man pregnant? Eat some rotten overdone Komodo steaks?"

"*Beans…*"

She twirled. "No, no, no, don't *defend* him on this! He's been wound so tight it's gnawing at all of us too, even McMaster said so to me, and we have a mission coming up, a bad one, a terrific explore in the hills of Alexander's soddy imagination, I reckon. Bit red in the teeth? Claws? Come off it, Bernie, tell mommy your precious cosmic sob story. None of the wisdom adding up? Feeling too old for a hike at sixty? Hair going gray? Bollocks going soft in the wind? Burning up from airship fever? *Well?*"

Gwafa held her back. "Please *madame*, easy…"

Bea became frantic. "No, no I will *not* take it easy, thank you very much. You don't know him like *I* do. He always holds something back like a *good* little ONI boy, a *good* little tin soldier, even if it means our very lives. We don't mean shite to him or his Yank leash-holders, we're expendable contractors with contracts up to our ears. He's a filthy—"

Alice slapped her. "*Beans!*"

Fists balled, Bea stared at her, shocked, barely able to contain her wrath.

At this, Bernie slowly sat in a chair and put his aching head in his hands, shaking, the Hoover Dam he had erected in his mind and soul began to crack, leak, then gush. He began to weep uncontrollably, unregretfully, as the edifice slowly burst. Grabbing two handfuls of hot sand and squeezing hard, purified grief and despair oiled his face.

Alice rubbed his shoulders softly. "Easy, old chappy, she didn't mean it…"

•••

Forty minutes later as the sun began to set, Bernie finished up his Portugal story, eyes red and hollow. "I only gave the facts in my report, not…" He gulped hard. "The colorful details. McMaster didn't know, no one knew, except for Hess, because…because *he* understood. Funny, the statue of Hekate and her handmaidens, her owl, the gear wheel…I remember now that I've seen it before, an exact copy. It's…on the top façade of The Museum of Industry next to the Smithsonian in Washington, a stone's throw from the Capitol building. She represents enforced ignorance, total control, darkness over all by the hidden elite few in the Anunnaki social club. It's right there for the public to see in plain sight under some sort of esoteric cosmic law or some such, but so very few of us do. How…bitterly ironic."

After biting her tongue bloody in order to keep steady, Alice slowly walked away and threw up, leaning on the big stones, coughing. The gruesome enormity of it all tearing at her insides, all the strange dots having connected at last.

In tears, Bea hugged and kissed him. "Sorry," she whispered. "Love you."

Gwafa had no words of comfort to give, he just laid his wide hand on a shoulder and squeezed, a gentle, manly connection of affection and respect between hardened warriors that meant the world. He could tell that Bernie usually took life by the foreskin and thrashed it just like he did, but this time the war and its unspeakable peripheral horrors had turned the tables.

Silent, mind far away, Bernie stared into the infinite pink distance for a lengthy period of heavy mental solitude, as if the answers to everything lay somewhere just beyond the vaporous desert's edge, unobtainable and elusive, a stunning white bird—fleet, svelte, broad wings—that is never seen up close or caught. A regal legend born of pastel twilight and pure thoughts.

Canteen slung, hat perched, Bea attached the rope around her waist and began the difficult and dangerous climb at the northeast corner. There was an easier passage on the southwest corner, but she didn't dare suggest it.

Gwafa went next, Alice followed him.

A minute later, Bernie attached the tarred bitter end and climbed one handhold at a time.

An hour or so later they all converged at the top to watch the sun slowly sink behind the infinite horizon, the surroundings painted a surreal deep golden orange. Not one word was said.

Beautiful, thought Lutz, wiping a tear. *Just beautiful.*

15

In the just-beginning lilac twilight, Bernie undid his rope, coiled it, then plopped it into the back of the Dodge with his rucksack. "Need a smoke and a piss." He walked off and turned a corner at the pyramid's edge.

Alice and Bea broke down the tent while Gwafa stored the canteens and books in the truck. Suddenly, he reared up and ran. "*Non!*"

Bea locked eyes on Alice. "Oh, *fuck* all."

"*No-o-o-o-o!*" Gwafa sprinted with every last ounce of speed he possessed and tackled Bernie, lifting him slightly off the ground before thudding the earth with their combined mass, the round from the Colt .45 auto burrowing into Bernie's head then hitting the stones beyond with a powerful *snap* and a *whir-r-r-r*.

Bea slid to a stop, removed the pistol from Bernie's limp hand, cleared the action, and dropped the clip into her palm. "*Gods*, no!"

Alice arrived with the medical kit and examined the wound with a flashlight. "Out cold. Just a deep graze, hold this torch for me. We're lucky, no skull penetration."

Bea looked to them with a face of pure determination. "No *word* about this… to *anyone*."

16

At nine forty-four p.m., a doctor arrived at the MI-6 mansion to examine Bernie's head in the small, makeshift infirmary via McMaster's strict order. Bea, Alice, and Gwafa sat on a Turkish inlaid wood bench reading newspapers and magazines next to the medicine cabinet; the newly-whitewashed room, smelling of onions, was formerly a root cellar.

"You slipped and hit a stone, is that it?" asked the doctor, removing Alice's dressing and probing and cleaning the wound, a big black bag of medicinals and bandages astride him. "He should have been taken directly to hospital."

Alice barked: "Orders. No unsecured hospitals, no reports, no German spies lurking about dressed as doctors or nurses with Scopolamine syringes. I did the best I could. Sulfa and ointment."

Slumped and dizzy, Bernie popped two more opiate-laced aspirin from a paper cup. "Just an accident, Doc, slipped…stones 'n shit…"

He began to set stitches. "A very…*precise* accident, I see." "I would say *ouch*, but I'm too s-s-stoned," mumbled Bernie.

"Prognosis?" asked Alice, not looking up from her ancient windmills article in *Practical Mechanics* magazine.

The doctor exhaled in exasperation. "No fractures of the skull, but I know a *bullet wound* with powder burns when I see one, young lady. This man needs two weeks in bed for recovery. He'll have memory loss, ringing of the ears, nausea…" He applied ointment, bandaged his head, and picked up the phone. "Orderly, please."

Sergeant Tillings came in and helped Bernie to the door.

The doctor pointed. "Put him in a bedroom upstairs for a few hours. See that he sleeps as much as possible. Lots of cold water and hot beef broth."

"Yes sir. Come along now, Captain Rodgers, that's a good lad."

Alice closed the door softly.

"Something amiss with one of you?" he asked, pulling off his stethoscope and tidying up.

"Plenty." Bea got up and folded her September 1933 *Vogue*. She smiled, and said in a hushed tone to his face: "Here's our problem, *Herr doktor*. We have a fun secret mission for the war effort coming up. We need him. It's crucial. If you decide to tell the Brigadier and Admiral he's not physically or mentally fit, they'll scrub it. That…would make me cry."

"I don't know why he would—"

"Dr. Walker, is it?" Alice placed a hand on his shoulder. "War's on full boil. We may lose. Rommel may sweep into Cairo for a cocktail. How's your…German and Italian coming along?" She kissed his cheek affectionately and put her head on his shoulder. "Japanese?"

He removed his specs. "Well, I would think…now look, just what are you three playing at? Hmm? I have orders from above to follow like everyone else. Now move out of my way. No one can dictate any—"

Gwafa stood, guarding the door with his back like the Rhodes Colossus. "We are all in this together, *monsieur le docteur*. *Nous sommes tous unis*."

"I said get out of my way!"

"That's right, we're all united in this effort, don't you agree?" asked Bea. She then revealed her Colt .45 and caressed the length of it under the light. "Tough going out there in the sandy sticks. All hands on deck 'n' whatnot, eh?"

"I don't care what's going on out—"

Alice slid her hand towards his crotch, speaking as if a little girl. "I'll say you tried to grope me with rubber gloves, that is, after you drugged and buggered me silly."

"Why *you*…"

"Brass tacks." Bea gently rubbed the pistol on his quivering forehead and looked him in the eye. "You *sure* you want to work for the Nazis dissecting children and pregnant mothers for the rest of your days?"

•••

After a lunch briefing on Iraqi culture and history, the three of them sat in McMaster's office playing Gin Rummy.

Admiral Cunningham and McMaster came in and sat down. They both eyed the three as if naughty schoolchildren caught in some sort of grievous prank.

"Five days' rest, *then* we re-evaluate him," blared McMaster sternly. "Obviously we've no *choice* in the matter. In the meantime, you three will have another chat with

Parkes-Jackson on ancient history every morning at nine precisely, then you'll brush up on small arms, short and especially long-range, wireless, overland and aerial navigation, aeronautical engineering, and lastly some bloody *physics*. I want all of you proficiently cross-trained on every single weapon and piece of gear, especially the sniper rifles, 500 rounds per person, bullseyes, all. This is a complex and demanding mission. No intoxicants whatsoever."

"Do we make ourselves *perfectly* clear?" demanded the admiral.

"Yes sir," they chorused.

•••

August 14

An angry Welsh sergeant-major stood over them at the desert firing range. "Breathe steady, damn your souls! I want dead center, black-boy. You lot too, you blazin' fuckin' she-hes, cycle them bolts. Smooth trigger fingers. Combat conditions!" He threw sand and rocks at them while another soldier fired in the air over and over. "Aim dead on, you swarthy gash-lickers! Windage, height, ranges set, crosshairs on."

Gwafa advanced with the heavy BAR on his hip, firing automatic five-round bursts at man-sized targets with a Malian yell. Then it was his turn on the sniper rifle.

The Sergeant-major yelled: "That's not good enough, not by a long yard. Another million rounds until you three prick-tasters make it right!"

Bea ejected a .30-06 shell and loaded another stripper clip. Thinking of her training years ago in Scotland, she whispered to Alice: "All this seems eerily familiar."

"I'll bet," whispered Alice as she struggled to lift the BAR.

•••

Four days later at 7 p.m., Bea trotted up the stairs at The Anubis Hotel, and with her key that he gave her, opened the door to Bernie's suite. She and Alice had taken turns sleeping in his room, that was the order given. Now narcotic-free, Bernie would be more lucid, but so far he hadn't uttered a word to anyone.

He was half asleep in polka dot pajamas, the radio on low playing jazz. International newspapers covered the bed and a tray of food from the night before sat on a table beside him, flies buzzing. He wore a silk paisley eye mask on top of his reading glasses, the frame of which peeked out. The rumble of cars, lorries, and people could be heard from the open windows, and a ceiling fan whirred on high setting, but did little to counter the day's dry heat, which was now finally easing.

Bea placed the tray in the hallway and settled into the stuffed chair beside the bed.

Pulling a book from her father's old briefcase that she had carried here and there since Wycombe Abbey, she opened *The Tale of Peter Rabbit*, fluttering pages and igniting her childhood innocence and wonder, a luxurious feeling she hadn't allowed herself for years.

Bernie awoke from his half-slumber and removed a crumpled sheet of *The Washington Post* from his stomach, tipping up his eye mask. "N-n-now...what?"

"Finally, Thoth speaks. When I was sick or sad as a child, Mumbly would read Mrs. Potter's books to me. Somehow they always helped. Away we go. '*Once upon a time there were four little Rabbits and their names were Flopsy, Mopsy, Cottontail, and Peter. They lived with their mother in a sand-bank, underneath the root of a very big fir-tree. Now, my dears, said old Mrs. Rabbit one morning, you may go into the fields or down the lane, but don't go into Mr. McGregor's garden: your father had an accident there; he was put in a pie by Mrs. McGregor.*'" Bernie rolled onto his side and moaned in wildebeest fashion.

"Remember our spiritualist friend Rudolph Steiner said that evil spirits will feed off depression and blackness, so don't feed them, old boy." Bea rolled along, modifying the text for her own amusement, hoping some of the prose would filter in between his tortured ears. "'*Peter was most dreadfully frightened; he rushed all over the desert for he had forgotten his way back to the Persian Gate. He lost one of his jackboots among the cabbages, and another one amongst the Lotus flowers in the oasis pond. After losing them, he ran on four legs and went faster, so that I think he might have got away altogether if he had not unfortunately run into Flash Gordon's gooseberry space net, and got caught by the large FDR election button on his jacket. It was a U.S. Navy blue jacket with brass buttons, quite new, with his recent medal for being the most clever Rabbit amongst his naysaying family.*'"

A painful: "Ohhmmm..."

"'*Mr. McGregor came up with a Luger, which he intended to whack Peter with the handle, but Peter wriggled out of the net just in time, leaving his prized jacket behind him.*

And Peter rushed into the tool shed, and jumped into a Tiger tank. It would have been a beautiful thing to hide in, if it didn't have so much sand inside.'"

A breeze blew in through the porch's open French doors, ruffling the sheets of newspaper, testing their poor aerodynamics in case a few decided to take flight. One did, and Bea caught it on the tip of her shoe.

"'*He tried to put his foot upon Peter, who jumped out of a window, upsetting three date palms. The window was too small for Mr. McGregor, and he was tired of running after Peter.*

After a time Peter began to wander about, going—lippity-lippity—not very fast, and looking all round. He found an immense door in a temple wall, but it was locked, and there was no room for a fat little rabbit to squeeze underneath the 500-ton polygonal blocks.'"

Bernie made no sound other than his breathing. She gently curled up next to him on the bed, sharing warmth, and kept on with a very soft voice.

•••

An hour later, chilled, Bea shut the book. She went into the bathroom and filled the tub with hot water. "C'mon. Let's get you up. Time for a wash. You reek."

Dizzy, he struggled. "N-no, want a…bourbon."

"Up! And no gin-juice, it'll make your pain and melancholia worse when it wears off, Herr Steiner." Helping him out of his dots and into the bath, she found a sea sponge and began to gently soap him up, the bruises that Gwafa had given him still blue. She could tell his vibratory spirit, his frequency, was at a low point, the oscillations rolling swells of stormy ocean. She kissed his forehead and sang her song about the seven cats and seven sacks, the one she would sing to her boys back at the orphanage in London, ones like homeless Charlie Martin who shook for hours in her arms from fear and neglect. "'*Kits, cats, sacks, and wives, how many were there going to Saint Ives?*'"

After dressing him and putting him back to bed, she called down for some mineral water, ice, fruit, and sandwiches. They both ate a little; Bea put ice in the medical rubber bag and iced his head for an hour. Soon he was out cold again, and she kissed his ear. "Love you Peter."

•••

Bea awoke on the chaise longue. She checked her watch: 6:31 a.m. In an hour she would report back for more training and lectures, which had been most intensive.

Bernie flushed the toilet and emerged fully dressed for breakfast downstairs. He fiddled with a cufflink.

"Tea 'n toast?" she asked, stretching.

He went over to the mirror to check on his still black eyes, tilting up the bandage that she had renewed from a med kit before going to bed. The wound was healing nicely, just not the one inside of him. "All right, Hopscotch, we go. I'll make it. *Finish* the damn job, I mean."

He turned to her, looking far, far older than his years. "But don't you be surprised if I decide not to come back."

17

♈

Midnight

Disguised well in indigenous robes, Prime Minister Churchill exited the privately-registered, non-governmental black Rolls-Royce—blackout headlights, hood mascot taped black—and entered the ancient mosque with three armed Egyptian bodyguards dressed in brown suits and claret fezzes. The driver guarded the car with a submachinegun. A trusted and vetted Imam led them down the long spiral stairs to the sub-sublevel and opened a heavy wooden door with a well-worn bronze key.

Churchill bowed slightly and muttered an old proverb: "'Know the world in yourself. Never look for yourself in the world, for this would be to project your illusion.'"

One of the guards translated, and the Imam bowed slightly in return, recognizing it from his youth.

In the dim oil lamplight, shadows danced along the intricate painted tiles and gold leaf of the magnificent octagonal-domed chamber that smelled sweet of incense and the ages. Attending to a small arabesque altar inlaid with ivory and rare woods was Aleister Crowley, dressed elegantly in a sharply-pressed oatmeal linen suit with a gold sash around his neck; it suspended a medallion, a rising sun symbol with the Templar hooked "X" in the center, an ancient symbol of higher knowledge kept secret. He looked tired, despondent.

Churchill sat while the guards stood by the doorway, arms crossed, pistols covertly drawn under their tight double-breasts of fine wool.

Precious moments of stillness passed.

"It's dangerous to meet here…but here I am," said Crowley, sweating in the heat. He dabbed his bald head with a red silk hanky and replaced his black pillbox hat. His eyes were dark, with bags under them sagging from struggle with the world and underworld.

Cigar was lit. "How's your health?"

Crowley coughed. He had lost much weight. "Sustainable."

Churchill blew a plume to the side so as not to sicken him further, then handed him John Dee's Speculum, a polished black mirror used for conjuring; he had liberated it from the British Museum. "I'm gladdened, old friend. We need you, history needs you, now more than ever before. How was your stay at Barrowgill?"

He beheld his sagging, aging visage and rubbed the mirror on his leg to brighten it. "Scotland was uneventful, the castle cold, clammy. Belial was unobtainable to me. Why is not clear. Dee's rituals were precise, the heavens in alignment. I am most...*bewildered.*"

"You are of the old royal bloodline. Was the Queen there with you?"

"Yes. But was quite...un-im-pressed."

"Lord Dowding and Archbishop Lang send their best, so does the rest of my salubrious 'Black Team' members, the descendants of the Orphic Circle of old. We've more dowsers and psychic assassins by the month."

A shrug. "I care not of this."

"I see. Well anyway, everyone likes your 'V' for victory finger sign. I use it to good effect."

He coughed. "Good. They should, and I knew they would."

"Speculate via Speculum. You met with Hitler twice years ago. You felt his black energy, his purified madness. Can you...enlighten me on current events as you see them?"

"A moment..." With a long match, Crowley lit two tall, thick candles at the altar, staring into one flame then the other, two pillars of light, a humble portal into unknown realms of thought and consciousness. Taking a deep breath and slowly exhaling as if tasting the atmosphere for poisons, he whisper-chanted an unintelligible poem in an unusual tongue, then said: "My liege, no guarantees exist within the rotating spheres of time and space, gravity and love, existence and nonexistence, and yet...I sense a distinct vibration in the æther." He paused, beheld the candle-lit Speculum, and gathered inner strength. He low-growled: "The rabid wolf has bitten off more flesh and bone than he can drag away to his den. Lessons will be learned, fates satisfied. Eventually the Slavic bears will devour...*him*, their strength and resolve second to none, their crack female snipers burning with the Divine Feminine, loins afire. In a dream I saw a great frozen metropolis that awaits the demon with jaws wide and black; in a pit of ruins death will ensue *en masse*, frostbite, black appendages, starvation, cannibalism. All have confirmed this in their visions, All will revel in hard-achieved balance and justice, The Law satisfied once more...and All is The *Law*." A low resonating echo ensued, a sacred octave, the chamber precisely attuned.

Churchill pondered the uplifting possibilities; he wondered if Moscow or Stalingrad were the ones seen in the visions since Sebastopol had recently surrendered to the Germans after a protracted and bitter fight. He then shifted topics. "I was rudely kept in the dark on certain particulars. The American blue file?" Winston easily recognized the hesitation, caution, and unfiltered euphoria that flowed through his personal magician as if pre-warmed intravenous drugs. Truth was at hand.

Crowley twisted his head repeatedly, eyes closed, neck vertebrae crackling slightly. "Formidable...in that it contains mostly accuracies...yet...dangerous in its naiveté." His jowls shook on the last syllable.

The Prime Minister's heart skipped and pounded. "We have a new general to take on Rommel, will he—"

"War, dust, blood, sacrifice—you already know the answers in your heart's flame, and if you do not trust your Higher Self then a negative result is almost assured. Ask me something of *importance*!" He sweetened his voice. "Ask me something of love..."

Churchill thought for a moment. "My grandniece, a mission to the Zagros. Will they achieve any—"

Crowley turned to meet his gaze, one feral animal to another. "She's supremely strong, unerringly erratic, and frighteningly fragile as I've told you, but she and the others will be supremely *tes-s-s-s-ted*. And I know the tall American, a fellow mountaineer of yore, a former young lover, an amateur follower of The Law. I've observed him of late from afar. He's inwardly wounded, outwardly scarred...but still an unbroken pillar supporting great weight, an Atlas, yet *only* at full strength in her presence, the other two members supporting flying buttresses, the blonde woman a cheetah, the blackamoor a lion. Rodgers' heart and chakras are pure hot violet and positive in vibration, perhaps far too much for a man of his ilk. On occasion emotional to a fault, and that can be...*fatal* in an unbalanced reality such as ours. Like Beatrice, Bernard is habitually stoic and irreverent in the face of pure darkness, sickeningly so, as many putrid Light Warriors tend to be when engaging in their annoying and meddling habits, though...even I concede we desperately need cosmic balance restored, and that means droves of them have awakened for work, just as that fat bitch Blavatsky had said many decades ago. Mother Earth's own vibration is on the rise as was predicted countless millennia ago, the resonance gong sounded by Herr Schumann, our ears ringing...ringing...*ringing*. The mismatched former lovers are two irregular pillars precariously supporting a crumbling edifice; an Hermeticist's erotic trance within a lucid tropical nightmare—the *both* of them."

A lengthy pause. "And?" he asked softly.

Eyes met Speculum. "I see...only vague probabilities...unclearly...they..."

"*And?*" he said angrily, causing a thundering echo.

Crowley slowly put head in hands, weeping softly. "Only if *Rodgers* survives, then so shall...they...*all*."

18

August 21
Iraq

The road from Basra had been a bumpy one; an Iraqi truck and trailer carried them to a crossroads up in the mountains twenty miles west of Yasuj on the old Royal Road.

Walking their mounts and stretching their legs, Bernie and Gwafa let the girls and their guide Nasim go on ahead; an excellent man, knowledgeable, fit, with one long eyebrow crossing his forehead. Nasim told the two girls wild tales of the mountains to pass the time, his English passable.

The six mules were packed with food, water, ropes, the two Springfield rifles, a heavy-hitting Browning Automatic Rifle with twelve 20-round magazines for Gwafa, Bernie's Thompson, an MI-6 issue long-range radio in a leather suitcase with a new liquid mercury antenna, tools, provisions dried and tinned, an electrical testing device Bernie had ordered specially-made in London, and one Leica camera. Dressed in Arab robes and Swiss climbing boots, they fit in with the landscape fairly well.

"Sure could use my old cowboy hat." Bernie knew well when it was time to get off and walk so as not to fatigue them too much. He led the fifth mule as well as his own. "I got a feel for horses and mules when I grew up on the ranch. No better education than nature, piles of shit, mountains, and farmland."

Gwafa slapped his hand on his leg. "For me the desert and the mountains of Mali and Morocco. Much to learn from. What was it like to live in a big city?"

Bernie caught eyes. "Believe it or not, for me it was hell. The death of the soul. Never could feel comfortable living in a box, no matter how fancy. Need trees, grass, birds, sunlight. Growing up privileged is nice don't get me wrong—big houses, yachts, plush beds, two wines and champagne with your buttery Dover sole, but it was still a gilded cage, a person gets soft in mind and body. I've been harassed and punished my whole life for thinking differently and being myself. I never really did fit in with the traditional elite, they...can be *boring*, self-absorbed, intolerant, and way too strict with rules and customs. I hate irrational rules. My brothers accepted me for who I am, a switch-hitting mystic gadfly, but not the rest of the family, or myopic high society for that matter." He smiled. "I needed structure. The Marines and Navy rewarded me for my diligent and loyal service, but I had to be careful not to rock the boat regarding my more...*outlandish* views. Now that boat's wrecked on a lee shore. The world's fucked up royally again and they task me with this crap, though I admit I begged for it. And so, here you are. Having fun?"

Gwafa returned the smile. "When a man drifts with the wind and ends up in jail, he learns what is truly inside of him. Punishment and solitary confinement do wonders for the soul of a young man who hated and blamed everyone else. I learned... to make peace with myself first, only then could I understand and forgive others. It is written that 'all answers lay within.'"

"I'm glad for you, I have problems forgiving others. You had a spiritual awakening most of us could only dream about. Hard knocks do wonders, I'm not kidding, pal."

"If by that...you mean I am strong from hardship, then yes. I first killed a man when I was fourteen, but I was big even then. He beat and raped my sister, so I beat him bloody, but he never woke up. That's when I ran. No looking back. As a sponge I absorbed the whole world around me. Never ask me for my real name, *monsieur*, never."

"I like 'Gwafa' anyway. Did you know that it's said the Berber people of the Atlas Mountains are said to be direct descendants of the Atlantis survivors?"

He pulled up a mule leg to inspect the hoof. "They are blond with eyes of cobalt-blue. Unique language. Yes, I remember."

Bernie shared a prized Army tropical Hershey bar especially designed for the heat.

"Did you end up in jail for stealing?"

"*Oui. Un petit avion.*" He laughed. "I read a book on how to fly and I stole it. When I landed far away in Libya I sold it to a man in the black market, but an Italian turned me in because he hated the fact that a black man could fly. After jail, I joined the French Army and became a mechanic. I could read the manuals, think independently, and that impressed them, but I was insubordinate too, 'a firebrand' they said. Officers want their men to fight and perform various duties without thinking too much. *Le capitaine* once burned all my books as punishment so I learned to be discreet. Very discreet. I then hid books in several trunks; each soldier would hide one for me at the bottom. Once a common man or woman can read, Bernard, a new world opens up and the mind follows, but that person must be careful where…" He looked around, admiring the distance and the craggy mountains. "…that leads them. This is how I feel when you and the women have shown me new wisdom, new knowledge. It is as if I am reading for the first time. My mother taught me to read and write when I was two; she died of fever five years later. I miss her."

Bernie itched his crotch. "Sorry for that. Gotta love a bookworm who can put knowledge into practice. That's the key point."

Gwafa stopped and tightened his mule's saddle strap, then looked Bernie hard in the eye. "Bea would *die* for you. Always remember that."

He became irritated. "Maybe so, but she can light my tinder like no one else." Moving on, the *clop-clop-clop* of the rhythmic hooves soothed them.

Gwafa said: "Her passion rules her sometimes, that is her stone to carry. Perhaps both of you have not found the inner calm you talk so much about. If you let others truly anger you, let them under your skin like a burrowing insect, you are not the master of yourself. I learned to be soft spoken and patient in prison to get what I wanted, needed, or the guards would rule me with a club while I starved alone in an iron box. Pain, fear, and hunger are together a great teacher, the best. *Pas mieux*."

"A philosopher and an aircraft thief, what could be better? Oh-h-h, I guess you have a damned point."

"The truth is we are all scared. We three *petites souris* were frightened in the tank at Siwa, but we found inner strength and did our jobs anyway; to face our fear with dignity and courage is what is important, to fight against the enemy odds, and Bea showed me that in a way I never knew. As for us today, four mice can cause panic for an elephant."

Bernie looked up at the unforgiving sun. "I know what you mean. I feel a strange inner calm in hot close combat."

Gwafa pointed. "We must keep an eye on Alice, she has not known the painful sting, the look in a man's eyes when you kill him."

He nodded.

Once they reached the top of the hill, a green valley with a small river surrounded by tall rocky peaks lay beneath them. Thorny shrubs tore at them, and walnut and pistachio trees dotted the landscape, the soft smell of them lingering in the breeze. In the distance a large town revealed itself from the morning's mist, peaceful, tranquil.

A lone French truck, an antique from before the last war, packed with sheep, slowly passed and ignored them; it had been two days since they had seen another; a boy waved. Most of the traffic had been friendly and helpful local people on foot or donkey, the war far away.

"Shepherds, no worries." Bernie then caught everyone up. He spread out a map on his saddle. "Let's head north, Nasim, get off the main road. I want to camp well north of Yasuj. If the Germans are up here and sniffing around, even in town buying goat's milk or lamb shanks, I don't want them getting a whiff or gander at us."

Nasim, short, thin, and wiry, replied: "*Nem sayidi*. A difficult trail. Steep, narrow." Looking over everyone, Bea panted under her black headscarf. "Well, we're not exactly First Skinner's Horse, that's for sure."

So did Alice, her scarf white with roses. "Nor an East India Company misadventure. Stunning view though. Pretty." They all moved along.

Bea unslung her canteen. "Rodger's Queen's Own Rangers on the prowl. Need a sippy."

"You look like you've lost a hunnerd and found a sixpence. Look old thing, go… just go and walk with him. Bend yourself to it. Kiss his falcon and make nice."

Bea saddled her canteen and led her mule. "Fine. My gunpowder lights easily I suppose. The canteen bit was overwrought." Shortish, she went astride the six-foot-three Yank colossus. "Lovely day for a highland stroll."

"How's your stamina?" Bernie asked. "Good. You?"

He grimaced. "What do you want?"

She rubbed the mule's neck. "The night before we pinched the Tiger, I fell asleep and had a dream."

"That's nice." He said it indifferently, coldly.

She pushed him slightly. "After I kick you in the plums, kindly go fuck yourself down a corpse-poisoned well. You never listen to me, not really, not attentively, but you will now by Zeus." She related her story of the night before the tank battle. "Lutz's in my head a lot helping me. Drives me bonkers, my deepest insecurities made manifest."

He puffed. "Lutz? Why are you telling me this weird horseshit?"

"*My* weird horseshit? What about all *yours*, Butch? Train robbers and airships, balloons and buffoons, trysting at 200 mph with—"

"Fair enough."

"Anyway, I wanted to explain myself. Spoke in haste days ago. It's not that I fully disbelieved you at all, it's just…that I wanted to get your goat, as it were."

He leered at her. "Oh?" Then fed a morsel to his mule, homesick for the peaceful, green Rockies and North American animals of all kinds. "I see, you were only trying to be under—"

She stopped. "Look, *you*. Something was eating at your soul's silk lining and it took me, yes *me* to wring it out of your tough ol' hide, you obstinate old boar. Aura and chakra cleansing the hard way à la Beansy. Sorry about the poor nippers, but now we all painfully understand the gist. No one should be beset by such horrors, but you can take it. You're not the only one who's *suffered*. Drummy's had it posh, but Gwafa sure has over his lifetime. She and I have lost our close-knits Dee and Peach. And while you and Aunt Walter were loo-shagging in Munich at the Sumerian Brotherhood those years ago nightclubbing it in a plush Maybach, I was being brainwashed silly in Austria, skiing and drinking blood in between squeezing off bursts of an MG-34 machinegun whilst my Alpine-chilled nipples hardened into diamonds as a sub-par SS *wunderkinder*! And to top it off I snuffed my Aryan husband as my first kill on the run, sorry, *on the lam* in your parlance. Lost my beloved Olaf and dear ol' Stick getting home, and ended up a fag of broken twigs in a basket for six months in searing pain whilst drowning in morphine and stomach-churning penicillin. Took months before I could even walk right or eat again without retching. And I was the *lucky* one, most of the young RN chaps were there in Scapa hospital nearly burned alive; I still hear their screams. You're not the only one who's felt like ruddy suicide. Get over it, and right this damn minute."

A few minutes went by, the words solidifying in his mind. "Suppose you're right. It was killing me inside." He then smiled at her. "You know, you look good in a veil."

She posed. "One tries to look one's best given the unfashionable circumstances."

Bernie tried to stifle it but couldn't, laughing.

"See? Can't be sore at me for very long, ol' soggy sahib. I'm your muse, a medieval sorcerer's assistant in desert couture."

"An alchemical pain in the ass." "'Tis true, that."

•••

Come night, they stopped. Bernie pulled out his compact sextant to get an exact position.

He penned notes in his Abercrombie and Fitch leather notebook. "Know where we are?" asked Bea.

Scribbling ensued. "Mmm, pretty close. Did you notice something in Yasuj today by binocular?"

She adjusted her small lantern. "Just the mosque. Incredibly fetching for a small town. Ornate in the extreme. Expensive."

"You've read a lot about T.E. Lawrence. He knew the Arab people and was accepted as one of them."

She longed for a potent French cigarette. "Yes, he was a spy like us in 1914, the Palestine Exploration Fund, an archeologist too. He'd been to Petra in Trans-Jordan, knew some of the deep secrets of the ancient world, and was amazed at the many rock-cut caves and ruins he found. I think he knew the boffins were lying to us about history. Walked all over Syria as a young man, and was obsessed with the Crusades and Knights Templar. A free-thinking romantic."

"Like you and me?"

She smiled. "Also the patron saint of Hermetic and Arab wisdom in my sticky-page book. He had an innate sense of his destiny as a desert fighter and hero against the Johnnyturks; he manifested it so, and was known as 'the man with the gold,' since he and his Arabs stole so much from them. Must have been a desert chap in a former life, or had many lifetimes out here. Cut the spine of the Turk's rail lines, guerilla tactics with the Bedouins, quite handy with Gelignite and Rolls-Royce armored cars—oh, he loved those alright. All our fighting tactics in the Middle East are credited to him. His unique talent was finding the right people with special skills that could get an impossible job done."

It was his turn to smile. "Similar to yours truly?"

She bumped hips. "Hardly. But it's a sad legacy that we Brits let the Arabs down at the end of the war. No Arab independent nation to be had, only English and Frenchy colonies, an aged policy that fed well of British bigotry. Hope it won't happen again, but I fear it may. Lawrence was then on seen as an embarrassment, a dangerous thinker. Sound familiar? Secret politics destroyed him, the brass hats victorious as ever. Poppy told me all that, his stint in Egypt was as indecorously horrid as mine, worse even; Poppy and

Lawrence were both friends with Middle East explorer Gertrude Bell, another girlhood hero of mine. She set up the Baghdad Museum after the last war, clever lassie."

"I didn't know all that."

"Parkes-Jackson told me the *Kahnnhar* said that the peoples of the desert, especially the ones here in Mesopotamia, are the protectors of vast knowledge, wisdom, and cosmic treasures known or unknown. A people, culture, and land to be conquered only at great cost if at all."

He sighed. "I agree, Lawrence was a fellow radical. He knew in the end it wasn't a desert war to be won, but an Aladdin's Cave to protect, and ultimately possess. We must take to heart his twenty-seven points for British officers in the desert. Have you read his book *The Seven Pillars of Wisdom*?"

"Long while back. Pretty sturdy reading. Had to read it three times before I got the gist. He was keen on palmy cosmopolitan Damascus as a pillar. Didn't work well." She took a last bite of her dinner. "Crikes, I've had enough Bully Beef and beans to turn the stomach of a shire horse."

"Be honest. Do you think we're out here chasing only shadows and legends?"

Bea looked to Alice and Gwafa by the fire. "I dunno, time will tell. We'll find something of value, even if it's only a lone Jerry in a tent rubbing a lamp in hopes of female companionship soon to be materialized. Speaking of, I see Queen Hatshepsup is drawing a bow at her target, the chase is on."

"I heard that, you incorrigible wastrel," said Alice. Gwafa came up. "I will take the first watch."

Bernie rolled into his tent and farted audibly. "Wake me at two for my turn."

"Hold on. Any wolves knocking about?" asked Bea with concern, warming up to Alice. "You just *had* to mention that," she said, unholstering her service revolver.

19

September 19

Twenty-six miles north of Yasuj and the Persian Gate, Bernie reached the top of a narrow ridge overlooking a remote and rugged valley beset with green scrub, the wind fresh and cold.

He set up his wooden box instrument, a Synchronized Electromagnetic Wave Gradiometer, a specially modified instrument from MI6's engineering works. With the sensitive instrument set precisely, he searched in all directions for any kind of unusual signal.

Puffing in the 9200 ft. altitude, Bea led her mule alongside Bernie's. "Anything?"

He adjusted minute knobs and checked the battery connection. "Nope. Just background noise. I thought I heard a blip of something, but…"

Bea took a sip of water and looked over the steep edge. "Don't chance our luck only on that. I'm not afraid of heights, but this spot's a bit precarious."

"Wasn't before, but I am now," said Alice, twenty feet behind, gripping the safety rope. Bernie searched with his heavy, powerful binoculars, then packed up. "We're done here. Let's make camp back down the way we came. God, it's beautiful up here."

"Well, *God* can have it!" cried Alice, shivering.

A hard rain chilled them on the way down, the fierce wind unforgiving. The cruel storm then moved off as fast as it had arrived.

•••

Gwafa roasted the last of the salted goat over a hot fire.

After having fed grain to the mules, Bea chewed her dinner, still cold from the rain. "Camping, trekking, searching, I've been eating so much goat I'm growing fur."

"Do not complain. Meat is meat. We are lucky to have some," scolded Gwafa, slicing with his knife. "Praise be to Allah for the bounty of nature. All we have left are dried beans and two cans of the sweet Italian cherries, courtesy of Rommel and his nemesis General Gariboldi."

"You'll have boar's head and Humble Pie with sheep's guts soon for Christmas, so no worries," said Alice, sewing a tear on her trousers.

Bea mumbled: "Somehow I don't feel any better."

Gripping his binoculars, Bernie looked down valley at the boulder-strewn green landscape and river, a small settlement in the distance. Behind the valley were the tall snowy peaks, making the whole scene look as if painted by a master landscape artist, the muted colors soothing and pastoral, a high-altitude paradise. "Tomorrow I'll send Nasim into the village; he won't draw much suspicion. Someone must have seen or heard something. Only a few highland shepherds have met us so far, let's keep it that way."

"We need salt, Bernard," said Gwafa. "And more water." "I know."

"It's been weeks. My hoofs are as sore as the mules'," said Bea, popping a vitamin. "There's more damned peaks and valleys around here than a French chef's meringue. The Germans could be hiding the entire *Afrika Korps* in a hidden glen and no one would be the wiser. We've made an arc of a hundred-sixty miles plus, and we're running out of tinned provisions. A girl can't survive on goat alone."

"The hell you can't," mumbled Bernie.

"What about heading due north? End up in Tehran via Arak?" asked Alice, yearning to see more than just mountains and valleys.

Nasim stirred the coals. "A long hard trip, sahib."

Bernie sat and chewed some overdone leg meat. "We can't give up. Something's out there, I can feel it in my bones. If there is an airship base and mining operation out here, they must be flying at night with no navigation lights. Maybe they float it up to altitude before using the engines. That's what I would do."

"I agree," said Gwafa. "But where to look?"

Alice pried open a tin. "I dunno, Bernie. Are you sure of yourself on all this? What if we just—"

Bernie took a firm tone, sensing defeatism. "Button it. We've been over all this already!"

"Look, we've missed something. Let's go back to the pass above Yasuj; The Gate must be relevant in some obscure way," said Bea. "Otherwise, I agree with Drumm, we should head up to Isfahan, somewhere." She popped a syrupy cherry. "Need a hot soak in a luxurious bath house or Harem."

"We need food for the mules too," said Gwafa.

Reading the map, Bernie thought deeply for a few minutes. They needed a sheltered rest and resupply at the very least, and his Gradiometer batteries needed recharging, the spare one for the pack radio all used up. Everyone was exhausted, even the mules he thought. "One more day's search, then we head north on the old Silk Road. Once in Isfahan, the soft beds and savory chickens are on me."

•••

The next morning, Nasim meandered about the small village of around seventy nomads. No one had seen or heard anything unusual in the sky. The women wore colorful and dazzling robes, and the children scurried about gathering wood for the roofs and fires.

Hidden well in a thatch of Gagea flowers and chestnut trees, Bernie watched him with binoculars from a hill. He scanned to the east, and on the narrow trail he spied a column of riders descending from the higher elevations via a small pass. By the look of them, they seemed well-fed with good strong horses; all wore robes and garments that blended seamlessly with the green and brown landscape, all had rifles and ammunition pouches, a rogue rival tribe bent on revenge no doubt. *This is all we need at the moment—a blood feud*, he thought. "Shit."

The mountain bandits dismounted and began rummaging through the village for whatever they needed, a softer target not found anywhere, thought Bernie. Goats were procured, but none of the bandits seemed willing to pay. Village elders protested them with Nasim, and a huge argument began. One of the riders drew a sword and ran through an old man. Nasim positioned himself in front of another elder to shield him. A bandit with a gold and black Keffiyeh headscarf dismounted, drew a revolver, and shot Nasim in the head, the bullet passing through into the elder behind. Two for one.

Two village men began shooting back with old rifles, a dust-up.

Bernie gripped his binoculars tight, the pain in his gut sharp. "No! No, goddammit!"

Infuriated, pride insulted, the bandits began to savage, rape, and pillage at will.

Everything of use was dragged out of tents and stacked rock dwellings, especially the young women, an expensive commodity soon to be sold. Whatever they didn't need was tossed aside.

Two riders made a circular reconnaissance of the village. One spied Bernie and yelled at him to stand up. As they neared, Bernie held up his arms in surrender, angry at having been caught with his pants down taking a much-needed piss at the worst of times. The taller man, laughing, weighted down by leather bandoliers of ammunition, made a sign to hand over the binoculars. Unarmed, Bernie did so, pulling his pants up and fastening his belt, smiling at them to help ease tensions.

The tall bandit suddenly fell off his horse to the astonishment of his swarthy companion and Bernie, shot in the chest as a sharp report sounded in the distance. The other bandit shot Rodgers in the hip with his pistol as his Arabian reared up sensing danger, the horses sometimes smarter than their riders.

The bullet exited out his ass cheek; Bernie dropped to his knees and howled in pain while another distant shot brought his antagonist down hard, his second pistol shot missing Bernie by inches. Rolling, Bernie evaded the panicked horse's hooves.

Bea and Alice were sighted in. Four hundred yards.

He grabbed the thrashing horse and hauled himself up in agony. "We're fucked!"

Great notice was taken in the village. Horses were mounted on the run with Arabic yells and whoops. They split instinctively into two groups to flank their unseen enemy—unwelcome infidels and perhaps rivals.

"Time to skee-daddle!" yelled Bernie, kicking his horse in just the right spot for full gallop. Six riders followed him at a ninety yards and closing, their rifle fire haphazard. Bernie's horse was hit on a steep rise and he fell forward as it reared; he rolled on the ground just as his father had taught him to as a boy, the many falls a badge of honor. "Dammit!"

Gwafa came down on the run. He helped him up and handed Bernie his Thompson and ammunition holster. "So much for keeping silent," hissed Gwafa, cocking his BAR as they took cover behind a large boulder.

"God, don't hit the poor horses if you can help it," said Bernie, shaking, ramming in a magazine with a blood-caked hand. They waited patiently, then squeezed triggers. All six riders went down, the hailstorm of automatic fire devastating.

One horse was wounded and went wild with pain. Gwafa reloaded a magazine. "Sorry." Bernie used his belt to tie a tourniquet, but with an entry and exit wound it was useless. "Shit! This is a royal fuck-up of titanic proportions."

Gwafa scanned for the enemy high and low. "I don't see the other riders!" Bernie held out a hand. "Help me walk. Let's find the girls."

•••

Far above, Bea looked through her scope; nothing. "Can't see 'em." Alice slapped her back. "Grab the ammo, they're down in the village!"

Bea twisted the front section of her optics while on the move, readjusting for shorter range. "There's Gwafa!" She reloaded with loose rounds.

Alice kneeled. "Enemy, left!" She aimed through her optics at the oncoming rider flanking them from behind a small hill, shooting from the hip with his Enfield. "Two notches down…that's it." She squeezed off a round and it found its quarry.

Bullets whined through the air; one grazed Alice's cheek. "Shite!"

Bea stood behind her back to back, dispatching the second man in a calm manner, cycling another round into the chamber as a rider jumped them from a grassy rise behind. Bea shot the horse's underbelly and the rider plummeted in front of Alice, who then shot him through the head at point-blank range. Bea grabbed the reins and calmed the beautiful beast. "Nice shot, Drumm. Ea-a-a-a-sy boy!"

Gwafa helped Bernie up the hill. "How many are left?" asked Bernie, bleeding badly. Alice guessed. "Two, three I think. Damned if I know."

Gwafa spied a rider heading back to the village. He fired bursts of three rounds, but at three hundred-fifty yards it was almost impossible.

Breathing heavily and in shock, Bernie said: "Down the horse—do it!"

Gwafa hit the horse and the man fell. As he ran, Gwafa emptied the remaining eight rounds into him with one burst. A dust cloud formed over the body.

Bea scurried up onto a big rock and pointed. "There he is! Raving marauder bastard!"

The man rode at full gallop back towards the village, slapping his reins on either side of the horse repeatedly as his crimson Keffiyeh took flight.

Alice came up beside her. She looked through her scope. "Three-seventy-five… four hundred…four twenty-five…"

"You can do it," whispered Gwafa.

"Can't see him—where is he?" Bea twisted her optics for range, then again for 700 yards. Resting the gun on a rock, she calmed herself, breathing slowly. Her friend Roxanne from the SS school grabbed her hair. *Come on, make it good, Hazelnut, or that goddess bitch Freya will bite your nipples off!*

"…five fifty…six hundred…"

Bea waited for the space between her heartbeats, Kirkaldy's hot breath down her neck.

Squeeze as if yer lover's manhood, ye randy square-pusher, he moaned.

"...seven hundred!"

"Got him." Reticle on target, Bea gently touched off the hair trigger, the Springfield's butt recoiling hard into her already sore shoulder. The bullet spiraled and arced, finally lodging in the small of the man's back. He plowed into the earth like a sack of anvils.

Heart pumping, Alice kissed her filthy cheek and whispered a loving: "Nice shot, Beans."

•••

Gwafa helped Bernie onto the horse. "Let's take a look at our marauders," said Bernie, lying almost prone. Alice had tended to his wound with the med kit; the bullet had gone through but hadn't hit the bone. He bled despite the stitching.

Alice covered both holes with gauze. "I need to sew you up better with—"

"I think we missed one! What was your count Bernie?" asked Bea, nervous. "I'm pretty sure there were fourteen, but…"

"The mules!" yelled Gwafa on the run. After a hundred steep yards uphill, he came upon the five wood stakes in the ground. "*Merde!*"

Panting, Bea came to a stop and fell to her knees. "Oh hell…" Gwafa examined the tracks. "To the west."

Alice led the horse with Bernie. "All of them?" she asked.

"This is all my fault. Dammit! Just plain dammit," yelled Bernie, caressing the long neck and inhaling the potent horse aroma that suddenly made him very homesick. He stroked its mane lovingly. "My fault…"

•••

Inside a stone house, Bakhtiyari villagers helped Alice sew up Bernie's wounded backside proper, then sealed both wounds with a hot iron; Bernie screamed. The elderly *Khalifeh* gave Bernie sips of mild opium tea for the pain; he spoke in a fluid tongue, but Gwafa shook his head at Bernie, the language unfamiliar. "I do not understand the Chief, Bernard." Gwafa spoke in Berber using hand gestures, but had no luck.

"Nomads, perhaps Lori dialect, it's Persian. They're patriarchal Shia I think, but may practice some Sufism," moaned Bernie. "Like the Kurds up north. They're heading south for the winter months, better pickings for the sheep and goats. 'People of the wind.'"

An old women in black robes spiraled red lamb's wool onto a special stick, the humble house used for carpet-making. Vibrant colors and intricate designs surrounded all.

"You'll be up and riding in about two weeks with any luck. Does this hurt?" asked Alice, moving his leg at the hip.

Bernie gripped a straw pillow. "Oww! Yes it hurts! Why are you damn women always torturing me?"

The observing elders laughed, their black bowl hats, wise weathered faces, and matching black moustaches giving them a proud, dignified look. They smoked Turkish cigarettes by the smell of it. Small conversations ensued; they were wary of outsiders, but clearly generous to honorable guests. Strong tea in small glasses was served along with ashy sheep's liver from a hot fire with rice. Nothing but the best for houseguests, a strong tradition of welcome.

Bea cleaned his face with a rag. "Shut it, Horatio Hornblower. And this is not your fault, even though I'd very much like to blame all our woes on your damned airship obsession." She ate some paper-thin flat bread and rolled her eyes from the fresh taste. "Yummy. Looks like we're spying on goat-herders after all."

Bernie grimaced. "You're both shitty nurses…but good snipers."

Alice taped the fresh bandages. "I'll live with that. I don't think the bullet hit the upper femur, lucky."

Another woman sewed Bernie's heavy twill trousers with patches of bright colors. "Aww, now I'll look like a damned circus ringmaster," moaned Bernie.

Outside, the villagers stripped the dead bandits naked, collecting all their gear and remaining horses; nothing was wasted, the horses and guns valuable trade items. Bea watched as the bodies were buried in a common pit, the tribal conflicts a sad part of life in the lawless mountains. Nasim was given an honorable rock mound burial by two able teenage boys, a headstone to mark his departure from this world to the next with honor. As she walked away, the very last body being dragged caught her eye. He was much taller than the others, with broad shoulders and knee-high laced boots. *The boots.* "Gwafa!"

He came on the run.

Amongst concerned Persian murmurs, Bea excitedly stripped off the dead man's twisted headscarf. The man was Caucasian and tanned to a caramel brown, with short-cut sandy brown hair and a thick beard. Franticly, she peeled off layers of robes.

"German desert uniform, SS senior sergeant, help me!" She stripped his right arm and looked straight into Gwafa's eyes. "*Gebirgsjaeger*, mountain troops. Edelweiss patch."

Gwafa unholstered the P-38 pistol, then held up the dead man's wrist. "What does this this say?"

"Cuff band. *Sondergruppe* IX, 'Special Detachment.' Never heard of it, but he's got an Ahnenerbe patch on this arm. Bloody bugger, he's the real thing, and riding with outlaws too. But why?" With help from the villagers, they carried the body to the stone house's threshold. Bea grabbed the dead man's hair and held up his head with a determined look.

Bernie could just glimpse their tan-uniformed prize, then fell asleep in a haze of poppy tea relief.

20

October 2

Dawn.

The cold morning got the chief shepherd and the flocks moving among the pistachio and walnut trees. Bleats and bellows from goats and sheep echoed in the crisp air, an ancient concerto. A young girl carried two kid goats by their feet; Bea and Alice helped out as best they could, the sound of many bells stimulating and soothing. The sun crested the peaks, and everyone's faces reflected the warm light as donkeys were loaded with blankets, rugs, and tents, the tribe ready to move down valley towards greener pastures.

Gwafa helped to load the horses, his broad smile and curious Malian songs endearing him well to the young. The nomad women sang; Gwafa didn't understand the lyrics, but the deep emotion was clear. He thought it might have been about separated lovers, a common theme in the vast deserts. The simple life was by no means simple, he thought, but it held the charm and satisfaction of one's hard work for the greater good of all. No selfishness had been evident, no greed. Mother Nature took as much as she gave, the rhythm, the ebb and flow of life a constant and nurturing hum. "Allah bless these fine people, or we would be dead," he mumbled to himself, tightening the straps of leather that held on the horse's blanket saddle. "*Principle of Rhythm.*"

There was a spiritual agreement between animal and human, Bea thought, and it felt perfectly natural. *We are all one in the cosmos, but I never thought I'd be one with a lamb.* Now she finally understood what Colonel Lawrence had been writing about in his books, the Arabs a noble people worth much more than the sum of their scattered desert parts. They were a golden race of remote nobles who held nature and family, Allah and tribe, as the greatest of treasures.

The tribe's single cow ate the last of the thinning sweet grass wet from dew; a young boy whapped it with a stick but it was slow to respond other than a fart. By the fire, an older man and his companion branded a sheep on its cheek, the mark difficult to hide if stolen by thieves.

"Bloody cold," said Bea.

Alice wiped her hands. "I told you it would be."

"I admire these folks, salt of the earth." Bea thought of home back in Kent. "If only Mr. Grath could see these flocks and us as third-rate shepherds. Rations on the move are slight, I'm always a bit hungry. Fine day. What I'd give for ol' Flippy and an aerial recon."

Hands on hips, Alice said: "My dear old bag, I think these nomads would shoot at you if you dive-bombed them in your old Moth for a lark."

"You do have a point," laughed Bea.

An older girl carried her baby sister on her back, leading a donkey with chickens atop tied to wool bundles. A small puppy followed her. She smiled at Bea and Alice, but the rhythm of mountain life also meant movement. Everyone migrated in a choreographed fashion, all knew their place, all did their jobs without hesitation or complaint.

Bea stopped, letting go her two kids. "You never did tell me how you felt after your first."

Alice picked up and cradled a soft white lamb, no more than two weeks old. She and Bea had been tending to the tribe's small wounds with the last of their medical supplies, using valuable cotton cloth bandages when needed. They had grown fond of the nomads, a beautiful yet durable people intertwined with animals at a basic level not seen in England for millennia; they traveled as one single migratory entity. "What the hell would you like me to say? I feel physically sick about it and can't sleep; I cried all day yesterday."

"I was the same way once."

"All life is precious, but we kill or eat it with abandon. I've shot deer and elk in Wyoming as a girl. There's no difference other than the animals have no malice in their hearts." A young boy relieved her of the lamb. "These people live a rough life close to the bone and closer to nature. Snake bites, scorpions, sickness, fast icy rivers to cross with frightened animals. Raising a family in a tent. Tribal rivalry. But they have true freedom, and it's intoxicating. We should *learn* from them."

Bea cleaned herself with a wet rag and a sliver of soap. "Amen to that, sister."

•••

With a wood crutch hewn from the strong part of a limb, Bernie watched as a horse's hoofs were sawed and mended. He could walk, but with pain. He would ride the horse intermittently, prone atop blankets to ease his backside agony. A young boy tugged at the brass zipper on his tartan wool jacket under his robe, having never seen one. They smiled at one another. Bernie zipped it up to the boy's astonishment. "C.C. Filson Pioneer Alaska, only the best for the mountains. After the war, I'll send some up here for you." Bernie imagined mighty Persepolis surrounded by the tents of nomads, tens of thousands of them bartering and bearing gifts for Great King Darius.

Bea came over, kid goats following her. "Don't forget the peanut glue you love so much."

"You just had to mention peanut butter, now I'm starving for some. Look, Alice was right. Let's head to Arak in a few days, then on to Tehran for supplies and horses. I've made sign language headway with the elders, one of the teenagers will lead us. I promised them my Thompson, no ammo left anyway, and I can't carry much of anything other than this Kraut pistol. Gwafa has three magazines left, how many rounds do you girls have left?"

"Between us, around seventeen."

"I'm exhausted. German mountaineer or no, we're done, really done. He could have come from anywhere up here, any direction." He pointed. "I see you have a furry fan club."

She pet them. "They sense my innate greatness. Look, you were right about Jerry being in these mountains. Let's keep on for a few days, we might see something of value."

"Alright, a few more days then."

•••

After a half-day of traveling, the tribe stopped for a lunch break, allowing time for stragglers to catch up. The bells echoed.

A lamb strayed and ran uphill; an elder pointed and ordered two boys to follow. Lugging her rifle, bored stiff, Alice followed the two boys while they chased it down.

Above them were steep peaks, some with snow. The highest around.

The adolescent lamb found a vaguely triangular passageway in the sheer rock face and escaped his pursuers.

"Yoo-hoo." Alice wandered in behind the two boys who had run down the wayward escapee with laughter. In the dark distance of the arrow-straight craggy tunnel she saw a pinpoint of light, an opening a quarter mile or more away she reckoned. She felt the walls of the seven-foot high tunnel; pick and chisel marks maybe. Once outside, she waved for Bea, then stuck fingers in mouth and whistled. "Up here!"

Bea struggled up the steep goat path. "What now?"

"A tunnel. Could be wrong, but I think it's man-made."

•••

Emerging from the tunnel's other end, Gwafa led Bernie on the horse.

Bernie hopped down and looked through his binoculars. "Jesus, a hidden valley! Lined on all sides by the steep peaks. About…eight miles long, two-and-a-half-wide, shaped like a canoe. Several streams and a small pond. Scrub oak trees and lots of thorn bushes. There goes a couple of ibexes, there, a fox. Great hunting up here. I don't see an easy way out, or any exit pass for that matter."

"Well that was simple. What's that in the distance to the left, behind that rise?" asked Bea, sheltering her eyes from the sun.

"Tents. I count around five. A truck or two. Could be more nomads, but… they're camped on a rise or something, a mound or hill. Sonofabitch, I think we've hit some kind of pay dirt. Hell, all those weeks chasing shadows…"

For fifteen minutes they moved closer, easing their way down slowly.

Bea borrowed the optics and re-focused, the images quite distant, the waves of atmospheric distortion acute. "Great Nelson's codpiece. No flag or identifier. But it's an expedition all right, a dig. The question is, whose?"

To the floor of the valley was an eighteen hundred-foot descent through pistachio and walnut trees, the narrow path serpentine. Once they reached a small grassy rise, Bernie got off the horse.

"I will be behind these rocks. Nature business," said Gwafa, leaning his BAR against a small tree.

"Bloody goat guts. I count thirty or so Germans, tan uniforms. Maybe sixty locals assisting," said Bea excitedly. "Now I see a small flag. Busy lot. Damn you, Rodgers, not bad work." She laughed. "Unbelievable!"

Alice took her turn. "Over there, see them? Two Kubelwagens. One heavy Opel truck. Now how'd they get them up here? A secret road or tunnel?" Bernie said: "We better make ourselves scarce befo—"

"Allo," said Gwafa, hands in the air with scraps of Basra newspaper falling. Behind him were three SS soldiers in tan uniforms, rucksacks, and forage caps, their semi-automatic Walther G41 rifles now cocked with authority. "At least they let me finish."

Marched to the dig site with their weapons tied to the horse, hands on heads, Bea caught sight of masonry blocks partially exposed, big ones. "Well I'll be a…"

"Shitty ol' Shieldmaiden," said Alice.

One of the SS let go a shot into the air to announce their presence along with prisoners. "*Achtung! Kriegsgefangenen.*"

"I knew it…" exclaimed Bernie with a smile. "I fucking knew it!" Adrenaline overcoming pain, he curved around a pointed ravelin, limped over the dry moat via a wooden bridge, struggled over a crumbling curtain wall, and touched the weathered ancient stones, melted together with so much precision that even his knife's tip could not penetrate far into the gaps of the angled wall. "Solid Quartzite!" Most of the site was still buried under meters of soil, much of it unrecognizable even from the air. Dust and debris suddenly fell from above onto his head. He looked up.

A pith-helmeted *Ahnenerbe* officer with a thick beard stood fifty feet above them on a huge star point bastion and put hands to hips, tunic unkempt, his jodhpur pants dusty and wrinkled, knee-high laced boots filthy. Arms outstretched in a welcoming fashion, he smiled and spoke in German with an amiable tone. "For *Gott*'s sake Uta darling, we've been waiting weeks for you!"

21

At the center of the five hundred-meter-wide star fort was an hexagonal platform with a series of wide stone steps on all six sides still showing some polished shine after millennia.

Twelve large, three-sided triangular standing stones each five meters high stood in the center, creating a wondrous henge for *mittagessen*, which was served on a long table under a camouflaged tent for the officers and guests, eighteen total. A white tablecloth lay beneath two large hams, assorted game birds and all the trimmings. In addition to the bottles of Italian mineral water, champagne was served cold from six ice buckets; tin cups sufficed for flutes. Silverware was Wehrmacht standard issue, tin plates same. A phonograph was wound up by an enlisted man. It played soft French jazz, a forbidden luxury within the SS.

SS *Standartenführer* Ernst Schäfer, *Ahnenerbe* zoologist, occultist, hunter, and chief archeologist, dismissed the need for guards, politely telling Bea and Alice that the valley and its ancient entrance were now sealed off and there was no place to run or hide, the steep sides and peaks inaccessible, virtually unclimbable, the nights freezing. He added that the odd brown bear or hungry Persian leopard might also be lurking about. They were free to roam at will, but would be closely monitored. Gwafa, however, would remain under arrest. "My apologies for him. Even though I regard the Aryan race as the most superior," whispered Schäfer, "a scant few of us Ahnenerbe could care less about socializing with lesser ones, and in fact it can be most stimulating and refreshing. The Waffen SS, well, that's another matter."

"I'll just bet," despaired Bea with arms crossed, taking it all in.

Alice stood silent, mouth agape as two hawks flew by, the abundance of nature palpable.

She noticed three graves off to the north with wooden man-symbol-shaped runes instead of crosses, an ancient symbol of the Wotan SS religion. Everywhere, spaded workmen proceeded with the archeological digging at a feverish pace.

"Now I've really seen everything," moaned Bernie, admiring the bespoke camouflaged Krupp field kitchen truck complete with ice boxes and a bakery wagon, the polished-clean stainless steel interior just catching the strong midday sun.

•••

Schäfer poured bubbly into Alice's cup while Bea scanned the table. Stocky, he was as ruggedly handsome as the day Bea had met him years ago in Austria, his brown beard the longest of all. Tunic collar frayed, he tugged at the cuffs of his non-standard pink silk shirt, his air one of confidence and informality. "Since the time of the great Aryan archeologist Gustav Kossinna, we Germans have been the masters of the great profession. My specialty is Ornithology, Miss Drummond, but I dabble in many disciplines. Occultism is the overarching doctrine of the SS and the Thule Society, and sitting here you have some of our best minds—minds that can easily mix raw science, metaphysics, philosophy, and hidden knowledge into a multifaceted tool for refining the near impossible, theoretical, and barely provable. A cutting-edge, mountaineering think tank of heretofore unknown levels of intelligence, hundreds of years of experience and wisdom. And now you three kindred spirits have kindly joined us. In Germany, I have gathered together an exotic seed bank, an 'herbarium,' from my Tibet expeditions in Graz, Austria, for the *Reichsführer*'s plan to increase crop yields in captured Russian lands—seven hundred varieties of oats! Our compatriot Jankuhn is now in the Caucasus doing just that. Perhaps you may be familiar with one of my famous books entitled: *Mountains, Buddhas, and Bears*."

Bea translated for her.

Alice crossed her arms in irritation. "No, I'm most certainly not fam—"

"Ha! *Bears*," blurted Edmund Geer, Schäfer's close friend and expedition leader since the early expeditions in India and Tibet. "How ironic."

Everyone laughed.

Schäfer slapped his hand on the table and grabbed Bea's arm. "As my former student here knows well, I'm keen on hidden ancient history, subjects that have greatly expanded our knowledge of who we are, where we came from, and what is our rightful place in the cosmos. How we miss the simple and noble Bon people and their animistic ways, gentlemen, yes? Those Tibetan traditions are now incorporated into the Thule Society and the SS for the spiritual benefit of all."

"*Prost*." Bea swilled her first glass, the bubbles intoxicating. "Gods 'n' sods, saved by the Ahnenerbe and its desert cellars. An uncommonly fine table this is. Dionysus would be flushed with pride. As for history I—"

"History obfuscated by the fucking Vatican Jesuits," said Geer in disgust. "Swine monks, quick with the scissors on ancient texts, then burned the rest in bonfires."

Murmurs of agreement.

A young, bespectacled Waffen SS junior officer with a squeaky voice, *Untersturmführer* Ötvös, a stickler, sternly retorted: "Always remember the Führer admires the Pope in secret since the Pope represents the Knights of Malta. We should all be thankful for Rome's assistance on rounding up the Italian and Romanian *Jews*."

Uncomfortable murmurs.

A botanist blurted: "Maltese Cross, Templar Cross, German Iron Cross. They're all the same. They're all ancient symbols of the sun when in a circle."

"And the center sun of the cosmos and creation. It's all hidden behind religion and lying secret societies," said a biologist.

"*What?* The Iron Cross? How can this be?" growled pudgy, clean-shaven Waffen SS Captain Schlapp angrily, an obnoxious officer loathed by all.

Bea, wolfing down German potato salad and French beans with hollandaise, her thirst for strong drink satisfied at last by excellent French vintage, broke the tension. "Oh, it can *be* all right. As for symbology and the occult, Herr Schäfer taught us Tibetan meditation with the help of his friend Kunchen, a Yellow Hat monk. Ace fellow, he was."

This is insane…a luscious luncheon with our opposite numbers. What, no salad fork?

Schäfer sighed. "How I miss him. A man full of cosmic wisdom and benevolence." "Pardon me, but I thought SS members didn't partake in alcohol," asked Alice. "All that pure bloodline, pure heart, and loyalty stuff." "*Prost!*" went the table, cups clanging.

"The SS *Sondergruppe* IX members here at our table, our vaunted *Gebirgsjäger* mountaineer protectors, may not partake, nor do Waffen SS officers Schlapp and Ötvös, but we Ahnenerbe are given some unofficial leeway from time to time for very special occasions out here in the field," said Schäfer, pulling off his worn leather gloves one finger at a time. "But it *is*…a rarity."

Sober Ötvös stood, his voice shrill. "As the Thule manual states clearly on page twenty-one, section three: 'An addictive poison and intoxicant. Fouls the liver. Burns the stomach lining and intestines while in sufficient quantities creating a pineal gland gateway in the brain for unbenign interdimensional intruders, sometimes referred to as…*spirits*.' Hence the old name for atrocious alcoholic beverages."

"I second that," said Schlapp. Mild chuckles ensued.

"Bravo, young man," said Schäfer, squinting at the sun. "But today warrants a minor intrusion."

Relishing fresh-baked bread with heaps of canned butter, Bernie looked to Alice and discreetly winked. *Play along.* "My compliments, Herr Schäfer, for a sumptuous meal of Westphalian ham and Spanish olives, the SS spares little for its exploratory subsidiary units I see, must be all that unfettered funding from the Reichsbank, Himmler's miraculous and unquestioned blank check and all."

The SS Mountain Division Detachment Commander, Piter Klemperer, a big-shouldered, muscular brown-blond-bearded *Sturmbannführer* with a tanned iron face and big ears, fused his eyes on Bernie. "How *dare* you…"

Bernie toasted him in English. "Here's lookin' at you, kid." Then drank.

Schäfer held up his calloused palm. "Ah-ah-ah, easy now, Klemp. Let us be truthful to our special guests. Yes, yes, our entire SS funding stream is off the books. A proud state within the state. We are grateful to the *Reichsführer* in no small fashion."

Ötvös suddenly stood at rigid attention with his water cup. "A toast…to the Führer and *Reichsführer*." Everyone smartly stood and saluted, officers and enlisted, even Alice after a moment of prodding by Bernie's elbow. "*Sieg Heil!*" everyone chorused.

Alice noticed that Bea was quick to stiffen her spine and quicker on the salute, a reflex. "What *now?*" asked Bea.

"Nothing," chirped Alice like a songbird.

"Sit, eat, and be merry everyone," said Schäfer, crossing his legs in commanding comfort.

Bernie sniffed a Sorrento lemon with eyes closed then took a luscious bite, not wasting one tiny bit. He looked at the huge standing stone behind Bea, its spiral carvings and double eagles with swastikas highly intriguing. "I see the Hittites were here at some point. How old is the fort may I ask? Any speculation?" *I'll be hornswoggled, dining like kings in the middle of the high Zagros,* he thought. *No one will believe us.* "Any sugar around?"

Schäfer snapped fingers as a waiter brought fine sugar in an SS silver bowl; he bristled with confidence. "Our estimates are in the fifteen to twenty thousand-year range, perhaps of the Heroic Age of Man. Many occupiers have come and gone over the millennia: Hittites, Babylonians, Parthians, Scythians, Armenians. But of course it was still active in Alexander's time, a time of Aryan conquest to the east towards India and

Asia. We believe his army marched into this valley through a small pass over there, now filled in by rockfall and time. *Sigh*. The Uxians drove him off of course, but how is still a question. We have found many layers of bronze swords, bones, and helmet fragments."

Impress them. Bernie thought deeply, and a memory exploded. "During the War of 1812 in America, our famous star fort, McHenry, held out against the British mortar and rocket ships for over a day defending Baltimore's harbor. The British never got close enough to land troops near the fort in defiance of their cannon, mortar, and rocket bombardments. Despite fierce resistance and a chain of sunken ships at the harbor's entrance, I wonder if the occult-savvy Freemason officers knew the fort to be protected by an unseen electromagnetic force due to its design, perhaps high-frequency waves, a force that helped to keep the British 'Limies' at bay." He shook the ragged lemon half to make his point.

"Why, *you*…un-continental Continental," grumbled Bea.

"Indeed." Schäfer took a proud tone. "I think the British officer occultists knew *exactly* what they were after, a valuable ancient port city and her star forts, just like New York, Charleston, Norfolk, Boston, and Philadelphia, important colonies of Atlantis, the infrastructure of canals impressive. Old *Norumbega* as well in Nova Scotia. You would make an excellent historian for the new Reich, Herr Rodgers. I urge you to join us of your own free will. Together we will unearth the entire hidden knowledge of the ancient world."

"I'll consider the offer." Bernie waxed poetically and arrogantly on all he knew about Alexander, the Uxians, and the Anunnaki Kings List. He and Schäfer sparred back and forth, the table lively with speculation and 'Star Civilization' theories, the uncountable fortified ancient towns and cities in Europe and elsewhere compared and contrasted, the expensive, beautiful heavy masonry star fort bastions and city walls hotly debated as to their quality, complexity, and original geomantic function—Naarden versus Palmanova, Munich versus Vienna, Neuf Brisach versus Bourtange, even Tokyo versus Jakarta. They were all connected, geoengineered with great care, contained vast geometrical formal gardens, defended themselves from floods and storms, and may have acted as one giant civilization in harmony with nature; it was Hitler's new European domain of old-world technology that remained little understood. "Even your sacred Berlin was once a star city with immense pointed bastions, ravelins, hornworks, crownworks, fortified moats, and impressive canals."

Alice asked the table: "Funny. You said that you were waiting for us for weeks. How did you know that dear old Uta was with us?"

"Our local spies on horseback that I personally recruited," said Klemperer arrogantly. "Crude but effective savages, especially when paid well. They would make excellent mountain troops if properly trained."

Shoving in food, Schlapp said: "Huh. They're not Aryans, just subhuman dogs."

Schäfer rummaged, held up a tattered book from his prized rucksack. "Those hired bandits easily made off with your mules and supplies, Miss Drummond. We allow irregulars to keep certain valuables of no use to us. However, in a bag...was this charming *book*."

Bea slowly stopped chewing, putting fork gently to plate. She swallowed hard.

Schäfer flipped tattered pages. "*The Island of Doctor Moreau*, by H.G. Wells. Such a *classic*! A tale of hybrid animal humans created by a mad doctor scientist. Obviously a cautionary allegory, one based on the late-era hubristic and hedonistic Atlanteans having genetically run amok with their slave-pet centaurs, mermaids, and hybrid dogmen, the Cynocephali. In the back I found a faded pouch with a folded card tucked in way-y-y at the bottom that reads: 'Checked out by one Beatrice Sunderland, March 18, 1932. Wycombe Abbey School Library.' Overdue by ten years no less."

Everyone exploded, even Bernie, who thought the whole mission had been thoroughly shipwrecked and he might as well join in for the roasting.

Bea slumped and leaned back in her squeaking campaign chair. "Drats and bats. Sorry, gang."

Alice leered. "You blithering toad! Operational security. No documents with *names*. Nothing to give away our..." She screwed up her sunburnt face in anger.

"Must not have noticed the back end, Drumm."

Gwafa sat alone a few yards away. A sergeant gave him a plate of enlisted men's rations of corned beef hash and sauerkraut. "Filthy black beast," the guard mumbled, spilling a little in Gwafa's lap.

Bea toasted Gwafa with her cup as he scowled back. She thought it best to polish her once shiny SS pin to ease suspicions. "He's quite a good soldier and manservant, but of course a subhuman pack animal at heart. Dr. Moreau would be proud."

The entire table laughed again save for Alice, who now leered twice as hard.

Funny lot... They were a varied group of scruffy scientists thought Bea, archeologists, geologists, climatologists, historian mystics and officers with proud Thule Society patches.

Schäfer's hand-picked team, the cream of Germany and Austria's best, but Alice and Bea sensed an uneasy tension among the civilian boffins, a nervous laugh, a far-off gaze, something amiss. No doubt like some of the physicists back in Germany, Poland, and Czechoslovakia, they were the usual nervous scientists under an ever-threatening SS whip, positive results and corroborating data at all costs. Spied on relentlessly. No failures tolerated. No excuses.

...*for a bunch of SS twits.*

Listening carefully, Gwafa mumbled disgruntled insults in French to himself. "*Je te déteste, madame...*"

Schäfer went on as if he had newborn twins. "The eight main star-point bastions of this octagonal fort design were of course determined by the sound frequency of the valley—its cymatic shape—that and the nodal point of electromagnetic Ley Lines that converge here shown on old maps. Show me a *crossing* of the Lines and I'll show you a sacred site with some hefty frequency and earth energy."

Bernie took a chance by revealing a bit of classified information in the hopes that life would go better for them as fellow historians and occultists in lieu of potential saboteurs. "As shown in the ancient *Kahnnhar*."

Silence. Silverware clinked on plates. Nervous looks.

"What?" asked Kisse, a gifted Sumerologist and Assyrianologist. "Nonsense," said head archeologist Klaus Schmidt. *Tap-tap-tap.* "*Liar.* He's trying to impress us," hissed Weinert.

"Impossible! It's only a *rumor* that it exists," said racial anthropologist Bruno Beger. "You're lying. What languages is it written in?"

Geer stood, arms on table. "Shut up everyone, let him speak. Are you telling us you've actually *seen* it?"

"Lovely maps and engravings," said Bea, dropping a fresh strawberry bomb into her champagne from height. "Belonged to that great fop Raja Chola. Gilt binding made of reed, papyrus, and crumbling leather. Had a great symbol on the cover, an embossed Sri Yantra, wasn't it Drumm?"

"The Vedas make good bedtime reading with hot cocoa," added Alice with confidence. "Flying Vimana stories, sweaty and sordid harems at high altitude and all that. Sundry Vedic Yugas and sheep's yogurt recipes."

Bea laughed as she translated.

Bernie smiled, spreading his palms apart. "Thick text, weighs twenty kilos, about yea big with a brass hinge and lock, much of it written in Sanskrit and Tamil, the latter the oldest language on Earth of course, the one we all used to speak before the arrival of King Anu and his wayward geneticists, but you all know that. A friend in Pakistan showed it to us a year ago. Quite impressive I must say, fine maps and etchings galore, Prediluvian spiritual teachings, Ley Line nodal points, trans-Arabian, Sufi, and Tibetan wisdom. Sacred geometry in Islamic and Indian architecture, formal gardens, fountains. In addition to coded Vimana technical information with pictures galore, it told the story of this very fort and its defenders. A splinter group of Uxians that held out against Alexander and his army on their way to sack Persepolis. Am I...wrong?" He took off his boot and dug into a secret pocket. He carefully opened the sealed wax paper and gave the folded page to Schäfer, who then passed it along. It showed a star fort etching with tiny Tamil inscriptions.

Raising an eyebrow, Bea asked: "You tore off a page?"

"Parkes-Jackson was in the head, the loo. I carefully used a razor blade." "That is indeed...*correct*," said Geer, shocked.

The Germans mumbled amongst themselves in amazement, carefully passing the parchment.

"*Gott*, then it does exist." "Pakistan? We must obtain it!" "At all costs!"

Schäfer slammed down his tin cup. "You impress me to no end, Herr Rodgers, you and fine and capable ladies here, we must have more exchanges of knowledge. The *Kahnnhar, Kahnnhar* ...what I would give to possess it, hold it in my arms, smell its odorous antiquity."

"Please, you were saying?" asked Bea above the excited hum.

Schäfer continued. "Hmm? Ah, yes, this fine fort. As I was saying, the bespoke cymatic shape was sound in four dimensions, if you will. We believe they must have grown the fort's foundation with sound frequency at first, then reinforced the earth works with strong stone for a harmonious and eon-durable result. The moat, as some refer to it, ran off the stream that flows through the center, resulting in electrical power, its storage, and water purification. Of course the fort had other more metaphysical uses like astral travel and portal openings and closings, the many dimensions of the universe available for journeys perhaps." He took a deep breath and exhaled lengthily, examining both sides of the parchment scrap. "This is the finest gift I have ever known, I shall frame it in glass with French gilt in Paris."

Beger added: "Most of us think Alexander was frustrated with the Persian Gate south of here…as it may have only been effective at certain planet alignments and times of the year. I'm assured he wanted personal contact with the gods and the greater unknown, and if he had captured this fort his wishes may have been fulfilled. The ancients knew all about this natural portal phenomenon, one not unlike tides and seasons, it's only today that we struggle with the dimensional concept, a legend steeped in much fact. The Near East deserts are said to be full of them at sacred sites."

"I'll bet the flowered women druids traveled dimensionally with aplomb, all that Celtic Divine Feminine and whatnot," said Bea.

Schäfer touched his tin cup to hers. "Especially at Ireland's stone circles."

Geophysical scientist Dr. Karl Wienert proudly added: "This so-called 'fort' must have produced immense electromagnetic power for this valley and its inhabitants, an important outpost in Prediluvian times. The mud-brick dwellings are long gone, a simple affair. We believe it was a last holdout for a group of people hiding from another group before the Fall and Flood. A high civilization hole in the wall, so to speak. Plenty of crops."

Bea pointed with her fork. "If memory serves, Ernst, you taught us novice Shieldmaidens that the Sons of Belial were in conflict with the positive, the Children of the Law of One. Atlantis would have been up to her tits in war in those times with dark forces, ones that embraced war, power, wealth, and materialism over benign spirituality and cosmic nature worship, you know, naked nubiles, bull rituals in temples, cornucopia food festivals, that kind of fun paganish thing. If it's true that the sonofabitching Belial Boys were after a splinter group hiding from them after the artificial crystal second moon had been destroyed, etcetera, etcetera, then this place may have thrived with its power plant, fields of grain, wild game, and fresh water."

"Shot down, that smaller moon probably crashed near the Yucatan peninsula," said Alice confidently. "Big hole in the ocean they say. Now all we have is our single hollow Moon."

Beger blurted: "How do you know all that? No one knows that but us, who—"

"Obviously, you're *not* the only ones," added Bernie, stacking their deck.

Bea plowed on. "But this is Anunnaki territory, especially Babylon over there to the west, and they and King Marduk were not happy with the rival bullyboy Belials by all accounts, but if an alliance *was* desperately needed, well then..."

Schäfer laughed, and grabbed Bea's hand. "How well you remember! An excellent student of mine, a former Shieldmaiden SS, gentlemen, once named Uta von Manstein, and yes, a relative of the general, 18th Infantry Division commander during the recent siege of Sevastopol."

"A Prussian noble. I hear he argues far too much with the Führer," spat Klemperer, fingering his Iron Cross with oak leaves.

Bea mumbled in English: "As it bloody well should be."

Schäfer continued. "Where was I? Ah yes, Persepolis to the southeast was an Anunnaki bastion of royal dignitaries and hybrid bloodlines as well, the capitol of ancient Persia even well before The Flood, but of course that's not taught by Berlin University now is it?"

Murmurs of discontent rumbled forth.

"Or dear ol' Cambridge," said Bea, slowly withdrawing her hand from his sweaty grip. "Yes, yes, it is my speculation that the alliance *was* made, and the last of the Children were cornered here to perish. They had erected powerful altars made of pure silver between the standing stones, an Atlantean specialty for astral travel using benevolent Moon Goddess energy, and we have found traces of them all over the fort."

Schäfer held up a tarnished silver fragment from his pocket.

Bernie asked: "Silver? But I thought—"

"*Silver*...is a noble metal that's an emanation of high spiritual frequency, one that matches the fort design itself, making it a 'divine machine' of sorts. But it was not to be, planetary vibration had entered its lowest point 13,000 years ago—the nadir of the Great Year 26,000-year cycle of the heavens—and The Sons and their various dark allies had become too strong in a world awash in low frequency. The Atlantis Empire was soon no more, and the war caused the deluge to spring forth through deliberate comet impacts and global earthquakes, two weapons of mass destruction we can barely imagine."

"Perhaps we shall be able to back-engineer the earthquake technology for the SS," said Klemperer. "Especially when we dig straight down through these stones. The Vril Works has developed a ground-penetrating radar at great cost; it has shown us a large void ten meters down through the solid granite." He pointed to a burly soldier fifteen meters away who held a device that looked like a mine detector, his backpack large and heavy. He swept back and forth with the large ring at the end of a rod. Nearby another soldier, seated, looked into a hooded television device that was connected via cable. "Impressive new technology, transistorized."

"Not everything we learn has to be made into *weapons*," snapped Schäfer as the table went silent. He turned back to Bernie. "In any case, after luncheon, I will show you and your ladyfriends some evidence of this now-proven theory. What an astounding piece of history we are dining in…a shining example of a once-mighty civilization of our advanced Aryan forebears, ones that enjoyed a fifth-density Prediluvian paradise world with all twelve of our DNA strands active with psychic powers for everyone… just imagine the *accomplishments*, the sciences alive and intertwined with philosophy, cosmology, and spirituality, ones that we can only—"

Alice motioned for more champagne from a waiter. "Any thorium about?"

The table went dead silent again, the element understood in all languages. Bernie grabbed a handful of his greying hair and pulled.

Ötvös stood and caught Alice's attention. "That is *none* of your business, *fräulein*." "Oh, but it is indeed our business," said Bea, diving in to her Linzer Torte, the best from Vienna with gold leaf atop; a crisp-uniformed waiter plopped a dollop of whipped cream beside it. "You see, we're here to negotiate the sale of good-quality ore, and hopefully we can reach a deal. Perhaps we can procure the almighty *Kahnnhar* for you in exchange."

"Now…why would we sell a rare commodity to an enemy combatant?" asked Klemperer politely. "Hmm? I'll ask you again, why—"

"Sold!" yelled Wienert. Laughter again.

Bernie sensed Bea's distraction and extrapolated. "You don't know what we're willing to trade. And we're not the enemy, not really. Yes, we carried arms, who wouldn't be in these mountains? We represent a private multinational concern, one that charged us to carry a heavy load of gold buried not far from here. Nice and chummy, an old moldy eastern syndicate and secret society based in New England. I'm their personal representative."

"Gold? Ingot or *powdered*?" asked Geer.

"Huh, the Reichstag has more than enough gold…" grumbled Beger.

A geomagnetic specialist lit his pipe. "The Allied atomic program is far behind ours. We have nothing to worry about if—"

"Be quiet, all of you!" yelled Klemperer, who angrily pointed here and there, his chair ejected behind him. He looked to Schäfer. "One of my mountain men is dead, Ernst. American, African, and British *kommandos*, pack radio and armed heavily. One *schwartzer* animal with an automatic rifle and a thousand-meter stare of a fucking Zulu lion hunter, a run-down middle-aged Yank occultist with a duplicitous Tom Mix smile, two highborn women snipers with precision rifles who would no doubt eat their own young if necessary, the auburn-haired one a bitch *traitor* to the Reich." He looked to Bernie. "Who do you think we are? Fools?" He waved, and an enlisted man smartly handed him Bernie's captured Gradiometer. He shook it violently. "What's this, eh? An MI6 *tin toy*?" He smashed it to splinters on the polished stones outside the tent using both arms.

"He's the equivalent to a Brit major?" asked Alice, mouth full of cream, trying hard to remember all the confusing German ranks and insignia.

"Oh, hmm," said Bea. "Bit of a temper on him, reminds me of Poppy."

"Oh, hmm."

Relaxed, Schäfer waved him off, his boots on the table's corner. "Now, now, Klemp, sit and cool down, *kamerade*, we're amongst honored guests, fellow historians and explorers, not combatants. The war is far-r-r-r away. Be polite, that's an *order*. After all, we are going to be living and working together for a very, very long time." He noticed with the keen eyes of a primatologist that Alice was taking a subconscious interest in the handsome Klemperer. He grabbed her chin gently, the cream dripping. "Perhaps…this fetching blonde beauty with high cheekbones and excellent fitness would make a fine Aryan housewife for you someday. Oh, but you have a slight bullet graze, my dear. *Tish, tish*, makes you even more lovely."

"*Hausfrau*? What did he say? A wife?" asked Alice, concerned, flapping her matted hair back and forth as she looked for an answer from someone. "Why you Goth gargoyles…"

Bea and Bernie laughed, then the entire table. *I've forgotten how amusing ol' Ernst can be with a few drinks in him*, thought Bea. *Hate to say it but he's almost likeable.*

Schäfer got up and poured glass after glass. "I'm kidding of course. More champagne. Come, come, everyone *drink*, we have much to celebrate today." Grumbles of agreement with nodding heads.

Everyone finished their dessert in a good mood as conversations shifted to the scientific. How the Anunnaki, a noble Aryan race of star being conquerors with six fingers and great height, could have created with their various genetic programs the races that became the Jews, Africans, and Arabs, was a hot topic—that and the hybrid offspring of the Anunnaki, the infamous and legendary *Utukki*.

The climatologist said: "The Anunnaki were from Nibiru, a planet in the Sirius star system. Nibiru was said to have male energy, as opposed to Mother Earth which is female. The stronger over the weaker, the Uttuki were created to control us, same old conquest story, divide and conquer, religions, racial divide, and a caste system. Boring in the supreme category."

Geer said: "Don't forget the many factions of trustee slave Uttuki and Nephilim. Our world is full of banking family and royal factions in every country. They're *ruining* this war for everyone."

Weinert said: "Fucking Rosicrucians, they dropped the metaphysical ball on *everything*."

Italian Zoologist Sarfatti said: "No, no, no, Neanderthal man was a strong and hearty hybrid human, one with ape, human, and Anunnaki DNA. He was a slave for them mining gold and other minerals in Peru and southern Africa, the Great Zimbabwe ruins. Why is it some of you dolts are ignorant of this?"

"*Nein, nein, nein,* my friends, the guttural Hebrew language is lower caste Anunnaki, while Sumerian was the royal caste language. That's why the Persians and Arabs hate the Jew dogs. Do you not understand the significance?" asked Schäfer of his underlings, holding a slice of ham on his fork and shaking it. "Look here. That cylinder seal we liberated stated that domesticated pigs had human DNA spliced into them long ago in the city of Ur when they were just wild boar, that's why they're so docile, smart, and make such fine pets today. Remember? The Anunnaki kings *relished* them." He then mouthed it.

"*Ja-ja,*" they chorused, blasé to a man.

"I have to admit, Jankuhn's Baghdad raid was a cylinder seal treasure trove for us," bragged Klemperer. "Anunnaki technology in quantity. Haushofer's astrology work on that mission proved fruitful…for once."

"Soon the other seals will be translated. Soon we can build new underground facilities in Ukraine of unparalleled sophistication, hydraulic engineering, and *power*," said Schlapp.

Bernie sat straight up. Suddenly he realized he was in the company of men who knew much more than he about the world's hidden secrets, and Klemperer's openness meant the Germans had no fear of their escape or potential mischief whatsoever.

Suddenly a little nauseous and realizing the significance of the traditional pork embargo by the Jews and Muslims, Bea casually pushed her half-finished ham plate away with discretion.

Alice did too. "*L'chaim*, as it were," she mumbled softly. "You said it."

Schmidt asked: "In honor of our guests, Ernst, is it true that the polyglot English language was purposefully limited in terms of deep description and thought when compared with Egyptian hieroglyphs, most of which can have multiple meanings on many levels? Aren't English and German…really derived from an Aldebaran subdialect?"

"*What?*" blurted Bea and Alice together.

Schäfer waved him off. "Yes-yes-yes, but the Anunnaki and Orion star people dumbed down all of our languages to keep us separated, conquered, and weak, even later Germanic ones. Their enforced caste system did the same. Well, no more of that in our Thousand-Year Reich. You know that as an expert on Anatolia and her ancients, Klaus. *Scheisse*! Who here actually listened at my lecture in Munich? *Anyone?*"

"French is from the Pleiades star system," said Klemperer. "The worst for the worst."

"Slavic is from the Orion system," laughed Geer. "Typical."

Others joined in the feverish debate, which morphed into other areas of intense speculation and wildfire theory.

Kisse said: "Greek is an offshoot of the original Atlantean language, and Santorini was also a colony. My thesis proved it. Then Greece went to war with Atlantis, they were rebels."

"Bonfires and torchlight festivals?" asked Weinert. "Witches of old rubbed psychedelic ergot ointment on their holly wood broomsticks and rubbed it on their vaginas in a fire ceremony. Pointy hats, especially the Aryan solid gold ones, upped their psychic ability. Just like Isis and her pointy head. Basque witches, sorry, women Druids, suffered terribly at the hands of the church for their Prediluvian pagan rituals, the poor devils."

Beger said: "Basque is from the Lyran star system. Unique."

"*Nein*! The sun is not a fusion reactor per se, it's more of an electromagnetic sphere. It gets its energy from higher dimensions. Stars disappear all the time without going supernova, they evolve to higher realms. Gravity is made by the sun's high-frequency electromagnetic radiation and our atmosphere filters the rays. Trillions of cycles per second. All the planets are therefore habitable. I'm the astronomer, I know."

Ötvös blurted: "The Tibetans could serve the Reich as part of a pan-Mongol federation against the British Raj in India. We could equip them with Vril psychic weapons and—"

"Nan Madol in the South Seas is proof positive of the megalithic Lemurian civilization. Half of it is underwater. The seas were much lower 55,000 years ago when it was active."

"One hundred-sixty meters lower."

"158.476 meters you mean."

"Geology doesn't lie, we have evidence of the Great Flood in the layers."

Geer said: "What if the Jesuits made up the childish Bible and everything else? We can trust *no* history book excepting the Vedic and Tibetan texts, the Norse Eddas, Kang Shuur, and now the damn *Kahnnhar*."

Cups were held high. "Prost!" Waiters scurried to refill cups.

"Catherine the Great was Prussian. *She* existed at least, therefore her father—"

"No royal is *great*," snapped Klemperer. "They're all of the Sumerian royal bloodline, that's it, end of story. These poshy Britisher women can attest to that. The *Order of the Garter* and its back-pocket-boy Churchill all wear black robes that signify the worship of Saturn and the darkness, just like the foul Jews. Why, why, why are the *incestuous* and pedophilic royal families always the richest in every culture?" He dabbed the table with his finger. "No taxes ever touch them. They're trustee slaves still, inbreeds, they kiss-polish their masters' boots while drooling from their misshapen Habsburg jaws."

Bea said: "Order of the Garter? How 'bout the black SS uniforms? Why you blackguard hobgoblin sons of—"

"Hell with the *Jesuits*, Karl, Adam Weishaupt and the Bavarian Illuminati had all the power in the Western world circa 1781, and via royal patronage in secret," said Schmidt. "They could have made all ancient history up as a fairy tale as far as the middling classes were aware. Foul deals were made with monarchies and the secretive Black Venetians in black robes. Profits to be shared. Factions at each other's throats. The only thing the secret elites ever agreed upon was secrecy at all costs!"

"Agreed." "Double agreed."

"Where's that fat fucking heroin addict Crowley when we need him?"

"He's kissing Churchill's *keister* in Palestine, no, *Baalbek*, French kissing on the Trilithon."

Bernie said: "The Romans didn't build the megalithic Trilithon, the Anunnaki did. Sixteen-hundred-ton stones? Try moving those with slaves and oxen. It can't be done, they must have had antigravity palettes or vibratory standing-wave carpets. All the idiot Romans built were military camps, *Lupinaria* brothels, and crude, thin-brick bath houses."

"I could use a hot steam bath, *and* a she-wolf." Laughter. "Prost! Prost!"

Bea put head in hands, pinching her nose bridge in disgust. "This is just a silly dream…just a dream."

A single scientist started it with one word, then others chanted in unison: "Giza, Giza, Giza…"

Schäfer bragged: "All right, all right. My latest theory on the Great Pyramids at Giza, you ask?" He collected his thoughts for a moment. "Bending *time* itself was their real focus, so as to provide, well, a *process* for priest initiation via self-created interdimensional portals. Come on! You know this. Atlanteans, Egyptians, Chaldeans, and Dareans, a multiple-use design created 42,500 years ago. And the manner in which this was accomplished provided other benefits for its people—increased crop yields, weather control, water management, a form of electrical power of course, and a learning institute for the study of the heavens: Astronomy, astrology and cosmic forces, mathematics, chemistry, inner-world dimensions, and the *Seven Levels of Initiation* we know well. It was a university campus, hospital, temple, astral travel train station, cosmic defensive platform, and powerplant complex all in one, the center of the Earth grid system. All were part of their incredible multifunction design. Mass meditation by thousands of enlightened people can manifest anything. Are you idiots listening? *Well?*"

"I knew it!" cried Bernie. "It all makes sense now…"

"Crop yields?"

"Hemp and Marijuana too?"

"Astral travel by priest initiates? Lotus flower tea, belladonna, and opium helped!"

Laughter.

"The usual mix with wild honey wheat beer! *Prost!*" Cups met cups.

Bea gulped champagne as the memory of the hallucinogenic tea in Schäfer's class came back to her in a rush. *So that's where the tea recipe came from…*

Drunk, Beger said: "No, no, no, it's the *Knights of Malta* who are responsible for this war. The Templars' foul descendants. They control the other secret societies via blackmail, and they're the gatekeepers of forbidden history. Special passports, secret goods across all borders with no questions asked. They can go to hell. Soon Malta and her megalithic star-fort bastions will be *ours*. May Odin bless the *Fallshirmjäger* paratroopers!"

"Crete was hell for them. Malta would be too costly," said Weinert. "That's a cowardly and *defeatist* attitude," said Ötvös.

"Easy, boy. You've never seen combat," scolded Klemperer. "Your outlook on everything changes. You'll see. Not for the timid of heart."

Schäfer toasted Klemperer privately with his cup. They had both been in an intense nighttime firefight with British Ghurkas in Nepal once in the mountains, and though it was a misunderstanding, it had been hell, the Ghurkas relentless and brave. Fearsome.

Bernie noticed the toast, and kicked Bea under the table. She nodded. Then kicked Alice.

"Oww!"

"Ernst was right, Jesus was a con man, Mohammad a loan shark, *scheisse*, was the Buddha a camel-racing bookie? Confucius had a *dozen* concubine wives and a hundred Manchurian children out of wedlock, and I think he was really a Caucasian Japanese *Ainu*. All of history is a *Gott*-damned lie, and it's up to us illumined Nazi few to unravel it."

"Triple agreed."

"A Sufi saying to remember, my dear fellows: 'Knowledge is but a single point, but the foolish have *multiplied* it.'"

Beger laughed. "Oh, *shut up*, Wienert. You wouldn't recognize a Sufi elder if he was sucking the gold leaf off your precious cock."

"Jesus died an old man at Masada with its defenders, a Roman officer found a sword in his hand with—"

"Which Jesus? There's plenty, all sun gods, all used car salesmen, the lot of them: Adonis, Eros, Mithras, Prometheus, Attis of Phrygia, Thor, Beddru of Japan, Indra of Tibet, Jao of Nepal. Christianity is based on the ancient worship of the sun and Mithraism. India's god *Krishna*? Try *Christian!*"

"You're not taking this issue seriously, Klaus. The so-called 'Ascended Masters' of history, corrupt to a man, were all in on the big game, the big lie, the pissing swine!" argued Geer.

Bernie interjected. "Ahem. Speaking of the ancients…don't forget all the old cathedrals built by Freemasons with unusual gravity technology, just like the kind the Egyptians used. Cathedrals are really sun temples and *analog waveform generators*, frequency from all that choir and organ music for the enhancement of health, love, and light of the soul. Nothing to do with religion originally since they're just brainwashing nons—"

A wave off. "Everyone here knows that. American scientist Eric Dollard published his findings years ago, I was there at Stanford at his symposium in '37. Who cares?" said Schäfer arrogantly. "Again, who actually *listened* at my lecture?"

"I was asleep."

"Laundry day, said my wife."

"The Hofbrauhaus was packed that night, free rounds of beer in honor of Goebbels' birthday. I forgot."

Klaus Schmidt added: "The Allies better not bomb our cathedrals in Germany or in captured lands, otherwise we'll annihilate theirs with *miracle weapons*."

By-the-book Schlapp pointed. "Watch your tongue, the *Wunderwaffe* is no joke. We don't need an *occultists'* war under the surface with the foul royals. Conventional warfare is to rule, it was *agreed* upon by all, the Allies included, said the *generalmajor*. Are you all listening? Our global civilization has not evolved for the better. We SS will *change* that."

Bea said: "Ahem. As for monarchies and bloodlines in general, I'd just like to add that my own family has ancient royal blood from my dubious ancestor Earl Kilpatricke, who must have shagged his way up the chain of—"

The table drowned her out. "Oh-h-h-h-h…" they chorused. "*Bitte*, stop while you're ahead, young lady..." moaned Schmidt.

Weinert stood, pointing, condemning. "This is the problem with British and French aristocracy, Ernst, their ever-growing entitlement and *arrogance*."

Laughter.

Bea threw down her fork. "Now *see here* you lot...ungrateful Hittite Hottentots, why don't you just go boil your bollocks in clarified duck fat with—"

SS Aryan ancestry impeccable, a hardened Thule member to the very core, Klemperer banged his fist on the table. "This man Rodgers is American Illuminati, he's no fucking better than his women here...I'll bet he's made a recent stone-kissing pilgrimage to the Temple Mount in *Jerusalem*. We have nothing to fear from America and her pitifully weak military, a nation of Jews, blacks, red savages, lazy Mexicans, Chinamen, and soul-sucking sodomites!"

Nervous laughter tapered off uncomfortably; everyone knew the Americans were advancing soon.

Bernie replied: "As a proud American I can agree only on the sodomite bit, Herr Klemperer, shameful, just plain shameful." *I know some Mexicans and Apaches that would slit your damn...oh, well, he is rather a tall drink of cool water...why are psychopaths always so handsome?*

Schmidt added: "The Columbia faction of Bavarian Illuminati took over the American Colonies. And the Yank sheep all worship that Isis goddess when they gaze upon the Statue of Liberty. No country is truly free. And they say *we* are the fascists."

"The Jew Rothschilds financed the American Revolution through the East India Company, they made money on both sides. They're from the Nimrod bloodline in Babylonia— they controlled the food and gold supplies in ancient times. Sound familiar?"

"Washington was a good tactician for a low-bred mongrel. He may have defeated our brave Hessians at Trenton out of sheer luck, but he was also a filthy goddess-loving Freemason," said young Ötvös, eager to impress the table with his limited knowledge.

Klemperer laughed in a sinister way. "Herr Field Marshal von Blücher and his Prussians would have wiped their asses with Washington and the Continentals if he was there at Yorktown when—"

Bernie stood in temper, pitched down his napkin. "Now see here, prisoner or not, I will *not* stand by while George Washington is made a fool of!"

Klemperer stood abruptly, exposing a six-inch neck scar under a white silk scarf. "I was my brigade's fencing champion in '35. Care to honor me in a gentleman's *duel*, Herr Rodgers? Or is that against your precious and cowardly American Navy honor code?"

Eyes enflamed, Bernie picked up a dull butter knife. "*Mutterficker*, I would if my backside wasn't shot to hell!"

Stares. A stand-off.

Bea looked to Klemperer, then Alice and whispered: "Not overburdened with excess charm is he?"

She smiled. "Oh, hmm. A thousand hells would be born if he bent himself professionally to the task. Good cheekbones though."

Klemperer pointed. "*What* did that blond bitch just say?"

"Enough!" yelled Geer, banging cup to plate, his authority second only to Schäfer. "Now, now, my friends, no romantic duels please…let us be cordial. Ladies are present, honorable ladies," said Schäfer in a soothing, melodious tone. "I myself have some obscure old Prussian bloodlines." He put a hand on Bernie's shoulder so that he would sit.

"Oh-h-h-h-h-h…" they chorused again as the table calmed. Most had had a glass too many, egos and tempers akin to spark plugs.

A mountain soldier changed the phonograph record to Vivaldi. Klemperer visibly relaxed.

Feeling diplomatic, Bea stood, cup high. "Gentlemen, we Brits are expected to thrive at the far corners of the world, and so…here we are. A toast to that fetching goddess Frigg and the fabulous Berlin Orchestra."

"Prost!" they chorused, clinking cups. "Lovely fat-titted Sif and her drinking horn too!"

Bernie changed subjects, a good tactic when thoroughly outnumbered. "Herr Schäfer, how big of an aircraft can your three-kilometer airstrip handle?" He pointed to the north where a heavily-camouflaged tin-roofed building and windsock stood. "It's around 2600 meters altitude on the valley floor, yes?"

"*Bitte*, call me Ernst. It is 2726 to be exact." Schäfer looked to his overbuilt gold wristwatch that had an altimeter function. He smiled. "Are you familiar…with the Swiss psychologist and occultist Carl Jung and his concept of 'synchronicity,' Herr Rodgers?

That all points of space and time are connected, and that there exist no coincidences, no moments of dumb luck or happenstance?"

"Yes, quite familiar."

Schäfer kept to his watch. "We are expecting supplies—frozen fish, French blue lobsters, my favorite *Gewürtztraminer* wine, sausages, fresh melons, various Alsatian cheeses, additional electronic equipment and honored guests fresh from Pilzen and the Skoda Works via Munich..." Thirty seconds went by while he slowly raised a finger. "... right about...*now*."

The table went silent again. The Germans looked to each other and smiled, some of the scientists loading their pipes with forbidden tobacco.

Bea's experienced ears perked like a hound's. "Aircraft! Multi-engine, a heavy." She gulped her champagne remnants. "Hop to it, Drummy. Let's have a look-see."

From the northeast a slow rumble filled everyone's ears, the valley and its steep sides reverberating the deep burbling sound. As they emerged from under the tent, a large speck along the northern peaks at altitude revealed itself.

"*Achtung*! *Transportflugzeug!*" Klemperer gave loud orders to his senior sergeant who blew a whistle. From their mess table SS men sprinted, tossing aside their checkered napkins.

A guard kept Gwafa seated, barrel pointed, then quickly handcuffed him. Bea looked back to him and nodded. Gwafa did so in return, the trust between them more solid than the surrounding stones. All will be well. Somehow.

With Schäfer leading, Bernie, Alice, Bea, and the Germans walked through an arched gate then down a makeshift wooden bridge that crossed the fort's dry moat. They all got in the truck for a short ride.

From seemingly nowhere, ten heavy trucks arrived at the airstrip with more Kubels, two motorcycles with sidecars and MG-42s, and a lone Famo halftrack towing a sizable cargo palette.

A twenty-man SS band set up, desert uniforms. Another one hundred troops stood behind them, rifles at attention, garrison caps straight and level. Officers gathered in front.

A Luftwaffe *leutnant* fired a green smoke flare from a small tower camouflaged as a clump of trees. All clear.

"They have a bloody *orchestra* out here?" asked Alice incredulously, hopping down from the tailgate. "Honestly..."

"This is one trip for the books," said Bernie, astonished at it all. "If we survive it."

Bea put a hand on his shoulder. "Well, no fanciful airship, old peanut, but they do have jolly good air support. Just look at the size of it, now that's the dog's bollocks."

He sighed. "Yessirree-bob." *Just what the hell is happening around here?*

On final approach looking like a giant condor, a massive Junkers Ju-290 cargo transport lowered its flaps as its four powerful BMW engines reduced power in the thin air, the long airstrip a necessity for one of the Luftwaffe's biggest cargo planes. It was painted in desert camouflage livery with Turkish markings. Heavily-laden, it touched down with two dust storm vortices trailing off each twenty-one-meter-long wing, the sturdy landing gear sagging a bit from the internal tonnage. In the forward turret, twin 20 mm cannons stuck out like tusks amongst the stick-forest of radar antennas. In small script, "Turkish Delight" was painted in German on the nose with swirling flourish and confident braggadocio. When the giant plane halted, a Luftwaffe pilot stuck out his head and waved at the ground crew chocking the big, rough-field tires. Engine shut-down. Doors open.

The band struck up a riveting *Aus Warth Zur Sonne*. Officers and men saluted with right arms thrust high. Boots sharply connected.

"Sneaks," said Alice. "False flagging it, I see."

Bea smiled, the aircraft magnificent, the exhaust smell pungent roses. "The Turks are neutral but chummy with Jerry. Clever ruse. All's fair in love and war, Drumm, all's fair."

From an arriving command Kubel exited SS *Generalmajor* Theodor Poppel, the overall Commander, a tall, exceptionally lean man with sharp-cut cheekbones, a fashionable razor-thin moustache, long lips, and Italian tortoise sunglasses under his SS-rune pith helmet; his uniform pressed and clean unlike his dusty command. He barked sharp, quick orders with a high voice that could scare a trained guard shepherd. Schäfer lazily saluted him; to all they seemed polar opposites in demeanor and ethos. They both walked to the rear of the plane where a large ramp came down with stairs.

The pilot and copilot came down first, adhering to safety protocol on landing. Schäfer shook hands and grabbed shoulders of the pilot, *Oberstleutnant* Kurt Baumann. A close friend and roommate from the University of Göttingen and one of the

Luftwaffe's best pilots, he had been pilot and cameraman on Schäfer's 1938 India and Tibet expedition. They laughed and carried on like schoolboys, drinking glass after glass much to the visible annoyance of the sober and fierce Poppel, who then rudely shut them up while they came to attention. Poppel loudly reminded Schäfer that his disgustingly inebriated scientific expedition was a secondary mission, despite the fact that Himmler had granted specific permission for it. Two for one.

Bea strained to hear them at twenty-meter distance. "Ernst doesn't care for the *Generalmajor* much, now does he?"

Bernie said softly: "Y-y-yup, and the opposite is quite evident."

Slowly, five civilians, four additional uniformed Ahnenerbe men, and a handful of additional Luftwaffe officers exited with hand luggage, some tired, some giddy and excited from the 3525-kilometer long flight that had started in the dark of the early morning at Fürstenfeldbruck Air Base near Munich. The side door was opened, and cargo crates were lowered down with a crane to awaiting personnel. Two iced crates of live blue lobsters were opened, the smiling cook holding a big one up by the claws for the cameramen.

As Poppel greeted the entourage politely, Bernie noticed one man in a three-piece grey suit and hat holding two heavy file cases, two well-dressed young assistants astride him carrying their own. He nudged Bea. "No airship, huh? That's Walter Gerlach, I'm sure of it."

"*What?*" exclaimed Bea. "Sneaks!"

Gerlach vigorously waved to someone still in the plane to come down. A tray of cold champagne was passed; Gerlach took two. An official SS photographer and newsreel cameraman captured the scene for posterity, a gift for the proud *Reichsführer* Himmler.

While their guards looked to the gaggle of dignitaries, Bea bolted like a greyhound. "Bea!" yelled Bernie, reaching for her and stumbling with his crutch. "No-o-o-o!" The two SS guards gave quick chase. "Halt!"

As the remaining passenger slowly descended the stairs mopping his brow, Bea barely dodged two swilling Luftwaffe officers in Wycombe football fashion—yet still managed to make them spill—then plowed through Schäfer and the Generalmajor, grabbing the last man off and kissing him on the mouth to everyone's amazement and shock as they both slowly fell to the dust. "Hallo Professor!"

22

"In *Gott*'s name! *You?* You!" cried Porsche.

Soldiers grabbed Bea at gunpoint. "Leave off! We're *friends* I tell you, *old* friends, like Napoleon and Wellington."

Poppel yelled: "What the hell's going on here?"

Doubled over, Schäfer laughed, then Gerlach, then others.

Porsche wiped his mouth. "Let go of her—I said let go! I know this young woman well, unfortunately."

"She's a saboteur and commando, like her compatriots over there," pointed Poppel. "And an aircraft thief," added Klemperer. "Shieldmaiden traitor."

Poppel addressed Klemperer and Schäfer for all to hear. "These allied saboteurs are your responsibility. Keep an eye on them round the clock with four armed guards. They're never to be left alone, ever. Clear?"

"*Jawohl*, Herr *Generalmajor*," they chorused.

Poppel asked: "You *know* this woman, Herr Professor?"

"Yes. Leave her to me. The war is *your* concern, Poppel, not mine." Porsche took Bea's arm and led her away. "Lady Sunderland, my dear Beatrice, what are you, why…?" He then took a tone of genuine concern. "What happened…what happened years ago to you and Lutz?"

They walked, two guards behind them. "We crash landed, can't say where or when. He died upon impact saving my life. Anton flew well and fought better, a fitting tribute to your older brother. As for Lutz, I loved him dearly, professor, I really did."

"I know he loved you. I'm so sorry. He was a nephew to me, my family too." *Anton would have hated war and warplanes…*he thought bitterly, he and his family all pacifists.

"We were to be married once in England." She turned to face him, suddenly emotional. "The racing years, the people, your engineers, the drivers, I…I was genuinely fond of you and your family, the lot. Well, maybe not Dodo-bird, she hated my guts. Yes, I know, a spy and aircraft thief, a liar, but before the SS got hold of me and twisted me into a pretzel, I had a great deal of fun with Lutz, he showed me a side of Germany I never knew, the people, the ordinary *volk*, and…I'll always remember that."

Porsche looked to the group of SS and German contractors inspecting the new portable crane, his heart sinking. He lowered his voice. "The SS? Yes, I…know. They've given us many thousands of starved Russian prisoners to work the VW factory since most of our workers have been drafted for service. The SS treats them horribly, shoots a few laggards, the weak and sick. Ferry and I despair in silence, but what can we do? Our young soldiers at the front, they need…we give them—"

She grabbed his lapels and said quietly, forcefully: "Don't *ever* cross them whatever you do, they'll imprison your family, shoot all of you as traitors. They're fanatical madmen. Their Norse religion and sick—"

A guard harshly pulled her away. "No touching permitted, *fräulein*."

Porsche put up his palms. "It's fine. What the devil are you doing out here in these dusty mountains, Beatrice?"

"*Me*? Well, I was taking a crack at herding goats when…"

A hand extended slowly and gently. "Professor, we've met before. Bernie Rodgers." He squinted. "Ah yes, the American who insured ships for Lloyds of London. And you, my dear?"

She kissed his cheek. "Alice Drummond. Bea's sister-in-arms, so to speak. We met at the mountain race in Austria."

Porsche smiled for the first time in a long while. "I remember. The Grossglockner Hill Climb. Yes-yes, I remember well the good times now past—Hans Stuck having fallen in the mud, Beatrice's fast run uphill, Manfred pissed as hell, Lutz laughing at it all. I'm so sorry to reunite in times of war, this…*horrible* war." The smile faded.

Schäfer arrived with Gerlach. "Herr Professor, an honor to meet you. I see you already know our dearest Uta. I was her instructor at the SS school in Austria. Zoology, anthropology, archeology, and metaphysics."

Porsche squinted at him too. "Uta? Ah, yes, the *school*…Walter here has informed me about the many odd SS programs. It seems my security classification has been uprated recently. Well, I'm no occultist or mystic, that you can be sure of. I carry tools." He pointed to a crate with his name stamped upon it. Next to it stood a Kriegsmarine chief engineer, *Kapitänleutnant* Banner, his assistant from his U-Boat engineering days.

"Come, Ferdinand, they're waiting for us, your famous tin can Kubel awaits," said Gerlach, his two young physicists behind him. "My right hand Lappe, and left hand

Rodmann. Berlin University, theoretical physics, newly drummed into the Vril Works." Bernie thrust out his hand again. "Herr Gerlach, Bernie Rodgers. All three of us are honored to meet you, and we are passionate enthusiasts of your Unified Field Theory and its various applications."

He shook it. "Huh? *Ja-ja*. Let's go Ferdinand, I need a bath, and so do you."

•••

Piled into a truck, Bernie looked up at a sheer cliff face as the lead car stopped and honked three times. *The tracks go right into the rock face. Doggonit, I don't get it, why—* Suddenly the rock wall split with a loud electric whirring sound. Two massive doors opened, craggy ones painted to match their rocky surroundings, a masterpiece of camouflage. "Jesus, they must be aluminum, and two hundred feet tall!" As they entered the facility, Bernie noticed the inner steel frames that held the aluminum skins, the doors on motorized tracks, the giant chains looking like oversized bicycle ones. From altitude the doors would be invisible.

After a hundred meters travel inside, Bea stood eyes wide, emotion coloring her voice. "By Athena's moist thighs, I'll never underestimate you ever again, old sod, *never*." Before her was a sight she would never forget. High off the ground, twin counter-rotating propellers on a single shaft, twelve thick blades each and both props eight meters in diameter, were rotated by hand, the six ground crew inspecting each of the twenty-four blunt-end blades for nicks and stress cracks on a tall gantry. Surrounding the props on the narrowed stern fuselage were twelve equidistant vertical fins, each painted red with a swastika in a white circle.

"Crikes, that's a big 'un all right," gasped Alice. "Nice job, Rodgers, Tesla would be proud of you."

"See the curved blades, Drumm? High efficiency at extreme rpm, I reckon."

"It's...dare I say, beautiful."

Jaw agape, Bernie had no words. The elegant fluted hull—an extruded, tapered octagon—of the 150-meter airship glistened a faint blue-silver under industrial electric lights like an oversized jeweled fountain pen, its beam an estimated fifteen meters, he thought. *Yes, fifteen for sure*. A row of port holes and rear observation windows showed much activity inside, and four large Kriegsmarine anchor chains, each link a hefty half-meter long, secured the floating craft to steel plates bolted to the solid iron mountings buried deep in the ground and walls. Luftwaffe personnel scampered up the midsection's stairway. Crates were loaded into a large cargo bay. At the bow, the many framed windows made the cockpit area almost 360 degrees transparent, a half-sphere of plexiglass. Four equidistant opaque hemispheres were built into the fuselage just aft the cockpit at the six, nine, twelve, and three o'clock positions, looking almost like aircraft gun turrets, their genuine function a mystery to him. On the outer skin was a set of Luftwaffe squadron markings, a *Balkenkreuz* cross, and a painted smiling Grizzly Bear with angel wings. "LZ-38. *Himmelsbär*, well I'll be double-dog damned," he finally said. "Now I get the bear joke at lunch."

"Himmels-what?" asked Alice, gripping the truck's railing.

"'*Sky-Bear*,' and he looks the part," said Bea. "What's with all the anchor chains?"

Bernie pondered. "Not sure. Could be they're securing him for an engine test or something. I can't believe how damn big it is. See there? Each of the fluted panels is made up of smaller flush hexagonal panels, probably for strength. He's a handsome sonofabitch. Looks fast standing still, or rather floating."

Schäfer arrived as if a film director. "Come down, my friends. Allow me to show you inside the Reich's greatest achievement in aeronautical engineering to date, soon to be our luxurious liner for parts due southeast."

Southeast? Bernie helped the girls off the back of the truck. "Who built it, may I ask?"

"Blöhm and Voss, the navy flying boat manufacturer," said Klemperer proudly, his four armed guards behind him, their escort. "The innards by Volkswagen, Arado, and *Luftschiffbau* Zeppelin. Electricals by Siemens and AEG." He laughed. "500 metric tons of cargo."

Bernie whistled. "Hoo-wee." *They really did it...Hess should have paid more attention to his various projects under development. Or did he lie to me?*

Alice and Bea stood there, mouths open as they gazed upwards, their youth ignited. It reminded Bea of the Graf Zeppelin airship that she had flown to Rio de Janeiro on when she was just eleven, her father half-drunk from fear of crashing and drowning. But this ship was aerodynamically leaner, more taut, more battle-ready than a passenger liner, hovering there with not one ounce of the flammable hydrogen gas inside that had torched the Hindenburg in 1938.

Here, the ship floated with torsion-field antigravity technology on a scale not known since Prediluvian times. It was graceful, elegant, svelte, like a polished silver torpedo ready for action.

"Buck Rodgers' fantasy come alive," said Alice.

"Blau-35 alloy. The whole thing's made of it!" exclaimed Bea. "Just like bloody ol' Anton."

"And faster than your precious stolen Heinkel, an amusing tale I might add. Well played," said Schäfer. "The Bear can presently achieve 880 kph with much more to come. Hopefully Herr Gerlach and Porsche can make that happen."

"Oh?" asked Bea nonchalantly.

"Any armaments?" asked Bernie. He swiveled around, marveling at the 100-meter or so diameter cavern which went on seemingly forever, the walls somehow made into smooth, polished-to-a-shine black anthracite. Wood buildings, barracks, mess halls, infirmary, and offices were built into one side, and a supply depot next to them. The sounds of winches, cranes, mining trucks carrying ore, and generators filled the void, the cavern smelling of beans, bacon, exhaust, and chemicals. Vent fans whirred above, exhausting toxic fumes through other hidden tunnels cleverly built by expert engineers. A generator shed had a yellow high-voltage sign, the electricity supplied by diesel, the exhaust plumbed into the ceiling. Far off, gangs of threadbare Arab slave workers marched in a long column. *Nothing fancy, it's all business here. Bad business all round.*

Klemperer said a stern: *"None.* Cargo only. A heavy-lift long-range transport. Recoil weapons are useless due to the electromagnetic plasma bubble surrounding him. He would become dangerously unstable in flight."

"That makes perfect sense to me." Bernie felt his neck cramping up from his head-high position. "How many round trips?"

"Over sixty," bragged Klemperer, hands clasped behind his back and tipping up and down on his toes. "Everything you see here was brought in by transport or the Bear. Ore and rare earth materials outbound, supplies and personnel inbound, five hours flight time on average to southern Germany. Minor onboard repairs and maintenance are in progress, timely efficiency is our goal."

Luftwaffe crew towed inside the Ju-290 in case any rarely-seen British reconnaissance planes were meandering about, the rough airstrip routinely camouflaged with cut trees, painted aluminum rocks by the truckload, and shrubs on mobile wood platforms. Within the hour it would blend in with the rest of the valley.

"Herr Schäfer, I need to visit the toilet," said Bernie.

Schäfer paused at the ship's forward stairway, a marvel of thin-tube cleverness in its own right. "You can use the marvelously-engineered one inside on our tour, they're pumping out the sewage tanks now." He pointed to a tanker truck that had a hose attached to the underside. "All the comforts of the HMS Queen Mary."

A smiling Kurt Baumann arrived with Porsche. "The Professor would like to join our tour before he takes a nap. He's an old hand from before the Great War regarding exotic aircraft. He piloted with Count von Zeppelin, the Kaiser, and Archduke Ferdinand on Zeppelin LZ-4. Can you imagine?"

"Im-pressive!" spat Klemperer.

"I will say the same, Herr Professor," said Schäfer, bowing slightly in Prussian fashion.

Porsche wiped his brow. "Hmmff. At my age it's a necessity to nap. Can't sleep on noisy planes, I keep thinking I hear the engines misfiring. The flight engineer and I knocked heads over the mixture settings and manifold pressures. Gerlach snored like a pig next to me the whole trip down. Thanks be to *Gott* for the pilsner and stinky cheese sandwiches."

"Your wife Aloisia always did make you the best ones," smiled Bea. "And with extra-hot mustard."

Passing them, a group of SS officers and cameramen accompanied Poppel on an inspection of the two-kilometer mine tunnel that lay to the east. Flashbulbs popped. One of the officers caught eyes with Bea and Alice; he smiled. Thin, he wore old cavalry boots and an older-style uniform, one Bea knew was worn by elite officers who had joined the SS before 1933. It was a subtle but potent message to the new boys that an "old salt" was present. The man's sharp features and piercing dark blue eyes gave him the look of a reptilian predator ready to strike.

Time slowed for her, voices sounded deep and strange, an anesthetizing moment of otherworldly déja-vu enveloped her like a warm, flower-scented bath. He blew a sluggish, sinister kiss their way, and it made her insides shudder. "Who's that cheeky colonel with the rumpled hat?" Bea asked Schäfer as time sped up to normal.

Alice leered.

"Hmm? Oh, him." Schäfer waved at the officer. "*Obersturmbahnführer* Hans Kammler. A contractor and builder, the best. An odd one, calculating, cold as ice, but Bormann and Himmler count on him to build the most challenging and complex facilities. An organizational genius, really. This is but one of his grandiose projects in the works, a difficult challenge for him and his team, his other projects are highly classified. Rises fast in the ranks, soon to be a general no doubt. He can literally move mountains. Leaves at five a.m. on the transport back to Germany. A taxi service we have."

Bernie looked to Bea and Alice. They had found their mystery genius.

Schäfer whispered to Klemperer: "A glorified civilian contractor. He's building the new concentration camps, an honor for him. And yet our doctor has to heavily sedate him, he's *scared* to fly."

Klemperer stifled the urge to laugh.

"Oh?" Alice put two fingers in and sharply whistled. She then gave Kammler the "V" sign, for *up your bum*.

Kammler and the others laughed. "Keep your filthy English whores on a leash, Schäfer!" yelled Kammler.

Schäfer huffed and puffed, tugging at his threadbare tunic. "My apologies for the crude, uncivilized behavior of others. He's a boor and a thug, a snake. People... *fear* him. Yet the ear of the adoring Reichsführer is his to kiss."

Two Luftwaffe officers nearby overheard and moved along.

Klemperer went face to face, whispering: "Be quiet, Ernst! You and your fat mouth... he can get us all on report, regardless of rank. He's a spy for *Obergruppenführer* Mazuw and Himmler, you idiot. Even generals fear him in private, Poppel too."

"You worry too much, Klemp."

Bea whispered to Alice: "Death camps, eh? Someday we'll have to find time to pay a social call on the cold sticky bastard, eh what, Drumm?"

They continued their procession.

Alice mumbled: "I'll wear my sharpened stiletto heels."

"Did he build this giant tunnel? How?" asked Bernie, amazed at all that surrounded him, like a boy introduced to a huge model train set replete with all the works. He wondered how they would ever escape their unusual situation, they were surrounded by hundreds of armed, fanatical *Waffen* SS and rugged *Gebirgsjäger* mountain forces, the best of the best. A solid ice nightmare.

Schäfer laughed. "No, no he did not, just the infrastructure, mining shafts, and buildings. Look around you, I did say I would show you evidence of our theories." He pointed all around. "This entire cavern and tunnel were built by the *ancients*. They must have used a gigantic free-energy tunnel-boring machine of some sort I'm told by a mining engineer, immense heat. The stone walls were melted into anthracite, a watertight and strong casing three meters thick. We found this cavern by accident on our first expedition to the fort in late '39 by mule just as you did; the discovery of quality euxenite ore was fortuitous, but that has always been a priority. When the Bear became fully operational a year ago, the engineers widened the entrance. Kammler's men designed and built the clever hangar doors, infrastructure, and airstrip. Porsche's design works designed the electric winch system of chains. Quite the…*ingenious solutions*, I might add."

Bernie exclaimed: "Impressive. From the air the camouflaged airstrip, tents, fort, and shacks are virtually unrecognizable in a vast sea of mountains." He noticed Porsche chatting with engineers over at the giant door electric motors. "Always some tweaking needed, I suppose."

Bea crossed her arms and whispered to Alice. "Funny. Never met that snake Kammler, and yet it's as if I had…long ago in some other lifetime."

"Pure evil," she replied. "A husband maybe?" Leering ensued.

Up the gangway they entered the cockpit compartment, and everyone held their popping ears.

"Normal. Higher pressure in the ship," said Klemperer. "Same when passing in or out of the electro-bubble. Pinch your noses and blow. Ingress and egress are not an issue when the bubble output is reduced."

Inside was a large cockpit area with two rows of aircraft seats behind a long curved panel with many gauges. Bea rushed in and sat amazed, gripping the Blöhm & Voss wheel in the center seat. "Standard panel and yoke for a transport—altimeter, radio direction finder, horizon indicator, oversized airspeed indicator to 1500 kph, tachometer that reads up to…10,000 revs? Holy Jesuit polecats, this rig can reach forty-thousand meters altitude!" To her right were several brass levers, one being larger with lightening holes up the shaft. "Must be for throttle, lift, descent, and maneuvering." An entire black panel of engine gauges lay in front of the copilot's seat, but most made little sense to her: *Torsion Bubble Diameter, Megavoltage Flow, Dielectric Medium, Gravity Pressure, Antigravitic Electron Voltage, Plasma Output.* The largest dial read *Power Reserve* with indications from zero to one hundred percent; a moveable red marker was fixed at fifty-two. "I say that's odd…" A circular glass instrument with a curved swastika in the center met her eyes. "An ionic sun compass. No way to use a normal one with all this electromagnetism floating around."

"Nice solution," mused Bernie, examining it. "They didn't miss a trick."

Alice wandered up to a large piece of shiny metallic equipment attached to the port wall bang up to the ceiling, the likes of which she'd never seen before. Glowing a reddish-gold, it didn't seem to belong. "Herr Schäfer, what's this odd antique-looking thing?"

"More evidence," he replied.

Bernie accompanied her, eyes wide at the beautifully-made concentric circle clocks and inlaid dials that reminded him of the Renaissance and its genius clocktower makers. "It's entirely made of red brass…it must weigh *tons*. It's as if a hundred master watchmakers cobbled this thing up on a king's endless budget. This dial here looks similar to the *Dendera Zodiac*, the four Hathor women holding up the heavens, a 24-hour dial with strange numbers, Egyptian, Babylonian maybe, and unknown figures of animals and some sort of numerology at play in the outer rings. Planetary energies and retrogrades must be part of the navigation. I think this entire machine is made of Orichalcum, with inlays of silver and pure gold. An absolutely exquisite work of art. These three animals surrounding the main clock, a lion, tiger…and *bear*. So that's the origin of the name."

Schäfer stood proud. "*Tellus Gravitatus*, we call it. It is a work of art indeed, and still looks brand new after 15,000 years or so. It computes navigation by astrology, cosmology, gravity, electromagnetism, torsion, the sun and time using the Fibonacci Spiral as a waveform guide, but we must adjust our calculations for millennia of ever-changing stars at night. We can theoretically fly in any weather, day or night, and land precisely on a target one meter square, even in heavy fog or blinding snow. It is directly linked to the aft power generator. Needed a polish of course, some minor repairs and lubrication of parts with mineral oil. It is our unique astrological and astronomical navigational system, wholly grafted on from the derelict airship in the adjacent tunnel. An *Atlantean* airship."

"You're kidding," said Bernie. "Wait, you're *not* kidding."

Porsche ran his hand over the intricate engravings, delicate dials within dials, the many bizarre ancient symbols and inlaid crystals a mystery to him. "It's remarkable, no, *incredible*."

Klemperer pointed to the three sizeable Kriegsmarine naval chronometers mounted on the navigation panel; below them was another sun compass and moveable chart. "We have three chronometers, one with a green face for time inside the ship, another brown one for the world outside, and the blue is for Berlin standard time. Time and space are directly affected by the electromagnetic bubble surrounding Bear. Antigravity affects time itself since gravity and time are linked at the hip."

"Well done," said Schäfer. "And here I thought you had been only reading *pfennig* novels."

Excited, Baumann came up the stairs. "The faster the ship goes, the slower time moves on the inside, our perception of it anyway, we must make constant adjustments. It takes four of us Luftwaffe flyboys to pilot him efficiently, still many gremlins to work out. I need a flight engineer and copilot on the right panel, and a navigator and timekeeper to my left. Lots of coordination between us at all times. The *Tellus* computer does the rest. No electronics at all, only crystals, gold wire, and strange gears inside. It…took some getting used to, I'll say that. We think the crystals are some sort of transistors, or perhaps storage devices for information."

Gold-faced dials expertly etched with astrological images spoke to Porsche; he traced a line with his finger. "There's nothing strange about gears, young man. It reminds me of H.G. Wells and his time machine, loved that book. I like clocks, repaired them for fun as a boy. But this…this is a masterpiece. I *must* know how it functions."

"What's this strange inlaid hand print?" asked Alice, thumbing the exotic outlined alloy panel that was warm to the touch; a glittering diamond festooned the center of each fingertip outline. "Bit flash."

Baumann said: "No one can figure that out yet, but we've tried and tried. Perhaps the ancients used it to connect with the Tellus telepathically. It's beyond my pay scale. What would a diamond be used for Professor?"

Porsche fingered them. "I have no idea, young man. But I'll figure it out." Schäfer placed his hand on the shaped indentation but it was too big to fit. "The Atlanteans wouldn't have used it unless it provided a valuable function. A mystery we need to solve, one of many. As of now, it's useless."

"Theosophist Manly P. Hall was right about Atlantis and her airships. Time I hit the head. Herr Schäfer, if you don't mind," said Bernie, pointing, who then walked aft several paces to the ship's toilet under guard, one of three facilities. Closing the door, he read the instructions for the new standard aircraft unit, the pale blue walls polished to a mirror shine; a framed photo of Hitler scowled down at him. The seat was equally polished. "Hmm, manufactured by the VW works, Wolfsburg, patent #334562. Push lever down." He wiped, flushed, and a rush of freezing compressed nitrogen and vinegar followed. "Jesus, that's gotta be a first."

Klemperer banged on the door. "Hurry up in there, I have the need."

"Hope your puny balls can stand it."

"Is this, uh, astro-thingy connected to that Tellus gizmo?" asked Bea, pointing to the planispheric astrolabe device just below and in front of the main panel; it was a megalithic yard in diameter with numerous celestial coordinates, strange numbers, astrological symbols, and directional arrows engraved upon it. It was infinitely more complex than any astrolabe she'd ever seen, and was made of the same exotic materials as the Tellus. Three perfect amethyst crystals were secured in the center of the concentric circle globe, glowing subtly but steadily with a slight hum.

Schäfer sat next to her. "It functions in cooperation with the analog computer, though I'm told by Baumann here it's still somewhat of an enigma to us as to exactly *how* it functions. Concentric circles move as we move, the arrows giving direction, but it's overkill. The entire propulsion system is intimately linked to it with cables of twisted copper and gold, the insulation some kind of green crystalline matrix fabric, beautiful. The Luftwaffe engineers grafted it on as a connected unit. Everything the ancients made is harmonious and stunning to behold."

Facing them, Baumann said: "Who cares how, Ernst? We're lucky it all works still. The Bear flies effortlessly and fast, with little G-forces. A pilot's dream. Lands straight down from high altitude on a pfennig. Outruns anything, even at only fifty-two percent of its potential power."

These idiots are only using bits and pieces, and they don't know what they're doing, thought Bea. *They're toying with science they barely understand.*

Gerlach puffed as he came up the stairs with his two assistants behind. "I'll see...that you get a *hundred*." He pointed. "See up there? The three ballistic glass domes around the cockpit section are Viktor's design when he was tinkering with—"

"Schauberger's design?" asked Bernie.

Gerlach shot him an arrogant look and shrugged. "Who else in the Vril Prop-Shop understands torsion physics, vortex compression, and unified electromagnetic fields? The Schmuck—I call him *Schmuck* you know—put a thin coating of powdered quartz on the inside of the glass, then the powder was coated with a special silver-based plasma I came up with, leaves a residue. The mixture is precisely placed between a nano-gold monatomic positive node and a lead-based negative node using the Sacred Cubit as a measurement table." He pointed up, twirling his index finger. "The domes rotate in flight with pulsed high voltage, and when activated this system provides tremendous power via sound resonance and torsion fields. Simple, effective field manipulation for thrust and maneuvering, like bow-mounted rudders and propellers on harbor tugs; the twelve stern fins are intakes for ship-wide cooling air. The older Prussian airship designs fifty years ago used odd discs, fans, and pinwheels which were rudimentary and inefficient for field manipulation, but…they *worked*. Hot, hot, hot out there, I need a damn *weissbier*. Baumann, call for some liquid reinforcement, damn you."

Bernie looked up. "Amazing. Quite a leap from his air and water tornado experiments." "The *Schmuck* knows no bounds, no rules."

"I'll stick with good ol' fashioned ailerons if you please," muttered Bea. "Didn't help you last time round, Miss Siwa," sneered Alice, arms crossed.

Bea leaned to her. "How'd you like it if I stuck your head up there between the two electrodes and ran high voltage through that thick skull of yours, O bride of Frankenstein?"

She went nose to nose. "Least I'm *married*." Alice then meandered over to another large piece of equipment. "Airborne Intercept radar. I say, a new variant."

Baumann came over to them. "Ah, yes. Lichtenstein B/C 202. The best. Multiple antennas are built into the nose section, very heavy duty. Seamless. Propulsion power levels must be accurate for it to work." He smiled at Alice and she returned it. "Not that anything would be a threat of course. The bubble deflects any and all weapons. We tested a 40 mm naval antiaircraft gun against a mockup of the ship, all rounds bounced off, even a few from a 120 mm cannon. We're unarmed, but literally invincible."

"Very interesting," said Bea. *He's certainly chummy.* "Be forewarned. She's French- poxed from farm animals since childhood you know."

Alice pinched her cheek. "Funny, old bitch."

Dodging maintenance crewmen, an SS steward brought a tray of Pilsner in etched glasses for everyone.

Gerlach swigged and licked his lips. "Get this one. A Nazi Party positron walks into a bar. The barman explains they've run out of peppermint schnapps. Positron replies:

'*Scheisse*! Oh well, it's no matter.' Ha-a-a-haa!"

Stares.

"What's wrong with all of you? It's a German physics joke, it doesn't have to be that funny."

Schäfer, Klemperer, and Baumann laughed. Porsche let out a: "Hmmff."

Utterly fascinated, Bernie kept staring at the above nodes, their inner workings visible via inspection glass. "I'm not sure I understand the physics involved with these things, but..." An engineer moved him out of the way to access a ladder. He put in a new part and closed the dome's hatch.

Gerlach huffed: "Huh. That was the simple part. Come, Ferdinand, let's inspect the engine room. We've work to do."

•••

Through pressure-locking round doors, the group walked the starboard-side companionway and passed the navy-issue U-Boat all-electric galley, three staterooms with cramped bunks, a radio room with a celestial navigation dome, a closed, guarded compartment marked: *Information Center,* and the compact medical compartment to enter the large cargo bay. Hordes of engineers, contractors, electricians, and crew scampered to-and-fro busily making repairs and modifications. Everything—all doors, compartments, storage bins, panels, windows, and minute items—were precisely designed, compact, and highly functional, the hexagonal patterns everywhere. Strength and simplicity.

Sacred geometry throughout, someone used their slide rules effectively, thought Bernie, more impressed than ever.

Inside the ten by twenty-five-meter cargo bay were aluminum and wood cargo crates lashed down, an emergency landing Kubelwagen and tents, a weapons locker, water and fuel jerrycans, spare parts, cases of combat rations, and an observation Focke-Wulf Autogyro that was in the process of being offloaded in sections with a crane, its rotor blades folded. Pallets of pine lumber from the Alps followed.

"Are my crates of finds and treasures loaded on yet?" asked Schäfer of the flight sergeant. "The Berlin Museum will be overjoyed, the Führer more so."

The sergeant checked a manifest and pointed to a stack of overbuilt crates being lashed down by two crewmen. "*Jawohl*, Herr *Standartenführer.* Extra sawdust. Ahnenerbe symbols as ordered. 400 kilos."

Bea walked up a mobile stairway and inspected the Autogyro's cockpit. "A whirlybird. British RAF desert markings, is nothing sacred?"

From below Klemperer scolded: "Our new observation aircraft. And by the way, I read the *Gebirgsjäger* reports from Oslo in your file. Your stolen Heinkel reportedly had both German and British markings. Who thought of that folly?"

Arms were crossed. "Well, we were in a damned hurry to leave Norway that day…" *Annoying bastard.*

"He's got a point," shrugged Bernie.

Alice added: "Amelia Earhart wouldn't have made that mistake if she—"

"Oh, do shut the hell up, the lot of you."

Schäfer waved his arm. "Let us catch up with our esteemed professors, shall we?"

•••

Porsche and his engineer unloaded a large crate with help from two Luftwaffe crewmen. Inside were horseshoe-shaped electromagnets of thirty kilos each, specially-made by hand at his Stuttgart design works. "I copied these as per specifications. A pain. No, a nightmare. Too many rare earth elements, a strange design. I felt like a medieval alchemist."

"No one can build powerful and exotic magnets like you and your wizards, Herr Professor. Just think, the propshaft has no contact with its electromagnetic bearings. It floats on a sea of magnetism. No wear. No burnt bearings," said his Kriegsmarine assistant, Banner. "Just think, a potential 10,000 revs."

Porsche marveled at it. "Each magnet must be aligned perfectly with a micrometer and welded into place. Whoever those ancients were, they were damned good engineers. Hand me that instrument, the one with the indicator on it." He adjusted it. "Thirty-six microns exactly."

An arc welder with goggles then attached the magnet.

A Luftwaffe flight engineer asked: "Herr Porsche, will it be able to handle the extra power? No one has yet been able to—"

Jacket off, tie loose, he replied: "Of course! You newfangled Luftwaffe boys remind me of your Austro-Hungarian forebears in the *last* war—always doubting my work. I've done the calculations over and over in my head. The hollow propshaft is made of the strongest steel alloy Krupps make. At two-thirds of a meter in width, it had better work, I designed it back at B&V to the specifications required and beyond. This big sausage of a...*machine* is more akin to a naval ship than an airship, and I've had much U-Boat experience. You *do* know what those are, yes?"

Laughter by all.

"Sound frequency from an oddball electric motor to turn the shaft? Where are the pistons I ask? The gearbox? Diesels? Hmm?" Porsche bent down to finish the installation inside the magnetic propshaft trench. "Thank *Gott* it has counter-rotating propellers and my variable pitch gearbox, things I can sink my intellect into. Unified Field Theory my fat foot! How all this damn—hand me the torque wrench—over-unity antigravity floating-on-air spacetime bubble blatherskite works is beyond me, and that, gentlemen, is, mmmphh, supremely *annoying*."

He laughed. "Come, I'll show you how," said Gerlach. "Our guests are in the engine room."

•••

Gerlach opened the round pressure hatch with a turn of the wheel. A steel wall separated the giant five-meter diameter electric motor from the propshaft compartment for safety. "Ladies and gentlemen, save for the floor, this engine room is almost a perfect sphere of specially-coated hexagonal ceramic tiles for insulation, a new process had to be invented. Engineering the space-time metric with antique components is not for the faint of heart or slide rule." He pointed to the large crystal, gold, boron, and copper motor that looked like it had been crafted by an Italian sculptor. "The massive electric motor was built by AEG, an exact copy of the Atlantean original." He patted it. "It's surrounded by these nine large quartz crystals sourced from the famous cavern in Mexico as per original specifications; each is four meters in length, and yes, they glow, even at idle. But the absolutely perfect cone-shaped zero-point plasma accelerator and magnetic field generator behind it is what is truly mind-boggling. It's ancient and completely original having perfectly survived the eons. The pointed top is surrounded by these bulging spheres, *mmm*....not entirely sure what they do at present, but we'll find out by Odin's arse. It sucks energy out of the very cell structure of the holographic universe around us by compressing energized plasma, one which then fuses with the lattice framework of space-time. It's bolted to the floor with these huge fittings, and these two large electrical cables running in tandem provide current to the electric motor. When the motor turns with its huge magnets, a special sound frequency is created, tuned, and amplified by the crystals, thus turning the propshaft with no physical mechanical interaction, hence the very high revs. A unique mixture of ancient and modern technology. Recently the American Navy figured out how to turn a driveshaft by sound, yes, Herr Rodgers?"

Shocked, Bernie stuttered: "Well, that is, I can neither confirm or deny…that they…I would know *nothing* about that."

The two physicists, Lappe and Rodmann, examined the control panels, wires and internals exposed. "The Bear's entire propulsion system, its overall…*simplicity* is the real marvel," said Lappe. "Once its exotic nature is firmly understood, that is. Philosophy is just as important here as physics. These machines are a form of art that must be appreciated with a new mindset."

"Philosopher's Stone in action," said Alice arrogantly. "Piece o' cake." Bea crossed her arms. "Alchemy, eh? Bit boring."

Lappe looked amazed, Rodmann too. *How could these foolish enemy women know?*

Bea placed her hand on the generator panel that had another embossed outline of a hand about half an inch deep. "Another bejeweled handprint?"

Rodmann said: "We tried it in conjunction with the smaller one in the control room, but nothing came of it. A mystery."

Gerlach tugged at his jacket lapels. "It's nothing very important, probably just an artistic touch, irrelevant. Now, as you can see, this output cable provides power for the antigravitic hull hexagons for mass reduction, thus the generator must provide a double output, but it's one it can easily handle, especially when it creates its own antigravity bubble as well. What's remarkable beyond the obvious is that this plasma accelerator is internally cooled somehow. The experimental units we have designed all needed circulating liquid nitrogen. The earlier one on board U-917 failed when it was attacked. A tragic loss."

"It blew up? The experimental submarine? All the work we…the engineering, the crew, a waste, a *pissing* waste! Why wasn't I told about that?" asked Porsche angrily. "*Dammt!*"

"Security reasons, I'm sorry. Your rating wasn't high enough then," said Gerlach. "Classified projects are hermetically compartmentalized by direct order of Himmler."

With concern, Bea looked to Bernie, they both realized at a snap it was the big one they saw back at Kiel shipyards in '39. Now they knew what happened to it, and to

Lutz's Uncle Albrecht. "Never seen the Professor cuss so much before," she whispered.

"In war, sailors die for the Fatherland, Herr Professor," said Klemperer. "Their sacrifice has advanced our science in no small measure. We should honor them as *heroes*."

"Agreed," said Porsche, suddenly emotional. "May a loving *Gott* condemn this war. *Gott*damn it! *Scheisse!*"

Bernie whispered to Bea: "You said it."

"Sadly, yes, Ferdinand," said Gerlach. "But perhaps…with new science we can save lives, end the war early for all concerned as you once said. Ladies and gentlemen, let us bow our heads for a moment of silence for those U-Boat sailors." Gerlach shook, putting a hand on Lappe to steady himself.

Everyone bowed heads, lives were lives.

Bea thought of Albrecht and Lutz, then instinctively reached out and held Porsche's hand. *I feel…strange.*

The Professor shuddered slightly, then squeezed back, tears in his eyes for Lutz and his uncle whom he had met several times. Helge too, Lutz's widowed aunt.

A strong humming sound, deep, guttural, electronic, organic.

Bea followed suit in tears, then Alice. "Damn, Professor," whispered Bea, suddenly overwhelmed, her hair sticking out.

Bernie tried not to with all his internal might, but cracked like a walnut. "Sorry. It's the many civilians….children too…every damn last…" His eyes moved to the field generator. "What's it doing?"

"What's happening to us?" asked Gerlach in tears. "It should be at idle setting."

The generator hummed like a beehive, electromagnetic energy swirling in unseen atmospheric rivers, the room energized with high-frequency vibration and static electricity. Unbeknownst to all, this provided a stimulating narcotic effect. Orange light emanated from deep within the ancient machine, boiling their insides with bittersweet grief. The nine quartz crystals gave out a high pitch, one that was almost silent, but Bea and Alice could just barely hear it.

It had reacted to their emotions, thought Bea, holding her ears. *This is most bizarre…what the hell's going on in here? We're all human, all sentimental. Bloody ol' Gerlach, Porsche, I…* "Oh, my insides, the pain…"

Everyone suddenly shed tears, finally even Schäfer who turned his back, stomach aflame. "I'm so ashamed…"

"There's no shame in tears for the *fallen*, civilian and soldier," snapped Klemperer, eyes red, emotional.

Klemperer's two soldiers shouldered their rifles and began to sing "Erika," the traditional *Gebirgsjäger* song they all loved. More tears, more unexplainable aches.

The generator went back to green. Idle. Calm.

When they finished, everyone regained professional composure, but with great effort. Alice said: "Well, that was certainly strange and—"

"*Achtung*! Attention, all. Let us compose ourselves. You were saying, Herr Professor? The generator?" said Klemperer, wiping his eyes.

"Uhm, I…well, of course, look here, this…this generator is entirely *sealed*, none of us could find an opening," said Gerlach, wiping his eyes with a hanky, his hand upon the smooth casing that looked like an eggshell. "The…satin white ceramic material it's made from is a mystery to us, we think it may be an organic material, strong. Lights from inside show through the translucent shell as we just witnessed—different power levels are indicated by color: green for lowest setting, then yellow, orange for mid-level. If we can figure out how to make it perform at one hundred percent power, who knows what color that will be?"

"Lipstick red?" said Alice.

"Flush with a tinge of pink I think, all the rage," said Bea. "Oh, hmm."

Unusual but welcome laughter by all. A pressure release.

"Are these Englanders intellectually qualified to be in here?" huffed Gerlach.

"Believe it or not, *yes*," replied Schäfer, slightly bowed with arms outward as if a courtier of old.

"What kind of generator has no service panels?" asked Porsche, revived to his usual obstinate self. "Nothing makes practical sense here. A strange antique powerplant that makes us weep, a crystal motor big enough for a battle cruiser. This is poppycock voodoo science, Walter. You and the Vril shop personnel designed one hell of an electromagnetic white elephant with no guns. Wait till I inform Hitler about your waste of precious wartime funds on this overwrought plasma gasbag of a delivery truck."

Gerlach wagged his meaty finger at Porsche. "It's spiritual science. Don't mock what you do *not* understand. You're here to do a job fixing minor details as a simple mechanic. Just wait till you take a ride in this cigar. Fast and smooth. Tight turns made at speed defying the laws of mainstream Jewish physics; Einstein was wrong, they all were. Huge lifting capacity, especially for new generation *bombs*. I invented and perfected Unified Field Theory, and this ship personifies it a thousand square. Quantum physics and antigravity are the future, not your tincan coal-powered dinosaurs!"

With no love for theoretical physicists, Porsche went ballistic. "Those *dinosaurs* are winning the war for us on the *battlefronts*, gears grinding in the sand, snow, and mud, not your fanciful Zeppelin prancing about with a crystal pipe organ for an engine!"

Fists were balled. "Why *you*..."

"I believe the term is 'Handyman,'" said Bea. *Peacocks, the both of them.*

Klemperer barked: "Enough, gentlemen, *bitte*. With respect, you are all under the command and auspices of the SS here. Full cooperation, decorum, and discipline will be maintained. Am I not clear?"

Coughs and stares.

The generator went into low idle, no color. The Bear sank two meters in altitude. "What's wrong with this moody contraption?" asked Porsche, pointing. "Blew a fuse?" Gerlach put himself between it and Porsche. "Leave it alone!"

"What language are the hieroglyphic symbols at the bottom?" asked Bernie, kneeling.

Schäfer rubbed the embossed Orichalcum symbols. "My colleagues and I believe this is some sort of proto-symbolic language, possibly a scientific sub-dialect of Atlantean. It may be a warning. I have decoded three of the twelve symbols, they read: 'Light of the heavens,' 'Sol, or sun,' and this one here that looks vaguely Aztec means 'gravity under pressure.' The rest are a work in progress. Symbols can have many meanings."

"So...this is what you're trying to re-create back in Czechoslovakia?" asked Alice. "To replace coal, synthetic gas, and oil?"

"I'll believe that when I see it," said Porsche, examining one of the glowing crystals, the ancient and exotic technology a mystery to him. "What we really need is a gemologist in here."

Gerlach rubbed his chin. "Shuttup, Ferdinand. Yes, eventually this electromagnetic implosion technology will replace fossil fuels. But it's a slow process. We only understand the basics of how this plasma accelerator operates. I believe inside this four-meter tall unit are three sets of counter-rotating drums of liquid Red Mercury or an equivalent. Thorium oxide is most likely one isomer, beryllium perhaps another, the nucleus in a high spin rate. Who knows what else? Once spun up to 50,000 rpm, it will pull energy out of the vacuum of space-time and produce an estimated 900 million volts, hence the need for this insulated room. As I said, the AEG-built electric motor is an almost exact copy of the original Atlantean unit that had eroded with time, leaving us only a few bits here and there to back-engineer. Soon we'll have it at peak efficiency."

Porsche smiled, slide rule in hand. "And an *engineer* figured it out. Took my men and I six months to re-design it from the various antique pieces before the AEG men got their hands on it for final assembly. Every copper and gold wire threaded by hand with myself as witness. Magnets and electric motors I know well from my early days in Vienna." The generator went back to green.

Gerlach tried to ignore him. "See? It's fine. Once up to optimal speed, additional plasma will be routed by this conduit directly into the hollow propshaft and out the edge vents in each propeller blade, thus providing the electrons needed for antigravitic horizontal thrust, otherwise the propellers would not work with the ship's powerful electromagnetic bubble. We call it *Magneto-gravitics*. But we must unlock more power to use this system at peak efficiency."

"Your Projects *Cinnabar* and *Chronos*," blurted Bernie.

"How irritatingly *knowledgeable* you are, Herr Rodgers," sneered Klemperer.

"Indeed," laughed Gerlach.

"Enough hokum-pocus. What's the damn horsepower rating of this rig?" asked Bea, uninterested in physics.

"Unknown." replied Gerlach lovingly, his hand outline glowing blue as he touched the white casing. "It reacts to the touch as if it were alive and sentient. If only it could speak…"

Porsche adjusted his slide-rule and made calculations. "By my reckoning…at peak performance…somewhere near 1.269 million brake horsepower."

•••

With Porsche, Baumann, and Gerlach left to their various duties, Schäfer led his group to a large alcove several hundred meters away from the hangar area. Wide, it had been carved out with precision. A large pile of twisted black and green metal met them.

"Here is what's left of the Atlantean airship, it was shaped like a pumpkin seed originally, about a hundred meters long by sixty wide. Most of the fuselage is made of an unknown verdigris-looking alloy."

Bernie touched a dimpled, crystalline-copper section that looked like a frame of a racing Bugatti. "It's astounding something this old has survived, but the dryness of this cavern must have preserved it. I remember that the Atlanteans used copper for their ocean ships, some sort of propulsive force from fresh water and salt water exchange."

"Yes, and the deluge of rainwater around 30,000 years ago diluted their earth energy sites, causing problems," added Schäfer. "The copper-lined seawater ponds."

Alice and Bea peered inside. "Not much to see in here, it's basically empty," said Bea. "No seats, no equipment, no cargo," said Alice, looking up to the roof which had large oval holes where glass once existed. On the lower sides were round holes; the entire craft reminded her of her father's 17th-century silver sugar, an elegant table implement with many small holes in various shapes for the disgorging of scraped loaf sugar. "Visibility must've been excellent."

Schäfer followed them inside. "Whatever was in here dissolved eons ago, nothing left but an empty shell. Everything was built using sacred geometrical patterns. We think most of the ship was made of biodegradable organic material. Astounding technology."

Alice asked: "Wicker seats perchance?"

She rummaged. "Not bad Drumm, they made excellent aircraft seats."

"What's this here?" Klemperer noticed a small image hidden under 15,000 years of corrosion and dust on a bulkhead. "Symbols. Runes. Odd letters. Graffiti? I wonder…looks like when they escaped to this place, they carved their names here for posterity." He kept wiping, revealing more. "Go get a stiff brush and a soapy water bucket with a few drops of mild acid," he ordered. A soldier ran off.

"We missed this, but how? Schmidt and I fine-combed everything. A most excellent find, Klemp," said Schäfer, wiping with his fingers. "I'll make an archeologist of you yet, by Buddha." Fingernails were next.

The soldier returned. Klemperer scrubbed off millennia of caked dust, corrosion, and grime.

After several minutes, the group beheld a hundred or so carved-in names in an unknown alphabet. Each one had a picture of a favorite animal beside it.

"Oh, how sweet," said Alice. "Everyone drew their favorite."

"Incredible. Actual *names* from Prediluvian times," said Schäfer, scribbling in his notebook. "And ideograms over here representing entire ideas. The Atlanteans took great pride in their collective memory, and intertwined every aspect of their lives with nature. Their soul forces were more nature than those of humans in the present, and the spoken word which they uttered had something of the might of nature. A few symbols here I recognize, but the rest..."

"Look familiar?" asked Alice, fingering the encrusted Holy Sophia emblem with the two lions and Metatron sacred geometrical crown, with Bennu birds at the bottom in an Egyptian riverboat. It was a perfect inlay, as if a giant hydraulic press had embossed it with precision.

"Just like the one Gwafa and I saw at Siwa." Bea gently ran her hand over the names below the symbol, sensing deep history. "Perhaps the animals they drew were nicknames. That's what I would have done."

23

♈

October 4
9:30 a.m.

Bernie ate a hard-boiled egg and slurped scalding coffee at the table, eyeing the two seated guards by the single window, his only view outside. Two more soldiers stood outside the small barracks, the wood on the walls freshly-cut, floors clean.

Bea and Alice awoke on stiff cots with mothball-scented army blankets. "Oh-h-h-h, the head," moaned Bea.

Alice followed. "Too much bubb during the midday will do that. Damn, I dreamt I was photographing flamingo chicks on a salt flat in Africa for a fashion rag. Now I've been whisked back here. For what it's worth, I officially retire from the war." She ran to the attached bathroom, the only privacy available.

Outside at attention, all personnel sang "Jupiter" by Gustav Holst, a favorite, the loudspeakers blaring.

Bea sat and yawned. "Are they torturing us? Bloody Jerry. Pour me a cuppa?"

"Now we know the name of Himmler's genius contractor, Herr Kammler." Bernie poured, gently adding canned milk drop by drop.

"Wonder if we can post a letter." She nibbled hard brown toast with jam. "My, my, what a bewigged gentleman you've become."

"Thanks. We need to find *Gwafa*. Bargain something for our release," said Bernie softly. She sipped. "Not with these four buffaloes on our chests. Will they do an exchange with us?"

He toasted the soldiers with his cup. "Perhaps once in Germany, but Gwafa will die here in the mines. Think they understand English?"

"Maybe. The Waffen lads are trained well. Let's switch to French. *Comment allez-vous aujourd'hui, Herr Obersharführer?*"

"*Bon, madame, parfait,*" he replied with a smile, taking the time to clean his automatic rifle with a rod and solvent.

"My Engleesh iss not zo batt," replied the other man, repairing his hobnailed boot.

"Cheeky sods. Hand-picked, eh?"

Bernie pointed to the overhead lamp. "They hear everything by the way." Alice sat. "Damned bugs."

Schäfer knocked and entered with Geer in tow as the song died down. The guards stood at attention. "Ah! I see you have rested well after your hot showers and a good sleep. Pour us two cups? Fresh beans weekly from Italy. Before we get started today, I thought Edmund and I would have a cordial chat with you." He blew into his cup, both men having chosen to speak in English, their world travels endowing them with plentiful language skills.

"Thanks be to Socrates, all that speaking German gave me a headache," moaned Bea.

Exhausted, disheartened, and confused, Bernie asked: "Alright Ernst, brass tacks, what the hell do you really want with us?"

Schäfer looked to the SS platoon leader. "You may leave us."

Once they left, Geer discreetly snipped an electrical cord on the lamp. "Privacy now. They have one in our barracks as well. The blame will be on you three, however." He handed the snips to Bernie. "Another little addition from Kammler."

Schäfer sat, his tone more serious. "Listen closely. The Reichsführer has given me carte blanche to recruit scientific and historical personnel, and in this capacity I outrank Poppel, much to his irritation. We have French, Polish, Norwegian, and English scientists working for us back in Europe so it's not that unusual. Tomorrow at four in the morning we depart aboard Bear for Pilzen with a load of thorium ore destined for I.G. Farben to purify. They ship it by night train. We scientists have been in the field for over a year now, and our group merits a two-week home leave with family. You three will go as well once you sign foreign national Ahnenerbe contracts, but you will stay on board under guard. Thirty-six hours turnaround. After my crates are unloaded and I hand in some reports, Edmund and I will join you and we'll turn southeast for Argentina with a contingent of new SS personnel and scientific equipment as per schedule, our vacations voluntarily nixed. The other scientists will make their way down by cargo U-Boat since there is a scheduled weekly service in place already. Now, I have an agreeable proposal for you."

"But of course," said Bernie mockingly. "Hope you lot have flight insurance," said Bea.

Schäfer ignored them. "Once at our home base in the mountains outside San Carlos de Bariloche, I want you three fellow occultists to work with me writing a new history of the world for the Reichsführer. Ten volumes, a thousand pages each he has ordered; I have a large comfortable house in town already procured. We will make—"

Bernie said: "I knew it, I just *knew* it."

Schäfer snapped his fingers. "The German aristocracy took over that program from the Prussians and the American side got involved with basic antigravity in the 1860's. In the Andes there was a large cavern complex for airships, and a deal was made by all in 1905, but that's all I know. Let us forget that colorful non sequitur and move on, shall we? Hmm? Now, of course some archeology work is waiting for us, not only in South America—especially Saqsaywaman in Peru—but also the Yucatan with its untold amounts of undiscovered jungle cities and pyramids, a lifetime of work in itself. Then eventually we venture to Antarctica under the ice and mountains just inland of the Princess Astrid Coast. *Neuschwabenland* Base 211."

"*What?*" breathed Alice softly.

"You're damn well *joking*," said Bea. "With the ruddy penguins and walruses?"

Schäfer held up a palm. "You'll be paid extremely well and treated as *equals*, as German citizens, as civilian Ahnenerbe employees, escorted daily as we all are, but free to roam the cafés of Buenos Aries, Lima, São Paulo. Your existing bank accounts and new salaries transferred to Banco Tornquist by Bormann and his financial underlings; I know the Deputy Führer well, and they've been quietly moving the Nazi Party's Berlin and Swiss gold reserves down there brick by brick. He's a financial genius, it's all done legally. German corporations and American banks are involved with the secret transfers, even Volkswagen, since Porsche plans to build tens of thousands of his *Volksautos* in Brazil and Argentina someday."

"Grubby little Handyman, I'll attend to *him*," growled Bea.

"But I'm afraid…even if the war concludes, you will not be allowed home to your respective countries, not for the first few years anyway under contract, and contracts are ironclad." Schäfer removed an ancient scarab gold ring and slid it on Bea's finger. "Trust me, once exposed to the most interesting finds in the history of mankind you will not *want* to."

"Add three Rolls Royces into the deal and we'll consider it," said Alice seriously, her mind wandering the romantic Old World streets of Buenos Aires.

Bea examined the weighty ring. "Amen to that, sister."

"Soon the war will end," said Geer in a dire tone. "The Allies will eventually make an armistice once an atomic weapon is dropped on Moscow as an example to all concerned. Gerlach said his fellow physicists in Germany are close to building a thorium-229, plutonium, and uranium weapon of ten kilotons yield using centrifuge isotope enrichment, probably no more than a year away at most since Farben has a chemical laser in operation, and you'd better believe the Bear can deliver the twelve-ton bomb efficiently from extreme high altitude. Secret agreements are being made this moment in Berlin, Washington, Bern, and London. No one will actually 'win' this conflict, but the war will end with certain small portions of the Nazi Party and the SS intact only in Argentina…but no Hitler, *nein*. Göring is slated for chancellor. Bormann wants to live in Buenos Aires. A 'holding action,' they'll call it in secret, a permanent armistice, the Russians halted for good at the Volga River or else smaller one-kiloton uranium *Nebelwerfer* rockets will be used on them *en masse*; Waffen SS units have tested one already."

"*What?*" asked Bea in disbelief.

Bernie put both palms on the table. "You're *lying*. There's no way—"

Suddenly emotional, Schäfer said: "Huge casualties! An entire Red artillery battalion wiped out—we saw a classified film of it. We emptied our stomachs on the floor, images of limbs and arms, pieces falling everywhere, melted guns and artillery, civilians horribly burned. The *Heavy Gustav* railway gun lobbed a crude, seven-ton experimental atomic shell on a Russian ammunition bunker at Sevastopol recently, and the operation was under the overall command of your cousin Manstein."

"That's just swell," said Bea.

"An *atomic* shell?" asked Bernie in disbelief. "Are you sure they—"

Geer added: "A massive fission explosion resulted, and the Russian battalion surrendered soon after, sick and irradiated. There's plenty of uranium in the Sudetenland and Silesia, and now the SS physicists can purify it easily. Now listen, new technology will be shared only with the Allies, a *select* portion only. Ask Gerlach, as a senior Thule member *he* knows the full list of secret weapons under development."

"You were *right*, Bernie," whispered Alice.

He exhaled all the air in his lungs. "I wish I hadn't been. Long-range railway guns now make sense, and *Gustav* is the biggest in the world, a twenty-six mile range. A perfect atomic testing ground, the Russian Front—no foreign press, no mention of secret weapons by Stalin for propaganda and morale reasons. It's no wonder the Reds threaten their own soldiers with death if they retreat from the Germans, they now have true weapons of mass destruction. Thermobaric air-fuel rockets as well?"

"Yes, with coal dust in them," said Shäfer. "They're throwing *everything* at Ivan, especially the experimental weapons. Hitler underestimated Stalin's resolve."

Bea added: "So *that's* why Adolph rashly declared war on America, he thinks he's invincible."

Geer said: "Soon he may well be, but it's still not enough. The new weapons are complex, expensive, and time-consuming to build. The Russians keep coming with more men, artillery, planes, and tanks every day, an endless supply. Europe could become uninhabitable one day from nuclear fallout radiation. I am to guess you three understand that peculiar horror."

"So it's a matter of time versus production, eh? Well, atomic weapons or no, the Allies will *only* want an unconditional surrender of Germany," said Bernie.

Shäfer slapped the table in fury. "They can *call* it whatever they *want*, a–a *big victory* with parades and fireworks and fountains, a glorious *Gott*-given jubilee with roses and fat cherubs, but the war will just simply end as he just said, an agreed armistice under the table with the typical dirty deals for war criminals, bankers, and madmen. It has always been that way. Stalin will probably get Poland and eastern Czechoslovakia, maybe more."

"How do you two know all this?" asked Bernie suspiciously.

"Our sources are *reliable*, they've proven themselves over and over. You're not the only ones with intelligence training and access to über-classified material. Our entire team has had exposure over many years abroad as *Order of the Black Sun* members, an elite secret group within the Thule Society itself," snapped Geer. "Plus Ernst and I are German Secret Service…at your shitting *service*. In the SS, everyone is a spy to one degree or another, that's why we gifted Ahnenerbe speak so many languages. Or didn't you know that, Herr Big Shot?"

Bernie shook a fist. "For a gifted scientist, you're a real knuckle-dragging—"

"Easy, Bern, easy," soothed Alice.

"Just how many secret circles are within the secret circles? I'm as confused as ever," grumbled Bea.

Shäfer gathered them all closer. "Please, *bitte*, let us trust one another, and trust is a two-way street. I will enlighten you on a very, very classified bit of financial information in order to win your confidence. Agreed? Good." He squinted. "Think back. Do you know, Herr Rodgers, who *really* financed the Nazi Party from the beginning? Ponder carefully now."

He scratched his beard. "Ha-a-ah, let me think here, Thule Black Knights, Vril folks, that esoteric Templar guy Lanz von Liebenfels and his Ostara magazine, industrialists, various wealthy hob-nobs in Germany and Vienna. What of it?"

"They did a little, yes. But why? Have you ever asked that of yourselves?" Schäfer looked to each. "You see my friends, Hitler…is really the illegitimate son of Kaiser Wilhelm, and the German secret societies and certain German Illuminati know this, but Adolph does not. He was adopted by a hand-picked couple, his future expenses paid for by Prinz Gustav von Thurn und Taxis, a Thule member and Teutonic Knight. It is not uncommon throughout history. Ragtag veteran or no, the Thule Society knew he was the chosen one in 1919. They followed him, nurtured him, protected him. The peaceful Vril Society had high hopes for an Aryan savior, one that could activate the burning Germanic 'archaic subconscious,' using Norse runic and Tibetan symbology as firewood. Hess was chosen as his nursemaid and they became close. But war and gas attacks had tempered Adolph, his hysterical blindness the result. Embittered, his mind malleable, he went on to greatness as a dark illumined man with a silver tongue, one who created a regressive occult bonfire that may yet consume the world."

Shocked, Alice looked to Bea and said: "In God's gritty…that *vagabond* house painter? Hohenzollern, Brandenburg, Saxe-Coburg-Saalfeld royals? That means…he's Queen Victoria's great-grandson!"

Bea put head in hands. "I'll not have it. This can't be true…why do I have to be related to Prussians? Why?"

"Son of a royal bastard," whispered Bernie, who then laid a hand on Bea's shoulder. "No wonder a few German aristocrats funded the rag-tag Nazi Party in the '20's, he was one of them by birthright, a royal. It all makes sense now, he was no accident of history. The banks were printing money fast and the German people were starving under the Weimar regime. He and the Nazi Party were the solution, *Hegalian*

Dialectics—problem, reaction, solution."

"Indeed it does make sense, but he turned out to be uncontrollable, megalomaniacal, and insane despite his brilliance. He wanted freedom from the world's banking families like the Rockefellers, Morgans, Rothschilds, Payseur, Duponts, and Mellons who financed this war against him, but unlike all the others in history the war has gone far off the rails, so to say. The German people are stool pigeons for the regressive Illuminati agenda of world domination, hired guns just like in a Roy Rogers wild west film, but just look at how many people currently oppose the Nazis—*millions*. The resistance movement has grown stronger in occupied countries, and now we will join them in a way." Schäfer pointed at Bea and Alice. "Sorry to shatter your fragile reality, but bloodlines must continue to rule the world at all costs for the Anunnaki royal bloodline factions, even in complete secret. Now, as for Nazi Party funding, the main source was and is an entity that doesn't officially exist in neutral Switzerland, never has, never will, it's called…the *OCTOGON Group*. It was quietly formed in the mid-19th century in Zermatt—fascist aristocrats, occulted royals, industrialists, nationalists, Thule members, and bankers—proto-Nazis if you will, ahead of their time." Schäfer drew on a piece of paper. "If one draws a Templar Cross and then connects the sides with straight lines…"

"You get an octagon," said Bea. "The Templars founded Switzerland in 1291."

"Bankers and mercenaries for God, or some such rot," said Alice.

Shäfer scribbled. "Correct, only this clandestine council spells their name with an 'O.' They control the entire European gold reserves, much more gold, artifacts, art, and gems than anyone can imagine, the world's biggest horde dug deep into the alpine bedrock in hundreds of secure bunkers; tunnels are accessed below the Palace Mont Cervin. That, my friends, is why the Kaiser and his bastard son Hitler never invaded or secured Switzerland, it is Adolph's private bank, all the Nazi plunder resides with *OCTOGON*, and it grows daily by the many tons. Top-ranking Nazis in many countries are modern-day Templars at their very core, even some of your important British and American friends. We are talking many *trillions* of pound sterling, enough for future wars to be funded, enough to bribe whole nations into vile servitude. You asked about Himmler's blank check? *This*…is why the SS has unlimited funding; look around you, see anything interesting? High technology research and implementation cost vast amounts of money. Swiss and Argentine banks will continue to swell with ill-gotten spoils, a financial Holy Grail if you will."

"Trillions?" asked Bea breathlessly. "I can't even begin to…"

Nervous, Bernie tugged hard at his beard. Suddenly he felt very small in a world growing bigger and more complex by the minute. "This…does make strange sense from what I know."

"Bloody Swiss—cheese, chocolate, pocket watches, and mountains of pirate booty," mumbled Alice.

A pause to take it all in.

"Well, new weapons and sacks of loot aside, what if the Allies capture Germany?" asked Bea.

"What of it?" asked Shäfer. "The Allies will probably join the Wehrmacht against the Soviets, push Ivan back to his Neolithic cave. Everyone hates and fears the Russians, bad for business. Germany will thrive, it has to for a stable post-war European economy, and everyone in power wants that at all costs. The same hidden power structures that put Hitler into power will continue to survive; they are intimately intertwined with multitudes of governments. You three must try to *understand* the bigger picture. Even if Hitler survives and is forcibly moved to Argentina, Uruguay, or Brazil with an entourage, who cares? He's a sick man, mentally and physically, a fanciful Teutonic figurehead only, but keep in mind it is rumored he has a child somewhere in secret, a daughter; an artificially inseminated woman was procured, clean bloodline, and Adolph knows not of her existence. He was drugged, and a sperm sample was taken."

"A daughter? Poor thing," said Alice.

"The royals will stop at nothing to continue to rule," said Bernie. "They're determined and ruthless. They treat us lesser American bloodlines like dirt. I've had enough."

Shäfer continued. "Anti-royalist Himmler will take command at Base 211 down there, a progressive *occultist* Führer, one that is not as fanatical, shallow, and *regressive* as Hitler. Heinrich has always been a fastidious and calm man who can get miracles done in a timely, organized fashion. He told me he doesn't care much about the Jews, told me so in confidence. He took on the genocide project *only* to please his dear friend and mentor Adolph, but he strongly argued against it at first."

"That sounds like a load of horseshit to me," said Bernie.

"This is utter *madness*," hissed Bea.

"God, what if…who's on board with this escape plan in Germany?" asked Alice.

With great feeling, Geer hissed: "Our Ahnenerbe commander Wolfram Sievers for *one*. He has influenced *hundreds* of scholars back home in secret."

"What about the existing camps? The SS genetic experiments? The missing? The sickening *genocide*?" asked Bernie. "Hess said to me that Himmler will always be loyal to Hitler while he's alive, especially when—"

Eyes bulging, Schäfer mashed his fist on the table. "I don't know, damn you! As a simple scientist I don't *have* all the answers, I only know what can be done realistically. Now. Hopefully the genocide policies will end via…via negotiation an-an-and *diplomacy*. It's nothing new, remember your history—Turks and Armenians, the Irish potato famine, the American Indian tribes. Himmler will eventually make things right and I believe in him…or I used to, perhaps that is my own naiveté to overcome. Think we like what's going on? Our hearts are broken as well. I've witnessed horrible high-altitude experiments on Russian prisoners; Klaus was one quarter Jew, he has relatives in Dachau—children! But he was the best archeologist we had, probably the best in the world because he understood the genuine truth of it, and in Berlin they make *exceptions* for such men." A minute went by as Schäfer shook a little from anger and frustration, having pitched his coffee to the wall. A guard peered in. "Science and society *must* advance, and there are always huge costs involved, history bears this out. Evolution comes only from severe *stress*."

Bernie said: "Swell, just plain swell. If this is a foretaste of what's to come, I don't want any part of it."

"What's in it for us?" whispered Alice nicely.

"Ditto," said Bea. "We're a cut above the usual cutthroats."

"For one thing, no *firing squad* in the morning," snarled Geer. "Poppel wants you gone, one way or another. He has the authority here to override a prisoner exchange with you three and you're not that important in the grand scheme of things. If he had his way, he'd send you back to Germany to be tortured and interrogated by experts, but there's no room on the transport plane for you in any case, full to the brim with Kammler and his men; they took off at five sharp. It's a practical decision. No loose ends. You are safe only with us. This is a highly classified operation here, strict timetables, if it wasn't for Ernst and I they would have—"

Bea said: "One condition. We want our colleague with us, Gwafa." "Non-negotiable," added Alice.

Bernie flew into temper. "Now wait just a damn minute, I'm not agreeing with these—" "Shh!" said Alice.

"Pipe down, hothead. What exactly do we have to bargain with?" asked Bea quietly but firmly. "Not much except what's in our collective memories. Our mission's scrubbed. Done. In the bin. I'd rather re-join the Ahnenerbe and work for the good of humankind—in a *fashion* of course—than die for zilch. This barmy plan *does* have a corsair spirit to it. To hell with McMaster and Winnie and the flipping brass hats, I've had a bellyful of their patriarchal head games and mislaid plans. We may not survive this war. I have absolutely no idea who we're fighting anymore. What say you, Drumm?" *Come on Bernie, follow my lead.*

"She's got a point, boss."

He stood, knocking over his stool. "To hell and back with both of you!"

"See you at dawn then," mumbled Alice.

Bea looked at Shäfer. "Find Gwafa. Bring him to us. We'll drop him off near, uh, Tehran or something, anywhere safe, then you'll have our full cooperation."

"Too dangerous. We can't land en route," said Geer.

She snapped fingers. "Wait a sec, wait…wait…wait, he's part Dogon. You know, the tribe with the Sirius star ancestors? He could be a valuable assistant for you, Ernst, he knows the stars, navigates by them in the open desert," pleaded Bea. "He's damn smart, probably smarter than we three chickens combined, that's why he's with us. Self-taught in the Arabic fashion, a bookworm, his breadth of mind vast. Quotes Rumi like a Sufi elder high on Allah's own ale."

Bernie moaned and griped, rubbing and pulling his hair. He couldn't muster any other solutions. "Bea's right. We need our friend, or no deal."

"Dogon? An assistant?" Schäfer looked to Geer. "Not a…popular decision, a *schwartzer*." "Don't do it, Ernst! A common negro isn't worth the risk," snapped Geer. "*Nein!*"

Bernie pounded the wall. "No deal, boys." "*Ernst…*"

Both girls shot the Germans a stiff look. "Fuck off, Geer," said Alice.

"This is getting too complicated, too *risky*," worried Geer.

Schäfer thought long and hard. "I'll make it a scientific decision, and he's not common, Edmund. With his genetic ancestry he could be most useful in our work, especially African cosmology. I'll smooth it over with Poppel, tell him Gwafa will be my bestial manservant in Argentina, he will not care a whit. Once in Argentina the black man can go his own way, I'll provide him ample funds. Poppel's not going with us down south once the mining operation shuts down. Good riddance to the swine I say."

Bernie slowly turned to face them. "Wait...why not? Poppel's not with you in this plan?" An uncomfortable pause; sounds of heavy machinery and work outside.

Geer cleaned his nails with a knife tip. "*His* responsibility...is the thorium mine here, but in five months they will have more than enough ore stockpiled in Pilzen for dozens of bombs and plasma accelerators. Then he will slaughter the Arab prisoners working the mine. He'll probably be assigned to the Skoda Works overseeing Kammler, the atomic scientists, and others under General Mazuw's overall command in Czecho. He's not...one of *us*." Knife tip met table, a wobble.

"One of who?" asked Bea. *What are these two jilly-jabbering twits up to?*

Shäfer drum rolled his fingers on the table over and over, thinking. "He's not... one of the *new* breed of Germans. But I will ask you to let this go if only to further our original—"

"Oh, *really*?" asked Alice. "Like a pure-bred Pekinese? For the life of me, I'll never understand your Byzantine nonsensical Nazi hierarchy." Bernie crossed his arms. "Ditto."

Geer said: "Why would you? You three cannot begin to unders—"

"New breed, eh?" interrupted Bea. "Your Aryan caste system expands *yet again*?" She leaned in and looked to Geer. "You've measured so many Tibetan skulls for racial purity with that idiot Beger, perhaps now you should measure your own for sanity."

Bernie and Alice chuckled.

"Spoken like someone who should *know*," replied Geer. "Go on, tell them all of it, Ernst. If we can't trust the 'enemy,' who can we?"

Digging up the last vestiges of her Cambridge drama club skills, Bea gave Schäfer a look of sincere fondness, then slid the ring back on.

Stressed, Schäfer sharply inhaled and sighed with vigor. "Fine, what does it matter at this point? I wanted to wait until...*dammt*. All of us scientists have quietly joined..."

"Go on," whispered Geer. "*Bitte*, Ernst. Please."

"...an underground breakaway group, the *Neuschwabenlanders* they call themselves. How do I explain this? It is so...con-vo-lut-ed." He paused for a moment, gathering thoughts. "You see, with great courage, the U-Boat crews, a few Old Guard aristocrats, and all the scientists left behind in Antarctica and southernmost Chile have recently voted on their permanent detachment from the Reich, *voted*, as is done in a *Constitutional Republic*. They changed the rules of the entire project. Back in '38, Hess, Göring, and Admiral Raeder made sure women and family members went with them because of the extreme remoteness of the 211 base under the Muhlig-Hofmann mountains; it's been an ongoing project for nine years, Hitler is most proud of the accomplishment, his…'southern Shangri-La.' But something strange happened, now the *Neuschwabenlanders* want an independent German colony, one free of the Reichstag and Führer…and eventually even the SS. One with a constitution no less. Fair Aryan laws. A relatively peaceful existence, disciplined, with occult science and spirituality at its core. No more western religions, only the ancient Norse Ásatrú solar cults that go back well before Atlantis. No prophets."

"I remember Ásatrú teachings at my SS school," said Bea. "Bit heavy on the sex ritual kundalini stuff, but I suppose that wasn't altogether too bad."

"Oh, I'm assured," mumbled Alice as Bea shot her a stern look.

Geer went on. "No more debt, a gold-backed barter economy only, trade with friendly Chile and Argentina mostly, and the *Schwabens* have stockpiled gold bars in quantity; FIAT currency is just worthless paper, always has been. That is the idea, large international banks print their own with abandon as was done in the Weimar Republic. Say what you want about Hitler, but he put us on a Reichsmark currency that was based on hours of work, not international gold, and that infuriated the Illuminati bankers who genuinely started this war. Anyway, the swastika and eagle will continue as a symbol for the 'Schwabens,' but the correct reversed swastika, the Tibetan *Yungdrung*. It represents the unifying force of the cosmos, the positive spinning torsion of creation and constant change for the better, as it was originally intended by the ancients."

"Oh, I'm quite assured," said Bea. "Lance the old Nazi ulcer and be done with it, eh? Sounds like just a different flavor of pure Fascism, no offense." "It's not!" snapped Geer.

"You're splitting atoms, Geer," said Bernie.

"Why of all places Antarctica? It's sub-arctic cold. Bitterly so," said Alice.

"My dear, there are as many reasons as stars in the sky," smiled Shäfer. "Remoteness, privacy, scientific wonders beyond imagination, valuable natural resources, and the fact that it's an entirely unutilized continent are only a few. It's the most secure and unassailable base in the world. They don't fight the ice, they *use it* to their advantage. Very little to see by air, now or in the future. They currently understand the importance of the female as the human prototype, the *original*, men being just castoffs of the Divine Feminine. Many women leaders will emerge triumphant, the men being much less intuitive and, dimensionally speaking, higher realm-capable. Hyperspace travel to the stars someday, our true *Lebensraum* destiny, will require many psychic female navigators."

"I like that bit!" said Alice. "Pssh!"

"This nutso plan is a *big* gamble," worried Bernie. "Why would they take the risk? If Hitler finds out there's a pocket of traitors he'll send the entire Kriegsmarine down there to wipe out the—"

Impassioned, Geer added: "Not all Germans are Nazis, many of us *hate* them, you three know that, and don't tell me your own countries are free of Fascism. Admiral Raeder was furious when he found out at first, but now he's quietly supportive say our Kriegsmarine contacts. We think *Grossadmiral* Dönitz may be as well, a high probability. Many high-ranking officers are beginning to lose faith, they want Hitler and his preening 'Tan Pheasants' in a mass grave, peace with the western Allies, their Prussian honor restored. Peace with Ivan. Poland split down the middle. Your cousin von Manstein too, yes?"

"Possibly. Many of the Prussian Old Guard do," said Bea, looking over her shoulder to Bernie. "Royal bloodline wars for top position are pretty common, even internally."

"Assassination attempts on Adolph are legion," said Alice. "He has to change his schedule hourly on that armored flak-gun train of his."

Leisurely, unexpectedly, Bernie began to softly laugh, which then rolled like thunder. "H-h-hold on a minute, this shit just gets better and better...you mean...you mean to tell us you're part of a group of *rebels*? Like us Americans in 1776? Tell the mother country—sorry, *Fatherland*—to fuck off so you can create a better way of life and government presumably under a thick sheet of ice? Smack dab in the middle of a raging world war? This stinkin' garbage makes no sense."

Shäfer went ballistic. "Keep your voices down! Yes, that's it, Rodgers, and it's perfect timing during the chaos of war—think about it. It was *inevitable*, too much centralized power, too much ambition, ego, conquest, too much gestapo, SD, and

Russian front madness. We Germans, we proud Visigoths are tired of being 'genocided' throughout history since before Roman times, then by Jesuit-backed alliances, foul royals and—"

"So I guess poor ol' Kammler and the downtrodden SS didn't get the internal memo on that one," snapped Bea.

Shäfer angrily said: "Don't forget your beloved Churchill, Uta dear, a genocidal maniac. And you, Rodgers, the American Indian slaughter and the cruel slavery of blacks. Jim Crow."

Geer sighed heavily and pulled his hair in frustration. "You English...I..."

"No nation is saintly, we all have blood on our hands. We're all responsible. Law of One." Bernie neared him and spoke softly. "Yeah, I get it now Ernst, I finally *get* it. This weird patchwork history is coming together rather oddly but nicely, *old buddy*. Let's get this shit straight. First the Anunnaki invaded, their caste systems, empires and wars flourished. Atlantis and Lemuria, Og, Khmer, and Mu. Fast forward. Courtly asshole John Dee summoned other space people, then secretly went to Prussia after Queen Elizabeth kicked him out of England during one of her frequent hissy fits. He illegally taught the Bavarian Illuminati Enochian Magick much to the disdain of the Holy Roman Pope and his winged monkeys from OZ. Well-read Prussians gained advanced engineering and alchemical help from the so-called 'angels' from outta town, but in exchange for human sacrifice, so I'd say most of those angelic types were demons in reality: *Raphael, Uriel, Anael*. Then it was the Thule Society and Maria Orsic who carried the torch by gaining more knowledge. But you industrious Germans are *just* a little itty-bitty different from anyone else—more technical universities, Gutenberg's printing press, NYMZA, clocks, airships, combustion engine, pharmaceuticals, Needle Guns, Krupps artillery, big-time physics, the whole pile o' beans. Pretty expensive black market stuff I'd say. That's why Europeans have always been picking on you Krauts, your special knowledge that can be used militarily, that and your warlike tribes with Thor's hammer thrust up their backsides, the ones who could implement those technologies better than anyone else, yes?"

"Don't forget the Steiff Teddy Bears," said Alice.

Bea whined: "Oh, I loved those..."

"Benevolent wisdom was deciphered as well," said Geer. "Don't forget that."

"*Ja...ja...ja*. And now spacecraft are crashing all over the world; someone wants us to advance more quickly during this war by retrieving the debris." This time it was Schäfer who went face to face. "You listen, fucking John Paul Jones, like us or not, my young nephew and our boys froze *solid* last winter from lack of proper food, fuel, lubricating oils, and warm clothing, and will again from Berlin *incompetence*. No stuffed bears for them! Horses pull trucks out of the snow, men eat the horses; guns jam at minus forty. Frostbite. Rommel's momentum and luck are running out, his supply lines bleeding from British naval attacks, but Goebbels won't print that. Any traditional German with half a brain can see it's starting to fall apart, a matter of time only. A year or so, two at the most since you Americans are now in it with unlimited war production and manpower. Germany will be ground to dust. The very minute Hitler declared war on America we knew it was probably lost, atomic weapons or no. Everyone knows a second front is coming, maybe a third. A death knell. We illumined few must prepare for the *inevitable*."

Bernie nodded. "Maybe. But what if your high command decides to drop an atom bomb on the Allies or London? What then?"

"Oh, *gods*..." exclaimed Bea.

"Once Hitler is dead or gone that won't happen," said Geer. "Göring admires Churchill's bulldog resolve in secret, he wants peace and cooperation with the Allies at all costs, a lion's portion of the entire Wehrmacht high command quietly respect Prussian aristocratic Hermann. A stable Germany. Hess knew that, both are high-born occultists, they had a plan together."

"That was over a year ago," said Bernie. "It failed."

"Even more reason to commandeer The Bear once over the South Atlantic." Schäfer pointed outside. "With this airship, free energy generation, and new Scalar-wave weapons we can hold off anyone in the near future, start a new civilization without help or interaction from greedy and untrustworthy foreign powers, the Vatican, and *grosser* banks. Develop a new culture based on the...the *wisdom*, spirituality, and technology of the ancients. It will make your eyes water and cock go stiff to imagine the many Atlantean and other high-civilization ruins to explore. Whole *cities* have been discovered intact under the ice pack, the legendary *Kadath*— twenty, thirty, fifty, a hundred thousand years old or more, the ice layers reliable indicators of geologic time having passed. Colossal pyramids and intricate star forts are strewn everywhere.

"Operational portals to countless dimensions in the cosmos...don't look at me like that, it's the truth! That's why the *Schwabens* have changed the rules of the game—

they see their situation and the wider world differently now, just as we do. Many are old aristocrats like you three, they hate Adolph and the Jesuits, and have joined with renegade elements of the Black Sun Society and certain intra-terrestrial and extraterrestrial Aryan groups to form a strong unity. They are tired of everyone wanting to wipe out all us Germans, and in the future they may even leave the planet for pastures unknown. Do you not see how all this is connected?"

"Aryan Intra-terrestrials? Extraterrestrials? I think we can connect the dots," said Bernie. "Sort of…"

"A hundred thousand years old?" asked Alice.

"Entire cities?" asked Bea. "Hope they have a few spacewoman-friendly mead and ale pubs."

Shäfer paced, rubbing his sore neck. "No alcohol permitted other than for special rites, nor is divorce or abortion, one of our contacts said that star nations in the universe that practice abortion die out in only a few centuries. All souls needed on deck, as sailors say. At Base 211 there are strict laws and customs, yes, strict racial guidelines, but imagine the new crystalline and consciousness-based technology to be fully understood, ones that could change the world overnight, end wars, injustice, inequality, poverty. That's why Antarctica is a hidden agenda within all the other filthy agendas. And don't think your American and British intelligence people don't know about it, Russians too, they all have their own expeditions going on. I flew over them in '38 with Baumann in a ski-plane." He shook a little, growling: "There…they…*were*. Admiral Byrd's little elves with their steam drills, huts, and tracked vehicles by the score; 'drill down far enough and you will hit something of value,' Byrd said to me with a Cheshire cat smile."

Bernie snapped: "Byrd? Don't give me that bull—"

"They were in cooperation with the Russians, Finns, Norwegians, and British, veteran arctic explorers, we talked with all of them upon landing, had tea together, vodka, one big happy circus." Schäfer procured a large photo from his rucksack. "But in a few decades the whole continent will be militarized, and conflict will probably erupt between factions over territory when the war in Europe ends. For now, the *Schwabens* are the strongest by far with the most underground real estate, manpower, arms, and important finds. *El Presidente* Ramón Castillo has visited from Argentina and was astounded. He said he will provide additional naval support for them. Mutual benefit. Bormann and Octogon's gold to prop up his economy."

Bernie scrutinized the photo. "Sonofabitch…that's Byrd with you guys all right." *What the hell?*

"*Scalar*, you said? That's Tesla's quantum invention, similar tech to our new Klystron radar systems," said Alice worriedly. "McMaster showed me the schems. Theoretically, on paper, it could melt a battleship. What if—"

"Gerlach said to us they are working day and night on it at Farben," worried Geer. "A directed energy weapon, no recoil. Couple that to Bear's generator in a few years and it could work. Whole cities could be destroyed. Atomic weapons are filthy-dirty with deadly radiation, but this new weapon leaves no aftereffects, no foul residues. Precise, a surgeon's scalpel."

Bernie sighed. "Yeah…the U.S. Navy's working on that idea full steam ahead, but we're way, way behind."

"Lovely, just plain lovely," mumbled Bea. "Another malodorous medley of maladies to nightmare on. This is starting to make frightening sense…"

He kept staring at the photo. "With my rarified clearance I would have been briefed if ancient cities existed under the ice," said Bernie confidently. "Or classified active Navy expeditions that included Byrd. They would have told me…if…when I was…"

"Piece it together, you idiot. Byrd was an incognito advisor on the secret '36 German Antarctic mission. He knows everything," said Schäfer frantically. "Our governments have been quietly cooperating with one another for over a decade on certain 'ghost projects' that are extremely classified, even now, today, this minute. Prescott Bush and the big banks continue to finance Hitler in complete secret. All three of you need to *grow up*."

"What?" asked Bernie. "No, no, no, when I was sailing with Bushy years ago he said he was against…he *promised* he would take on…"

A moment of deep thought by all.

Bea gave Bernie a forlorn look. "Though you'd think we'd rate it by now… McMaster and Menzies don't tell us everything you know."

Alice added: "Nor FDR or Uncle Winnie, Bernie. ONI, G2, the lot."

"And soon the goddam OSS." *At least Hess was honest with me. I'll punch Simpson's lights out if I ever get home. He lied, I just know it. But why?*

"You sure you have all the dots connected, Bernie?" asked Bea. "Well I was—"

Schäfer went on feverishly. "Wrap your minds around it, extrapolate! Marry the man or woman of your choice, help raise a–a *new* generation of knowledgeable children not falsely programmed by schools and universities to be mindless sheep, drafted soldiers, or slaves to debt. No more royal authority, no more ignorance of the cosmos; they will learn Atlantean metaphysics, advanced transgenics, responsible ecology, zoology, and true world history—a new generation of enlightened Aryans will evolve. South America will be ours in totality, and peacefully so…as I said, *mutual benefit*."

Bernie sat, deflated at having been compartmentalized and kept out of the loop by his own people, the war a convoluted, enigmatic puzzle created by rival factions for profit, territory, and occult death rituals, the raw Vril energy of millions sucked dry by unseen vampires from many dimensions. Bea was right, it was utter madness, but on a scale they could barely grasp.

After decades of hard field experience, he could sense Schäfer was telling the truth, perhaps his own *Ahnenerbe*-tainted version of it, but the truth nonetheless. Bernie didn't want to believe it, but he did have to strongly consider the frightening possibilities. Now he was the one feeling naïve, and it stabbed him like a hot knife.

"New generation? I'll just bet," snapped Bea. "Sounds a lot like the zesty *Lebensborn* project, the one with all the pretty blond girls and boys singing and shagging in the haystacks with no—"

Geer pleaded. "Listen to us! For years they have been growing crops and forests under the ice, plenty of food and animals for the already 63,000 people there, more arrive every month by steamer from northwest Spain: Germans, French, Basque, Spanish, northern Italians, Ukrainians, it doesn't matter as long as the woman is Aryan, fetching, and strong, the bloodline pure, and believe me the SS can test you reliably now. A few men even, the lucky bastards, four women to one man. *Antarktische Siedlungsfrauen*, or 'Settlement Women,' the-the *pale* blue uniforms, Italian-style garrison caps, special insignia. An ASF training camp was set up in Estonia, on a peninsula near Ristna on Hiiumaa Island in the Baltic Sea. It is a combination finishing school and boot camp, where the ladies take lessons in charm and housekeeping along with their courses in polar survival, science, and weapons."

"Housekeeping, eh?" asked Alice.

Bea asked of Shäfer: "What about us Shieldmaidens?"

"A few have volunteered," he replied. "They train the others there, but that's all I know." Geer went on. "Empty temperate caverns were found in Antarctica, big enough for all of Munich to hide inside; they've begun an improved Aryan soldier program using retroviruses, but we have few details on that other than it's run by General Walter Krüger. The caverns are warm, moist, heavenly—cold dry skin heals in minutes. Hothouse pear trees. Oranges. Milk cows graze on grass fields several kilometers in length. Rabbits galore. Pigs. Almond trees. The U-Boat men pack their hulls to the brim when returning to Saint Nazaire, they eat like kings! Even Spanish horses roam freely. Date palms grow with a new form of artificial sunlight. Humid warm air from geothermal springs and plenty of fresh water. Communal hot baths. It's a *Gott*-damned paradise, a miracle. We've *been* there, Ernst and I witnessed it."

"Horses? Really?" mused Bernie. "So that's where all those cargo ships are bound from A Coruña. A supply line. McMaster and Menzies were right." *Improved Aryan soldiers? Krüger? Must be genetic programs...*

"Wouldn't mind a hot spring bath," mumbled Alice.

Exasperated, Bea said: "Miracle my soggy arse. This is a fattest load of crackpottery the likes of which the world has never witnessed before! Octagonal gold piles? Aryan eugenics? Bizarre equine transgenics? Orange-stuffing Black Sun civil servants? Cowpat pyramids and palm tree forests in steamy caverns? I'll thank you not to exaggerate to us any long—"

"Let the man finish," scolded Bernie, the bizarre, uncomfortable puzzle pieces falling together one by one like snowflakes.

"Don't pour scorn upon it. It can *succeed*, you know it can, Uta, but we need your help for the long term. You three can become our ambassadors for England and America, the big Illuminati wheels will listen to their own," pleaded Schäfer emotionally, holding her hand. "Many Tibetans will join us as fellow Aryans. Some of the Berlin ones are there now as spiritual teachers for the families, the ones who fully understand mankind's duality and place in the universe, the ones who became disillusioned at the Reich Tibet Institute. Positive Bon rituals are performed daily along with ancestor worship. Someday soon we'll build Stupas and gold-domed temples to amplify cosmic worship, the spiritual positivity growing daily as it did in ancient times. The universe has four fundamental vibrations: Love, harmony, wisdom, and *freedom*." He pounded the table. "We Aryans... must...be...free!"

Bea squeezed back, sensing an opportunity. "Sorry, I...sounds amazing, Ernst. It really does. Bit of a long bow to draw, all that, but..."

Bernie got up to look out the window. *He's in love with Bea, always has been, why didn't I pick up on it before? No wonder he wants us in on the deal. This is nuts, insane, but what choice do we have? Sweeten the pot.* "Okay, okay, let's…let's say we agree to cooperate fully and with honesty and integrity, tread the middle path as it were, but I say to hell with Himmler as a new leader down there, no chance, he's a psychopath like the rest, let him perish on the clipped vine with Hitler. What you need is a kindred spirit. A brilliant mind, an occultist leader with some semblance of ethics and morals. Hess, for example, I've known him for years, just saw him. Fit 'n fierce."

"That's your idea of a middle path?" asked Alice incredulously. "Told you the Hermetica was rubbish," mumbled Bea.

Shäfer mused the idea. "He co-sponsored the original expeditions to the ice in '36 and '38, he's one of us, maybe the *original* one, Edmund. This breakaway concept may have started with him well before he left for England. *Ja-ja*, it makes perfect sense. Perhaps it was to be part of his agreement with the English King and Mountbatten."

"Count on it," said Bernie. "But something went awry on the Brit end. Maybe Antarctica was one of the bigger problems…yes, yes, maybe *that* was it, they couldn't manage a fair agreement amongst themselves for post-war territory. Hess even alluded to that."

"In some ways Rudolf is perfect, Ernst. But England is far off our course," worried Geer.

Bernie finger-dabbed the table again. "I know *exactly* where he is. The three of us can spring him in fifteen minutes flat at night. Hover that Zepp over Wales and we'll nab him."

Shäfer shook his head. "*Nein*. Sorry. Too risky to fly over there, the radar you know, and you might flee while in England, no offense. But once we're in Argentina, we will negotiate hard for his release. I promise you that. Britain will need gold after the war, lots of it."

"This is no time to be thinking of Aunt Walter," said Bea. "Honestly."

"Well I was just…"

Alice slumped with mental exhaustion. Inside, she couldn't help but be intrigued by the utopian idea, and possibly with Klemperer at her side. It would be high treason, but she was becoming disillusioned by the hour. "I'm in. Anything for a soft bed and proper jam biscuits. Love penguins."

Bea slowly raised a finger. "Hol-l-ld on a tick-tick-tick, just how are you going to get this frozen daquiri of a nutjob plan done?" she asked of Shäfer. "Sell everyone in this cavern equal value real estate shares? A holiday home in an ice cave replete with seal fur furniture?"

Bernie crossed his arms. "You know, I-I-I was wondering the *same thing*. Who else is in on this teacup revolution? Erik the Red? Beowulf?"

Shäfer replied confidently: "Besides all ten scientists, Baumann is with us, so is his navigator and copilot, he said. Porsche we need for a long while. We'll take him for a year or two, but if he wants to go back to Germany in peacetime to his family that's fine, my word upon it. A mechanical engineering genius will be paramount. Building out many caverns under the ice for airship hangars, ship quays, science labs, schools, and U-Boat pens will require new technologies, new ideas, firm solutions."

Geer added: "I doubt Gerlach would be interested, he's a Nazi through and through, a hardliner. Too much trouble."

Bea said: "Sedate Porsche heavily is my advice. He'll pop his cork but good when you tell him where we're headed."

Geer poked Shäfer. "The two Vril assistants with Gerlach, we'll press them into service as well; he groomed them. We need quantum physicists who understand metaphysics, temporal, and trans-dimensional science. They're unmarried they told me."

"This is just...what about the Luftwaffe crew and armed Waffen boys on board?" asked Bernie with deep concern in his voice. "All the pistol-wielding cargo handlers?"

"Leave that to Baumann and me," said Shäfer, pacing, stretching. "We'll need muscle, especially with the new personnel *en route* to Bariloche. Our knight errant Klemperer is 'on the fence' as you say, undecided, he's most unhappy at being passed on for promotion three times and quite vocal about it when prodded with flattery and schnapps in private; oh yes, he drinks a little, so do some of his men, just not to 'evil spirit' excess. He'll be on board Bear with ten troops for our protection in transit just as was done on the trip down here."

Shocked, Geer asked: "You told him? Of all...why, Ernst?"

"Cal-l-l-l-m yourself. I've made it a point to get to know him better like any good expedition leader, we're friends, and we both admire Himmler's forward thinking, on science at least. A hundred mountain troops are under his command here. He may be a stiff-arsed soldier, diligent, proficient, but he's not stupid or ignorant. Despite his rude outbursts and *Das Reich über alles* bravado, he patiently listens and learns in between tirades, unlike his more shallow subordinate officers, new boys *Hauptsturmführer* 'Pickelhaube' and that nasty little squirrel Ötvös, both regular-issue Waffen SS, eager idiots who would rather be gloriously fighting Cossacks in the Caucuses and winning Iron Crosses than babysitting us weary bone-diggers. I only broached the idea as a possible future concept post-war, Klemp knows only the long-term broad horizon view, and I was vague on precise details, but he did listen carefully those many months ago when—"

Enraged, Geer grabbed Schäfer by his collar. "*Scheisse!* Why would you have—"

He broke the grip with a quick, two-handed upward thrust. "Quiet, Edmund! If he suspected even a whiff of conspiracy among us eggheads he would have *turned us in* by now, eager for promotion. Don't you understand? Klemp is the *keystone* in our arch, we must have him on our side when the time comes, he's the only officer his mountain men will listen to when the going gets hellish rough, they display utter devotion to him, you know that. He's a *Thule*, like us, remember? His mother is Austrian, father Sudeten German, a Moravian. He's spiritual, enlightened, educated, and knowledgeable with a—"

Geer pushed him hard. "So what? He's a hard, pig-eyed—"

He pushed back. "Keep your head! The tiny *Gebirgsjäger* fraternity is as tight as their fucking rope knots, Edmund, an elite group, 'mountaineers first, SS second,' he said in strict confidence. They're not fanatical, dishonorable, an–and psychopathic *Einsatzgruppen* in Russia slaughtering Jews and Slavs and civilians by the thousands behind the lines, they are mostly Austrian alpine farm boys…from the Norway Ski *Jäeger* battalion, did you ever notice that? No? Recruited under a bit of pressure into the SS, Klemp's company never made it to Norway, most were assigned to the Ahnenerbe first by order of Himmler, knowing full well that we needed the best on rough-terrain expeditions, especially in the high-altitude snow." He rapidly pointed to his chest. "I know because I *personally* asked for them before we left Germany, Klemp especially, knowing this mission would be dangerous and difficult in British-held territory. We've climbed and skied with a few of them from here to *Gott*-damned Nepal, remember? Shared hardships, frozen tinned food, frostbite."

"But Klemp, he's a mad dog of a—"

"Mad dogs? Are they? One of them, that…that corpsman Naso, he splinted your broken foot outside Kathmandu in a blizzard, sewed up your festering wound, saved your miserable life; we carried you unconscious for days with fever, we were all sick. Remember the firefight with the Ghurkas that night near the remote temple? British swine, it was all petty *jealousy*, they wanted our stash of finds, our maps, our unique knowledge, the lazy dogs. Klemp and his five men saved all our shitting lives. But unlike us, they've truly *earned* those Edelweiss patches on their caps alpine-fighting the Poles and French!"

Geer sat, confused, stressed, stroking his leg. "Yes, the Austrians, they...the Ghurkas were..."

"Klemperer's a horse's ass, a Nazi cinder dick. I don't think you can turn an indoctrinated and branded Waffen SS officer," said Bernie. "Not a chance."

Bea added: "I trained with the *Gebirgsjäger* in Austria, a tight group of special chaps, indeed a breed apart compared with the rest of the army. But I have to say, Ernst, I wonder if you can really—"

"None of you fully understand," blurted Shäfer. "His association with us Ahnenerbe the last year has slow-w-w-l-y but steadily affected his overall outlook on the war, eroded some of that hastily painted-on SS indoctrination, I can tell, psychology is one of my specialties, it has to be as expedition leader." He put his hand on Geer's shoulder and took a lax tone. "When pure warriors leave the intense battlefront for calm rear areas or relaxed duty, they tend to soften a bit and regain some humanity over time, though I admit he doesn't show it, not much." He then got up and gently put his hands on Alice's shoulders. "And yet...he's quite taken with Miss Drummond here thankfully, a healthy schoolboy crush perhaps, but that means he's thinking about love, marriage, and adoring children, not combat."

"She does sport a nice set of smooth flanks," said Bea. "Why you—"

"Though it's immensely difficult to imagine given our circumstances, human beings are really creatures of love, kindness, inventiveness, and tolerance, not brutal warriors, not at our very *core essence*. The ancients knew that, you do as well, Uta, because I taught you all this years ago. The dominating patriarchal energy in this installation has been suddenly affected by the presence of you two females, and I sense many who lack sufficient male–female balance would love to steal your life force, your precious *Vril*, by forcing themselves upon you, but that won't happen of course, severe discipline and punishment are good for some things."

"Such a charming notion," said Alice in disgust, head in hands.

"As for Klemp, he's unhappy I tell you, unfulfilled, and as third in command of this base, he's always being pushed around and overworked by an even more ambitious Poppel. They hate one another with zeal behind the scenes he told me. Poppel's a sycophantic Party member bar none, a boot-licking bureaucrat, not a soldier. Given what I know, I think I can *sway* Klemp once airborne."

"In other words, you believe he's thinking mostly with his John-Thomas, not his Thule Society-addled brain," said Bea.

He sat. "My, my, always so charming and full of aristocratic grace. I like that," squinted Shäfer, smiling, nodding.

"I hope you know what you're doing, Ernst," whisper-yelled Geer. He kept staring into Bea's eyes. "Trust me, old friend."

"I can work on him too," said Alice. "Charm the bastard. I'll Frenchy kiss him so deep and hard he'll choke on my tongue."

"Quite operatic, all of this." Bernie then looked to Bea. "Well? This is right up your weird alley, kid."

Bea looked at all of them with wide eyes. "Why the hell not? I'd rather be a pear-eating live troglodyte socializing with Aryan *frauleins* over hat sizes than a shot-dead saboteur."

"That was easy," chirped Alice, head resting on fists. "Make my Rolls butter yellow."

24

Driven to the fort's huge zig-zag outer glacis ring to watch, Bea, Alice, and Bernie stood stunned. The tall crane had a sizeable bomb attached on a cable at thirty meters' height.

"Looks to be around 300 kilos in size. The pointed tip is hardened steel. A 'bunker-buster,' I reckon," said Bernie, shielding the sun with his palm. "I think they stole that idea from you Brits."

"Are we at a safe distance?" asked Alice with concern.

Schäfer pleaded with Poppel nearby. "Why wasn't I consulted on this plan? This is destruction of an important find. It will *destroy* what's below. Please, Herr *Generalmajor*, don't do it!"

Ignoring him, atop a rock, Poppel addressed the dozen aggravated scientists in a group.

He pounded a boot. "Our timetable has been moved up! Your pitiful jackhammers and picks have failed to do the job, the quartzite too thick and hard. This very morning I have received by telluric ground wave communication that the Reichsführer himself has given the go-ahead for rapid penetration of the fort's sub-levels. That bomb has been specially designed to penetrate thick amounts of rebar concrete in modern fortifications. Once a hole has been opened, pack up any finds in crates and load them aboard The Bear within a twenty four-hour window." He motioned to Klemperer. "Give the order."

Klemperer motioned to Ötvös, who blew a whistle. "Everyone into the slit trench!" Soldiers scampered about.

"Please, no!" shouted Schäfer, running towards the fort's center in protest. Two soldiers tackled him, then brought him back to the trench under protest. "This is not *science*, it's barbarity!"

"He's under arrest, *Sturmbannführer*, keep him secured," yelled Poppel to Klemperer. "Proceed, *leutnant*."

Ötvös picked up the receiver on the pack radio. "Achtung, achtung. Bombe—los!"

A quarter second before release, a small solid-fuel rocket motor ignited, sending the bomb downwards at high speed. It penetrated three meters of stone, the shaped-charge warhead digging deeper. A huge explosion resulted, sending rock and debris everywhere for three hundred meters in all directions.

"*Scheisse* on toast, that's one way to do it," cried Bea over the din, dirt and debris covering her in a hailstorm.

Alice had her head in Bea's lap, Bernie covering them both. A small earthquake erupted, then quickly faded.

Boots splayed apart, Poppel stood over the trench on top of a pointed glacis wall. "All you so-called scientists listen to me, they say in Berlin you're all geniuses to a man, well, *prove* it. Get to work!"

•••

At the end of a long rope, Klaus Schmidt wiggled through large chunks of pink granite with a flashlight. When he hit bottom fifteen meters below, he yelled: "I'm in! There's room for three men. The floor is made of ornate tiles—they're something to behold!"

A small tremor hit, then dissipated.

"What's going on, Ernst?" asked Bea, as everyone at the edge of the round crater began to mumble.

"I'm not sure..." He cupped his hands and shouted below. "Edmund, check for any odd vibrations and irregular frequencies."

Geer and a fellow geologist rammed probes into the ground of the sunken dry moat. With earphones he listened, then watched a dial on the Waveform Tester. "Nothing."

"We found something!" yelled Schmidt. Bruno Beger and Karl Weinert accompanied him.

Beger used a pick axe to pull away debris while Weinert held an electric lamp on a long cord. As they dug furiously, something black emerged from a wall. Geer used a rock hammer to carve a small furrow on the hard object, most of which was still buried. It glowed a shine. "It's silver...it's silver, by *Gott*. We found a silver pillar!"

Schmidt yelled up the hole. "Ernst! We found one!"

Geer listened carefully with the headphones; suddenly a signal sounded, then many of them, a torrent. The dial needled off the scale. "*Nein...nein!*" He threw down his headphones, and looked to his colleague. "The nodal point, the fucking Ley Lines...the tectonic plates!"

A tremor began, then slowly intensified as everyone became nervous.

Panicked, Geer clawed his way up a crumbling point bastion. "Ernst! The tectonic plates have been affected by the blast. The fort is at the epicenter of the nodal lines, *Ernst*!"

"Get them up!" yelled Schäfer, suddenly realizing the horrific geologic implications. He and the others had been correct about the correlation of Ley Lines running along the edges of tectonic plates and the infolded scalar energy of nodal planetary physics. The bomb's blast had sent a shockwave to the nodal point, causing ripples of frequency to fan out in all directions, pounding ancient fault lines under intense pressure. "Up-up!"

Weinert and Beger were hauled up on the rope at the quick by five soldiers. As the tremor matured into a genuine earthquake, the hole began to collapse. Schmidt shrieked as he was buried alive.

Schäfer grabbed his arm. "Klemp, order your men to take them out through the valley entrance. Do it, man. The cavern will probably collapse too, everything."

The ancient fort began to crumble, the once strong stone masonry loudly cracking apart like artillery fire as fissures formed.

"Klem-m-mp!" screamed Schäfer.

Klemperer thought fast as he stumbled to the ground. He scanned the airfield with his binoculars using a standing stone to steady himself. A huge fissure opened up, it spread like a lightning bolt in all directions, a snowflake forming under a microscope, consuming two trucks full of his soldiers and Poppel's command Kubel near the landing strips' tower. Down they went thirty meters or more. He pointed at Ötvös. "They're all dead! We're done for. *Leutnant*, take those forty men and lead them all to the entrance, I'll follow. Take the field packs and supplies. Go!" He then turned to Bernie and the girls. "Your choice. Go with me or Ernst."

"The valley entrance still exists?" asked Bea, leaning on Bernie who then stumbled with his crutch.

"I lied!" yelled Schäfer over the rumble. Tables and tents collapsed. Equipment fell into the moat.

With a dire expression, Bea looked to Bernie. "The Professor, Gerlach, Gwafa…"

"Come on, Beans. Let's hightail it!" yelled Alice, suddenly panicked, attempting to flee with Klemperer and his men.

Bea grabbed her mop of blond. "You're coming with us, *Dolly*. Hope you brought a damn *parka*."

Klemperer turned. He quickly re-thought his situation. "What the hell, I'll go with you." "You won't regret it." Schäfer then waved to his scientists, who pleaded with him to join the exodus. "I'll see you there someday," he yelled. "Hot *schokolade, kameraden*. Paradise!" "You're a damn fool!" yelled Weinert, who then grabbed his rucksack and ran. "Fuck you, Himmler, *and* Antarctica!"

Geer said to Ernst: "I go with you. No point freezing and starving with them."

"Come on, Ernst, let's go!" yelled Bernie, leading the girls by the hand and descending a bastion. "The Bear is protected by his electro-bubble, yes?"

"Theoretically, yes," said Klemperer, dropping down and rolling in the dust. "We'll find out!"

Everyone ran as the earthquake intensified. Two trucks stood waiting.

As Bernie opened the door, a fissure opened and swallowed him and the truck. Bea and Alice grabbed his bad leg and pulled. Dirt filled his mouth.

Klemperer and Schäfer grabbed his other leg. "To the other truck," yelled Schäfer. They piled in. "Let Bea drive!" yelled Bernie, mouth clear, spitting blood and dirt.

Bea put her foot on the starter pedal. It whined and came to life. Alice rode shotgun. "Easy old girl, mind the socking potholes," said Alice in a calm voice. "Just like the hill climb, smooth and fast."

In first gear she floored it, both sets of double rear wheels spun dust, the diesel Mercedes engine roaring. As the valley floor began to liquify with vibration, Bea evaded fissures and sinkholes, weaving hard, the steering wheel vibrating, the wheels slipping as if on ice. Second gear. She sped up, gaining speed. Third gear. Faster.

As the surrounding hills and peaks shed streams of boulders, the left hangar door unfastened itself, buckled, and crashed down as dozens of personnel ran for their lives in all directions. Many were swallowed by pits or flattened by multi-ton rolling boulders. A bloodbath.

"Look out!" cried Alice as Bea yanked the wheel hard. A boulder the size of a locomotive rolled just ahead of them, then shattered into chunks. One chunk grazed them, smashing into the side-mounted spare, cracking the windshield.

Bea spun the truck in an arc almost running over a few soldiers. She crunched into reverse and reversed into the cavern, weaving around. "Out of my damn way people!" Backing up to the rear stairway of the airship where Luftwaffe personnel were abandoning ship, she cried: "All stop!" The air brakes hissed.

Baumann, head bleeding badly from a fallen lump, grabbed the truck's doorframe. "What are you idiots doing? The cavern is coming apart, it's Old Testament shit." Huge chunks of the anthracite tunnel casing came down, killing many with their glass-sharp edges. Barracks and sheds were smashed in the onslaught; fires erupted. Many chunks rolled down from having hit the protective airship bubble. "It's a giant grave in here!"

Klemperer and Schäfer carried Bernie. "Get to your cockpit, Baumann. We're taking the Bear out in reverse," ordered Klemperer. "My men!" He waved at some soldiers, slowing them down. "Into the airship, that's an order!"

Rucksacks donned, two of them looked back into the tunnel. "With respect, we ask permission to take our chances in the mountains with our comrades, Herr *Sturmbannführer*. If we are going to die…"

He thought for a moment, surveying the disaster all around him. "Go! Make your way north to Turkey, then to Greece. I'll see you in Munich at the *weinkeller*."

The men saluted and ran off.

"Porsche's finishing the last few magnets in the propshaft trench. There's no time," pleaded Baumann.

Schäfer grabbed his collar. "The whole valley is disintegrating, Kurt! Take your chances with us, or take your chance out there."

"I don't know where my flight crew are, many are dead," said Baumann frantically. "Most were in the mess eating when—"

"Bea, you and Alice help Baumann in the cockpit. Do it, run!" yelled Bernie as Klemperer and Baumann helped him up the gangplank, his bad leg in serious pain. "She's a pilot, the best, she can help."

"She had better be," snarled Klemperer. "Ummphh…you weigh a ton, Rodgers, how tall are you?"

Woozy, Bernie gave him a dirty smile eight inches away, a tooth missing. "Six foot three, just like George God-damned Washington."

"Hightail it Beans, I've got him," said Alice, now assisting a woozy Baumann.

With the ship undulating to-and-fro, Bea ran through a hatch and plowed into Gwafa at full gallop as he was carrying a load of tools. Prone, she kissed him, then Alice did. "Thank the soddy gods—you're alive!" yelled Bea, pulling at his cheeks.

"*Vous deux idiots!*" He pulled them up. "*Monsieur* Porsche removed my handcuffs with a set of picks. I have been helping him, what happened?"

"Earthquake, you silly goose," chirped Alice, who then kissed Gwafa once more.

From the propshaft compartment, Porsche yelled: "Hurry, Beatrice! We're finishing the last magnet. One broke."

The girls bolted down the companionway, pulling an unsteady Baumann with them. "C'mon you, pull it together, flyboy," growled Bea.

Geer came up the stairs. He yelled to a panicked Luftwaffe officer below carrying a wounded enlisted man. "Hey! Come with us!" The officer hesitated, looked the ship over, then shook his head and ran, leaving his comrade for dead. Geer hit the switch and the stairs retracted with an electric whine. "Everyone has fled, who can blame them? They think we're insane!" Gerlach helped fit the magnet with small titanium hex nuts. "If we survive Ferdinand, the *Bockbier* at the *Berlinerhaus* is on me. You too, Herr Negro. I may be a hard-edged Nazi, but I don't discriminate in a crisis."

Gwafa proffered tools. "*Merci*, but I prefer sweet mint tea."

"Check the generator, Walter, I'll finish with Gwafa. Who's with us?"

"Just Lappe. Where's Banner?" asked Gerlach.

Sweat poured from Porsche's brow. "He's dead. The officer's mess."

With eyes of shock, Gwafa looked out the aft set of windows. "The entrance just collapsed...we are entombed, *messieurs*."

Porsche and Gerlach watched in horror as the last of the sunlight faded to a pinpoint.

•••

The girls sat in the cockpit area. Bea ran her hands everywhere. "Uh, shite, lessee here, where's the ruddy starter button? How the hell do you *fly* this crate?"

Alice frantically searched the large panel that had dozens upon dozens of switches and dials. "It's all in German. What's this one say?"

"That's the external running lights, fore and aft. Get 'em on. All internal lights too," said Bea.

Baumann stumbled at the railing; Bea helped him. "Gads and zooks, what a mess." She pressed a bandage to his bleeding head. "Right as rain soon."

Alice flipped all ten safety switches. The cavern and its anthracite rain shower became partially visible. The airship weaved and pulsated on its anchor chains, the dull thunder outside so loud it penetrated the usually noise-absorbing hull and insulating electro-bubble.

Bernie arrived with Klemperer and Schäfer. "Rig for red!" cried Bernie. Bea found the switch for the red cockpit lights. "Saves our night vision."

Gerlach's voice boomed on the intercom. "*N Porsche's done. Generator normal. The static dielectric field is stable, zero amps. Get going, Baumann.*"

Baumann sat beside Bea, bleeding badly, semi-lucid. He pushed the main throttle lever one click forward. "Standby mode, yellow light. Field Effect Generator safety switches off, one, two, and three. Landing buffers disengaged. Current bypass switches to flight mode, hull plating electrified to megavolt level one. Throttle detent disengaged, pushing elevation lever one notch up. The props rotate automatically once off standby mode." A green light came on. He pushed the throttle forward one click at a time, and the propshaft rpm dial moved off its peg. "Go slow, then push the...no, this...altitude lever up while pulling back on the yoke. This lever is for the maneuvering node power level, they will activate according to the y-yoke pitch and yaw p-p- position. Full power to...electro-bubble on the g-gauge. Move...up...the t-throttle...as..." He coughed and gagged, then puked on the panel and passed out on the floor, convulsing.

"No!" cried Bea.

Alice examined him. "Shite! He's out, possible concussion. A coma maybe. Where's the med kit?" She dug through it, searching for an adrenaline syringe. None.

Eyes wide scanning the panel, Bea moaned: "Why, why, why can't I catch a break..."

Porsche watched in disbelief as the huge propellers came alive, the anthracite and rock chunks bouncing off an invisible electromagnetic field surrounding them, the stern lights illuminating. Suddenly the entire ship began to shudder from the powerful earthquake's soundwaves. "How did this happen?"

In the cockpit, Schäfer said: "The earthquake's high frequency patterns are affecting the hull. We're shaking apart!"

Bernie growled behind: "Wind this tin toothpaste tube up Bea, and get us the *hell* out of here!"

She turned. "Where to? We're bloody well trapped like rats in a constipated drainpipe if you hadn't *noticed*."

Schäfer pointed ahead. "Down the main tunnel, we explored it for kilometers, it's endless. Push the rocks out of the way, *push* them."

"Underground?" asked Alice, two fingers at Baumann's throat. "He's had it."

"Go! Go!" yelled Bernie.

Bea moved up the throttle but the airship didn't move an inch. "What the flying fuck— the *anchor chains*, how many did they release?"

"Two. I saw mechanics run after ditching their tools. That means two left," said Klemperer.

"Full power now!" yelled Bernie, inches behind Bea. "Otherwise we're all mummies in an anthracite sarcophagus for shit's sake."

The power reserve indicator showed fifty percent. Then sixty. Sixty-five. Gerlach's handiwork and realignment of the quartz crystals had gained them power. Porsche's new magnets successful. Still, it wasn't enough.

"They missed something, we're not going *anywhere*," yelled Bea.

Schäfer and Bernie looked to the Tellus. "What can it be? What about...?" asked Bernie.

Schäfer searched and spun dials. "Maybe this dial? Move the zodiac, no, maybe this lever? I..."

Bernie adjusted a series of numerical concentric dials using small levers. "Maybe we missed—"

"*Nein-nein*, it can't be that simple..." said Schäfer, looking in Bernie's eyes. "A precaution of some sort?"

"Some sort of balance mechanism? A balance of Vril energies is needed?" Bernie put his hand on the embossed handprint. "It's a probably power limiter of some kind, a safety measure. Mine's too big. It needs a...Alice, come here!"

Alice put her hand on the imprint, it then glowed green. "What's it for?" A rush went through her, causing her pupils to dilate. She inhaled loudly as if in orgasm, tilting her head back. "Ahhh!"

"An equal male-female connection is required I think, the Principle of Gender," said Schäfer. He clicked the intercom. "N Gwafa, are you there? Put your hand on the generator's palm outline panel, the panel—do it!"

When Gwafa placed his hand on the generator panel, it fit almost perfectly. The panel glowed. "*Zut! Something is happening here.*" He then felt a warm, indescribable hallucinogenic connection to Alice, the universe a warm golden metallic bath swirling around them.

Alice slumped on the floor, dazed. "Helluva jump start..."

Bernie held her. "You okay, kid?"

"Sort of..."

The dials suddenly went off the scale and the generator hummed loudly as it went hot pink.

"Welder's goggles," said Gerlach, handing them out. The four men exited the engine compartment, shut the circular hatch with a *hiss-s-s-s*, and watched from behind the protective glass panel. Screaming, the generator went a blinding white hot. A small explosion erupted.

"Lappe! No!" yelled Porsche.

One of the cables came loose and thrashed about in violent sparks. "I have it!" Lappe grabbed it with electrical gloves and reattached it to the generator. A flash. He instantly faded out from existence.

"An arc! He's lost!," cried Gerlach. "Lost to another dimension!" "It is blinding, *monsieur!*" yelled Gwafa.

A pale blue sphere of light emerged from the generator with the Flower of Life pattern; it surrounded the spherical compartment, a harmonious sculpture made of interdimensional plasma and unknown cosmic energies.

"It's true! Quantum physics have triumphed!" yelled Gerlach, his hand moving through the holographic flower image. "The building blocks of the universe..."

The propellers gained rpm fast. Eighty-five percent power. Ninety.

Porsche and Gwafa saw the iron anchor chains go taught, then a few links began to stretch with a groan. Both port and starboard chains snapped in an instant, thrashing the hull's bubble like angry pythons with dull thuds. The two men both reeled. "Young man, I've seen many things in my life, but this takes all..." said Porsche, who then pressed his nose to the interior view window of the propshaft compartment.

Gerlach entered the generator room, something else had happened. "I need help!"

They ran to help Gerlach. Porsche balanced the electrical flow matrix. "We're being buried alive, Walter."

Gripping a large custom-made wrench, Gerlach twisted a quartz crystal with Gwafa's help, a two-man job. A meter showed improvement. "Ninety-five, six…we've got plasma running through the drainpipe!" yelled Gerlach, barely able to see even with his goggles. "The blades are finally ejecting it."

Fed from a rapidly glowing propshaft, a blue halo of energized electrons ejected out the blades' edges and surrounded the spinning propellers, providing massive amounts of antigravitic rearward thrust in a spinning torsion field where the scant air pocket fell short for the blades to bite on.

"One hundred!" yelled Gerlach.

It was beautiful, an azure tornado, thought Gwafa. The edges of the surrounding rocks began to glow red from heat.

"That did it," yelled Porsche, nose to glass and drunk with awe. "My variable pitch gearbox is working as designed, 20,000 rpm. Over a million horsepower!"

The Bear inched forward shaking and vibrating violently, plowing through mountainous heaps of rubble like a giant mole.

"We're moving!" yelled Bea. "Speed five kph." The power reserve indicator read full. "Incredible machine," gasped Klemperer, gripping a railing. "*Unstoppable.*"

Schäfer slapped a hand on his shoulder. "And subterranean as well as airborne."

After 800 meters of agonizingly slow going, the ship finally burst through the last of the rubble, gained speed, and outran the earthquake's deluge, bouncing off the smooth walls as Bea struggled with the yoke and the ship's slow response. "Whoa-a-a-a Nelly! Twitchy sausage, I can't get him to fly straight!"

"300 kph," said Alice. "400, 500, *700…*"

"What are you *doing*?" cried Bernie. "Adjust the power to the maneuvering nodes. You're wagging the damn dog."

"He doesn't want to slow!" cried Bea. Alice eased off on the lever. "Better?"

"Yes I…" All became calm. "We're losing altitude." Bea then reduced power to twenty percent and adjusted propeller pitch to normal cruise setting. "Fifteen degrees down angle at the bow. The tunnel's descending. Altimeter reads zero."

"Speed now 55 kph," said Alice, as the ship finally smoothed out. "Where'n hell will we end up?"

She leered. "You're asking me? It's like being swallowed up a horse's arse."

Noise soft, the view out the windows showed nothing but a black hole ahead, the only visible clue of their progress being the eerie yet sublime reflection of the running lights off the smooth, shiny tunnel walls.

"Who knows?" Now it was Schäfer's turn to grip the railing. "These legendary tunnels stretch from one part of the Earth to another. Tens of thousands of kilometers."

Bernie clicked the intercom. "*✎ Any damage back there?*"

"*✎ Lappe is gone, dead, Bernard, and le professeur is much shaken,*" said Gwafa. "*Monsieur Gerlach asks where we are headed.*"

"*✎ Gone? How? I have no idea where we're going. Will advise.*"

25

"Make your speed one hundred," said Bernie, now seated behind Bea and Alice. All three men opened the hatch and tossed out Baumann's corpse.

"My poor old friend…" wept Shäfer in tears. "Oh *Gott*, why?" He then tightened the seal.

Saddened, Klemperer sat on the stairs and said a few words from the Bible that he remembered from his youth and consoled his friend. The immense loss of life, both German and prisoner, had stunned them all. "So many dead within minutes, a sad affair, Ernst. Pull yourself together, we need you in top form. Where's Geer?"

"He hid in a stateroom I think," said Alice.

"Who can blame the sonofabitch," grumbled Bernie.

Shäfer sat next to Bernie and composed himself. "Plenty of air in these tunnels, Rodgers, a cool breeze came up now and then in the hangar. It was refreshing to say the least. Many explorers have spun tales about these passages over the centuries, but we could find little about them other than it's a vast network; some are three kilometers wide read one text." He looked to a set of pressure gauges. "Outside air pressure almost matches our own, one-point-two-six atmospheres. As ranking officer, I now charge you with the responsibilities of the ship's navigation. Have you any naval ship experience on the high seas?"

"Well, I took a ride in a Navy blimp once, did a one-year tour on a destroyer in 1918, five years on a cruiser, I'm a decent sailor on a yacht, my friend Red and I did some rum-running in an admiral's launch once or twice, and I piloted an Elco PT boat off Rhode Island for three months…"

Bea turned around. "He flies effortlessly now. Still descending, and the tunnel is getting slowly wider. The compass is useless, Herr Kappy-taine *leutnant*, maybe you can radio the Newport Yacht Club for directions."

Bernie held up a middle finger. "See this? It's got your name on it."

"How do we figure what direction we're flying?" asked Alice. "Or…tunneling, is it?"

Bernie asked of Shäfer: "You said there's tens of thousands of kilometers of these tunnels?"

"Find us a way home, Ernst." Klemperer exited the command compartment. "I'm heading to the engine room to see if they need help. I'll inspect for damage along the way." A *whoosh* sounded from the rubber seal upon closing.

"Yes, many thousands, but I have never seen a map," said Shäfer. "Beger said with conviction one exists in the underground Vatican archive, but it's just a story. The ancients, and I mean ones that far predate the Atlanteans or Lemurians, were said to have dug these tunnels billions of years ago, the Hyperboreans and Paa-Taal, the Founder Races. Supposedly they needed a secure and safe network of them between caverns and cities that exist down here. Safe from weather, asteroid and comet impacts, the sun's radiation, safe from intruders or rivals. They are also said to have been conduits of trade with the surface-dwellers. I've read accounts by explorers and geologists from all over the world, but their expeditions all ran out of food and water since the tunnels are endless and dark. As for subterranean navigation, I…"

The crystal astrolabe made a humming sound, and a few concentric circles moved. "What's this fancy doohickey on about?" asked Bea. "Ancient technology worries me."

Shäfer looked to the Tellus computer. "This dial with symbols moved as well. Perhaps…it knows where we are heading. I think the astrolabe is for navigating under the Earth."

Bernie stood next to him. "This dial with number markings moves with it at a different rate. I think it's a nocturnal of some sort, see the stars? This one next to it is perhaps the underground version of it. The Atlanteans must have navigated these tunnels. If I had to take a wild guess, it's showing direction and depth."

Shäfer asked Alice: "Time elapsed since engine start?"

She looked to a small clock with engine hours and stopwatch time. "Forty-seven minutes."

Shäfer rummaged his prized rucksack and pulled out his large notebook. "Tamil…Tamil. I think I can decipher some of the symbols, at least a few Egyptian-looking ones." He moved to the navigation chart table. "Now, Rodgers, if we were here at the base, then in the tunnel descending in a northeast direction…I think given our speed and time we are somewhere near…"

Bernie used a triangle and plotter. "If my navigational skills are still good, I'd say somewhere under the Caspian Sea by now." He thumbed a chart wheel calculator.

"Maybe…fifty kilometers depth, but it's a wild guess."

After several hours of Bernie and Shäfer's attempts at deciphering symbols, Bea said: "We're leveling out. I see something ahead. I'm killing the forward lights."

A tiny green dot could be seen in a sea of blackness. "Now, what in the world is…*that*?" asked Alice.

Bernie sat anxiously. "Whatever it is, it's getting bigger." Ten minutes went by as the dot became wider and wider. "I'm slowing to fifty," said Bea.

Shäfer stood from his seat. "It's a…cavern."

As the ship passed into the huge void, Bea slowed. "All stop." Then reversed the twin airscrews. "Let's hover a bit."

"Alice…kill all the non-navigation lights," said Bernie as he beheld an awesome sight. It was a roughly spherical cavern with water below. "Look at the mist in the distance. Must be five, no, six kilometers in diameter, I can barely see the other side. Tunnels go in every direction." One of the tunnels was a waterfall, disgorging a flow a thousand meters long; another tunnel glowed bright with plants and trees. "I count around…mmm, forty-eight tunnels."

"Fifty," breathed Gerlach with emotion, overwhelmed with the possibilities of a honeycombed Earth. "Countless caverns await, many civilizations. The Vril people were right."

Shäfer walked down the three steps to the forward windows. "It is entirely lit green with bio-luminescence of some kind, I've seen it before in a deep cave in the Yucatan. The ancients called it 'Lightstone.' Most interesting."

Porsche and Gwafa arrived. "Unbelievable," muttered Porsche. "Jules Verne was right in his book. He must have known."

"Indeed, and so was Bulwar-Lytton when he wrote *The Coming Race*. The underground world is as *real* as he imagined it was," said Gerlach with conviction. "Just wait till we hand in reports to the Thule and Vril department chairmen. Where's Baumann?"

Alice pointed to the blood trail that lead to the forward hatch and shook her head. "*Gott*," muttered Gerlach, looking to Porsche.

"I would ask you, Bernard, where we are, but I imagine you are not too sure," whispered Gwafa.

"No I'm not. Jesus, your *hands*." He felt the calluses and blisters. "A life in the mines is not for the faint. I will endure."

Bea looked back at them. "You'll live. Still happy you signed on?"

"*Oui, madame.*" He gazed into the ethereal distance, his imagination alight. "But only slightly."

"Which tunnel should we pick?" asked Porsche.

Bernie pointed. "What's that? Lights ahead." A sizeable ship emerged from a lower tunnel that was at water level. He grabbed the binoculars. "One stack. Two cargo cranes. A damn freighter!"

"What the hell do you mean a *freighter*?" asked Bea.

Bernie adjusted the dial for focus. "Hold on…I see…Swedish flags. *The Pelikanen*…Port of Sundsvall. He's low on the waterline, full cargo holds. He's shining his spotlight on us." The ship blew its foghorn three times while illuminating the Bear. "He's saying hello. I'll be damned. Somehow these waterways connect with the oceans. Alice, the radio. Get him on the horn if you can."

She sat at the radio station and slid on headphones, twisting dials as the tubes warmed over the course of a minute. "Static. Some strange beeps. Background noise only. All megacycles, nothing."

"Perhaps we could follow him?" asked Porsche at the windows.

Gerlach pointed. "Look at his exit tunnel, too small for us to navigate safely. He's lowering his radio mast and heading off."

"A shame," said Klemperer. "We must contact *someone*."

Bernie handed over the binoculars. "They must modify the ships that navigate down here for different sized tunnels. Amazing idea." *Why the hell wasn't I informed about this? Someone must've known…*

"It must be true that gravity can be manipulated differently down here. The tunnel must rise to meet sea levels," mused Shäfer.

"How can that be?" asked Porsche, attending to his pocket watch winder.

Gerlach rotated his hands. "Gravity, ladies and gentlemen, is *not* what we think it is. Our sun sends electromagnetic waves at the Earth a trillion cycles a second, which then create gravity. Matter itself is really held together by various other gravitational forces we are only beginning to understand. A hologram in a holographic universe. From all directions it comes, a million varieties."

"Photons as units of light?" asked Porsche.

Gerlach smiled. "I'll make a physicist of you yet, Herr Boilermaker."

"And all atoms have a soul," smiled Shäfer. "As do stars and planets, galaxies even. Baumann isn't dead, his soul will travel the universe forever."

After a half-hour of communal scientific speculation, Bea snapped: "*Achtung*! Can you three wisemen dolts figure out how to get us the flippin' hell out of here?"

Shäfer said: "We must find a tunnel south to Argentina. Then on to Base 211. It's the only—"

"*Nein*! We must find our way to Europe, *Germany*," yelled Klemperer, cocking his pistol and pointing it at Bea. "To hell with your obsession with Antarctica. You've been poisoned by the enemy, especially this arrogant child *Beatrice*."

Gerlach grabbed Porsche and hid them both behind a bulkhead, yelling: "Idiot! Don't put a kinetic bullet through the hull, you might destabilize the field!"

Shäfer eased his way up the steps. "E-a-a-a-s-y now, Klemp. No one has been poisoned. There are no enemy here. We're all in this togeth—"

Flushed with malice, he pointed his Luger at Bernie. "I am in command! Find a way to Axis territory, those are my orders!"

Calm, Bernie folded his arms in defiance. "Oh? Any keen ideas? What bearing should we take with no compass or underground charts? No idea? I see. Well, as ranking military officer, I hereby commandeer this ship under the regulations and auspices of the United States Navy. And you, sir, are under *arrest*. I say we head west to the Atlantic."

Alice put fists to hips. "Excuse me, but Bea and I claim ownership of this vessel under the rules of engagement set forth by the Foreign Office, His Majesty's Government, and MI-6. And if you would be so kind as to—"

Bernie snapped: "Nuthin' doin', I say it belongs to the Navy and—"

Cracking under pressure, the stress of the day one ounce too much, Klemperer pushed the barrel into Bernie's forehead. "A dead man you are!"

With vigor, Shäfer pleaded. "Klemp, no! Think of the future, *kamerade*, think of your family free of the corrupt Nazi rulership. All of us can be free of tyranny and oppression, free to behold the wonders of the universe while creating an improved human race with—"

Shaking with stress, he pointed the barrel at Shäfer. "Traitor! Filthy idealist idiot, enough of this insanity! Your—"

"*Au revoir Bosche!*" From behind, Gwafa lifted Klemperer with a barrel hold, squeezing the air out of his lungs.

A shot passed by Bernie's head and lodged itself into the Tellus. Dials spun, noises rang out. A low tone descended from an hexagonal organ pipe like a dying water buffalo.

Bernie put a fist in Klemperer's face. Down he went. "The tool box in the cabinet, I saw wire in it." He held his aching hand. "Ahhnngghhh. First my ass, then the leg, now I've hurt the hand…oh, why did I…shit!"

Gwafa found steel wire and tied Klemperer's hands. "*L'Armée Française* can learn much from German efficiency and preparation."

Bernie put his boot on Klemperer's upper back. "Easy, Herr Dipshit. This chap knows how to tie the legs of a goat well, then quote some pithy Rumi poetry."

Klemperer struggled. "*Autsch, verschwinde!*" Gwafa rattled his memory as he wound the wire.

"'*Out beyond ideas of wrongdoing and rightdoing, there is a field. I'll meet you there. When the soul lies down in that grass, the world is too full to talk about. Ideas, language, even the phrase 'each other' Doesn't make any sense.*'"

A struggle. Klemperer yelled: "*Schwartzer* animal! Nigger-lovers! Traitors!"

Geer pushed through the air lock hatch. All eyes landed on him. "Ernst, we have *stowaways*…"

• • •

Bernie pry-barred off the lock to the weapons locker adjacent to the cargo bay. "Enough of this candy-ass screwing around." He armed himself, Gwafa, and Alice with MP-40 submachineguns. "One bandolier of extra ammo." He shoved in a magazine and shut the action with the back of his hand. "You two eggheads stay clear and stay put."

Gerlach huffed: "Gladly. And mind that you don't—"

"I know, I know, no rounds through the damned fuselage." He handed Geer a pistol. He refused it. "I'm a scientist only."

Except for Shäfer's crates and some extra lumber, the Kubelwagen was all that was left in the cargo bay. Porsche proudly showed off his camouflage-livery prototype to Gerlach. "It's all electric. A battery compartment is in the front. Four-wheel drive. It charges off a solar panel I invented for the *Afrika Korps*, desert-use, lots of sun. Rommel loved the idea, there's a struggle for fuel."

Gerlach checked the unique battery array. "You're not as much of an idiot as I suspected. Ingenious."

With a limp, Bernie led them to the Information Center compartment. "They must have hid in here during the evacuation. This it?"

Geer replied: "Yes. But it's…"

Bernie kicked the door open with his good leg. "…already open."

Alice put her weapon dead on target. "Ello, gents."

"*Guten tag*," said one of the twin brothers calmly, both over seven feet tall in matching grey suits with short white haircuts, black ties, matching waistcoats, Nazi Party pins on their lapels, and Luftwaffe sunglasses hiding their eyes. Sitting on a stuffed Victorian-era, whorehouse-red banquette, their pale white complexions gave them a theatrical look; they played cards and smoked foul-smelling Russian cigarettes.

"Gin," said the other twin. "You owe me ten marks."

"You cheated again," said his brother, sucking a strong one and exhaling a fetid cloud. Alice looked to Bernie, completely bewildered.

Bernie clicked the intercom. "Ernst, can you…come down the hall please?"

"𝒩 On my way."

One of the twins pointed, lowering his glasses to reveal his reddened pale blue eyes. "O-o-o-oh, I've never actually met a black man before. *Ein Afrikaner, ja?*"

"And he's so-o-o-o handsome," said his brother, who then switched to Alice. "Ah! An Aryan beauty to rival Até, goddess of mischief and folly." He bored into her mind with a psychic drill.

Alice gasped, her mind probed with a cold clammy hand, her innermost secrets and desires laid bare under the holographic onslaught. She grasped her head, letting the gun fall slack on its leather shoulder strap. "Ah-h-h-g-g-n-n."

The brother said: "Naughty, naughty, *fräulein*. Oh, I see that your very first taste at the fountain of love you took it up the buttered backside at Wycombe so as not to get pregnant that time with the groundskeeper's son in the garden shed, and you never… told…Bea…either, because she liked him too. So-o-o déclassé. And now you secretly crave dear old Klemp, our mountaineering hero all tied up and ready for your sadistic pleasure. You shoot well at long distance, an Annie Oakley. Most exciting."

"They're psychic brigands—typical." Regaining composure, she ran her barrel along his sleeve. "Nice check suits chaps, who's your tailor?" Then stuck her barrel into a chalky, buff cheek.

The other brother said in perfect upper-class English: "Huntsman, Savile Row don't you know. Just like Bea's dear old…Poppy." The brothers then looked at one another and snickered like devilish schoolboys.

Gwafa shouldered his submachinegun and frisked them for weapons. "Comedians, Bernard. Shall we shoot them?"

One of the brothers opened his legs wide. "Try frisking down here, I may be hiding a gold-plated Derringer, Dogon-man."

"Not...yet." Bernie scanned the ornate, wood-paneled room, the fine joinery and millwork in stark contrast to the rest of the austere alloy ship, his memory sparking. He admired a Winslow Homer painting of a fisherman calling out to a schooner. *This looks strangely familiar...*

Shäfer arrived. "Edmund, who is...?" Shocked, he looked them over. "*Scheisse.* What are you doing here? How...?"

"Who are they, Ernst?" asked Geer.

Bernie snapped his swollen fingers. "Hess told me...the Nazzaro, no, the Nazzara brothers. Albino twins. Contractors and advisors, yes?" *Pretty strange looking hombres...*

"I'm Stew."

"I'm Lew. At your service, Herr Rodgers. Proud contractors and Party members. Thule and Vril Societies. Black Sun representatives. Himmler's personal trade confidants and plenipotentiaries." He toasted with a wine glass. "Good to see you again, Ernst. You look pale. Try some liverwurst and tomato paste on rye toast. Good for the hemoglobin. We relish your *Gewürtztraminer*, a tad on the sweet side, but...a clean finish."

Shäfer sat at the table. "What are you doing on board?"

"That's not a cordial *tone*," pouted Stew, lower lip extended. "Poppel gave us permission, not that we really needed it. We're your old friends. Fellow racial archeologists and spelunking cave explorers. Your regal ambassadors to exotic and lush parts below." He tasted his glass. "Hints of Alpine flowers, I should think."

"Mmm, yes," said Lew. "And some elderberry—"

"It can't be!" exclaimed Bernie.

Alice sat in an overstuffed chair, exhausted. "What is it now?"

"They grafted it on, *wholesale*. The whole shebang—paintings, the organ, the millwork, even all the books." He pointed. "This is the library room from the *Magellan*. I've been in here before. The Germans don't waste anything, if it works it works." He stamped on the fine Persian carpet. "Son of a gun!"

"He's so excitable, Frau Drummond," said Lew, passing a tray. "Canapé?"

She took one, then poured herself a glass. "That's my boss, bit of a cowboy romantic. How'd you chaps get so tall? Gigantism run in the family?" "Our *sisters* are even taller," said Lew.

"Very rare genetic condition," said Geer.

The intercom came to life. "*♩ Just what the hell's going on back in—*" Bernie shut Bea off.

"Herr Nazzara?" asked Shäfer.

Drawing cards from the deck, Stew said: "Ah, yes, well we decided to inspect the installation with Kammler and his entourage as per the *Reichsführer's* request—it's in our contract—but we were disguised in uniforms and kept out of sight for the most part. While you were digging up your precious bastion fort—not the most impressive example I might add, but truly an historic one—we were tasked with an inspection on behalf of our…*upper* management. I must say, it was going swimmingly well until that dried sea sponge Poppel blew it to pieces, such an inflamed hemorrhoidal Neanderthal." He then shuffled like a pro. "But of course, even with the Atlantean silver altars aligned just so, the portal would not have opened up. It went into disuse about 750 years ago due to union demands and planetary shifts; the local universe can be so unforgiving and unreliable in its natural gifts to us. Our reports will list your valiant efforts though, high praise for you and Edmund and the rest of the academic dilettantes. Oh, and so sorry about Klaus, a decent fellow he was. Once the earthquake hit, we stowed away in here for the fun-as-ever ride to who knows where? We relish unscheduled adventure, bored to tears. Need a distraction. Ah, four jacks, Gin."

"Now it's you that's cheated," said Lew.

"I thought higher dimensional inner-Earth dwellers didn't drink alcohol, eat meat, or smoke," said Shäfer calmly. "The *Vril-Ya*, that is."

Alice gasped. "You mean…?" "*Gott*…" breathed Geer.

Lew drew an unsatisfactory card and frowned like a cat. "Within your treacle-thick lower third dimension and, yes, due to our fourth-dimensional physicality being held together by these bejeweled multi-alloy bracelets, we are subject to 'dimensional dysphoria.' Hence the fun partaking of alcohol, liverwurst, and tobacco. Just a tad, though, since it further lowers our vibration, albeit deliciously so." Snickering ensued.

"I knew it! Offworlders and wartime interlopers," snapped Bernie. "Vril-Ya Aldebarans. The real McCoy."

Alice spat out her wine. "*What?*"

Gwafa pointed his weapon point-blank. "*Merde!*"

"You ingrate." Stew stood, lowering his head so as not to hit the ceiling. "We are certainly not offworlders! Human as you are, well, mostly. Aldebaraners we may be, but we were born here on this nugget just as you were, though two hundred kilometers beneath the surface of Australia of course. But I admit our distant ancestors came from the Taurus star system."

"And we were born 917 years ago," wheezed Lew, examining an Ace of Spades. "Middle age can be so disheartening."

Bernie snarled: "The famed 'Gizeh Intelligence.' I'll bet it was you boys who sold the SS their new technology secrets."

Lew smiled. "We are but mere businessmen, dear sir, and only two of many. A rogue group of nasty Pleiadians are also on our payroll, plus a few cutthroat cast-offs from Sirius-B, a shadier star system I know not."

"*Gizeh Incorporated*, if you please," said Stew. "Oh-h-h-h, many other star nations are also involved in trade and conquest, liberation and rebuilding, always have been over millions of years. Your ancient legends bear this out. You surface humans, or should I say *Terrans*, an indignant group of mutt-like misfits, have the genetics of twenty-two star nations, hence your unique twelve strands of DNA, though only two are active at present by design. Only seven strands for us, so we're quite jealous. Quite an expensive race to manufacture you were, so many patents and contracts, so many differing creators, the ritualistic and royal Anunnaki, well, being so difficult to work with at times. They hate the other 'parents' with zeal, and claim you as their personal legal property. Just think, we're distant cousins of a sort, you and us. Were you worth all the trouble? Time will tell."

Shäfer exclaimed: "Twenty-two DNA star nation parents? That means we are galactic genetic royalty. Then it's true that—"

Stew slapped his hand as a teacher would to a child's. "This…*outer rim* of the galaxy may be a miasmic backwater swamp, but many are now taking an interest in you 'topsiders' and our lush, green Earth, the hollow Moon as well. And yet I hear real estate is becoming quite dear up there, and the SS has brokered a sweetheart deal for a cavern facility. But be so advised, there are many others claiming to be us Aldebaraners when they are not. Shabby knock-offs. Poseur confidence men in holographic masks. Noncredentialed amateurs even. They create havoc in our trade."

"Businessmen? Really? And just who *else* do you represent?" asked Alice.

Stew held her hand but she quickly withdrew it. "A few interested parties my dear, that's all. And it is entirely legal, especially when the top Germans *asked* for help in these matters, no one can force their will upon those with the *divine gift* of free will, and that's you lot. It's the Wild West here on Earth, no rules apply. Law of Consistency as you well know. Ask Dr. Gerlach and his cohorts Dr. Oberth, Otto Hahn, Heisenberg, Dornberger, and Dr. Debus—we provide them with advisors of tremendous expertise, otherwise their own attempts at free energy generation, scalar weaponry, atomics, and antigravity would take many more decades to mature if at all. Simple toys for petulant children. As a gift of goodwill, we helped them cobble together this crude airship with antique spare parts, and here we are, floating in the bowels of Earth without a care." He stretched. "Ah-h-h. Back in the eighteenth century we had to obtain written permission for our involvement on parchment no less; so many contracts, thousands, so much champagne fanfare, royal masked balls, orgies, *Gazette D'Amsterdam*'s foul gossip, vice-laden Vatican dinners and occult Parisian salon-hopping, our powdered wigs full of lice, our silk pockets with pink macaroons. Jansenism versus the philosophers. Nowadays in wartime, well…it's ever so much more…*streamlined*."

Alice gasped: "You mean you two dressed up and shagged—"

"Ahh-h-h, those were the days, and we were so young. Secretly kissing *Les Bas-Bleus* Madame Recamier, the ultimate *salonnière* when natural philosophy was discussed, her bold personality, classic beauty, and heaving bust bearing the stamp of voluptuous elegance. Pastoral pleasures, coquette boudoirs, courtly picnics, King Louis' syphilitic trysts, the Oranges of Holland, Pope Pius VI, the delightfully duplicitous East India Company and their inexhaustible gold…" wheezed Lew fondly. "Count St. Germain was such a preening prig when he opposed us at every turn with his sniveling young protégé *Le Marquis de* Lafayette, drumming up support for the upstart-rich American Revolution—the sure-shot guerilla Virginia Riflemen under Morgan, cases of fine wine and claret for General Greene, cannon and shot, rum and powder, Admiral De Grasse and the French fleet." He sighed. "Such a dreadful fop for a lewd lampooning Light Warrior, the Count."

"A lame fizzle of a man, but a worthy adversary. Excellent taste in frolicsome brocade coats and velvet breeches though," remembered Stew fondly as he toasted. "His

Madame Recamier

silky-smooth stockings were always the best."

Bernie pointed at them in accusation. "Time travelers, eh? Businessmen? More like the Mafia. You're nothing but low vibrational low-lifes dealing in the cosmic black market, and at bargain prices for black arts military technology. What did the SS pay you with? Human genetics probably. Jews? Poles? Slavs?"

"*Bargain* prices? We engage only in a barter system, an exacting one." Lew stood proudly next to his brother and took a haughty, sing-song tone. "You're so uncouth at times, a piss-ant *parvenu*, mind your insolent tone as you were taught as a boy, Herr Poncy. Time travel, timeline hopping, stargate access, and spacefaring are all part of the same tourist travel brochure. Your dunce-hatted Einstein knows that, ninnies John Trump and Oppy too, well, at least *partially*. We have nothing to hide. If you must know, it was…urchin children mostly, a hundred thousand per annum, poor, filthy, and unloved by your cruel and heartless societies, their physiology clean when compared to an adult's lifetime of tobacco, pharmaceuticals, disease, and alcohol. Scores of young females of a specific ethnic and age group are traded for breeding and pleasure, just as was done in the old scented markets of Babylon, Hattusha, and Aphrodisias, the spices and gems trading hotly along with expensive human flesh; some things never change. Average men are considered foodstuffs mostly, but are also valuable slave labor offworld. Mining is big business in our galaxy, and a goodly portion must be done intelligently by hand."

Gwafa said: "So, we are all slaves regardless of color or caste, *tout le monde?*"

"Smarter than you look, *Monsieur* Darkie, and that's annoying. Indeed, all of you rank as slaves. The best slaves are those who don't think they are—field marshals, kings, queens, prime ministers, Hitler, the Pope even. Oh yes, and high-intellect scientists are captured in national parks for new jobs hundreds of light years away, their souls bought and paid for like Podunk politicians; many refuse to return, their new lifestyles more lavish and intergalactic than anything conceivable here. Certain tree and plant genetics are popular goods as well. Rare earth materials. Silks of course, all colors. Chocolate and coffee by the metric ton, everyone likes a hot cup of Joe with illegal Centauri sugar-vine. A particular strain of blue corn and potatoes as well from Peru. Tasty."

Stew added: "A big demand exists for avocados in the Orion star system this year."

Lew neared Bernie. "Yes, forgot about that, dear brother. And do you think in your 'infinite unwisdom,' as Bea often says, that your own President Roosevelt has not also asked for certain technological trade goods via select intermediaries—mere beads and blankets mostly from our pansy competitors, you know, the sissy-pants 'benevolents' like the Adromedans, Telosians, Lyrans, Cassiopians—with which to fight the mean old 'evil' Germans with? The beastly Russians and Stalin? What about fat Signori Mussolini? Slanty-eyed Hirohito and Black Dragon Tojo? The recent spacecraft crash in Louisiana alone will yield much when your scientists back-engineer its systems under Dr. Van Bush's watchful eye, but that will take precious years even with lawful galactic advisement. Very precious time the Allies don't have. It's all just a game in essence, tit for tat, a balance of power, but the Germans are far, far ahead. They comprehended their gifts of cosmic technology sooner thanks to the Vril Society's keen tutelage, an historic penchant for philosophic and materialistic science they have. All those technical schools and clandestine castle Teutonic roundtables. It's a deadly game of multisided five-dimensional chess, winner takes all, and all's fair…in love and war."

Bernie said: "So it's true that spacecraft were purposefully crashed in the Black Forest in '31. They've been analyzing exotic equipment for over a decade. Son of a…"

"Spacecraft?" asked Alice, suddenly flush with mental images of Flash Gordon in a Turkish harem.

Lew said: "Many vessels have crashed since the 1300s. Galactic visitors sometimes forget that when they enter your dense third dimension their craft have to suddenly abide by the local laws of physics here, so sometimes they slam the earth as a result. Then it's easy pickings for anyone who wants to gather up the debris. Where do you think John Dee's scrying tablet came from?"

"The Dogon elders will hear of this," said Gwafa angrily.

"They're sadly off limits," sighed Stew. "The Nommo people from Sirius-A protect them under treaty. It's a complex universe, but we *do* cherish visiting the Serengeti on occasion. Giraffes and elephants are a hot commodity in the Kappa Draconis star system. Your overlords giveth and then taketh away, so to say."

"You leave our loveable giraffes *alone*," pouted Alice.

Lew pointed. "You're in a bind, Herr Rodgers, we're just the middlemen in the deal, not the...*primary* stakeholders, not the secret societies per se, although they *can* be useful at times. The cold, amoral Nazi hierarchy tend to pay more and on time, that's all. All that Swiss *Octogon* gold, Russian refugee what-not and death camp genetic what-for, oh deary me, it's a hot market. The Anunnaki pay us well for high-quality Earth gold much in demand out there yonder for planetary atmospheric protection and the like. The expensive rare genetics help other star nations survive and thrive on their harsh-environment planets when they splice DNA generationally, colorful chimeras and hybrid offspring being all the rage in *Haute Couture* circles at the much-populated Galactic Center. Out here, well, it's as if we were back with your slave-raping hero George Washington on the Ohio frontier dealing with unwashed savages and bloodthirsty settlers."

Bernie said: "Yes, but he—"

"It's business, just commerce," added Stew. "You should understand that, Herr Illuminati-man. Perhaps you can insure us through Lloyd's of London?"

"*Nein!*" exclaimed Geer, realizing it was all true as he connected uncomfortable dots. Shäfer stood in anger. "You filthy swine, you never told us you—"

Stew stood abruptly and held out his curled hands like a movie monster. "Yar-r-r-r-r-r!"

Enraged, Bernie pulled his trigger. "Kneecaps only, wound them!" He re-cocked the action. Nothing.

Gwafa pulled a dry trigger. He could hear the brothers laughing in his mind as he lay on the ground as a naked child while they kicked scalding sand in his face. "Get out of my head!" He welled up in tears, kneeling on the floor. Then it suddenly stopped, his mind twisted like bread dough.

A dreadful pause in conversation.

Stew wagged a long, bony finger, the electrified brass gas lights reflecting in his sunglasses. "Tsk, tsk, tsk. We removed all the firing pins with a mental file, so to speak.

Bullets could do much damage inside the ship, dear old *Himmelsbär* we've come to love, such a quaint vessel, almost all the comforts of home. Other than minor things such as that for safety, we cannot interfere with your fine little war or your pitiful exploits here. Neutral we will remain. International, Galactic, and Universal Law say so, and we abide by all. Just drop us off in a neutral city. Non-combatants have rights, just like your Standard Oil representatives that sell to all parties with an unhindered straw-man hand." Facing each other with knees bent, the brothers snickered childishly again, a sickening chorus. "Don't forget Ford Motor Company repaying the Germans for their Ford truck factories that the British bomb by night!"

"And the Allies by day. What a strange little conflict you have going on." Lew bowed and held out his palms. "We prefer to stay in this cabin until further notice. Call on us anytime for questions. Answers, however, may be subject to our discretion. Law of Non-Interference, as it were. Feel free to peruse the library or play the organ. We do so cherish music, especially Mozart and Wagner. Our talented cousins, yes?"

"Twice removed," said Stew.

Bernie drew a knife, but Gwafa held him back. "Easy, Bernard. They have shown no real aggression."

Shäfer turned to his friends. "He's…unfortunately correct, under cosmic law they *are* protected, even by the fine print of the Geneva Convention, if you can believe it. Diplomats of a sort. Unethical trade representatives. Shrewd and amoral. Everyone in the universe abides by law despite their polarity, at least mostly so. Harm them and we are no better than they are."

"The Law of One is for suckers, boobs, and wimps," sneered Stew. "It's flexible citizens like us that make things happen on a snappy timetable. Evolution being slow as molasses in a Siberian winter."

Bernie gained composure. He plucked a book on Hermetic Law from the shelf that he recognized. "You're too generous, Shäfer. The 'benevolents' of the universe abide by the Law of Non-Interference, but not the 'regressives.' Angels versus the demons, the Old Testament." He read a line. "'A higher-dimensional star nation cannot directly interfere with a less advanced one lest they cause harm in their natural evolution.' But the bad guys don't play by the rules. They profit from the suffering of others, nourish themselves off the Vril energy of mass death, natural evolution be damned." He shut it with a *clap*.

"Well said!" gushed Stew.

"You two murderous louts disgust me," growled Alice.

Lew leaned over and licked his red lips. "So judgmental you are. Pretend I'm Dagwood, give us a Frenchy kiss, Blondie."

Bernie replaced the book. "It's all about the damned loopholes in Earth Law, Cosmic Law. All right Gizeh boys, cut the jive. What's the point of all this? The whole war? What are we learning? Can you at least tell us that?"

The brothers sat. Stew dealt new cards from Crowley's Thoth Tarot set, flipping them over as if to solve enigmatic fortunes. He drew deep breath and spoke in a higher tone. "The point of all this? This fine war? Just as it was at Yale when you were a young man hiding in closets and attending lectures, Herr Rodgers..." He then held up *The Fool* card. "Philosophy class is now in *session*."

26

Bernie looked in the mirror, rubbing his thick beard. "Really could use some Burma-Shave." Not one razor could be found.

After securing Klemperer—with a swift kick to his rear—in the storage room with Gwafa's help, Bea slid a pair of handcuffs on him and removed the painful wire. Down the hall, she then slammed open the salon door eating a ham sandwich. In the galley she'd made them for everyone.

"Usually a knock is polite," said Lew, dealing cards for Manila.

"Well, well, Drummy informed me *all about* you two twin parakeets." She sat, and poured a glass of mineral water, finished, and dabbed her mouth with a napkin. "Now it's just the three of us. How's business, may I ask?"

"Oh-h-h, you're an *in-ter-est-ing* one," said Stew, smiling, not looking up from the cards. "Always spreading your squid-like ink everywhere, fouling the pot. Your mind a feast of indelicacies. I sense you have more advanced psychic abilities than most, and that's quite arousing. A gen-u-ine Divine Feminine Light Warrior, talented pilot, iffy Panzer driver, well, all right, you can lob a few decent rounds, but you're also…a drunken, unreliable, gossipy, rebellious-to-a-fault poxy-doxy with questionable taste in men and eveningwear. Brava to you my dear." He unfolded a card: *Strength*. It showed an enlightened woman with a lion. "Balance of power. Mind over matter. Strength of character. My, my, how fitting. You should be—"

She swiped away all the cards in one go. "Which way out of here to goddam Ireland?" McMaster had told her and Alice that Ireland was the more secure landing zone, especially Achill Island. "*Well?*"

Lew frowned. "Such crude manners for a Lady. We wanted to tell your fortune. Astrologers, the both of us. In the guild."

Stew went to his ear. "Let not her foul tongue sway you, brother."

She grabbed Lew's hand-sewn lapels and shook. "I'm not afraid of you subterrestrial cod-pale mad hatters! Get us the hell out of here and I'll make it worthwhile to both of you. I represent Great Britain here, and she's the most energetic place on Earth—Stonehenge, Avebury, Harrods at Christmas. Biggest cabbages anywhere, heaps of sheep wool and tartans, sweetest toffee biscuits, silkiest clotted cream, finest oatmeal stout in the soddy ol' galaxy."

Stew probed her mind for weakness, but she pushed him back mentally, a Spanish bull knocking down an over-curious Matador. "Ow! She's got talent, brother." He tried again, making Bea wince with pain while she held her head. A battering ram.

Sensing his brother's struggle, Lew joined in. A cape buffalo. They both pinched her carotid artery with their minds.

"*Arrggnnnnnn…*" Bea fell to her knees in agony, screaming, her darkened mind under fierce attack by Stuka dive-bombers, her limbs bleeding red, but within seconds she remembered how to align her chakras and breathe deeply Shieldmaiden-style, focusing her mind and spirit for a fight. Slowly arising with new vigor, she punched Lew in the gut and pitched wine in Stew's face, the ram and buffalo meeting a giant granite bull with horns of Krupp steel. "Don't even try me with that consciousness claptrap, I'll mentally *bare-knuckle* the both of you to the floor! That's right, I'm helter-skelter, a fritzy, a discombobulated booby-hatch. As a Shieldmaiden, they tried to break me psychically time after time. Drugged me silly. Red lights, electronics, hypnotherapy. Torchlight satanic rituals for Moloch, Hel, and Odin. Rape and torture. Guess what? Didn't *work*. This ship's weird vibrations have somehow sharpened the old brain box, as it were. Don't know how or why, but they did. Now, given all that, kindly stand down, or I'll circumcise you both with a rusty mental razor."

"Oo-o-h-h, I like this one, she's got hutzpah," wheezed Lew, aborting his attack. "How rare, how exciting, a true descendent of the infamous Madame du Barry. Sit, sit and be cordial."

Stew rubbed his stomach and sat. "*Ooch*. You'd have made an excellent boxer, *madame*, or, more likely you *were* one in some other lifetime. Fine. But what do you *really* have in trade besides rotten oatmeal and sticky toffee pudding?" asked Stew, calmly folding his hands, not one for being outplayed by a lowly surface-dweller. "What are you really interested in?"

She held up the *Justice* card. "Wrongs righted."

•••

Porsche and Gerlach attempted to fix the bullet damage on the Tellus. "Hand me a needle-nose plier," said Porsche. He pulled out a gear and mainspring. "I'll have to fix this on the workbench. So intricate."

"These two crystals are damaged. They'll need replacement," said Gerlach. "Plenty in the storage compartment. The Luftwaffe boys may be new to metaphysics, but they didn't skimp on spare parts."

"Walter, have you met our distinguished guests before?" asked Porsche.

"I saw them at a distance with Himmler once at Farben. We'll win the war with their help."

"Can it be fixed?" asked Shäfer worriedly.

Porsche snapped: "Leave the clock repair to the expert. My hobby in younger days."

Bernie stood by the chart table. "Change of plan. There's gotta be a tunnel to America, east coast."

Bea ran in and sat at the yoke. "Right. I've got the directions out of here to Allied territory. On my mark, we make way through that tunnel over there to port. Third one up."

"How do you know that?" asked Bernie.

"Mark!" Bea accelerated, the astrolabe rings and arrows moving. "I won a round of Manila with the twit twins, mmm, so to speak."

Alice exclaimed: "You *what?*"

The dials and zodiacs on the Tellus began to move. "We're trying to fix this thing, Beatrice," said Porsche. "You're making the Glockenspiel unhappy."

"Never you mind that. I know the way to Ireland."

Bernie slammed a palm on the world map. "Ireland? No dice. That's McMaster's bullshit fallback plan. We're going to the Bahamas, a secret U.S. Naval base near the *Tongue of the Ocean*. Don't needle me on this, Bea."

"Hell with that." Bea put the ship into the new tunnel after crashing through a cascading waterfall. Darkness enveloped them, the water splashing off the electro-bubble.

"The tunnel's going deeper," said Alice after a few minutes travel. "Ten degrees down angle on the bow."

"I sure hope you know what you're doing," snapped Bernie. Shäfer added: "As do I."

After three hours of flight at 400 kph, another dot of light lay ahead. The ship finally emerged into a vast cavern of dark green ice with white mineral veins marbled throughout. Mountains loomed, and switchback rivers plied their trade below. Patches of fog lay everywhere.

Alice said: "Well, it's emerald green all right, but it ain't Ireland old girl." Bea slowed to 25 kph. "I don't understand…it's another cavern?"

Bernie paced. "But I do. Those two pale monkey-boys are not to be trusted or dealt with in any manner. Does everyone understand clearly?"

Gerlach put his hands on the forward windows. "A whole new world awaits us. We must be at eighty kilometers depth or so."

Bernie checked the television rear monitor. A fuzzy but recognizable wide-angle image of the stern came up. "One, two, three, four—you idiot, Bea! There's got to be nine tunnels behind us. Which one did we enter from?"

"The temperature has dropped considerably," said Shäfer. "I say we keep going ahead. Going back is useless."

"Why those lying, lecherous, boil-sucking demons…I'm pulling over by the side of the road," said Bea. "All stop."

Alice wound the camera and pointed. "Over there by those long vines, move near them, I want to take a snap of them."

Bea maneuvered dead slow among the five-meter-thick vines that hung from somewhere above the light fog. "They look as if someone wound them together like rope." Birds flew by, a flock of grey-looking seagulls with very long beaks; one of them relieved itself atop the canopy; white streaks and drips. "Well, that's not very polite."

"Beatrice, pull over to that outcrop, I want a sample of that green ice," said Shäfer. He and Geer walked down to the cargo bay and opened a hatchway to the outside, icy-cold air met them and their breath froze. With a pick axe on the extendable platform, Shäfer cut off a sizeable chunk of around five kilos. "Risky, but it's worth it," said Schäfer.

Back inside, Geer examined it on a pull-out workbench with gloves and a pencil. "It looks almost like frozen algae, or some kind of microscopic plant life. It's melting…a gelatinous matrix of some type, thick like treacle."

"What about the white parts?"

"Unknown, a mineral vein of some kind. How can an entire cavern and mountains be made of this?"

Shäfer pulled at his beard. "We must explore further. Take chances in the name of science."

Porsche and Alice stood by the forward windows. She took two photos. "Almost like giant stands of hair," she said.

"Something's not right, Ferdinand," said Gerlach, gazing upwards. "My instincts tell me that."

"I hate to agree with you, but I will," muttered Porsche, checking his pocket watch. "No sun, no sense of time, only twilight. By the way, how much water do we have, Rodgers? I'd like a hot spritz bath."

"No chance." Bernie strained his eyes ahead. "2500 liters, we need drinking water, not…what's that to the starboard, Bea?"

Bea slowly plowed through the hanging forest, the vines parting. "Not sure. I'll get closer." Through the fog, they could just make out what looked to be a vertical cliff. Suddenly, the Bear bumped into a brown rubbery substance that filled their entire view. "What in God's gritty…"

"I'm no expert in geology or forestry, but that looks like wrinkled bark," mused Gerlach. Bernie grabbed the railing. "It's a tree! A giant tree! Christ, it looks almost like a Redwood in California, only much bigger. Bea, float up a few hundred meters to the canopy." The fog began to thin. Bea eased up on the lift lever.

"It must be three hundred meters in width. That branch is as big as this ship," said Bea. "Check out those needles, long and thin like canoes."

"A Sequoia of some sort, pinecones as big as a Volksauto," said Porsche. "Imagine a cross section of the trunk."

"Or it being a Christmas tree!" said Alice, snapping away. "I could ring up Saks Fifth Avenue, see if they could cobble up some sizeable gifts and silk bows."

"Where's Paul Bunyon when we need him?" asked Bea. "This might be a daft idea, but how about an expedition onto one of the branches? We could all use a fresh-air kip and tea."

Shäfer and Geer arrived. "She's right, Rodgers," said Shäfer. "We should make use of our being lost while we can. Scientific wonders are not to be ignored."

"Agreed," said Geer. "We are all exhausted. Ernst and I will check the surface for safety. Poisons may be present."

Bernie clapped his hands and rubbed them. "All right, not a bad suggestion. Let's don jackets and bring our friend Klemp along. Maybe a little nature will be good for him."

•••

Geer gave the all-clear sign with his hand.

Using the extended gangplank, everyone made their way onto the thirty-meter-wide branch, its undulating fibrous bark a challenge to traverse. Cool mist passed by smelling slightly of mint leaves and cloves. Large ice crystals lay in cracks.

Schäfer examined some of them. "It's a theory that ice crystals and snowflakes form sacred geometric patterns from the electromagnetic frequency of a particular environment."

Porsche leaned in. "Amazing, and so large."

Alice took her turn guarding Klemperer. "Where you from?" she asked sweetly, twirling her hair, the stump of bark a decent bench. She opened a thermos of hot coffee.

He sighed. "A small town east of Graz in Austria, Köflach. My father and I climbed mountains together, skied too. My mother is Moravian, an excellent cook. Both taught me well."

Bernie unlocked his handcuffs. "Play nice and we'll get along fine. Word of honor as an officer?" He waved his pistol.

"Ja, word of honor." Klemperer looked the tree over and quoted from an SS propaganda film. "'Eternal forest, eternal German volk…we must stand in eternity. Make space for the Fatherland…'" He then turned to Alice, rubbing his wrists and accepting hot tea from Bea who had made a fire. His demeanor softened. "Call me Piter. No need for such formality." He then nibbled a Zweiback with canned butter. "Huh, reminds me of childhood."

Another seagull pack flew by. "*Scheisse!*" yelled Porsche, covered in a gallon of white liquid excrement, a dive bomber's pass made good. "What are those damned Pterodactyls eating, anyway?"

Everyone laughed. Gerlach rolled on the ground, breathless.

Bea removed Porsche's parka. "Easy, Professor. I'll clean you up." She gave him her jacket, having donned a wool turtleneck Kriegsmarine-issue sweater and hat from the storage locker.

Gwafa cleaned his Homburg with a cloth and canteen water. "*La!* Good as new." Then plopped it back onto Porsche's head.

He patted it. "Never go anywhere without a proper hat, son. Serves me well."

After some easy chit-chat, Alice asked of Klemperer: "How do you feel about our…*illustrious* passengers in the organ room?"

Bea sat and translated, but her intermittent tutoring had improved Alice's German.

At this he thought deeply, swallowing hard his biscuit. Suddenly, everything in his reality had changed completely. "I'm a loyal officer and soldier, and I'd like to think I'm honorable…but the things I've seen and…well, Rodgers explained everything in exquisite detail, thus I…Kammler, the camps, those two strange men they…" He looked at both women, a concerned look in his eyes. "It's far beyond disgusting, and completely unbelievable, *unconscionable*…if I had known…if only every German soldier knew the foul truth of…" A tear dropped and he immediately wiped it away, ashamed. "I've lost my humanity for many years, my sanity. Brainwashed or no, *Gott* will punish all of us for our crimes. How could I have been so naïve? So…"

Bea asked: "You were never aware of the death camps, experiments, and murder squads?"

"I don't expect you to believe me, but no. Dachau, yes, but…not us dusty *Gebirgsjäger*. We all wore the SS badge, but every division and section is sealed off depending on their duties. No one talks about their jobs, even the officers, *especially* the officers. Odin-kissing Himmler fanatics like Poppel are everywhere. It's completely different from the regular army. Everything is compartmentalized, everything is so damned secret…but you understand, you were one of us. I didn't care, it was an honor to protect the *Ahnenerbe Dienst*, interact, fight, and travel with them. I've learned so much." He looked to Shäfer, who was chatting with Gerlach and Bernie. "Huh, Ernst may be an egotistical arse, a dandy, but he's been a good friend and mentor, and a good climber."

"I'll leave you two alone," smiled Bea, walking off. "He needs to earn our trust, Drumm, be so advised."

Alice squeezed his arm, and laid her head on his shoulder.

After a minute or two he asked softly in English: "Do you…haff a knife?" Alice waved. "Bernie, he wants a knife."

Bernie hovered over them. "Okay Klemp. But no sudden moves, pal."

She handed him her folding knife, then quickly extended her full lips and kissed him, their chemistry undeniable, a passion about to blossom. Alice could not help herself, emotions ran high.

"I knew it! I just bloody *knew* it!" cried Bea amongst laughter.

Klemperer pulled off his anorak and began to saw away at his uniform's SS patch. When he was done, he handed the knife to Bernie handle first. "*Danke*."

Bernie folded his Buck knife and hissed: "I'll be watching you, SS."

•••

Bea sat, sharing cold chocolate. "Lovely mist today, smells like Black Forest pine. I read a report in my spare moments stating that Himmler presented you with the SS Death Head ring. Wear it sometimes?"

Porsche leered. "I keep it in my tie pin and cufflink drawer. Official occasions only. You were in the SS too. Where's yours, may I ask?"

"I was a dragooned member, kidnapped. Threw it into a pond in Norway. The woodland spirits liked that."

"Hmmff. For the best."

Bea opened one of Poppel's personal files that she found in the chart room. "The *Generalmajor* really liked to keep scraps and bits from the battlefronts." She found a Moscow *Pravda* newspaper clipping from March with the photos of two female pilots. "These two birds flew the Yak-1 fighter. Damn…can't read what it says."

Porsche examined it with his reading glasses. "I learned a little on my trips to Russia ten years ago. I think it's saying…that these two are decorated fighter pilots, Katya Budanova and Lydia Litvyak. Many kills between them apparently. Impressive for women."

"I'll be damned! Knew the Russians had some imagination." "Poppel wrote here they must be desperate for pilots."

"The hell with him, we women can handle it all. Oh, I hear via songbirds you plan to build *Volksautos* in Brazil after the war."

"So? My family deserves to profit on my and Ferry's genius. Anyway, inexpensive lightweight cars will help those of little means. In addition to Europe, my plan is to 'automobilize' the third world countries for the sake of progress. Racing will flourish."

"Jolly good, I suppose. Oh by the way, had a go in your fancy tan Panzer back in the desert at Siwa Oasis. We lobbed so-o-o many tungsten core shells at—"

"You *what?*" exclaimed Porsche, mouth at utmost capacity.

"Not bad, shot well, swam better, but we broke down after forty minutes or so. Damned hot in that tin can. Basically impregnable. Beastly old thing. The Afrika Korps has a price on our heads you know, Gwafa and I."

"Madame, you…*you* and I seem to be inextricably linked in some unusual and irritatingly cosmic way, but now I'm exhausted trying to make any real sense of it, not anymore." He sighed. "That idiot Hitler, I told him we should copy the Russian T34 and make it better, but he insisted on a complicated heavy tank of German design. He's a madman. We had less than a year to develop it. Many problems arose. The electric motors needed more development."

"Perhaps electric tanks are a bridge too far."

He mused the idea. "I'd prefer no tanks at all after the war. Hopefully we won't need—"

Bernie addressed the group. "Let's conclude our business here. Time to weigh anchor."

27

Two weeks passed, but to most it felt like six.

With no sun or calendar to mark the passing of days, all crew members had a different current date in their minds. Discussions over dinner had been lively and full of conjecture, but as to what direction they were going, that was up for debate. Despite only two meals a day, the food stores were down to one week's provisions including army-issue Iron Rations.

As the Bear silently hovered above, Schäfer picked green and lavender-colored plants. "I don't advise eating any of these. Water can be tested, but plants must be digested for poisons to cause a reaction."

Bernie smelled them. "Well, none of us should be guinea pigs. Too risky."

"And the rodents may have eaten the plants," worried Geer.

Bea washed her undergarments with Alice in a cold stream while Porsche and Gerlach bathed naked thirty meters away. She and Alice had piloted them through uncountable kilometers of tunnels into a large temperate cavern with lush tropical trees and rocky terrain bathed in a dim orange iridescence. Strange animals were many: Armadillos with yellow spots and golden eyes, small red birds with shiny white wings, tiny mice, a fat, loud-croaking frog-like amphibian that was a shiny metallic light blue, and an amazing, four-foot bipedal reptile that Shäfer said resembled a prehistoric raptor of one genus or another but was friendly enough.

"Good to be clean again. I reeked," said Alice, combing her hair.

"Ernst sure likes feeding those clever lizards mice, but I'll not go near them. Hand me the soap. Ahh, what I'd give for a bar of Mumbly's pink French variety, smelled of orchids."

Alice tossed it to her. "Geer's got at least ten dozen species of flora and fauna stored away. If we do make it to Ireland, at least we'll have been successful as a zoology mission."

Bea combed through knots. "I hope we make it anywhere on the surface, it's an intolerable labyrinth down here, a test of resolve like none other."

Gwafa sat and began to wash his shirt. "Cold and clear, and smells good. Never have I been so glad to see potable fresh water in my life. Even the Sahara has its magical wells and streams. I am very glad for Ernst and Edmund, their testing equipment."

Bea handed him the soap with a smile. "We may be an ark at present, but at least we won't smell like animals for a while. And yes, I consider our two stowaways animals of the lowest sort."

Gwafa asked: "Why do they not attempt to take over the ship if they have psychic abilities enough to kill?"

"They said they're not interested," said Bea, yawning. "They enjoy the ad hoc adventure and only want to be dropped off in Axis territory. Bit queer, them, well, *more* than a bit. Maniacal, unethical, greedy, addicted to gambling but lazy-minded. Profit and prestige are their main interests, political intrigue a close second. They said they're only 'going with the universal flow,' whatever the hell that means."

Gwafa looked into Bea's eyes. "Are *we*?" She held his soapy hand. "Hope so."

A distance away, Lew and Stew splashed each other like children. "Yoo-hoo, over here ladies!" yelled Lew, bending quickly up and down so his large penis flapped against his wet stomach repeatedly. "*Weisswurst!*"

"Wankering dim bulbs," muttered Alice. "Law of Unattraction describes them well." With Klemperer's help, Bernie lowered a hose into the water to fill the ship's tanks. "Now Porsche and Gerlach can take their precious hot showers."

Having finally befriended Bernie, Klemperer laughed for the first time. "And together diddle themselves silly while saving water."

•••

At midnight the berth wall shook.

Klemperer lifted Alice by her silky moist thighs to the wall of their compartment, pressing a slight hexagonal pattern into her back. He thrusted hard, bending his neck and biting at her stiffened nipples. She screamed in excited agony, her womanhood split by his more than ample manhood, nails dragging skin off his sharp buttocks till blood ran. Breathing was hot and deep; passion off the scale. Despite the exciting embarrassment of close quarters they kept on, tongues buried, long-awaited orgasms at the quickmarch.

On the wall's other side, Porsche and Gerlach attempted sleep. "Did I ever tell you that I traveled on the Hindenburg to South America?"

"Argghhn-n-n-n-n!" groaned Alice.

"No," replied Porsche, pillow over his ears. "But I'm sure the *Schweinebraten* was delicious."

"Four Jacks," exclaimed Bea, laying down her poker cards in front of Stew. "Funny story. Had a similar winning hand whilst skiing at Gstaad in '36. Imperial loser Price Bernhard handed me the keys to his bespoke blue Talbot-Lago with leopard seats. Took him a week to win it back from me. Fun with snow chains, Peachy and I entered it into a local winter rally. Dented the shite out of it hitting an ice wall but came in fourth overall. He was no happier than you, Stew. Tish-tosh."

Folded, Gwafa laughed, the 9 mm bullet pile of chips enormous. "So glad we are not waging real money."

"Let's change that," said Bea. "Play for real stakes." She pinched Gwafa's thigh to let him know she was scheming.

"Agreed, this is boring." Lew poured the last ounces of a hidden half-bottle of apricot brandy he had saved. "She's cheated you again fair and square, brother. Her mind is a blank."

"Texas Hold 'em my pink pearly *ass*," grumbled Stew, patting his chest. "Wait I…I need a loan." He picked up a bullet. "If only these were real gold…"

"Speaking of, you already owe me 700 gold sovereigns," said Lew. "It was that solid week of *Piquet* with Empress Maria Theresa in Vienna, the palace garden, mmm, spring of 1747, I think. She won, but owed me plenty from months earlier. A wild cheetah in a Jacquard daybed."

"You still hold that chit? Insolent dog of a brother."

Bea tossed back a shot and burped. "Pardon *moi*. Lovely Nelson's tot that is. Anyhoo, that's going to cost you *beaucoup* interest, your royal lowness." She pushed a small pile of bullets his way. "Fifty."

Stew fumed. "Only fifty? Lascivious vamp. Double or nothing next hand."

Shäfer and Geer could not sleep, their four-man berth donated for the private moment of love. They attended to their finds in the cargo bay and recorded drawings in their notebooks. After writing letters destined for home someday, they fell asleep against crates.

Bernie stood watch in the cockpit, lights off, the expansive view of lush treetops glowing in the scant amber light. He thought fondly of his family. Like a southbound Laplander wishing for snow and reindeer, he wondered if they would ever see the surface again. He mumbled a pathetic: "An entire world at war and here I am, an unlucky sailor being slowly digested in the bowels of the Earth."

∙∙∙

All was quiet at 0300 hours.

Psychic poker was not for the timid. Since no one's mind could be read except Gwafa's, Bea had discreetly marked the cards the old fashioned way as her father had taught her years ago, not for cheating per se, that was beneath a Sunderland, but in order to tell if someone else was.

Stew and Lew had been used to cheating psychically for centuries thought Bea, but they had not noticed the slight tell she had used by indenting the edge ever so slightly with a fingernail. Now they were playing for very high stakes. *So they have gold fever, eh?*

Gwafa had long since dropped out. He dealt. "All right *madame, messieurs*, the game is Follow the Queen, Aces high." The bullet pile had grown to three hundred-seventy plus. "Each bullet is now worth a Reichsbank-issue gold bar of 11.33 kilos. All agreed? *Bon.*"

"How much is your fuddy-duddy father worth again?" asked Stew. "We have ways of checking you know. Bankers we know well."

Bea leaned in and took a firm tone. "Twelve million pounds or so at the Bank of England, his estate, and another ten in a Swiss account. Two for myself. I'm good for it, my word upon it. Can you tell if I'm lying?"

Lew looked into her eyes. "She's not lying, I can tell that at least, the rest is a murky mess. She definitely drinks from Loki's golden cup."

"A trickster, eh? Pick up the cards then," snarled Stew.

∙∙∙

0430 hours.

"All's quiet with fecund and feral Drummy back there." After many hands, Bea pushed her entire pile to the center. "All in, gents. I count 465 chips."

"Don't do it brother," said a frustrated Lew having folded. "You've an incurable passion for losing money."

"Silence, dog." Overly confident and fuming with machismo and boredom, Stew went all in. "And everything I owe you as well. I call."

Bea deftly flipped a Queen, then lay down a winning wildcard hand. "That's how it's done back at Cambridge."

Stew fumed hotter. "I don't buy it. My cards are perfect. Where's the book?

What's the *ruling?*"

Gwafa pulled down the 1892 Poker Rule Book from the shelf, opened the proper page, and showed it to a much more sedate Lew.

Lew leaned in. "It's close, but no cigar, brother."

"Shit from a camel!" cried Lew, pitching his cards to the air.

"Your penchant for reckless gambling has reached a new nadir, brother. What will the commerce guild chairman say?"

"This is intolerable! How could..." Stew pounded the table, then stood abruptly. After a pause he calmed. "Books. Rules. Dogon treachery. Britisher *femme fatales*. We Aldebaraners are *shrewd* businessmen my dear, but...we're always good for our debts and our word." He straightened his suit jacket and fluffed his pocket square. "Commerce and diplomacy are exacting." He turned to his brother. "Fine, fine, fine then, what's our lump in Zermatt worth?"

Lew took a deep breath and made calculations on a piece of paper. "By my reckoning, including two Monets and one Van Gogh, about..." He checked a notebook on the current value of gold on international and galactic markets. "Oh, 35.166 million pounds sterling thereabouts, including silver and platinum. Not quite enough, we're...23.246 percent shy. Oh damn."

Tired and hungry, Bea's inflamed imagination begat images of Swiss chalets, cars, clothes, and yachts after the war. *I'll buy out Dior and Chanel, buy back Bentley from Rolls-Royce, then build my own Le Mans racecar with—*

"*Madame?*" asked Gwafa, holding her hand and squeezing.

"What? Oh, yes. Right, yes, of course. What say we...umm, make a trade?"

"What...kind of trade?" asked Lew in a kind voice. "I keep the books, he's the diplomat." "Oh, nothing much. How-w-w many people do you have in custody awaiting shipment?" she asked casually, drum rolling her fingers.

Stew looked at his brother. "You topside Earth humans?"

"*Oui*," said Gwafa. "Law of Gender, otherwise known as The Law of Balance. We intend to uphold it."

"An Hermeticist, eh?" Lew flipped pages and sighed lengthily. "One hundred sixty-five able-bodied young men, mostly Russians and Poles, a few Czech and Ukrainian women, tall, blond, blue-eyed, good genetics for breeding. Three scientists bound for a research facility near Alpha Centauri, two extremely talented artists to be time-traveled to the past, and a thousand plumpish children. What of it?"

Bea leaned back on the plush banquette. "You two take much more than you give back, that's for damn sure. Balance must be kept. I'll trade the lot for their freedom."

Stew hissed: "*What* did you just say?"

"You can't be serious?" asked Lew, lifting his sunglasses. "Their collective value is much higher due to market demand, blame it on the *Orion-Draconis Concrete Consortium*. How about our entire zoo's worth of animals instead? They're flash-frozen in temporal glass cubes and will last forever. Open one up and instant gazelle."

Bea laughed. "Nothing doing, but now that I think upon it…I'll take *them* too. If not, then you two bleached hyenas better find a lot more gold under some tropical rainbow."

Stew wiped the table clean in one go. "Why you little poxed poppet—"

Gwafa instinctively stood. "Fair and square. Fine yellow gold, *beaucoup d'or*. Pay up. If you were dishonorable cutthroats you would have killed us all by now. If you have honor, present it."

Bea added: "Tsk, tsk, add the two Monet paintings for that outburst. Manners please, or we'll let it known through the grapevine that you monkey-business chaps welched on a payment due. You *do* like Monet, don't you sergeant?"

With clenched teeth, he replied: "Indeed, Madame. I will raise money for my village by selling them, but only after one of the two artists copies them for my wall someday."

Lew held his arm. "Take it easy, brother. They strike a hard bargain, you have to respect that at least. We need our precious gold at the moment for pending deals, the overheated market is tight, and Earth gold is the best quality found anywhere. Don't fret, it's going to be a very lo-o-o-o-ong war."

Bea laid down the Tarot *Balance* card and tapped it. "And no chits or fine print, snowmen, I want a *signed* ironclad contract on permanent parchment."

28

"Okay, we've spent two days searching. We need to pick one," said Bernie. "In three days' time we begin to starve, and I ain't gonna start eating strange rodents and unfamiliar roots until I have to."

Alice stood by the forward windows with the others. "One goes into the ground, another goes into the cliff, is there a third?"

Bernie looked to the river below. "In the wilderness back home if I was lost, Dad taught me to always follow a river or stream downhill until it reached some kind of encampment or settlement with people. The river here goes down over that rise and into an underground tunnel. Can this ship swim?"

Gerlach pointed. "It's a sealed pressure vessel, plus the electrobubble should protect us, but I would not venture too deep if we hit an underground aquifer. I'll have to reduce the bubble a little at the screws so they can bite the water. Should work theoretically. Air and water are both fluids."

"Good. I'm not even going to bother asking those two untrustworthy albinos for their opinion," said Bernie.

"I don't think Blohm & Voss designed this blimp to be a *U-Boat*," grumbled Porsche.

Klemperer held Alice's hand and said: "It's made it this far without incidence. How many hours of oxygen are in the tanks? Baumann said they replenish themselves automatically."

"Around twelve hours," replied Gerlach, tapping two gauges on the wall. "That's for high altitudes, but if we don't venture too deep the air won't compress much further. Spherical tanks, strong."

Bea ordered: "Let's get it done." Easing up on the lift lever, she set the Bear down on the half-mile-wide river with a gentle splash. When they reached the end there was a waterfall into the tunnel. "Here we go."

"All set back here, the props should work fine," said Gerlach.

"Hang on everyone!" yelled Bernie. "Running lights on."

Nervous, Porsche struggled with his lap belt. "Jules Verne…20,000 Leagues…

Nemo the tyrant…"

The Bear eased over the cliff and floated with the intense rapids as they entered the tunnel. Frothy churning water was all they could see. Vibration was minimal but steady.

"Descending, eighteen degrees down at the bow," said Alice.

After an hour of churning water and no visibility, they entered a massive aquifer; the forward view became all dark green. Tiny white creatures danced and moved out of their path by the tens of thousands.

"Albino Krill, *Euphausia superba*, millions of them," said Geer, palms to plexiglass. "Can you maneuver Bea?" asked Bernie.

"Controls are sluggish and all dials read zero. He's not designed for water. I think we're moving forward, but I've no reference. All ahead slow, we're nothing but an oversized cork in an underground river."

Bernie sat. "Steady as she goes." *Hope Dad was right…*

•••

"Last of the Iron Rations," said Alice, handing them out at the mess table two days later.

Everyone was hungry and had lost weight.

Porsche patted his diminishing stomach. "Not a bad thing for Walter and I."

Excited, Geer came in with a large pan. "I sucked some Krill from one of the fresh air intakes and used a screen for a strainer then fried them in oil. They will keep us alive anyway. The underground water is fresh and tasty, no worries there."

"Bitter but not bad," said Alice.

"Edmund and I have eaten much worse in the Amazon," said Schäfer, pouring the last of the apple juice. "Snakes, insects and such."

"All the power in the universe back there and no food. What a mess," said Bernie, examining a tiny .04 centimeter specimen, then crunched it between his teeth. "Needs salt. Nice job, Edmund."

Bea ate a spoonful. "Well it's certainly not Dover Sole Meunière at the Zürserhof Hotel, but it'll—" A hefty bump jarred everyone. "What the *hell* was that?"

"*Everyone to the cockpit—now!*" yelled Klemperer over the intercom.

As they scampered in, Schäfer scanned instruments. "Outside temperature is minus five and dropping."

"Jesus, icebergs, that's just goddam great," said Bernie. "All stop." Giant ice chunks reflected the ship's lights with an eerie green glow.

Bea took over the helm from Klemperer. "The bubble setting was on low, I'll increase it. What now, Cap'm Bligh? Torpedoes?"

Bernie rubbed his beard. "Let me think. At least now we have a reference for forward movement, but we need some kind of navigation. Anyway, let's keep moving."

Porsche arrived with no tie or jacket—a first for him—carrying a small tray of parts. "Perhaps I can give you some when I fix the Tellus." After many hours of slow going, he carefully attached the last planetary gear and accompanying crystal with a pair of pliers and a magnifying glass. "All done, it's back to factory specs. Best I can do without a diagram."

"The astrolabe is humming and moving again," said Bea. "Nice work Professor."

"Fine job even for a genius." Schäfer adjusted the zodiac wheel to what he thought was the approximate date. "Alice, if you would be so kind…"

She came over and placed her palm in the outline; it glowed. "I feel something, a tingling. I think it knows me intimately now."

"I wonder about that," mumbled Porsche, organizing tools in a tin box.

"Try this: Clear your mind, relax. That's it, deep breaths. Think of the surface, where do you want to go?," asked Schäfer calmly.

She became euphoric, her voice soft. "Well, the Bahamas did sound nice…"

"No! I demand we end up in neutral territory. That's a compromise we can all adhere to," said Klemperer. "Anywhere in South America would…"

Suddenly a moving map appeared on the Tellus under a glass dome.

"It's an old map of some land masses," mused Bernie up close. "Four land masses with intersecting rivers and a circle of water in the middle."

Schäfer said: "That's an old map of the North Pole. I've seen sixteenth-century ones that looked just like it. The North Pole must have been an ice-free island or islands in ancient times, the maps re-copied over the ages."

"Could it be we're under the Pole now?" asked Bernie. "That would explain the ice—"

"It…it's confused I think," said Alice, eyes closed as the Tellus hummed and whistled.

"All I see are places I don't recognize. Mountains and snow, odd circular cities, huge megaliths covered in gold, black sand beaches, rivers…places of the distant past perhaps."

"For Stalin's sake, think of someplace sunny with tropical fruit, rum, palms, and plenty of solid food. Think Tahiti," said Bea, avoiding an ice chunk. "I hereby quit the war."

Klemperer sat next to her. "Agreed. All I want to do is climb mountains with my future children and eat fondue."

Alice collapsed into Bernie's arms, her palm still connected, eyes rolled to the back and quivering. "Sun…trees…farms…"

Schäfer held her head. "Alice? *Gott!*"

A shrieking alarm sounded from the top of the Tellus' organ pipes; the astrolabe cast out a repetitive thrumming sound then pointed downwards and to the left, the arrow extending as if to make the direction clear.

The yoke fell forward and to the left out of Bea's hands. "It's gone rogue. Hard to port and descending, power's up to fifty percent." She pulled hard. "It's stuck! Christ, it's on some sort of autopilot!"

"Try harder!" yelled Bernie. "It's taken control of the helm."

Klemperer tried to reduce throttle. "The lever won't move!" Muscles strained.

Porsche helped him. "Something's gone horribly wrong here…maybe I fixed the wrong…"

Out the forward windows was a horrible sight. Bernie grabbed the railing. "The icebergs are moving around us, it's a whirlpool. We're dropping fast into a whirlpool!"

The rushing sound of raging water intensified like a hurricane. Vibration became strong. Swirls of light green energized water currents encompassed the ship with flashes of lightning.

Gwafa came on from the generator room. ♪ *"What's happening up there, Madame?"*

Gerlach could be heard yelling in the background.

Despite the protection of the electrobubble and the power of the maneuvering nodes, the Bear twirled helplessly in the huge whirlpool as the lights and power suddenly went off. A battery-powered alarm klaxon went off and harsh G-forces became evident for the first time. Bea could feel herself slowly passing out as a strange sound emerged from the hatchway; Stew and Lew were welcoming their inevitable collective death with laughter.

•••

Klemperer awoke with a mouth of puke next to the starboard bulkhead; the ship was listing to starboard, half submerged in a dim light. The hull gently scraped the side of the anthracite-lined tunnel as it moved with the gentle current. Water dripped from the top node onto his face, an obvious leak in the seal, but the cold drops had done the trick; he looked to his watch and thought maybe five hours had passed but wasn't sure. Behind him in a pile was Porsche, gagging. Klemperer quickly dug into his throat, clearing the blockage. "Professor, wake up! Come on, damn you!" He then used a Heimlich maneuver. "Are you alive?"

Face painted red from the emergency light, Porsche vomited and coughed. "I'm...not sure."

Klemperer found a canteen slung on the wall and gave sips to him. "Wash it out, good, good. Drink some. No injuries?"

"I'm fine, bit bruised. *Cough*. I've been through two wars, one wife, ten dogs, three hundred races, one Führer, and two children. I'll live."

"Klem-m-mp..." softly moaned Schäfer nearby. "My arm...won't work."

He examined it. "*Ja-ja*, a clean break. You'll be fine once I splint it." He gasped slightly at a large pool of blood. "You have an exposed femur, a broken thigh. Don't try to move!"

Schäfer licked caked blood from his lips. "Hel-l-lp the women. You always were the strongest of all of us, now I'm so glad of it. Jealous...before, a fine...friend am I."

Klemperer found Alice huddled with Bea under the helm. "Alice my love, *liebchen*, wake up." He kissed her then shook her shoulders. "Alice!"

"Mmm, oh-h-h-h...I...I love you, Piter."

He held her tight. "*Scheisse*, we're in bad shape."

Gwafa awoke to the generator's slight hum; it glowed a soft amber at idle speed. He felt the large lump on his head. In his arms was Gerlach; he'd saved him by grabbing the man before he hit the wall. "*Se reveiller, monsieur.*" He patted his stubbled face. "*Achtung!*"

Gerlach awoke at a snap. "*In Gottes namen*...get your filthy hands off me you blacksnake!" He arose, then stumbled. "Sorry, I...We are listing. Power...we must get the electric power stabilized...or..." Before him lay a pile of disconnected cables, popped fuses, and ruptured conduits.

Bea moaned as Alice wiped her face with a wet handkerchief. "C'mon old girl, wakey-wakey."

She arose unsteadily. "Oh-h-h-h, the head. I was enjoying the Bahamas for a while." Geer came in; he was fine. "The Nazzara brothers are missing, I checked. I passed out. What happened?"

"What *didn't* fucking happen?" asked a much-bruised Alice in a cracked voice.

"Rodgers? *Rodgers!*" yelled Klemperer. "Wake up you…" He felt his throat; Bernie was ice cold with no pulse, his head cracked apart, milky eyes half open. "Oh, *nein-n-n-n*. He's…dead. No pulse."

Porsche leaned in for a second opinion having seen a few dead men in the last war; he looked to Bea and Alice and shook his head.

Bea wailed in grief; Alice held her in tears.

Hearing the cry, Gwafa crawled over the Kubelwagen and its broken wood palette, much gear had broken loose and was now pooled by the dented cargo door—tools, weapons, lumber, tents, tires, jerrycans. When he entered the cockpit he saw Bernie and Schäfer in a bad state.

Geer asked: "Gwafa, help me get Ernst to the sick bay. I have to operate *now*."

•••

With two flashlights Alice opened every cabinet in a hurry, tossing out bandages and arranging instruments. She then poured wood alcohol on Schäfer's wounds; he growled like a shepherd dog. "Morphine, I'll inject him."

Geer ripped off Schäfer's clothes. "I'm not a doctor, but I can perform field surgery in an emergency, fucking SS is good for something. Good thing you're trained too."

Alice yelled out the door: "Gwafa! Tell that arselick Gerlach we need power and lights or this man will die too."

Gwafa gently dragged a liquid Bea away from Bernie's body. "He was a brave leader, a man of great morals. Come, we must help the Professor, or we may all die."

She squirmed and writhed in his arms. "'Where shall w-w-we three meet again in thunder, lightning, or in r-r-rain? When the hurlyburly's done, when the battle's lost and w-w-won.'"

In the engine room, Porsche found another flashlight. "This is a mess. How did the power go out?"

Gerlach pointed. "Never mind how, it's all gone to hell. Can you splice this cable into that one?"

As Porsche worked, Bea and Gwafa held the two heavy cables for surgery. In the dim amber light Porsche could see her streaks of tears. "He was a good man, Beatrice. We'll all miss him. The war's over for us."

"Hold him tight," snapped Geer as he pushed the two bones back together with a snap inside a bloody hole.

Schäfer's scream echoed throughout the ship. The arm bone was next.

Geer sewed him up with an alcohol and sulfa cleansing. "Give him the rest of the morphine so he can sleep. I'll find a wood plank to splint him."

•••

After three hours hard work, Porsche said: "The C-cable is done."

Gerlach replaced blown ceramic fuses one by one. "Fifty amps, one hundred amps, five hundred amps, one thousand."

Porsche spliced the last bit of heavy copper wire and covered it with gutta-percha rubber insulation. "A-cable attached, 'B' is next. Done. Try it now."

Gerlach flipped the auxiliary power lever, the generator hummed pale green with a small power draw. Lights and ventilation fans came on, and the ship automatically righted itself with minimal bubble output. "'Piece of cake,' as the Britishers say, *ja*?"

Bea just sat on the floor slumped. "*Ja*."

•••

Klemperer and Gwafa hammered away building a wood coffin out of the pine lumber.

Placing his body in a canvas tent, they rolled Bernie up and sealed the crate.

After cleaning and organizing the cargo bay back in order, they lashed the coffin down next to the secured Kubel. Everyone gathered except for Bea. Words were said, kind words, and Klemperer sang his beloved "Erika." Bernie had been a fellow mountaineer and officer.

Geer, Bea, Alice, and Klemperer searched the entire ship, no trace of the wicked brothers could be found. Even their briefcases were gone.

"I don't get it, where would they have escaped to?" asked Bea. "Bet they won't honor our deal now."

"I honestly don't care," said Alice, looking under an access panel. Klemperer hissed: "Swine. I hope they drowned like rats."

•••

They floated along in the tunnel's darkness with dimmed running lights to save power while the emergency battery array charged.

Bea hung her head out the round, port-side loading hatch near the galley, her voice weak. "About eight or ten knots I'd say, the river's probably a mile wide or so now."

"I miss England and our families." Alice moved in and put their heads together. "So decidedly boring. How long have we been riding the current?"

"Almost thirty-six cheerless hours now. The Professor said they'll have full antigravity power soon they think. I don't care anymore. Hope we die soon, sick of it all."

Alice kissed her cheek, not knowing what to say. Hunger pains were setting in, the situation bleak. She then left Bea alone, something she always did since childhood when Bea needed it. Bea wept again.

Klemperer sat by the radar station reading the ship's manuals. Alice sat on his lap. "I think we can exceed the maximum setting on the forward radar array, it's incredibly overbuilt for some reason with immense power capability for long range, not that it matters much."

She twirled his hair. "That's nice."

He shut the book. "Strange how war is. All four of you were my sworn enemies a month ago, but I now consider you my dearest friends. I even miss Rodgers, he…was kind to me."

Her German was getting better, she thought. "Is that all I am?" "No. I love you in the fullest, and you had better know that."

Cleaning his hands with a rag, Porsche sat next to Bea. He had no comforting words to give but thought it best to spend time with her. After all, his life had been saved time and again. *Pity, for it seems I cannot ever be a help to her*, he thought. "Shäfer has a bad fever, not much we can do for him, a bad infection. How I miss my wife, my home, and her cooking."

Bea smiled. "Yes, the mushroom soup…the arguments with Ferry, Ghislaine and nephew Anton, Lutz and his middling manners, how I loved it all before the war."

He'd cracked a thumbnail, and it reminded him of the Tripoli Grand Prix in the pits. "Have you dreamt of Lutz lately? I have. We were racing again in the warm sun."

"No. I probably imagined it all anyway." She led Porsche down the companionway to the cockpit.

Klemperer came over to them. "We voted. I am in command, it was the four of us against Alice and Gwafa who wanted you."

Bea turned to look at him. "Fine and dandy. Well, Herr *Grossadmiral*, what now? What are your Thule-approved orders of the day? Hmm? You see I could give a fat shite if—"

"We've got more problems!" yelled Alice, face to a forward window.

Porsche bolted to the engine room. "Whatever it is, I'm going to light a fire under Walter's ass."

Klemperer went with him. "Keep us informed."

Bea and Alice watched the tiny dot of light ahead. "Distance and time?" asked Alice. She inhaled and sighed. "If the tunnel's a mile wide and we're moving at eight knots, maybe an hour or two, but it's a guess."

"It could open up as just another river at the bottom of another cavern."

"Or it could be one of those mile-high waterfalls, and over we go." She hit the button.

📢 "*Attention all hands, there's a pinpoint of light ahead, possibly an exit. You clever chaps back there have an hour plus to get us airborne.*"

•••

Finishing up the repairs, Gerlach said: "The only explanation I can think of is that the powerful whirlpool created its own electrical torsion field storm, one powerful enough to disable the magnetic field couplings. Something like that."

Gwafa helped Porsche adjust one of the large crystals in the electric motor. "Hold that ladder steady my good man." The Professor tightened bolts and retaining screws. "That's done it."

"A strong ship," said Gwafa.

📢 "*Are you bloody well done yet? We can hear the falls up here!*"

📢 "*Stop yelling at us, Beatrice!*" yelled Porsche.

"Here goes." Gerlach flipped the main power switches. The dials spun upwards.

Bea pulled back on the yoke. The strange-looking exit was huge and bright with swirling colors at the center as if a giant fish-eye lens was trying to focus on something. "It's not enough, we're going over the precipice. Goddam you Porsche!" Her eyes reflected the kaleidoscopic liquid light.

A slight electric shock filled the ship, causing everyone to momentarily scratch at themselves. The ship pitched straight down in free fall, then slowly righted itself as it passed through a waterfall.

Alice said: "Good power on the dial, seventy percent. Leveling out. Altimeter's working again, 3560 meters." Suddenly strong light bathed the cockpit as if someone had opened a curtain.

Bea reduced throttle. "All ahead slow, 45 kph."

Geer and Schäfer went to the wet forward windows. "It's the sun—we made it to the *surface*. By Freya, Bea, you did it!" yelled Geer.

Schäfer pounded the Perspex. "Unbelievable! It feels so warm…and pale blue skies. But how did we…?"

The Bear passed through a white cloud with a slight buffeting.

Alice joined them. "Look down there, no, that way, I see *fields*, rows of trees…and over there, buildings, houses. It looks like East Anglia." She squeezed Klemperer's hand. "I see a lake, and what looks like orange tree rows. Maybe California? Oh, it's so beautiful!"

Klemperer banged on the window. "Descend a little, Bea. Let's take a closer look."

Gwafa looked to their rear using the retractable outside mirror. "A mountain waterfall of immense size with green all around it. Bea was right. But we have only thus far descended…not much makes sense to me."

Porsche and Gerlach stood amazed. "Those rectangular fields…they go on forever to the horizon," said Porsche. "Perhaps we *are* in South America."

Gerlach tapped the window. "Is that a mountain range in the distance? No, it must be Mongolia or China. I've seen photos."

"Angels two." Bea leveled out at 2000 meters.

Schäfer grabbed the binoculars. "Citrus trees of some kind, and over there, rows of corn or barley, we must obtain some seeds, Edmund. I've never seen such perfect grids and fields in my life." He focused for distance. "That huge mountain in the haze, it must be 4000 meters high or more. Bea, head to port ten degrees."

Geer looked through them next. "No Ernst, we must be somewhere in Indochina. I see canals feeding the agriculture. Many grids and canals…like Hanoi or Luang."

"It reminds me of East Africa, the cassava fields, but these are so straight and perfect," mused Gwafa. "The small hills over there, the Ethiopian lowlands perhaps?"

"*Afrika? Gott*, Bea, we should land for some food," exclaimed Klemperer. "Fresh game, sorghum, bread, millet and melons…"

Bea set the autopilot. The Tellus and the astrolabe were silent. She moved next to Schäfer and held out her hand. "May I?" She focused the lenses for maximum distance. "Palm trees of some sort, I see a building, no three. A Siamese temple with a gold dome. Then we are in Indochina somewhere. Let's land."

As they descended between crop fields, Geer shouted: "People are waving at us! Is this Japanese occupied territory? Must be. They seem excited. To them we're Axis Allies."

Shäfer turned to Bea. "Set us down on that sandy stretch near the fruit tree groves. See it?"

"Got it." Bea eased them down and set the landing buffers.

At two meters off the ground, the Bear suddenly became surrounded by a crowd of around a hundred.

Shäfer extended the bow stairway. "Come on, Edmund, let's greet them. I know some Burmese. I'm going to suck down ten oranges."

Geer descended. "Swastika flags! They're Buddhists then…"

Tibetan-looking people, prayer wheels and horns greeted them in a cacophony. Shäfer shook dozens of hands. "Hello, hello. We are lost travelers. *Ni hao, ni hao.*" A jeweled gold bracelet was placed on his wrist, then Geer's.

The bracelets shrunk to fit. "Tight! I can't get mine off," said Geer.

Shäfer observed: "Strange. I was feeling as if I were somehow splintering apart, but I'm fine now."

Alice folded her arms as she and Bea stood at the top of the stairs with Gwafa.

"We do not want to be permanent guests of the Japs."

"Agreed. I'm taking us back up if we see any," said Bea, accepting a gem-encrusted gold bracelet from a smiling woman. Everyone in the ship's company had been given one. Bea examined it. "Not bad."

Alice rubbed hers. "A tradition of some kind? This looks to be a 200-carat ruby."

Gwafa scanned the scene with the binoculars. "I see no soldiers. Only people in colored robes and fine hats." He marveled at the gold inlay on his copper bracelet, and thanked the woman. The men's bracelets had engravings of intricate symbols instead of gems.

A small crowd lifted Geer up and down on a yellow blanket. "Amazing!" he cried.

Locals eagerly flowed up the stairs, filling the ship. They examined everything with great curiosity, especially the Tellus and astrolabe.

Bea and Alice gorged on oblong melons and unrecognizable fruit. "I've never had anything like it," said Bea, mouth dripping. A smiling child wearing a golden conical hat gave her more from a woven swastika-festooned basket. "Thanks, old man. We were a bit lacking." *Love the headgear.*

Alice gulped and peeled. "Tastes like mangoes, champagne, and coconut."

A band of long horns and drums erupted. Chanting ensued. A vibratory celebration.

Porsche, Klemperer, Gerlach and Gwafa slurped vegetable soup at a large table under a colorful tarp lean-to. "Delicious! *Gott* be praised. We should unload the Kubel and go for a reconnaissance," said Porsche. The other men made grunting sounds, starving animals filling their bellies.

"Warm. Must be twenty-five or so," said Klemperer, removing his stained tunic. Gwafa tilted the whole bowl and chugged it down.

Alice dug into a bowl of warm green soup proffered by an elderly woman with a long copper ladle. "Tastes like a Parisian pea soup with mint and cilantro, and this flat bread seems to be made of lentils." Spilling a little, she looked to the ground. "Bit odd. Beans…where's our shadows?"

Bea looked up. "Well, the sun's at twelve o'clock high, must be noonish." She looked far and wide. "Everything's lit up equally, see those fruit trees? You're right, I see no shadows. Oh, who cares? I say, no meat to be had anywhere? That's downright uncivilized."

•••

A half-hour later Gerlach and Porsche flew off towards the mountains in the electric Kubel with a high-pitched whine.

Alice put palm to forehead. In the distance she saw three dots approaching at fifty feet altitude. "Incoming bogies."

Bea strained her eyes. "Not any aircraft I recognize, and that's all the Japs have to my knowledge. They're…"

"Foo-Fighters!" exclaimed Alice.

"I suppose the antigravity party is growing in popularity by the day."

Three silent spheres arrived, their outer hulls burning bright white in the sunlight with no shadows. Hemispheres and protrusions of all sizes that shined like mother of pearl glowed a soft pink, with six icosahedrons protruding from the hulls in equidistant placement. No windows could be seen. They hovered, then one of them maneuvered towards the open cargo hold and extended a transparent tube that melded to the door like warmed rubber. Locals carrying Bernie and Shäfer loaded them into their sphere ship.

Alice cried. "They're taking the men!"

"Perfumed soup? No shadows? Just what the bloody hell's going on he—"

Porsche barreled in from a sandy road, swerving around the locals, beeping.

"Beatrice!" Gerlach stood in his seat and pointed. "Those are not mountains, they're *pyramids*!"

29

With a horde of locals accompanying them inside, Bea piloted the Bear at 200 meters altitude slowly following the white spheres; a light shower commenced. "Must be one big-as-hell cavern to contain all this," said Bea. "Twenty thousand meters high or more, I reckon."

"No wonder it seemed that all we did was go deeper," said Alice. "I'm so turned around we could be on the Moon."

Passing the massive central pyramid, they all took wonder at the shiny white exterior with a crystal capstone on top which beamed light up to the central sun. Many smaller pyramids of varying sizes, pitch angle, and widths surrounding it made a perfectly geometrical mountain range that almost defied imagination; pyramids melted into one another, with some having tetrahedron, octahedron, and hexagonal footprints; some were pure pale blue crystal while others changed colors as they passed.

"Pure Vril energy," muttered Gerlach. "Mixed with telluric and cosmic energy. Impressive. Inexhaustible."

"Now that's engineering," added Porsche. "No seams or stone blocks at all."

In the distance, gentle green foothills studded with aqueducts loomed, then a city with tall buildings and spires—Turkish, Tibetan, Indian, Asian, and Arabic in style. Below, octagonal buildings and gold-domed stupas peppered the outlying areas with the open spaces lush with trees, lakes, bridges, and rows of plants; grids of flowers bloomed like Holland's tulips.

Everywhere, people on the ground waved.

Geer sat behind Alice. "Ernst was right, Agartha is as real as he imagined. That city ahead must be Shambala, its capitol. If only my fellow scientists could witness this."

The locals in the cockpit all repeated the phrase: "*Shambala al tea-onna-sah.*" Buddhist yellow hats were tipped.

"I wonder what it means," asked Klemperer.

"As long as I can have more soup and bread I'll not complain," mumbled Porsche, winding his pocket watch. "I suppose time is measured differently down here as well, how annoying. Oh, forget it."

Eight-sided star-shaped towers with translucent pinnacles atop lined the way to what seemed like the central portion of the metropolis. In the distance, a large pyramid-shaped building loomed, and Bea followed the leading ships onto a multi-kilometer-long landing ground where craft of all shapes and sizes were parked in rows alongside polished pink granite obelisks. She touched down behind where the "sphere-ships" had landed. "All stop. Shambala everyone, passports please."

"The film was partially correct, the temple complexes on the hills do look a lot like Lhasa," said Gerlach, referring to *Lost Horizons*. "Schäfer said the yak butter tea was horrendous."

"Mind the gap." Bea led the party down the front stairs. Coming at her was a large group of Agarthans; tall people with pale blue skin, short ones that looked vaguely African, and Tibetans by the score in hats of every color, shape, and size, adorned with voluptuous robes with bedazzling patterns of silk and unknown fabrics. Horns fifty feet long blew strong notes of welcome. "Well I'll be a drunken Brewer Street harlot…Kunchen!"

Alice mumbled: "I've no doubt upon your occupation in a former life."

Bea was so excited she didn't hear the usual *slur du jour*. She was just so happy to see a friendly face from her Shieldmaiden days that wasn't a Nazi SS psychopath or mad scientist.

Kunchen smiled and bowed, his yellow hat the largest amongst them. He spoke telepathically and clearly in her head. "*It is agreeable that we meet again, Uta. We must gather in the sun temple, for the council wishes to meet with you and your compatriots. Your arrival is an unexpected surprise.*"

"*So nice to see a familiar face!*" she said silently with a smile. "*Oh, we were so lost!*"

"Who's this chap? A friend?" asked Alice.

Bea kissed him on the cheek. "Oh, he was my instructor at the school alongside Ernst, Herr Kunchen. A friend, a Tibetan monk."

"Ask him about Bernie and Schäfer, where are they?" said Gwafa, bowing to the dignified group which was doing the same. "Why are some of these people pale blue?"

"Probably the effects of the artificial sun," said Gerlach, looking up at an eight-foot-tall woman with small delicate features, a bald head, and large ears. She smiled and winked at him, her cat-like eyes bright green. "I hope."

Porsche put palms together and bowed, repeated the greeting: *Namaste sah-*

lamor. "The food too probably. High in vitamins, minerals, and fiber for growth. *Ja-ja*, I'll bow to you too!"

Kunchen motioned for Bea to follow. "*I will show you to your wounded companions.*"

The group walked the seven hundred meters to the main entrance which was forty meters high and shaped like a horseshoe painted a dark glistening red. Rows of fruit trees and flowers lined their way, and blue flame-ponds crafted in sacred geometrical shapes glistened with azure and cream white tiles. A great marble hall adorned with lapis and coral surrounded them, with people coming and going and carrying on conversations as if an ambassadorial convention was taking place, which was soon evident. Thousands of large silk animal oriental rugs decorated the floor which had intricate inlaid geometric patterns in wood and stone of all varieties. The main fountain of the *Sacred Threefold Flame* was the very center of Shambala; many waded into warm water that dripped all the way down from Mount Kailash above, its snow pure in vibration from the unseen quantum field on up.

A delegation of three unusual pale-skinned bald men in patterned blue robes came over and grilled Porsche telepathically. He grabbed his head as his Homburg fell. "They're talking all at once so fast! Tell them to stop! No, I don't know where you can find high-sulfur bitumen in northern Asia…"

Kunchen waved an arm and the three men went away. He spoke in German. "Apologies, Herr Porsche. They thought you were a dealer in such minerals."

"I'm an engineer, not a *Frankincense* merchant."

Bea soothed. "Pretty sturdy stuff, telepathy, not for the faint." Gerlach handed Porsche his hat. "What else did they ask?"

Porsche took a deep breath. "I'm not sure…something about why my hat is so strange and my vibration is so low. Hmmff, they should have seen some of the racecars I built, now *they* had high vibration."

Gwafa took a glass from an offered tray as people and exotic animals swirled around them. "Tastes like honey mixed with flowers." A two-headed jet-black camel led by a short man whisked by. One of the heads turned to meet his gaze. "I know this isn't a dream…but it would make a fine one." Lavender llamas were next, a small herd led by a smiling boy.

Alice sniffed then sipped. "Mix up nice with gin and lime." From behind, an Indian elephant with a crowded Howdah atop lowered its trunk to drink from her glass.

"Hey you! Get your own ambrosia…"

The elephant roared, trunk high. The Howdah gang laughed from above.

"I've never seen an elephant so big," said Klemperer, patting its side. "Magnificent beast."

Geer took a photo with the Leica. "No one back home will believe us."

"What luck!" Gerlach recognized a suited German businessman in a mixed group of delegates and ministers. He went up and shook hands, chatting away.

Herr Flugelrad grabbed his shoulders. "Walter, why are you here? How did you…?" "I flew in by airship, the *Himmelsbär*. You should see my genius at work in the engine room. What is this place? Are we really in Shambala?"

He smiled. "Yes we are. I'm here on behalf of Speer to negotiate rare-earth materials, exotic mineral oils, and trade for citrus products bound for the Russian Front, tinned of course. Allied representatives are here too, bit of a competition."

"*What?*"

Fluglerad laughed. "We're in a neutral country of sorts. Anyway, we came by Norwegian freighter with some monks via a long tunnel near Svalbard. I didn't know you were cleared for Inner Earth Duty. There're only six of us, I thought. You need much spiritual preparation and a Buddhist's sense of calm. Strict permissions too."

Hands in pockets. "Errgh! It was not in my mission briefing, that's for sure. Nor Porsche's either. Two brothers were with us, the Nazzaras, both Aldebarans, traders. We're on board with enemy personnel, ex-Iraq, the Zagros mining base. It collapsed in an earthquake. A long story. How does one get clearance for this place?"

"You'll have to ask Himmler when you get home. It's classified above all other programs. Why in *Gott*'s name are you with Porsche?"

"Like me, he was brought in by transport plane as a contractor to fix the propshaft magnet problems we had. He's an egotistical ass, but a good mechanic."

A whistle. "This way gang," said Bea, grabbing Gerlach's arm.

A distant gong sounded; delegates moved off. "I have to go. Let's catch up later in the jade dining hall," said Flugelrad. "Stalingrad was lost. We need a *miracle* now."

Gerlach looked shocked. "What? The Sixth Army? How?"

Far off in a crowd he yelled: "Marshal Paulus surrendered despite the Führer's orders. Our boys froze and starved. I'm a Bohemian mystic diplomat, not a soldier. Who knows how?"

"That Prussian coward!" yelled a furious Gerlach, pitching down a bundle of flowers that had been given to him as a gift. Swirls of Shambalans backed off; many were shocked by the negative outburst, the foreign vibration irritating and unwelcome.

Suddenly, a circle of fifty surrounded Gerlach. "What are you people doing? Out of my way you subhuman beggars!"

They began a low chant, then a hum. "*Oh-h-h, so-o-o, hum-m-m-m...*" The air tingled with high-vibrational energy, as if the sun had shown through a hurricane's eye.

He pushed against a Shambalan, then another. Soon he was inexplicably calm, even slightly joyous, an odd feeling for him. "*Gott*, what a strange *volk* you are...oh, our poor frozen boys now lost." Gerlach processed the grief and felt cleansed.

"*Oh-h-h, so-o-o, hum-m-m-m...*"

Porsche gently grabbed his arm. "Come, Walter, they like you now." He wiped tears. "We've lost to Ivan at Stalingrad."

"I know."

Kunchen led them out of the crowded Great Hall into a tunnel walkway that led downwards. The surrounding light from embedded crystals painted everyone a pale green, while their hands glowed a swirling metallic violet.

"*Not to worry,*" said Kunchen to everyone in their minds. "*Just a precaution to eliminate toxins and viruses. Our healing chamber, what you would call a hospital.*"

At the bottom of the walkway they entered a large domed room about 300 meters across. Large tube-like structures lined the outer walls; they glowed a dim orange and then changed hues at regular intervals. The floor was a spongey grey.

Doctors in pale blue robes with a Merkabah insignia whirled every which way, tending to spherical holographic instrument panels that appeared brightly before them.

As Bea's wide-eyed group gathered around one of the ornate tube structures, they saw Bernie laid inside one. A high-pitched whine could be heard, then silence. A cylinder of geometrically-etched glass revolved, revealing his body in a fetal position. He awoke, stretched, and yawned, his thickly-bearded face red as a blood orange; eyes opened slowly. "Errmmmphhh. What the hell is everyone lookin' at? Hey, why'm I naked? What happened?"

Bea fell to her knees. "I don't believe it..." *They've achieved resurrection technology...death is an illusion.*

Nothing ever shocked Alice for long, it was just how she was wired. She kissed him. "Oh! You stink like garlic-almond paste. What was it like being dead, old thing?"

Bea laughed, then hugged Bernie in tears.

"Rodgers! Alive? How can this be?" asked Klemperer.

Porsche and Gerlach stood stunned. Physics and engineering had never prepared them for something as spiritual and metaphysical as this.

Bernie wrapped himself in an offered blue silk robe that warmed him instantly as it shrank around him. "Dead? What? I was knocked out by the whirlpool, that's all. Why is everyone so damned emotional and…hey, where are we anyway?" He looked up and down.

"Shambala State Hospital," said Alice. Bernie gaped. "This place is…?"

Kunchen addressed them all. "*Since corporeal form in fifth density is malleable, the photon-matrix, we can use light, color, and vibratory frequency to capture a holographic portion of the body's chakra system that used to be healthy once upon a time. In a space of utmost neutrality, we then graft that temporal image onto the lifeless body to reanimate it by letting it zero-out; the cellular structures then realign and re-crystalize in the new holographic vibrational state. Using our consciousness and his, we can then recreate the younger whole. Vril energy is the fifth element of spiritual alchemy. Bernie is now fifteen years younger and perfectly healthy. The liver and gluteus maximus especially.*"

Bernie felt for his hip wound. "It's gone! Just a tiny scar. Well, I'll be fucked…" Schäfer came up in a similar robe. "I'm all healed. So good to see everyone. I told you Agartha was real and—"

Klemperer hugged the man. "Christ, Ernst!"

Geer pinched Ernst's face in wonderment. "My friend, you look red as a lobster." Gwafa looked Schäfer over. "It is a miracle…"

Schäfer shook hands. "These people live in a different reality than us, a higher-dimensional one. To our backward eyes, they can achieve anything imaginable, Herr Dogon. Here in this realm our potential future awaits, peaceful and war-free."

Gerlach examined the ornate machine that responded to his touch with colored outlines and warm humming sounds. "Living plasma. I cannot even begin to understand…"

"Hmmff." Curious, Porsche looked inside the tube that still glowed orange. "I wonder if it can heal my ragged nerves and constant constipation."

•••

At a long communal table in a hall made of jade, they all ate a common stew of vegetables, spices, and bean purée. Crusty bread and exotic fruit accompanied the main dish.

Alice took a bite. "It tastes like Tandoori lamb!"

Mouth full, Bea pointed. "Kunchen said they can make any dish you want in that wall over yonder, but it's all made from vegetable matter goo. Sure tastes like mutton à *l'orange*."

Alice saw a long line of hungry delegates and Shambalans. "Make my Connaught Hotel roast beef under-done if you please."

Bea added: "At the SS school, they taught us that when we eat meat, the trauma of the animal's death is also absorbed. That's probably why everyone here is a veggie."

"Lovely."

Two astonished American pilots sat next to them. "Say, heard your accents. What're you two English gals doing here?" asked a rather fat Army Air Corps captain. "Nice to see a white dame's face 'n all."

Alice asked: "I should ask you two Yanks the same."

"Cap'm Daniel Golonka, and this here's my copilot Eric Davis. Tenth Air Force. We were flying 'The Hump' over the Himalayas. We had engine trouble and crash-landed in the snow. Some villagers brought us down here through a narrow tunnel. We have to stay for the duration of the war they said. Food's not bad, but there ain't no beer or cigarettes."

"No movies either," said Davis. "No Betty Davis gams, no Mickey Rooney and Judy."

Bea shrugged. "Thruxton, ferry pilot m'self. If there were any butts, beer or ale, we would be the first to join you. Equipment type?"

Golonka shrugged in return. "C-46 Commando, loaded with canned food and medical supplies. Our navigator bought the farm when we hit hard in a snowy valley."

Davis asked: "Wanna dance the Lindy? They got music in a domed place here somewhere."

Alice said: "Well we have—"

Bernie sat. "Ha! More refugees, eh? Captain Rodgers, U.S. Navy. What news of the war, gents?"

Golonka dabbed his mouth. "Sir, all's I know is that the Japs are giving us hell on all fronts, we're losing our shirts. Halsey's taken command in the South Pacific. We've been here for two months. The yellow-hatted guys in charge say we can't leave till the war's over. Something about soul contracts, destiny, and 'karma,' whatever the hell that cockamamie horseshit is."

"Are you in command of that slick Nazi airship?" asked Davis.

Bernie said: "Yes, we commandeered it, but that's all I'm allowed to share. Our mission's classified. We're trying to get it to Allied territory, preferably Pearl. Halsey, eh? That's a good choice. Tough and creative."

"Take us with you, sir. We'll hide aboard," asked Golonka. "Drop us off at Waikiki Beach."

"I'll give it a whirl. Sit tight."

Porsche asked for the loo and ran. "The medical tube machine worked too well!"

"Looks like his irritable bowels just got cleansed," laughed Bernie, dripping stew.

•••

After dinner, meditation was held in a spacious, padded carpeted room with incense. Large bells the size of a small house were rung; glass bowls were twirled to make soothing music. Thousands sat cross-legged and comfortable on large silk pillows. Blankets were issued to those in need.

Suddenly, everyone's consciousness became one with the people of Agartha; all became calm, all became well.

Her spine melting into the soft floor, Bea drifted off. *I've never been so serene in my life...*

•••

Ensconced in Kunchen's lavish private quarters high above the city center on a hill, tea was served the next morning. All sat in a circle on overstuffed couches; plants and trees surrounded them by the hundreds, birds cooed. Colors seemed more vibrant; sounds seemed more clear; smells and fragrances seemed more acute; there was a heightened state of awareness and vitality. Inner stresses and worries morphed into calm states of being. The war and its harsh realities melted into the background almost as if it didn't exist at all.

Three elderly men and two women sat with Kunchen, silently talking and using their hands to illustrate points and topics. Bright holographic images flashed one after the other between them, the colors otherworldly.

Kunchen addressed the group telepthaically. *"My friends, the council elders and I have discussed your unusual situation, one that should not have occurred at all, but cosmic fate has a schedule of its own, therefore we must all adjust our expectations and reality to suit such moments of inexplicable excitement and passion."*

Dressed in a gold dragon and dark green silk robe of many luxurious layers, a stocky elder with a long white beard said: "*You are most welcome in our realm as are all visitors, ambassadors, trade representatives, and galactic plenipotentiaries. Agartha is a neutral land, Shambala a peaceful, pan-race meeting ground, a diplomatic free-zone with no judgment as to polarity or intent. We exist in a temporal bubble, a land outside of time and space. The Terran conflict above is not our concern, nor are its goals, politics, and expectations. We cannot and will not interfere according to Cosmic Law, the Law of Non-Intervention. However, unexpected and unvetted guests such as yourselves are always a puzzlement, for how you came to be here unprepared for such a trans-dimensional journey is most perplexing. But surprise can be seen as a positive vibration this day.*"

Another elder, a woman in yellow silk, added: "*We surmise your two former stowaways are the genuine cause of your surprising visit here; the water tunnel was a restricted portal, which is why you felt as slight shock going through it. It opened only due to the unique frequency of the Bear's generator, a recognizable high-pitched one from Atlantis times. By using quantum teleportation in the tunnel, the brothers bilocated their atomic structures and relocated here, wrongly thinking your ship was doomed and you with it, but eleventh density non-corporeal beings, the Shahh-Malaah, thought it best you live out your destinies as planned by Source, 'God' if you will. The two brothers Nazzara are of negative polarity and have been heavily fined accordingly for their malfeasance, but are equally welcome here to raise their vibration if they wish. That is our custom. They have trade business to conduct and are known pranksters. Some galactic races view that as a necessary trait for contract completion and hard-won alliances.*"

"I'll box their ears but good," thought Bea, arms crossed. "*They're slave traders and Nazi reprobates.*"

"*We do not condone slavery, and violence of any kind is not permitted,*" said the third elder in a tall solid gold hat. "*Slavery as a concubine, soldier, or ordinary citizen is a soul's choice, and that soul is to be admired for bravery. As hard as it may be for all of you to understand, those performing their duties as regressives are doing an important job for the cosmos. Without the darkness for contrast, no one would fully appreciate the light of Source, no one would understand the difference, not to mention the infinite shades in between. The many hearty souls who have agreed to be part of the slave trade, wars, and the regressive agenda throughout time immemorial have done so willingly and without regret in order to learn from those painful experiences via soul contracts. Their acute wisdom will be passed on to others not only in the past or present but in the future as well, otherwise balance between the forces of light and dark will favor the darkness in perpetuity. As the torsional Yin-Yang symbol represents this balanced concept, for there is always some light in the darkness and vice-versa."*

Bea and Alice sat silent, the metaphysical philosophy made perfect sense, but their expanding reality only kept becoming more complex day by day.

"What about Davis and Golonka, the American pilots, can they come with us?" asked Bernie.

Kunchen replied a somber: *"No. Their destiny was to crash-land and experience life here until the war ends. Then they will live out their lives as Shambalan ambassadors of a sort, educating small intimate groups of awakened Americans on our way of life and philosophy at the Eranos Conferences and beyond. They have much to learn in the meantime, especially ego eradication."*

"Those two flyboy meatheads? I hope you picked the right men for the job," said Bernie, confused.

Kunchen smiled. *"People grow and change with new experiences and challenges. As will all of you."*

"All this blather in my head unnerves me," grumbled Gerlach.

Impassioned, Schäfer stood. "He's saying our visit here is a mistake, but is it? This place has been my life-long dream to experience firsthand. Synchronicity brought us here, it's meant to be!"

Bernie looked out a window. "They're making repairs to our ship in a dockyard. I hope they don't skimp on provisions. You heard the man, Ernst. Grow up."

An hour of back-and-forth questions and answers made the time pass quickly.

Bea shook Alice awake. "Well, I'd like to stay for a long while, never been so relaxed and happy in my life," said Alice, stretching. "Love being a veggie guru."

"Snap out of it Rip Van Winkle, we've a mission to complete…don't we?" asked Bea of Bernie.

Bernie shrugged, palms outward. "Don't look at me, kid, I'm not sure which way is up or down, north or south. I'm still getting used to being alive again."

"I wish for *asylum*," said Klemperer. "The war is unjust. Germany has fallen by the wayside with amoral psychopaths. There are mountains down here I would like to climb. People to meet and learn—"

"Turncoat!" snarled Gerlach. "I'll have you arrested once back in Germany."

"Shuttup, Walter," said Porsche, examining what looked like a Ming vase of the Jiajing period. "Who can blame the man? Don't worry Piter, I know Hitler and Himmler much better than our dear Walter does."

Gerlach went face-to-face with Porsche. "Greasy hobnobbing mechanic!"

He smiled. "The Führer loves my fast cars, airplanes, and big tanks. He could give a nose hair about your befuddling physics."

Kunchen said: *"I know how you all must feel, but your destinies and soul duties must be completed as per cosmic schedule, and staying here is out of the question. Your disappearance from the war reality above has changed the current and most favorable timeline ever so slightly and it must be healed for all concerned, even for us Shmbalans, or a less than positive historical timeline may develop. This is the final judgement of the elder council. In two weeks' time you must leave; the exact moment in time is crucial. You will then have no memory of your visit except for your dreams, and in them you will find answers to your many questions."*

Schäfer begged: "Please, Kunchen. Let us stay for a few months at least. That shouldn't make much difference. Geer and I need to record as many species as we can."

"Humanity above will benefit greatly," added Geer.

Kunchen slowly shook his head. *"None of you understand what's at stake here… but in time you will."*

•••

Separated, Bea, Alice, and Gwafa roamed the main hall. Humming with activity, the private salons were packed with dignitaries making trade deals. Legendary Indian Nagas traded with African merchants, their racial features the same as Gwafa's, but their skin brownish red akin to an Anasazi. Gwafa tried to talk with them, but only confusion resulted since they communicated via holographic symbols not words. In the end he gave them a smile, and they warmly returned it.

Gwafa rubbed his beard. "Some distant cousins of mine, I think." "Indeed so," said Bea.

Robed Aryan men with Black Sun-symbolled crimson capes moved as a rigid column with high-held swastika and Knight's Cross signifiers, the negative and positive groups at peace with one another, the followers of the Black Sun—the void of creation—and the Left-Hand Path versus the Right-Hand Path Golden Sun. But all had descended from Hyperboreans eons ago said Kunchen, all were considered as equals; Shambala had become the teaching and learning center of the world, the wheel hub of contemplation and spiritual Vril energy known throughout the galaxy and beyond.

"The Iron Cross, a symbol of the godhead's inner light," said Bea. "I remember that from the Austrian school."

"Glad I didn't attend *that* one," mumbled Alice.

Animals roamed freely, and small machines scooped up the various piles of dung, spraying perfume to mask the odor.

"Stinks in here," said Bea.

"I stepped in something," said Gwafa, lifting a boot.

A man handed out sticks of fruit. Skipping, Alice ate one. "Everyone's so darned nice and…" She spied two white heads above the crowd. "Them! Ooooohhh!"

Bea forcibly parted the robed seas like a Spanish bull. She pushed Lew back into a pile of Shambalans. "Liars! Thieves! Pale psychopathic lizards!"

"Easy, old thing. Positive vibes and the like. Make nice," soothed Alice, who bumped into something huge. "Oh, excuse me, I was…" She gazed up. "…was…"

A fifteen-foot-tall muscular man in a thick, braided black beard and glistening winged armor stood with his wife, she a mere twelve feet in height and covered in a magnificent translucent gown of woven gold and silver thread; their skin was oily and reflected light, hence *The Shining Ones*, or the *Followers of Horus*. Beside them was an ornate chest made of black stone and a two-man druidic entourage of lesser stature; all were unarmed yet had somber faces. Their skin was treacle brown under many dense gold bracelets and rings, their eyes light blue and piercing. Golden leather serpents spiraled up from their sandals, and the royal couple wore chiseled crowns of polished orichalcum and gems.

"I'll not scream bloody murder if you don't," whispered Alice, somewhat alarmed, squeezing Bea's arm.

"Anunnaki at last," mumbled Bea. "Bit gaudy but grand."

Stew made hand gestures to the two giants, and quartz cylinders were exchanged.

The Anunnaki colossus clenched his ceramic wings shut behind him with a loud *clack*, unnerving a few dignitaries. He bowed his head sharply in agreement.

Sensing what she thought were slave underlings, the wife turned to the girls and made a hissing sound; Alice trembled.

Bea felt a primal genetic urge from times long past, a déja-vu of sorts, to descend to her knees in devotional respect as she had done in a former lifetime, but also fought strange feelings of projected avarice and dominance with a determined grit of modern-day defiance. *Nice try, but no genuflect, Apollo and Aphrodite, you majestic twats. What a mess you've made of our history with your pathetic patriarchal master, slave, and enemy sensibilities. I may be part of your hybrid elite, but I won't be a two-bit mindless god devotee. Nor Dolly here.*

The hissing grew louder; the crowd backed off.

Kunchen arrived, and telepathically spoke. "*Please be polite, Uta, they hear every thought. They, Alalu, are a royal-line couple from 6750 BC in your time scale, and are here in peace to do business for their master Enki. They will not harm anyone, nor do they aspire to. All they wish for is some quality Green-Gold from Lyra, a very rare commodity indeed.*"

Bea crossed her arms tight. "Time traveling for basement bargains? I'll just bet."

The crowd calmed. Stew opened his briefcase and handed her a red leather binder. "Ah! Finally. Fair and square. We always honor our debts, ladies. *Adieu* and farewell."

Bea and Alice smiled when they saw the signed and red-sealed parchment agreement.

The brothers followed their valued herculean customers. Lew turned to the girls. "Hope you enjoy the gazelles."

•••

Days passed with many lectures, diplomatic feasts, meditation retreats in the mountains, farming exhibitions, and genetic plant laboratory visits much appreciated. Shäfer and Geer were given bags of seeds for the surface world of agriculture. Rice, bread, fruit, and food were loaded onto the Bear, the ship repaired, cleaned, and readied for flight by gangs of Shambalan engineers and specialists with vacuums. Lavender toilet paper made from naturally antiseptic vines was stowed away; laundry was pressed; water tanks were filled; the quartz crystals in the electric motor re-vitalized with sound resonance tuning equipment.

•••

Gerlach fumed in his apartment mostly, only going out for meals to meet with his friend before the man left for Germany. The Shambalan officials in charge of Herr Flugelrad's mission refused passage for Gerlach on the freighter, but a letter to his wife was granted. Permissions, agreements, contracts, and protocols were tightly observed—

no exceptions, no special treatment. After that disappointment, he spent time in the vast libraries of scrolls and tablets, learning all he could via holographic translation devices.

A knock. When he opened the door, a robed man stood in the dim; he unfurled his hood.

Flugelrad whispered: "Walter, take this device. One of my colleagues took ill and it's his own. Hurry, I must leave, I'm due in Berlin in a week's time and our ship embarks in two hours. We can't take you with us, they watch us like hawks."

Gerlach examined carefully a small half-centimeter cube of greenish gold with tiny inscriptions on it. "What is it?"

"An Aldebaran holo-cube that acts upon the aura, our bioluminescent electromagnetic intelligence field. It's illegal technology and will lodge itself in your gut for weeks. You alone will remember your visit here. For the good of the Führer and Reich, swallow it!"

•••

Bernie accompanied Geer and Shäfer on hilly hikes with a local guide, the distant views magical, surreal. They gathered insects for study, but had to return them to the wild quickly after sketching them. Nothing biological could be removed from Agartha, and mineral specimens and crystals by strict permission only.

Geer took a photo of their smiling guide who was seven and a half feet tall. "Say *gesundheit*!"

"How do you feel?" asked Shäfer.

Sitting on a boulder, Bernie rubbed his calves. "Amazing! Like I was forty again, except for the grey hair."

"Myself as well." Panting for air, Shäfer admired the pyramids in the distance, his soul expanding. "Like a dream come alive. No one will believe us."

Bernie drank from a canteen. "Some might…those who understand the much bigger picture."

•••

Later that afternoon after much-needed pedicures and green algae skin treatments, Bea and Alice meditated in oversized stuffed armchairs that hung from giant ceiba trees at the humid botanical gardens; acupuncture and foot massage were mandatory; they felt their bodies melting like warm butter into the ultra-soft crimson fabric that seemed to breathe with every breath. The misting central fountains resonated softly; longtail birds chirped and whirled and sang; glowing crystal prayer wheels were spun by denizens who strolled about. Many teas were served, aromatic sweet to spicy hot. Heaven.

"I'm staying here for the duration of the war," wheezed Alice with the slightest of effort as a diminutive tree frog crawled up her arm one sticky digit at a time.

"Amen to that…siss-ter-r-r," whispered Bea, lungs deflated. With one eye left open, Bea saw Kunchen sitting across from them.

"*Time for some peaceful healing slumber,*" he whispered.

Bea fell fast asleep, the green hills of Kent in the distance, her feet on moist cool grass.

30

Elaine screamed at the top of her lungs. "Bea-Bea, pull up! Pull up! We can't make it."

The small bridge was veiled in fog wisps. Bea flew at treetop level at full power, he scarf fluttering behind, stretched to the limit. She felt her mother needed some stiffening of the spine. "Hang on, mums!"

"No! Please don't! Pull up!" cried Elaine. "Stop showing off, stop being a bloody *child*!"

Bea felt her exhausted eyes closing up; she headed for the bridge's underside. Her wheels hit the water causing spray as the Moth strained with both wings, the new Porsche V-16 engine far too powerful for the wooden airframe. Tunnel vision gripped her. When her top wing hit the bridge she blacked out.

"Beans! *Beans*! Wake up! Goddammit old bag, we're going to crash! *Bea-a-a-a-ans!*" Alice slapped Bea awake, then again. Woozy, Alice fell on her ass between the chair and panel.

Multiple warning claxons sounded: Altitude, speed, and electrobubble alarms and lights lit up the panel.

Bea's eyes were blurry, the tunnel vision still active. "W-w-what? Can't see!" As her eyes slowly cleared, she saw their fate fast approaching. They were on the deck in the high desert at an altitude of ten meters, their speed a shocking 2750 kph. A huge dust trail fell behind. Closing in was a mountain range. She pulled at the yoke, but it was frozen.

"Sabotage, Gerlach," moaned Alice. "Too woozy to stop him…" Porsche, Schäfer, and Bernie were strapped into chairs still passed out.

Klemperer awoke; he saw Gerlach jamming a tool into the throttle gap. He struggled to rise, then hit the man square in the jaw. "I've been waiting to do that!"

Gerlach hit the floor. "Traitor pig! Do you want the Allies to benefit from this airship? We need to destroy it!" Blood poured from his mouth onto the floor. "Germany's what's important, the Third Reich, not our damn lives!"

Klemperer struggled to remove the large screwdriver that Gerlach had bent with a hammer into the slot, freezing the throttle wide open. The Power Reserve gauge read 100%. Their speed increased, 2970 kph. "He's jammed everything!" He struggled with the maneuvering node power lever, but it was frozen.

Bea looked to Alice. "I can't gain altitude. Wake up the Professor!"

Bernie awoke in a snap with a huge gulp of air. "Aaahhhhgg…now what? Shit!" "Professor, wake up!" yelled Alice, shaking him.

"Hmmff?" Stop shaking me!" said Porsche.

"Porsche! *Ferd-in-and*! Take the bottom of the damn panel apart. Gerlach's jammed all the fucking controls!" yelled Bea over the blaring claxons.

"Suicidal maniac!" yelled Porsche, groping for the back of a chair to steady himself. "I could use some herbal tea."

Gerlach arose and yelled at Porsche: "Time to die for the Fatherland you coward!' Klemperer socked him square. This time Gerlach reeled, then fell to the floor passed out cold.

Bernie grabbed what was in the toolbox and began to furiously unbolt the bottom of the control panel with a socket wrench and hex screwdriver. "If we disconnect the wrong cables—If the Luftwaffe built this like all the others we…*scheisse*, transistors." Porsche took needle-nose pliers and began to pull apart a cable attached to an electronic panel; the panel sparked violently. "Damn all this newfangled *Wunderwaffe* technology. Altitude, we need altitude first." He cut a cable housing, exposing the inner coiled cable. "Here, pull gently…gently!"

Bernie did so carefully so as not to break it. "Try it now Bea!"

Bea pulled up hard, the yoke stiff in response. "It's going to be close…" She skimmed the foothills then scaled up the face of the steep range. The Bear bumped hard as it hit a snowy section. Bea aimed for a gap between two peaks. "Hang on Mumbly…" She shot through the gap but the Bear's underside hit a rack face; suddenly the ship began spinning violently end over end. "I need reduced power now!" Gravity forces were still minimal but felt.

"We're working on it," yelled Bernie.

Alice struggled to reduce power with Klemperer's help; they got the level down a few notches but it was firmly stuck.

Bernie unbolted all he could. "I've never seen so many wires and guts and…"

Porsche began to disembowel the panel's underside, pulling at everything. Then he saw a standard electrical cut-off switch he recognized as his own design. "They rigged the main power for maneuvering and throttle on one safety switch." He flipped it off. "That was simple."

Slowly the Bear regained composure. Bea levelled him out as the power dropped to almost zero. "We're drifting slightly...power's at idle, altitude 3006 meters, heading east at fifteen kph."

•••

Hours later Bernie and Porsche buttoned up the bottom panel. "Everything's done, but some of the transistor panels are shot," said Porsche.

"He's sluggish and slow, but he responds now," said Bea, testing the yoke.

Alice unjammed the screwdriver's tip out of the throttle gap with a hand crowbar and a chisel. "Finally! All the gubbins are busted up pretty good I reckon."

"Where are we?" asked Geer.

Schäfer looked out the windows. "It's Mongolia. I recognize the terrain, Altai Mountains. Nothing quite like them."

Geer pointed at the range. "Are you sure it's not another cavern?"

He handed him the binoculars. "This time Edmund, I can say absolutely yes."

"The sun compass is working," said Bea. "Ernst is correct."

Geer looked to the Tellus. "No power, nothing. Nor is the astrolabe working." "I remember nothing since the aquifer incident," said Gwafa, rubbing his head.

Bernie rubbed his chin at the forward windows. "Let's not land in Russia, they imprison everyone, especially downed American air crews. We're not too far from the Pacific coast with—the radio! Alice, get on the horn and see if you can raise anyone. I wonder..." He pulled up his shirt. "Anyone know how I got this scar? It itches."

"Can't remember shite. What the hell happened?' asked Bea. "Why did we all blackout?"

"The whirlpool and lightning, that's all I can remember," said Schäfer. "And yet the sweet scent of flowers intoxicates me..."

Klemperer stood next to Alice as the tubes warmed. "I officially surrender to the Allies. I've had enough of this war."

"I'll surrender with you," she mumbled, headset tight.

Fixing the throttle quadrant, Porsche shrugged. "I'd prefer a ride back to Germany, but I like America, especially Detroit. I'd like to see the wondrous GM Hydramatic automatic transmission in production. If it's good enough for a Cadillac, it's good enough for tanks. When the war ends my wife will fetch me."

"They'll wine and dine you at the Waldorf if you help the Allied war effort," chuckled Bea.

"Hmmff. Better than a prison camp. No, I cannot do that. Perhaps Henry Ford will let me stay with him under guard. He and I can design efficient postwar cars together like we did years ago."

Bernie stood behind Alice. "Let me think...it's like my brain is made of bubblegum. Try, uhm, try this frequency, 11.652...no wait, try 11.775. They should be listening in San Diego and Pearl Harbor, Station HYPO."

"I hear some Japanese, now some Russian." She handed him the earphones. "11.775. Light static only."

"I've got to try and remember...flap...no, flapper...Mount Fuji, no-no, that's not..."

"C'mon Rodgers! Get it together damn you!" yelled Bea.

"Got it!" Bernie spoke into the mic. ⚡ "Flapjack Five to Mount Weather, Flapjack Five to Mount Weather, come in Mount Weather." He adjusted the dial for a finer signal and repeated the call sign.

Porsche adjusted the throttle a bit. "How's that?"

Bea looked to the airspeed indicator. "Fifty kph. Is that all?"

"For now, yes. The transistor panel is burned up. I looked for spares but found none. Expensive gear, experimental too."

Bernie kept at it. ⚡ "Flapjack Five to Mount Weather, Flapjack Five to Mount Weather, come in Mount Weather, over. Come on dammit, answer you lazy bums!"

A distant scratchy voice. ⚡ *"Mount Weather to Flapjack Five, Mount Weather to Flapjack Five, glad to hear from you, over."*

Bernie asked: "Can you boost the signal?"

Alice turned the receiver power dial to full. "Try it now."

Excited, Bernie spoke strongly and clearly. ⚡ "Flapjack Five to Mount Weather, western Pacific, western Pacific, Apache Eagle on the move, I repeat, Apache Eagle on the move, over."

Static and atmospheric hisses. ⚡ *"Flapjack Five, Flapjack Five, message understood, message understood, vector to Corral Six, I repeat, vector to Corral Six, over."*

"He means Midway Island. They know we're airborne, not on the deck. Hot damn!" Bernie clicked the mic. ∕ "Flapjack Five, received and understood, I repeat, received and understood, over and out. All right people, we're in business."

Porsche adjusted further. "Any better?"

"A little, thanks," said Bea. "Speed now 212 kph."

Bernie plotted on the chart. "Make your heading 0-7-8 degrees. Let's be well north of Japan, then we'll turn southeast."

"Okay, 212 kph. I can live with that," said Bea, gaining a little altitude. "Course 0-7-8 degrees."

Porsche wiped his brow. "That's all I can give you without burning out something else."

"Rum and canned pineapple here we come," said Alice, tuning in some Hawaiian music which she then put on the loudspeaker.

"Beautiful!" said Geer. "The ukulele, island girls, old Lemuria."

•••

Hours later, they passed over Sakhalin Oblast peninsula. "On course over Russian territory," said Bernie, making adjustments. "Bea, what's our altitude?"

"8200 meters."

Klemperer tied Gerlach's hands to the seat's armrests with rope. "No more sabotage today..."

Alice watched the radar screen. "In God's gritty...bogies from the south. Climbing. A decent-sized wing of aircraft."

Schäfer turned to Bernie. "Where is the demarcation of Japanese territory?" "Well, I..."

Russian and Japanese fighters and light bombers clashed all around them. Bea evaded, the controls sluggish. "Bloody ol' hell, we've flown into the Pacific War! Damn your half-arsed navigation Rodgers!"

"The swastikas on the stern!" cried Alice. "We're Germans!"

Russian Yak fighters zeroed in, firing at them; Japanese planes defended the Bear, an ally.

"This is most bizarre..." breathed Schäfer, watching the scene at the forward windows. Bernie said: "I knew I should've plotted a more northerly route...the Japs must be on a bombing raid, a Russian port or something. Or they saw us and...I thought they weren't fighting each other much, they signed a non-aggression pact."

"Well they're aggressing now!" exclaimed Bea.

Hit badly, a burning Russian fighter started his suicide run. "He's going to ram us!" yelled Geer.

Everyone watched in horror as the plane barreled in.

Alice noticed the warning yellow light on the panel. "Did anyone notice the cargo bay door was open? Why did—"

"Sound collision!" yelled Bernie as the plane hit them in the cargo area. The ship shuddered hard. Another alarm claxon sounded, then more.

"The electrobubble must be weak at the cargo bay, it should have *protected* us," said Porsche, horrified. "Walter's done more sabotage—I'll never trust a physicist again!"

Gwafa and Bernie examined the cargo bay; parts of it were on fire with plane debris, the cargo door bent outwards; cold air rushed in. Part of the port side wing was lodged into a bulkhead. The automatic fire control gushed CO_2 and foam from the ceiling, killing the fire in minutes; toxic smoke was thick. "Still some fuel on the floor," coughed Bernie. He tapped a gauge on the wall which read empty. "Lucky for us the Luftwaffe takes fire seriously."

Gwafa coughed violently. "Hopefully the outside air will evaporate it soon."

"Walter must have reduced power to the ship's bubble," said Porsche, wet hanky over mouth. "The hatchway to the engine room is blocked. *Blau* Aluminum melts only at very high temperature, but it can deform out of shape at a much lower one."

Klemperer tried to prybar the hatch open behind the hot smoking debris. "The aviation fuel…it's melted the bulkhead's alloy!"

"As I feared…" said Porsche.

Bernie and Gwafa helped. "No dice. The door's fused shut," moaned Bernie.

Gwafa strained with all his might to pry it open. "All this way…and we are attacked by one ally only to be defended by an enemy. There must be, *mmphhhh*, some philosophy at play here, Bernard."

"Errggnnnn…must be I reckon. Bea's Law of Confusion and Bewilderment…" He pitched his crowbar to the slick floor. "Forget it! We have other issues to contend with."

Bea checked their altitude as they lost their pursuers. "We're losing a meter every couple of minutes. Just a guess."

"So much for Planter's Punch," said Alice, who went to the intercom.

"Hey back there, we need a new heading."

"What goddam catastrophe do we have now?" asked Bernie as they came back to the cockpit. He plotted a new course. "Come to course 1-1-2 degrees southeast. It's 4352 kilometers to Midway. That's around twenty hours' flight time at 212 kph if we can maintain it." He went to the radio and relayed their ETA for Corral Six.

Alice made notes over the course of ten minutes. "Our current rate of descent is one meter every two minutes. Altitude now 8295."

Geer passed out rations and water. "Keep your energy levels up. There's plenty of fresh fruit and vegetables in the refrigerator units. We must have picked them up somewhere."

Gwafa ate what looked like a purple starfruit. "But where? Étrange, this tastes like lemon with Kiwano melon. I think I remember rows of fruit trees somewhere..."

Bea slurped from a coffee cup. "Well wherever it was, thank gosh for mint-pea soup. That's odd, the taste reminds me of sitting on large oriental carpets."

Alice tilted the cup and chugged. "And tall trees with pearlescent pink birds."

Klemperer grabbed Gerlach's shirt and pulled hard. "What did you do back there? A Russian plane hit us in the cargo bay."

Woozy, he replied: "The savages are good for something after all..." Klemperer let go. "Always loyal to the shitting SS no matter what, eh?"

Porsche wiped the crusty blood from Gerlach's mouth. "Walter, think of our wives and families. Tell me what you did so I can fix it."

"Fuck you, mechanic. I also locked the small access tunnel to the engine room. The Americans cannot be privy to my non-linear physics and antigravity propulsion." He then smiled in a sinister way. "We'll all drown for the Fatherland. Just think...you'll be a hero."

•••

Thirty-six hours passed into sunrise. Conversations were at a minimum; everyone ate. "Rate of descent has increased," said Alice.

"Speed is dropping, 146 kph," said Bea. "139 kph."

Bernie did some calculations. "We're not going to make it. We'll be 122 kilometers short. Son of a..." He went to the radio station. ⚡ "Flapjack Five to Mount Weather, Flapjack Five to Mount Weather. Received battle damage, received battle damage. Losing altitude, I repeat, losing altitude. Headed to Davy Jones. Estimate we will ditch 1-3-4 kilometers short of rendezvous on a heading of 1-2-2 degrees, over."

Thirty seconds of silence commenced.

⚡ *"Mount Weather to Flapjack Five, received and understood. Set your time to 07:12 local. Plan Victor-X Ray in effect, repeat, Plan Victor-X Ray in effect. Will advise, over."*

Alice adjusted one of the 24-hour clocks to Midway time. "Set." Schäfer asked: "I wonder what day or even month it is?"

"What's Plan X Ray?" asked Bea, looking behind.

Bernie looked confused. "I have no idea…"

31

09:12 hours. Mist.

"Altitude 950 meters and dropping," said Bea, her concern growing as the visibility dropped. "Airspeed dropping too, 46 kph. Rain shower ahead."

"Will this rig float, Professor?" asked Alice of Porsche.

At the chart table, he made some paper calculations, drawing an outline of the Bear. "The cargo bay is sealed off via the doors, but it will fill with seawater. It's the biggest compartment on the ship, and with the door hexagon skin damaged, the bubble is compromised in that section. We might stay afloat, but I presume we will be half-submerged. It's a guess."

Bernie looked out the raindrop-covered window at a submarine ahead of them on the surface; he adjusted for focus. "Interception course. It's American, Gato Class. We're barely outrunning him for now. He won't have security clearance for us, which means he doesn't have the word, and probably under radio silence this far out on patrol. Our mission is far above top secret. Christ, if we land on water he'll probably put a fish right up our ass and call it a day."

"I see a second submarine!" cried Geer at the Starboard windows. "It's a wolf pack!"

"*Gott*, what else is following us?" breathed Klemperer. "Fucking Yankee Navy."

Bea said: "901 meters. Speed 22 kph."

Bernie tuned in the radio. ⌕ "Flapjack Five to Mount Weather, Flapjack Five to Mount Weather. Losing altitude fast. Sharks are closing in, repeat, sharks closing in. Please advise, over."

Silence, static.

⌕ "*Mount Weather to Flapjack. Help is on the way. Repeat, help is on the way. Use flares if necessary, repeat, use flares if necessary. Warn them off, warn them off.*"

"Come on Gwafa!" They ran to the cargo bay and rummaged for emergency flares. "Why the hell didn't I think of that?"

Gwafa opened the life raft stowage compartment. "Flare guns and flares. Will this work?" "I dunno, worth a try," said Bernie, stuffing flare cartridges into his pockets.

"Sometimes it's whether or not a sub captain had a good night's sleep."

As Bernie and Gwafa returned, Bea yelled: "Twenty millimeter fire, both subs!" Tracer rounds bounced off the nose. "They definitely don't have the flippin' word!"

"C'mon! You fire to starboard, I'll do it to port." Bernie lowered the forward stairs halfway; he and Gwafa let go two red emergency flares, then two more. Outside the electrobubble's protection, .50-caliber tracer rounds pinged the stairway's lower edge. "Damn, they're pissed!"

20 mm rounds could be heard exploding in the cargo bay; the fire re-ignited. They let go two more flares in two directions and the shooting stopped.

"What's that dead ahead?" asked Alice.

Bea replied: "I'm not..."

A large ship and two destroyer escorts came into view at five miles distance through thick haze. They fired green flare rockets.

All the men crowded at a lower window. "They're submerging...well done you two," said Schäfer.

"A light cruiser, it's ours. Two anti-sub destroyers," said Bernie. Alice asked: "What's that flying towards us?"

"Probably going to blow us out of the sky and then *sink* us," grumbled Bea. "612 meters and descending fast."

"We need life vests," panicked Geer.

Bernie grabbed the binoculars. "It's a...Jesus H. Christ, a dirigible...it's the Crazy Horse!"

The smaller Navy airship with colorful nose art maneuvered underneath them, then rose to mate with the Bear's underside with a loud *clunk*.

•••

At the helm, Captain Simpson ordered through the communication tube: "All right chief, pour on the coal!"

In the Crazy Horse's crowded-with-gear engine room, all personnel wore radiation suits with thick rectangular glass in their helmets.

The chief petty officer yelled: "All right you horse-fuckin' peckers, open those pipes to max flow and lash down the safety valves!"

All six crewmen opened the valves for the liquid nitrogen tank to cool the small plasma generator which had been updated over the years for more power with a spiral of insulated cryogenic cooling pipes. Condensation froze on all surfaces.

The chief pushed the power levers to *all ahead full* plus. "Let's get our asses outta here!" He then shut the pressure hatch and sealed it tight. The generator went hot orange. Through the porthole, he saw the indicator dials pass maximum redline. Escaped nitrogen fogged the compartment, now a winter's scene. "God give us full lift…"

Simpson threw a series of switches on a newly-installed panel. "This magnetic field dampener should punch a hole in their bubble. All right Seaman First, hop to it."

Through the upper hatch, a goggled machinist's mate began to cut a hole in the Bear's hull with a gas torch; sparks and hot metal bits flew every which way. "This alloy's damn tough, sir." He then cut through a second and third layer. "We're through, Cap'm." With pure strength, he and another gloved sailor bent the cut metal disc over to make a hatchway; rice poured in, they were in the Bear's galley and had nicked a storage bin.

The first officer, a junior lieutenant remarked: "Why's this rice orange?"

"Lieutenant, the ship is yours. Marines with me!" yelled Simpson, cocking his Colt .45 auto. As he clawed his way up a ladder, he and two Marines slipped on a pile of mashed exotic fruit. Simpson kicked open the galley door into a smoky companionway. "You four men aft, secure the engine room. *Cough*! You six men with me; shoot to kill only if you have to."

"Allan! *Allan*! We need foam chemicals…the cargo bay is on fire again, Av-Gas," yelled Bernie down the companionway. The lodged Russian wing had leaked more fuel when hit.

Simpson gave orders to a Marine coming up the ladder. "Pass the word down to the Chief. Class-B fire extinguishers. Av-Gas!"

A Marine with Gwafa at gunpoint said: "Sir, I don't think this man is a German either…" "No shit, son." As Simpson turned, Bernie socked him hard.

Two screaming angry Marines pointed their Thompsons directly at Bernie; he held up his arms. "I surrender. We're old friends." He looked them over. "Navajos, eh?"

Sailors with fire extinguishers squeezed by in a hurry.

Simpson arose, rubbing his jaw. "Volunteer job. High Security. I needed the best in case some Waffen SS guys were on board with some weird technology. And with a name like *Chief Crazy Horse*…"

• • •

15:50 hours.

At the northern spit of Midway Atoll, Bea put the Bear down on a long sandy stretch of beach after the Crazy Horse had disengaged from below. Landing buffers set to a standard three meters, she shut down all switches on the panel. "All stop." Warm moist salt air filtered in from the forward stairs, displacing the cold, dry air conditioning. Laysan albatrosses were interspersed with their chicks; a Great Frigatebird peered in from the stairway's edge, tilting its head with curiosity. It squawked.

"Hello, bird," said Bea as her heart warmed. "Oh, how sweet!" said Alice in high pitch.

Schäfer and Geer examined the galley. "Orange rice, unidentified flat bread, strange fruits by the score, and a green vegetable soup that's delicious. Where did we obtain such fresh stores?" asked Ernst, tasting everything.

Geer slurped cold soup. "I don't remember, no one can. Cilantro and nut paste, this is *haute* cuisine."

Schäfer let go a handful of rice through his fingers. "I hope the Americans let us go home after the war."

Alice kissed Bea's cheek. "Land ho! Lovely holiday with you as always."

She hugged her. "You said it." Bea then saluted Simpson in a nonchalant fashion. "Herr Kappy-tain."

Simpson shook their hands. "Ladies, an honor." He then went to the Tellus to examine it. "Amazing stuff, pretty fancy gear for the Germans."

Bea and Alice fled down the stairway, giggling.

Bernie twisted a dial or two. "That's because it's not German. It's a 15,000 year-old gizmo. Wait till you see the engine room, they really—"

"Fifteen *thousand*? Look, where the hell have you been, Bern? It's been ten months since you left Cairo. You're damned lucky we had someone at HYPO checking that frequency daily, most of us had given up on you months ago. I was at Pearl on other business; it was dumb luck we had the Crazy Horse in a hangar ready to go and an escorted cruiser on patrol in the Midway area. The Horse can achieve 680 mph and 50,000 feet altitude now, it was headed for an important mainland Japan reconnaissance with *me* on board. I took a big risk and guessed you had stolen a valuable German aircraft of some type, maybe an airship, so I had to scramble en route to get this rescue operation in gear, the admirals were all over my ass with questions and roadblocks. Security posed a problem, so I radioed Train who called King who then called Nimitz, who finally gave the green light. Rules were bent, security was relaxed on wartime emergency grounds. It was a miracle of timing and logistics."

Shocked, he replied: "Ten months? That's impossible…by my reckoning only six or seven weeks have passed, although…it was really hard to measure time underground."

"Underground?" Simpson handed him a Chesterfield and lit it. "Buddy-boy, it's June 14th, 1943. We're advancing on New Georgia in the Solomons. The Aleutians have fallen, we now have Attu Island in hand. Admiral Yamamoto was shot down by P-38s over Bougainville."

An instant tobacco high hit him and he smiled. "Seriously? Yamamoto? Then we're pretty much winning this war now…"

A Marine handed Simpson a roll. "Pink toilet paper, sir. Very odd. Felt like it was alive or something."

Bernie examined it. "Lavender actually, with a Vesica Pisces symbol on the sheets. You know, lots of strange things were—"

"C'mon, pal." As they walked down the stairway, Simpson lowered his voice so no German could hear. "Rommel and the Africa Corps are done for too. Be cautious with that intel, but yes, I'd say we're on the move upwards." He looked back. "Jesus, what a first-rate ship! You four did a helluva job. I hope FDR kisses all of you on the lips. Wait till Botta and his crew lay eyes on this fancy tugboat, they'll pick it apart."

He laughed. "In Cairo you did tell me to steal something." "I remember that!"

"Ten months gone? Then…" Confused and exhausted, Bernie inhaled the salt air, just glad to be alive as the low sun painted his bearded face. "I'll figure that out later. Need privacy. Let's walk over there for a minute." Stepping gingerly around albatross chicks under a palm, he bent down and grabbed two handfuls of sand, letting the grains fall through his fingers as the chicks sped off. In privacy, he then went face to face. "On behalf of everyone, thanks for the rush rescue job, I mean it as your friend. But you lied to me, Allan, why?"

"On what?"

"Antarctica for one. Schäfer explained all about Byrd and the underground ruins and such. The *Schwabens* have an entire under-ice colony with—"

"The who? Look, I told you I—"

"…Swiss gold, atomic railway guns, Aldebaran spice traders, fucking Prescott Bush and his bullshit—"

"Listen up. What precious little I did know I wasn't allowed to share, orders. *Orders!* You need to grow up and take it on the chin like I have, we still have a big war to win, so forget what Nazi propaganda bullshit you heard, especially about the South Pole. Everyone upstairs expects us swabby peons to do their jobs perfectly and quietly. As I said in Cairo, ONI and OSS security across the board is now tight as a dog's asshole. Secrecy at all costs." He pointed back to the Bear. "You want the Russians to have our atomic and airship science? The 'Celestial Devices' shit FDR talks about? Trust me, we'll be fighting the Reds next, this war could go on indefinitely. From now on you need to respect protocols with honor and discretion, or *else*.

"Everyone you see around here, enlisted or officer, has been given extra pay, everyone signed newly-minted ONI, G2, or OSS security contracts with a capital punishment clause for spilling any loose beans. Two men have been recently imprisoned on *my* order! It's the only way to keep security extra tight—fear and intimidation. I don't particularly like it either, but I agree it's the only solution. You could end up in Norfolk Brig with a life stretch or shot dead, so watch that big mouth of yours. Am I clear?"

Bernie chested up to him. "I just love your bedside manner when—"

"What? Are you gonna punch me again? Go ahead. Or did those Krauts on board sway you to *their* way of thinking?"

Bernie walked off. "We're really done here." *Learn to forgive unconditionally someone said, if that's even possible...*

"What? Can't take the heat?" An albatross mother pecked at his leg. "Hit the road, bird."

He turned. "*Principle of Correspondence.* As above, so below. And believe me, you're the one below decks, you and your secret upstairs pals calling the dirty shots. Every little action has bigger consequences in the cosmos. Remember that."

•••

Palms swayed in the distance. Olive drab Packard staff cars and two deuce-and-a-half trucks were parked in a neat row. A medical tent was quickly set up; several of the Crazy Horse's crew had mild radiation burns and frostbite.

Three Quonset huts were fifty yards off the Bear's bow, and a platoon of Marines and sailors secured the area; most just admired the airship, their jaws wide open. Even with a huge open scar, he was still impressive, glittering in the strong sun. Men walked underneath it, amazed.

"Watcha lookin' at? Ain't you flea-bitten mutts ever seen a joyman airship before?" asked a grizzled chief petty officer of decent years from the Brooklyn Navy Yard. "You there! Stop touchin' that damn ting or yoose burn ya hand."

"Over-curious Seabees, huh? Give 'em hell, Chief," said Bernie, shaking out butts for both of them and heading for the latrine, the lavender paper trailing from his pocket.

"Tanks, sir. Dese here greasy barn animals wouldn't know ah split coconut from a pissin' lug nut."

Marines escorted the Germans off the Bear and into one of the huts to be debriefed.

Despondent, bonds cut, an exhausted Gerlach hobbled along shoeless in the deep sand behind Porsche. "Intolerable situation—a prisoner! The shame of it all...Hope they have cold pilsner at least."

Weary, trousers ripped in several places, Porsche fluffed his ragged Homburg. "Hmmff. I'll second that, Walter. Oh, and if you have any designs on killing me again I'll have my son Ferry sabotage your Mercedes drop-top."

"Remember...the *palm gardens* by the Canyon River in Shambala?" asked Gerlach in a whisper.

Porsche furrowed his brow. "Gardens? Where's 'Shambala'?" He laughed. "Nothing...nothing at all. Just a dream I had."

Schäfer looked to one of the Navajo Marines and laughed. "Cowboys and Indians, Edmund, noble red descendants of Lemuria. The great Geronimo. Cochise."

"*Ja-ja...*" he replied. "If only they would allow us to measure some craniums."

"Move along and keep your yaps shut, you Kraut pricks," said the gruff Navajo Marine, menacing Garand pointed.

Inside the main hut, U.S. Naval officers, ONI, an OSS woman in an Army uniform, and two Army G2 intelligence personnel greeted the Germans warmly as guests, not POWs. Cold Budweiser and root beer were served from an ice bucket along with Spam sandwiches on G.I. white bread. Light conversations ensued: Rations and crew comfort, flight duration and places visited, engineering discussions, sightings of Russians and Japanese forces, underground tunnels and rivers described in detail, hometowns and family, caverns, strange animals and tall trees, the mysterious disappearance of the odd and disliked Nazarra brothers during the whirlpool storm, Geneva Convention protocols, varieties of Pennsylvania Dutch and Bavarian bratwurst debated.

Peeling back a slice of bread, Geer asked an officer: "Is there a vegetarian dish we could have instead of meat? Fruit? I used to like meat, but now..."

The doctor gave him a blank look, then turned to an Army nurse who was examining the Germans for wounds and sickness. "G.I. rations. A can of fruit cocktail. Top shelf."

She sped off. "Yessir."

"A handsome nurse," whispered Shäfer to Geer. "Fine cheekbones and mandible." "And quick-legged!"

The imposing, six-foot brunette female OSS officer meandered over and went face to face with Schäfer speaking pitch-perfect German. "I'm quick-legged too. I know much about Beger, Kisse, and Herr Geer, professor, the whole bunch. Major Bradley's my name, archeologist, historian, and occultist, Humboldt University, Berlin, 1934. My father was a diplomat at the embassy, so I've met all the top Tan Pheasant Nazis who think taking a bath is optional in life. We are going to have some ver-r-ry long conversations together about your precious Thule Society and *Ahnenerbe Dienst*."

Schäfer tugged at the pockets of his filthy blue Luftwaffe mechanic's overalls. "I hope you enjoy *silence*!"

Geer hid slightly behind him. "I, well we..."

When they all sat, an admiral stood behind a long table with many documents on it. "I'm Rear Admiral Swift, and you can address me as such. Gentlemen, in twelve days' time...you will be flown to Alaska by a sizeable Navy Mars flying boat. Takeoff is before dawn at Eastern Island a few miles south of our position. At Anchorage Harbor, you will be met by a long-range German transport plane—Swedish markings of course—which will take you over the North Pole to Trondheim Norway, then on to Germany; it's a Blohm & Voss flying boat with six engines they told us, a 3763-mile journey. They will have important Allied prisoners on board in exchange for you. After you've been debriefed and you have signed top secret release documents, you will be shown your overnight billets, showers of course, clean uniforms, anything you need. Now, unless you have any specific—"

"Over the *North Pole*?" asked Porsche nervously with a beer burp. "But how...?"

Gerlach laughed. "Let's hope the Kriegsmarine mechanics have the engines in good order for you!"

Schäfer stood. "Herr Admiral, would it be possible for Edmund and I to explore these islands under guard? Perhaps with Major Bradley here? There must be many new tropical specimens that we could take back to Ger—"

The official group translator, a Navy commander, stood. "*Nein*! You're all Nazi SS members, close friends of Hitler and Himmler. You're damn well lucky we don't imprison you for the duration of the war and force you to work for us. But our orders come from the top, FDR, so be thankful for that. This top-level exchange is without peer."

"Take it easy, commander, sit down," ordered the admiral. "These are civilians mostly."

Pulling at his long beard, Geer said: "Actually, I've never met Hitler, but our dear Heinrich is a most misunderstood indiv—"

"Do you *know*...exactly who I am?" asked Gerlach incredulously, his eyes wide and menacing, hands flat on the table. "I'm Walter Gerlach, non-linear physicist, University of Tübingen, Kaiser-Wilhelm *Gesellschaft*, quantum mechanics. The Führer and Hirohito will have you weak-kneed, Jew-loving pond scum by the balls soon. Why you filthy ungrateful Yankee swine, I—"

"Oh, shuttup, Walter," said Porsche, inhaling a sandwich. "Any hot mustard about? You see my wife makes—"

Klemperer abruptly stood at attention and spoke with authority. "*Sturmbannführer* Piter Klemperer, *Gebirgsjager* SS. A mountaineer by *Gott*. Serial number G.21817. I wish for asylum—I want to defect! I will cooperate to the full extent but will not divulge military information. And if you are amenable, I would like...permission to be married to my shipmate Miss Alice Drummond, soon to be divorced. She has since accepted my pre-proposal, my insurance for engagement, my oath and dagger upon it. I will wait for her in an American prison camp of course until such time as—"

"Traitorous dog!" snarled Gerlach. Porsche, Geer, and Schäfer laughed.

After the translation, the American officers looked to one another, stunned and bewildered. A Navy photo reconnaissance technician handed the admiral a single eight-by-ten photo.

"Mr. Geer's Leica camera, sir. Only one negative developed, the rest were unrecognizable."

"It's Major Klemperer here...and an *elephant*?" The admiral looked to the Germans and pointed at the photo. "The biggest God-damned world war in history...

and you people were on a fucking tropical *safari?*"

Wide eyes and stares.

Outside, a young ensign passed a tray of rum, bitters, and iced pineapple juice cocktails in tin cups. "Ladies, with the admiral's compliments. Over the radio they said you—"

"We're saved!" Alice grabbed two and swilled one after the other. Bea followed suit. With a mischievous look, Bea looked to Gwafa and Alice. "Last one in swallows Himmler's high hard one!" She bolted fast, peeling off her tunic down to her bra and panties, then ditched the bra. "Waahh-hoo!"

Alice did same, screaming. "Or Uncle Winnie's shriveled bollocks!" Breasts gloriously revealed, Marines and Seabees whistled and cat-called at the girls. Pandemonium, cap waving, and clapping ensued. "Divine Feminine at work for the good of morale!"

"You said it."

"*Vive la* France, *vive* Timbuktu!" yelled Gwafa, diving into the cool heavy surf in his underwear. After he cooled off, he returned to the beach feeling truly victorious for the very first time. He fell to his knees, and said a silent prayer to his family and ancestors.

Suddenly, Lutz stood next to Bea in polka dot trunks and a wet Kriegsmarine garrison cap; he shivered. "I'm so proud of you and Alice, everyone. Go to him. I vill wait for you in ze future. War is the opposite of love, find your balance at his side."

"Law of…Balance." Bea trembled, and stood motionless in the surf. "Stick, I only…" "Beans? What's wrong?" asked Alice.

"Nothing, I…"

"Do not look back my love, ze past is only history." Lutz swam off, disappearing in the burnt orange waves as the sun gloriously set, his cap floating away.

Bea's trembling slowly stopped over the course of a minute; somewhere deep inside she found the courage, real courage that had been lacking for a very long time, courage of the heart.

Gwafa slid on trousers in the company of Bernie and Simpson.

Bernie said: "You've been officially turned over to our Navy as a French civilian advisor. However, there's an idea floating around that you might be eligible for a negro flight program in Tuskegee Alabama if you want it, but secretly as a two-stripe ONI lieutenant under my command with a top secret clear—"

Simpson added: "It's controversial, but with some study and training you could—"

At full speed Bea jumped onto Gwafa from behind. As they fell onto the sand she kissed him deeply with all her might and passion, pinning his strong arms. He returned it.

"I knew it!" yelled Alice from the surf, splashing furiously. "I just bloody *knew* it!"

"C'mon," whispered Bea, eyes alight, smiling, leading Gwafa by the hand back out to sea as if a mermaid of long-ago legends. "Love you."

Bernie laughed with full vigor.

Simpson pitched his cap to the sand. "Aww, for cryin' out loud, Bern, you and your damn team really know how to screw regulations up but good."

Chugging his rum, he pulled off his damp Luftwaffe undershirt. "What the hell…" He took off buck naked after them, kicking the water like a little boy without a care.

Also from
John W. Warner IV

All author profits go to wounded veteran charities.

"... a historical thriller... a propulsive war story." – Kirkus Reviews

Little Anton, prequel of *Lion, Tiger, Bear*, is a gripping historical novel series that discloses covert technological inventions and the prominent leaders who exploited them during the turbulent years leading up to WWII and the Battle of Norway in 1940. Part love story and part satire, the book masterfully interweaves a fictional adventure within factual reportage, revealing in greater detail why Adolf Hitler tasked his personal hero Professor Ferdinand Porsche and his brilliant engineering mind to build the world's fastest, almost invincible racecars and potent military machines.

Author, artist and historian John W. Warner IV writes historical novels in his studio in Virginia. To learn more about John and his novels, visit www.johnwwarnerivauthor.com

Tune in to the BLA podcast.

John's podcast series "Beyond Little Anton" is available on these leading channels:

Listen on **Apple Podcasts** · **Spotify** · **SOUNDCLOUD**

FOLLOW US ON
SOCIAL MEDIA

A strong feminist, John shares hidden historical details and little-known facts about the women of WWII who were spies, ferry pilots, nurses and inventors, entertaining memes and interesting interviews on:

@JohnWWarnerIV
@Warner_IV

@JohnWWarnerIVAuthor

John W Warner IV

Made in the USA
Middletown, DE
10 October 2021